GRAND CENTRAL PUBLISHING

D0710127

Dear Reader,

I am pleased to share with you *Twain & Stanley Enter Paradise* by the late Oscar Hijuelos, a historical novel that focuses on the unlikely friendship between two of the most famous and admired figures of the nineteenth century. Oscar Hijuelos, who won a Pulitzer Prize for *The Mambo Kings Play Songs of Love,* published eight novels and a memoir before his untimely death in 2013.

Twain & Stanley Enter Paradise was a great labor of love for Hijuelos, who worked on the manuscript off and on for ten years, spending time personally scouting the book's far-flung locations and immersing himself in the documentary record covering the long-time link between the literary titan Mark Twain, the famed African explorer Henry Morton Stanley, and Stanley's wife, the painter Dorothy Tennant. The result is a book unlike anything else Hijuelos ever wrote—an exhilarating blend of fact and fiction in which the author vividly conjures up a vanished world and the everyday voices of the larger than life characters that inhabited it.

It is truly an honor to have had a hand in publishing this novel. The experience of working with a manuscript by a great writer who is no longer available for the usual colloquy between author and editor has been bittersweet, but I have worked with his widow, Lori Carlson-Hijuelos, who knew him better than anyone and who knew his work from the heart. This has been a rare privilege that I wouldn't have missed for anything, and I am thrilled that *Twain & Stanley* is finally seeing the light of day.

Gretchen Young
Vice President and Executive Editor
Grand Central Publishing

TWAIN & STANLEY
ENTER PARADISE

to come

TWAIN & STANLEY

Enter Paradise

OSCAR HIJUELOS

GRAND CENTRAL
PUBLISHING

NEW YORK   BOSTON

Grand Central Publishing
Hachette Book Group
1290 Avenue of the Americas
New York, NY 10104

www.HachetteBookGroup.com

Printed in the United States of America

RRD-C

First Edition: November 2015

10 9 8 7 6 5 4 3 2 1

Grand Central Publishing is a division of Hachette Book Group, Inc.
The Grand Central Publishing name and logo is a trademark of Hachette Book Group, Inc.

The Hachette Speakers Bureau provides a wide range of authors for speaking events. To find out more, go to www.hachettespeakersbureau.com or call (866) 376-6591.

The publisher is not responsible for websites (or their content) that are not owned by the publisher.

Library of Congress Cataloging-in-Publication Data
[TK]

CONTENTS

AUTHOR'S NOTE

Twain and Stanley Enter Paradise is about the way the lives of Mark Twain and Henry Morton Stanley, two famous nineteenth-century Victorians, intersected. Frankly, I began writing it because their characters, as I researched them and from what I had deduced from their writings, seemed a perfect pairing. They in fact were good friends, even if (eventually) they held quite conflicting views about imperialism and the colonization of Africa. And there is something else: No one else has ever written about their lives together, and that simply appealed to me.

The spine of the book involves the trajectory of their relationship: the way Stanley first came to know Twain as a newcomer to America from Wales in the late 1850s, their very similar careers as journalists in the American West, and finally, after each had achieved great fame at about the same time, how their friendship over the years proceeded.

It is a fact that Henry Stanley's wife, one Dorothy Tennant, was a highly regarded artist in nineteenth-century London. A flamboyant aristocrat of bohemian proclivities, she painted a number of portraits of Stanley, one of which is quite well known. Later, as I have configured the novel, she paints Twain's portraits—she has him sitting for her as he talks about the poignancies of his existence. Along the way, though he is certainly deeply in love with his wife, Livy, a quite frail, constantly ill woman, Twain, tired of his life's adversities, becomes hypnotized, as it were, by Stanley's wife, a voluptuous seductress at heart, whom he came to dote upon. In that way it is a triangle, with Twain, as I imagine him, unconsciously falling in love with Tennant despite her many eccentricities and his unflagging loyalty to his wife.

I am also fairly convinced that, in London of the 1890s, when Twain and his wife were grieving over the tragic loss of their daughter Susy, it was Dorothy Tennant—whose brother-in-law, Frederic Myers, was the head of London's Society for Psychical Research—who took them around to various mediums and séances. To help ease Livy's suffering, and out of curiosity, Twain played along, but rather skeptically so. Despite an earlier experience with the supernatural—namely, a premonition he once had as a riverboat pilot on the Mississippi, foretelling, in precise detail, the death of his younger brother, Henry in 1858—Twain doesn't buy any of it. When confronted with a spiritualist who seemingly "channels" their daughter's ghost, he still refuses to believe, as Dorothy Tennant certainly does, that there might be something to such a phenomenon. Not to throw around ten-dollar words, but thematically speaking, the novel pursues that dichotomy in Twain. Recording that premonition about his brother's death extensively in *Life on the Mississippi,* and often retelling that story during his life, he remained in denial, and rather doggedly so, of the supernatural: And yet, at the same time, he somewhat envied people, like Dorothy Tennant, who, however deluded, took solace in such beliefs.

Then there is the notion of "paradise," as alluded to in the title. For Twain it came down to his memories of his fairly happy, carefree youth, the sweet energies of which he put into his most famous book, *The Adventures of Huckleberry Finn.* (I have Stanley taking this book with him on his 1886 expedition to rescue Emin Pasha in Africa, a notion I latched on to based on a statement Twain once made to that effect.) Twain's "paradise" also entailed his love for a family that, as the years went by, simply vanished— two of his three daughters died, then his wife; I find it a supreme irony that a man who brought so much joy into the world, and whose own beginnings had been so happy, suffered so unfairly. What paradise remained for him came down to what he had captured so beautifully in his books and in his lingering friendships.

For Stanley, whose life began so badly—his childhood in Wales spent in a workhouse as a ward of the British state; his dangerous but successful enterprises on behalf of King Leopold in Africa eventually, perhaps unfairly, linked to the atrocities committed in that region "for rubber and ivory tusks"—this "paradise" came belatedly, in his later years. In the mid-1890s, Stanley and his wife adopted a son and retreated to a country estate in Surrey where Twain and Livy stayed as guests on at least three occasions. (To quote Twain himself, "Stanley's was the last country estate in England I ever visited.") There, after a lifetime of wanderings, he found his contentment in the company of his affectionate adoptive son. Of course, even Stanley's autumnal happiness had its limitations. Shunned by polite society over his African exploits, he became a recluse save for the company of certain friends such as Mark Twain. Plagued by recurring bouts of malaria and other "Africa-borne" diseases, he eventually entered his decline, his only solace coming not from any nostalgia for the past but from the love of his little family, the achievement of a lifelong solitary's dream.

Of course, much more happens. There is Twain's failure to persuade Stanley to write a book for his Charles L. Webster and Company publishing house upon his triumphant return from Africa in 1889, a fiasco that their friendship somehow survived; their mutual admiration for each other as writers (for a time, with Kipling, they were the most famous authors in the English-speaking world); their bouts of bad health (it was Twain who put Stanley on to the dubious holistic wonder cure known as Plasmon); and their mutual hatred of slavery—Twain was the head of an antislavery society for many years, and Stanley, as far as he was concerned, had done much to limit slavery in Africa, lecturing all over England for that cause. There were also their public lectures together and the soirees they attended—in London, Twain at one point introduced Stanley to a "promising young Scottish writer" by the name of Bram Stoker, author of *Dracula*, and Stanley introduced Twain to one of his wife's American friends, a demure fellow named Henry James, who often came to their house and met Twain on several occasions.

However, as a writer best known for certain subjects, I also intend the book to give a glance at nineteenth-century Cuba, mainly through the journeys the men made in their lifetimes to that island. Stanley went there in the early 1860s, during the American Civil War, a time when Cuba, with its strong Havana–New Orleans sugar-tobacco trade and many southern inhabitants, seemed an extension of the South. (Had the Confederates won the war they would have annexed Cuba as a state.) In that regard, Stanley's travels there draw a picture of Havana circa 1864 or so, when the Confederates had filled the warehouses of the harbor with ammunitions and supplies and when surly southern brigades, knowing how the war was going, stoically manned the docks. Twain journeyed there in 1902, in the aftermath of the Spanish-American War, and having invited Stanley along by way of a letter to England—Stanley was too ill to make the transatlantic voyage—he toured the island from one end to the other aboard a yacht, the last great adventure of his life (Twain was in his late sixties by then).

The novel extends from the late 1850s to 1910 and somewhat beyond and before, skirting back and forth in time. It culminates in Twain's last visit to London, in 1907. Stanley, a little more than five years younger, had died in 1904, and Twain, in England to receive an honorary doctorate in letters from Oxford, spent an afternoon with Dorothy Tennant for tea. (It's in the records.) She had remarried by then, to the very surgeon who had attended to Stanley in his last days, but the house remained filled with remembrances of her late husband. After some niceties, tea served, she persuaded Twain to sit for her one last time, for a fast "wishy-wash" of a portrait. And so Twain, still enchanted by the lady, who had not aged a day since he first met her in 1890 and for whom he still felt some furtive longings, sat for her again. What did they talk about? That's something the novel will tell.

TWAIN & STANLEY ENTER PARADISE

You once asked me, "What is time?" I don't really know, but the other day, for a moment I had the oddest impression that you and I were walking along the levee in New Orleans again. It was many years ago, but the dense memory of it, unfolding with all its details, seems to have taken place in the moments that it takes to blow out a ring of smoke.

—CLEMENS TO STANLEY IN A NOTE
FROM HUNGARY, JULY 10, 1897

When I was younger I could remember anything, whether it had happened or not; but my faculties are decaying now and soon I shall be so I cannot remember any but the things that never happened. It is sad to go to pieces like this but we all have to do it.

—SAMUEL CLEMENS, FROM HIS AUTOBIOGRAPHY

To lie is considered mean, and it is no doubt a habit to be avoided by every self-respecting person. But the best of men and women are sometimes compelled to resort to lying to avoid a worse offense.

—FROM *THE AUTOBIOGRAPHY OF*
HENRY MORTON STANLEY

Part One

DOROTHY'S QUESTION

IN AN 1889 ENGRAVING FOR the frontispiece of *London Street Arabs*, Dorothy Tennant is posed in profile, her jewelry-laden left hand just grazing her plumpish chin. It captured her well. She had a high, gracefully rising forehead and a great head of curling, perhaps graying hair, pensive brows, a nose that was prominent but not oppressive, thin and pursing lips, delicate and fleshy ears, and eyes that were dark and alert, her features bringing to mind a classical portrait of a Roman or Greek lady.

Tennant was a woman of wealth and high social bearing who lived in a Regency mansion on Richmond Terrace, off Whitehall, in London. This rendering of her was made but a year before her marriage to Henry Morton Stanley, explorer and "Napoleon" of journalists, whose roots had been so humble that his childhood experiences and poor upbringing in Wales would have been an abstraction to her, for her own experience had never included want or deprivation. That she, the artistic and lively pearl of London society, had become involved and happily betrothed to Stanley after a well-known period of difficulties between them was one of the great mysteries of Victorian courtships.

Like just about everyone else in England, she had been caught up in the national frenzy over Africa, having followed with rapt interest the careers of Livingstone, Baker, Cameron, Speke, and Burton, among others, whose exploits were reported in all the newspapers and commemorated in books. She had been in her adolescence when the first of these explorations began, but by 1871 the greatest of all such explorers, Henry Morton Stanley, had emerged. He first became known for his search to find the Scottish missionary David Livingstone. His later activities in the region, principally in the Congo, where he had spent many years leading other expeditions, often under impossible conditions, had only increased his stature as a heroic figure in the public mind. Stanley had been so successful in opening the equatorial center of the continent that he had become one of the most famous men in England. ("Before Stanley there was no Africa," Tennant would later write.)

Despite Stanley's mercurial personality and the burden of his many maladies, such as chronic gastritis and numerous bouts of malaria—"the Africa in me," he called it—their marriage had flourished, and they became one of the most famous couples in England. Tennant's haughty circle of friends intersected with Stanley's colleagues and acquaintances—professional relationships, for the most part. But now and then there surfaced the occasional true friendship, such as the one he had with the American writer Samuel L. Clemens, or Mark Twain, as he was most famously called.

Tennant first met Clemens at a dinner in New York City while accompanying Stanley on a lecture tour of the United States. It was an introduction that culminated, in the month of January, 1891, with an invitation to visit Clemens at his Hartford home on Farmington Avenue, where Dorothy and her mother, Gertrude, spent a most diverting few days with him and his family (at the time, Stanley was away, lecturing in Trenton and other cities in New Jersey). Thereafter, over the next decade and a half, she and Stanley saw them on various occasions, principally in London, where the Clemenses lived in the mid-1890s, then later, at the turn of the century, when they had taken up residence in England once again.

In those years, paying socials calls to the Tennant mansion on Richmond Terrace, Clemens passed many hours in their company, giving impromptu recitations for their friends at dinners, shooting billiards, and occasionally withdrawing into her studio, a canvas- and prop-cluttered room known as the birdcage, to sit as a portrait subject for Dorothy, who, in her day, was greatly admired as an artist.

It had been her wish to present a portrait of Clemens to the

National Portrait Gallery, as she had done in 1893 with a commendable rendering of her explorer husband, whom she had captured in all his splendor. Dolly had made dozens of studies of Stanley during their early courtship and dozens more in the years after their marriage—each session an immersion, she felt, into the spirit of her subject, for once he had become trusting of her, fruitful conversations ensued, and his tortured soul poured naturally forth.

The same kind of exchanges took place with Clemens, from whom Dolly had learned details about his private life—his joyfulness and pride in his family; the pain of certain devastating events that made his later years difficult. She had spent perhaps twenty hours sketching him. He had been an occasionally distracted subject, fidgeting with a cigar, getting up at any moment to stretch his stiff limbs, often staring out the window to look at the Irish perennials in her garden and sometimes losing patience with the whole idea of sitting still. Yet when she got him to talking about the things that made him happy, mainly his youth in Hannibal— the perpetually springlike wonderland from which his most memorable characters flowed—time stopped, his discomforts left him, and a serenity came over his famously leonine countenance.

⚜

"AS YOU SURELY KNOW, DOLLY, I have always been fond of Stanley. Not that he's the easiest person to understand, but he kind of grows on a body. His convictions, his work ethic, his knowledge of many things—these qualities appeal to me, even if I do not always agree with him. He's not the easiest person to get along with, by any stretch, which, by the way, I do not mind. And he is one of the moodiest people I have ever known, besides myself, and has been so ever since I first knew him. Our saving grace is that we have similar temperaments and can disagree or feel gloomy or cantankerous around each other without standing on ceremony; we are just that way."

He had paused then to relight a cigar, drawing from his vest pocket a match, which he struck against the heel of his shoe.

"Somehow, ours has been a friendship that's lasted. I cannot say that he is as close to me as my best friends in the States, but I hold him in considerable esteem just the same. The fact is we go back together to simpler times, an enviable thing. As much as he has changed over the years, he is not so different from the young man I met years ago, on a riverboat—you know of this, do you not?"

"He told me once that you met long ago."

"Indeed we did. It was a friendship that commenced by chance—on the boiler deck of a steamboat heading upriver, between New Orleans and St. Louis...in the autumn of 1860, just before the Civil War, during my days as a Mississippi River pilot."

A plume of bluish smoke.

"Stanley was traveling in the company of his adoptive American father, a merchant trader who plied the Mississippi port towns. He was Stanley's mentor in New Orleans and a great influence on his manner of dress and grooming, and he did much, as I remember, to advance his son's education, which by my lights was already considerable. Stanley was one of the better-read young men on that river. Of course I already knew some bookish types; Horace Bixby, a fellow pilot, got me to reading William Shakespeare, and occasionally I'd meet some traveling professor or any number of journalists with whom I could sometimes talk about literature. But Stanley, in those days, with his good common-school English education—one that he was modest about—was quite a cut above the average Mississippi traveler. And he seemed the most guileless and unassuming fellow one could ever encounter, to boot."

He puffed on his cigar again, and even as he was speaking, conjured, in his mind, the sight of drowsy still waters at dusk, campfires along the Mississippi River dotting the shore with light, the stars beginning to rise.

"He always had a book in hand and seemed anxious to learn about the world: I found myself beguiled by him, and I was touched that he seemed to be in need of a friend. We were both young men—I was twenty-five or so, and I believe Stanley was then about nineteen, the same age as my dear recently deceased younger brother, also named Henry. I suppose I was ready and willing to befriend Stanley for that reason alone, though who knows how or why chance happens to place a person in one's path. Whatever the mysterious cause, our friendship blossomed and eventually led to a quite interesting run of years. I am surprised that he has not told you more about our beginnings."

                              ◈

SHE SITS DOWN TO WRITE a letter in the parlor of her mansion, the interior unchanged from the day Stanley had died, three years before, at six in the morning, just as Big Ben was ringing in that hour from a distance. In its rooms many of Stanley's possessions and keepsakes remain where she had put them; in the hallways, framed photographs of Stanley on safari, Stanley in Zanzibar with his native porters, Stanley poised on a cliff in the rainbow mists of Victoria Falls. A bookcase bears a multitude of first editions and translations of his African memoirs. Atop the numerous tables and travertine pedestals are a variety of ornate freedom caskets from cities like Dundee, Edinburgh, Glasgow, Swansea, and Manchester, each honoring Stanley for one or the other of his African exploits. Here and there, hanging on a wall, are plaques that Stanley had particularly liked. One of them, harking back to 1872, when he had become famous for finding Livingstone in the wilds of Africa, reads:

A COMMON COUNCIL

Holden in the chamber of Guildhall, of the City of London
On Thursday, the 21st day of November, 1872,

RESOLVED UNANIMOUSLY

That this court desires to express its great appreciation of
the eminent services rendered by

MR. HENRY MORTON STANLEY

To the cause of science and humanity by his persistent and
successful endeavors to discover and relieve that zealous
and persevering
Missionary and African Traveller,

DR. DAVID LIVINGSTONE,

The uncertainty of whose fate had caused such deep anxiety,
not only to Her Majesty's subjects, but to the whole
civilised world.

There are framed maps of Africa and bronze busts of Stanley lining the hallways and several Minton biscuit figurines of
Stanley—the kind that were sold for years in the tourist shops
of Piccadilly—set out on a parlor table. On a desk in Lady Stanley's own study, just down the hall from her painting studio, sit
her commonplace books and a manuscript of her own writings—
the fragments of a memoir (never to be completed) called *My Life
with Henry Morton Stanley*—alongside a plaster cast of Stanley's
left hand, which she keeps for good luck. But there is also much
more about Stanley—diplomas, royal decrees, gold medals (the
Order of Leopold and the Knight Grand Cross of the Order of
the Bath from the late queen; the Grand Cordon of the Imperial
Order of Medijdieh from the khedive of Egypt)—to come upon in
that house. There are also many other keepsakes—old compasses,
sextants, and other instruments as well as various native African
artifacts, such as Zulu fly whisks, spearheads, and phallic oddities
brought back by Stanley after his journeys—on display in a curio
cabinet.

As she writes, his presence is inescapable. Even as she is about
to remarry, in a few weeks, Lady Stanley has never gotten around
to removing a thing from Stanley's private bedroom—they had
sometimes slept apart. His wardrobe closet still contains the Sav-
ile Row suits he favored, along with his shirts, his lace bow ties,

his vests, suspenders, stockings, his walking sticks, and many pairs of his distinctively smallish-size shoes. Even his bedside table has remained as it was the morning he left her—a pair of wire-rimmed spectacles sitting atop the pages of a Bible, opened to the chapters of Genesis. Nor has she touched the mantel clock with Ottoman numerals, except to rewind it nightly; nor has she removed from that chamber the other books he had taken much comfort in: Gladstone's *Gleanings of Past Years*, a volume of autobiographical essays that Stanley admired despite his personal dislike of the man ("I detect the churchgoing, God-fearing, conscientious Christian in almost every paragraph," he had written); the histories of Thucydides; and two novels, *David Copperfield* by Charles Dickens ("That boy was me, in my youth" he once said) and another by his old friend Mark Twain, *The Adventures of Huckleberry Finn*—the very copy Stanley had carried with him on his final expedition to Africa.

And along with the framed photographs he had asked to be placed near him as he had lain in his bed, beside those of Denzil, Queen Victoria, and Livingstone, there are several oil studies made by Lady Stanley in earlier days: Stanley sitting on the lawn of their country estate in Surrey; a portrait of Samuel Clemens that Dolly had commenced some years before in her studio.

From Lady Stanley to Samuel Clemens

May 11, 1907
2 Richmond Terrace, Whitehall, London

Dearest Sam,

I have been going through Henry's many papers and notebooks in my attempt to fill out his history. In his study, he kept several large cabinets of facsimiles of letters, old manuscripts, and notebooks. He was a hoarder of all things pertaining to himself, perhaps for the sake of the historical record, and so, as you may well imagine, there has been quite a bit to consider. Lately, I have made it my habit to spend a part of my days searching for materials pertinent to the story of his life— no easy task, given their volume. It is a labor I have conducted in slow but steady measures.

In any event, I have come across a manuscript that I had never seen before. It is a manuscript I believe Henry had commenced shortly after we had visited New Orleans in the autumn of 1890, while on tour for dear Major Pond, when Henry's memories of his life there, after an absence of thirty years, had been freshly reawakened. Since much of it was written out on stationery from hotel and steamship lines, with which I am familiar, having accompanied Stanley on his tours of the States and Australia in 1891 and 1892, I date its composition to that time. At first, I had thought the manuscript a preliminary version of the chapters regarding his first years in his adopted country, which Henry would later refine. But as I read on I was surprised to see how much it diverged from what he later left as the "official" version, for these pages contain an untold story. And that story has presented me, as the amateur compiler of his life, with a very great dilemma.

And here it is: In the completed sections of the autobiography, which he approved for publication, he plainly states that Henry Hope Stanley, the merchant trader from New Orleans whom he considered his second father, had vanished during a journey to Cuba, where he had a business: "He died in 1861. I did not learn this until long afterward," is how he summarized it. Yet the "cabinet" manuscript, if I may call it so, seems to be an elaborate explanation of Henry's search for his father in Cuba, a journey he claims, in these pages, to have made in the days of late March and early April of 1861, with you.

Samuel, as delighted as I had been over this unexpected revelation, you must imagine the state of perplexity it put me in. For in this manuscript contradicts what Henry once told me about his experiences in Cuba, which he claimed to have

*visited only once, in 1865; he said that he made that journey to
see his adoptive father's grave for himself, the elder Mr. Stanley
having been buried "in some churchyard near Havana." And
the only time he had mentioned you in relation to his early
days in America—in fact, while we were strolling down the
Vieux Carré of New Orleans during our 1891 journey there—
he referred to your chance meeting "along some stretch of the
Mississippi," aboard a riverboat, years ago. But he never elaborated about your early friendship, nor did he begin to hint at
the extent to which he had, in fact, privately written about
you. Since it was obviously Henry's wish to exclude this narrative from his official story, I am assuming that he had his
reasons, upon which I hope you will shed some light. I have
taken the liberty of sending you a typescript version (Henry's
original, often written in a post-malarial state, suffers from
stains and an addled penmanship). Once you have read it, I
hope you can answer this question: Was it so, Samuel?*

THE CABINET MANUSCRIPT

My Early Days in New Orleans, 1859

WHEN I ARRIVED IN NEW Orleans from England, aboard an
American packet ship, the *Windermere*, it was as a despised and
loathed cabin boy without a friend in the city. Prior to my voyage I

had worked for a butcher in Liverpool, such as was my own father in Denbigh, may God rest his soul, and like all children who are raised without the touchstones of paternity and in poverty, I had become overly trusting of complete strangers. Some seven weeks back, on a solemnly gray day, while the *Windermere* lay in port, I had made the delivery of some meat goods to the ship's cook, the blood bleeding into my coat sleeves, and because I had been so respectful in my dealings with him, the captain thought me a fine candidate for a life at sea. In truth I was not happy with my current profession, so when the captain offered me a position—that of a cabin boy, with its promise of adventure—I believed him and signed on eagerly.

The reality turned out differently. Aboard the *Windermere* the same kinds of abuses I had endured at St. Asaph Union Workhouse were repeated. Landlubbers such as I were held in the lowest regard by the seasoned mates. It had not helped my situation to have often fallen ill with seasickness; that was one thing, humiliation and grief another. For even in my illness I was often rousted from my cot by a mate who said he would skin me alive unless I scrubbed down the deck for no good reason. After some fifty-two days at sea, with stops in the Canary Islands, Jamaica, Haiti, and Cuba, had come into New Orleans, my romance with the wild seafaring life had subsided.

We had anchored off one of the four mouths of the Mississippi River at a point called La Balize, after which we were tied to a tug that steamed us upriver for about one hundred miles, as I remember. When we finally came to the port of New Orleans itself, about midday, the harbor was glutted with merchant vessels of every kind. Along the levee, which stretched some three or four miles, forming a crescent-shaped wall against the water around the city, freight lay in mountainous heaps everywhere, and an army of workers—of every color—moved in great packs around them, mules and carts and wagons loaded up with barrels, cotton bales, and hogsheads. Sailors, pilots, captains, and laborers, sacks slung over their shoulders, were making their way down the wharves toward the city (for some reason I fancy it a possibility that my friend Samuel Clemens had been among them).

As the *Windermere* was the fourth in a row of ships berthed parallel to one of the piers, no sooner had we laid down a walkway of planking to the next ship than did a contingent of New Orleans harlots flock on board to make arrangements with the men who paired off with their ladies and headed off into the saloons and boardinghouses fronting the riverside.

I remained on the *Windermere* with my cabinmate on that voyage, a handsome English lad by the name of Harry who was my own age but far more seasoned than I. Having been to New Orleans several times before, he had been anxious to go ashore, but he and I had been kept on day watch, to guard against thieves slipping aboard. I was not entirely displeased with the prospect of remaining behind, but Harry wanted to show me around. He knew of a boardinghouse near the commercial district where we could have a very fine New Orleans–style meal at little cost. When night fell we descended onto shore. I had no watch to keep time, but I had heard only moments before some distant church bells ringing the hour of seven. It was a few minutes after that, on February 17, 1859, that I first set foot onto American soil.

The joy of my young heart cannot be adequately described here, but suffice it to say I was overwhelmed. As we bounded across the levee, taking in the balmy air, I was struck by the many scents emanating from the shore. Occasionally there came the aroma of magnolia blossoms and flowers from some distant garden or patch of trees, a whiff of crisp sea air cutting through the doldrums.

GRADUALLY WE MADE OUR WAY into the city. Its physical aspect was reminiscent of the "Spanish" style described to me by the sailors who had been to such places as Málaga, Cartagena, and the city of Havana, which I had only seen from afar—our ship having remained anchored in its harbor because of a cholera quarantine. The torch-lit streets teemed with people, who, walking along in the languidness of the air, were soothed and serenaded by all kinds of music.

Moving with a certain gait, which seemed quite "un-English" to me, these citizens, slave and freeman alike, were casual about the mixing of classes. Even the black men, Harry explained to me, were at liberty to roam about and to partake of such things as they wanted, for in that place the mightiest banker walked alongside the lowliest slave and common worker. This I had never seen in England!

Through these crowds we made our way to Tchoupitoulas Street and, at long last, came to the boardinghouse that Harry had mentioned to me. The owners, recognizing him from before, treated us with the greatest hospitality. Shortly I sat down to my first American meal—a feast of grits, corn muffins, okra soup, sweet potatoes, and other fixings, followed by helpings of rice pudding (which I had never eaten before, and hence, even these many years later, I especially remember it). Then I joined Harry in a cigar.

Afterward, with our hunger sated, I would have been perfectly content to return to our ship, but Harry, hungry for another kind of experience, led me to a boardinghouse on another street. In my trust of Harry I had evidently allowed myself to enter a bordello, for no sooner had we sat down than did four young ladies, in silk bloomers and stockings, assail our persons: I was left speechless. And while Harry seemed to be enjoying himself, it brought to my mind the terrible and lowly stock of the transient women I had seen interred within the walls of St. Asaph's, among them my own mother, who had abandoned me at birth.

I fled from that house and, with Harry's voice calling after me, made my way contritely back to the ship.

Now, the captain who had tricked me aboard in the first place perhaps hoped that I had indeed jumped ship, for it was a strategy of such men to gain an additional profit from their voyages by making conditions so intolerable for temporary seamen such as myself that the workers simply bolted without their wages. And so the next day, when the captain found that I had not "vamoosed," he put me to work at some very harsh labors. He worked me so hard that I could not so much pause for a moment to wipe the sweat from my brow. Alone in my cabin at night, while pondering my plight, I decided to leave that ship for good, come what will.

Late on the fifth evening, when Harry returned from one of his rambles through the city and collapsed, dead drunk, on the bunk above me, I lit the cabin's pewter lamp, packed my few possessions into a sack, and, slipping off the *Windermere*, made my way onto the levee. About a half mile from the ship I lay down by a pile of cotton bales to sleep and had wistful, odd dreams.

☼

AWAKENED AT AN EARLY HOUR by the clanging of bells and first mates' whistles coming from the harbor, I left the levee and made my way toward the commercial district, moving among the din of passersby. My general distress was only alleviated by my trust in Providence: For whatever reasons I had been brought to that juncture, I believed it part of some kind of design. I had no money, not even enough for a simple breakfast. My situation was perilous: Had I been struck down by a bolt of lightning, what would have been found on my person were a few letters that I had intended to send to Thomas and Maria Morris, my aunt and uncle in Liverpool, each of them signed, "Yours, John Rowlands." And I had a certificate of graduation from St. Asaph's, folded into quarters; a passport saying who I was; and my Bible, which also bore my name.

And yet despite my many faults, luck smiled upon me that day. As I came up from the harbor and made my way to Tchoupitoulas Street, Negroes were everywhere, sweeping the sidewalks and attending to the arrangement of goods and barrels in front of the many stores, which seemed to become progressively larger as I walked farther along. Among them was a warehouse from whose facade hung a great sign that read:

SPEAKE AND MCCREARY, WHOLESALE AND COMMISSION MERCHANTS

There I saw an immense and bearded man of middle age in a dark alpaca suit and stovepipe hat sitting in a chair in front of its doorway, newspaper in hand, a slave standing by his side fanning him. Sucking on a thin black cigar, his dark blue eyes focused intensely upon his reading matter through a pair of spectacles, he had been, at first, indifferent to my approach; but then when I, taking him as the proprietor, finally piped up, asking if he needed a "boy," he could not have been less interested.

"What would I need with a boy when I have my slaves?" he said. But then he noticed my Bible.

"And what is that?"

"My Bible, sir."

"Then let me see it."

Opening it, he was pleased by what he saw: Inside its cover was an inscription that read: PRESENTED TO JOHN ROWLANDS BY THE RIGHT REVD. THOMAS VOWLER SHORT, D.D., LORD BISHOP OF ST. ASAPH, FOR DILIGENCE TO HIS STUDIES, AND GENERAL GOOD CONDUCT. JANUARY 5TH, 1855.

"Most commendable," he said. "So you are from Wales?"

"Yes sir."

"And this 'St. Asaph's'?"

"It was a parish workhouse: I was sent there as a boy."

"What are you doing here in New Orleans?"

I then told him the tale of my misfortunes on the *Windermere*.

"And why do you carry a Bible?"

"I carry it because, whatsoever are my difficulties, I have the faith."

"And your favorite sections of the Bible?"

"The book of Genesis. The beginnings of this world impress me very much. And, of course, the New Testament, which contains the good teachings."

"A fine response. It happens that I am a former preacher and would have answered the same." Then: "And you are looking for work?"

"I am, sir. Or for any advice about how I can find it."

"Can you read?"

"Well enough."

"Then read this."

And the gentleman handed me his morning paper, the New Orleans *Daily Picayune*, an article from which I began to recite aloud.

"Enough. That is a correct reading, but are you aware, young man, that you have a very strong accent?"

"I do. But I would strive to correct it."

"I see." Then: "Can you write?"

"My script was said to be the finest in my school."

"Then take a brush and a can of black paint to those coffee bags piled against the wall there and affix my trademark and their destinations to them. Here, I will show you how."

I shortly set to work, and after his example, I inscribed his trademark, a letter *S* inside a quadrangle, onto each fibrous covering, along with its eventual destination upriver, Memphis, Tennessee. I did so in a firm hand and with the most beautiful letters. When I had finished addressing about twenty such sacks, this gentleman, greatly satisfied, told me that I indeed possessed an elegant and legible script.

"I could not have done better myself," he said. "Well, let me see what I can do for you. Mr. Speake, the owner of this warehouse, always comes in after nine. Until then, we will have ample time to discuss the nature of his business. Perhaps he will have a use for you."

We stopped in a restaurant, where, famished, I ate to my heart's content; and because I was in such a disreputable state we then visited a barbershop, where, at my benefactor's suggestion—and expense—I was cleaned up, my hair shampooed and trimmed, and my face shaved: Then a Negro boy dusted off my coat, pressed it under an iron, and polished my boots. By the time we returned to the warehouse Mr. Speake was in his office. I do not believe I have ever seen so thin a man outside of a circus or one who used so much hair dye and tonic, for, parted in the middle, his hair glistened like wet coal, and he possessed a nervous twitch, which made his sharp nose seem skittish.

He conducted a short interview with me on the spot, asking if I could add. When I told him I could, he smiled and, winking at his gentleman friend—my benefactor—posed the following question:

"What say you of the following addition: If there are twenty-seven cases of soap at four cents a bar, with ninety-six bars per case, and a markup of one and one-half cents per each—what profit would that yield per case?"

"One hundred and forty-four dollars," I said after a few moments of calculation.

Mr. Speake hired me that day, on a temporary trial basis, for what seemed at the time like the princely sum of five dollars per week. I would be a general assistant in that place, to perform at first many menial tasks until I learned the ropes. But he told me that he would be away for a month or so, traveling upriver with his consignments, and that he hoped to hear good accounts of my work upon his return.

That same evening, after acquainting myself with some of the inventory in the store, since I had no place to go, I was given a cot and a blanket and shown to a storage room in the back. Resting in my cot that night, I had the strange thought that just a few days before I had been in a more or less untenable situation and that my status as a ship's lackey was changed by the simple possession of my Bible. Though I was kept awake by the buzz of insects and the scratching about of mice as they investigated the dark corners of that room, I couldn't have cared less at the time.

☀

NOW, IN THE DAYS THAT followed I was put to work alongside the two slaves—Dan and Samuel—preparing all manner of items for shipment. It was my direct superior, Mr. Richardson, who prepared the bills of lading, and it was my responsibility, being able to read, to retrieve such goods from storage. Many of my hours were spent up on a ladder with a slip of paper in hand, sorting through the disorder of the inventory, which seemed quite arbitrarily arranged, in one or another of the three lofts that stretched above the ground floor some one hundred feet along the length of the premises. Cases of wine and brandies and syrups and other groceries were stacked randomly without concern for order: Bottles of Scotch whiskey might be found in three or four different locations; a crate of a certain brand of rye would be sitting under a stack of crated candles or soaps; tins of chewing tobacco would be lost somewhere under a pyramid of English tea tins. The ground floor was no better organized.

"Little boss, why you want to work so hard? Better to leave something for tomorrow," Dan and Samuel would say.

But in truth I was incapable of lying idle for even a few moments; the disorder of the place disturbed my peace of mind. Even the respectable Mr. Richardson, who filled out the bills of lading, dealt with steamship pursers, and kept the ledger books, had a maddening tendency to throw all our completed invoices into a barrel that he kept behind a counter without much concern for the possibility that they might be needed again. Several times he set me to work sorting through them. On one occasion, when a cotton planter, up in a place called Attakapas, claimed that he had been shorted of certain items, the finding of the original invoices, made out some months before, took—and wasted—several hours that might have otherwise been constructively spent. (My readers may be wondering why I am mentioning such things; but it is because from such disorder I learned the importance of keeping proper records and inventory, a lesson that would serve me well in my future provisioning of my Africa expeditions.) And there was something else: Aside from my tendency toward work, I wanted to reflect well on my benefactor's faith in me.

I did not know very much about him at the time: I only learned his name, Mr. Henry Stanley, by asking. But it was from the shipment manager, Mr. Richardson, that I ascertained, through conversations with him, the exact nature of Mr. Stanley's professional life. The brunt of his business was in trading cotton. He would travel upriver by steamship, bargain with cotton planters on behalf of the New Orleans merchants, and offer the planters grocery goods—the necessities that were sold in the most remote outposts and settlements along the Arkansas and Saline Rivers. Loaded up with consignments of everything from coffee to combs, tooth powder to razors, he set out north and returned with huge shipments of cotton, which, processed through his own cotton press, he then sold to the merchants of New Orleans. And sometimes, his route took him to the West Indies, and principally to Havana, Cuba, where Mr. Stanley's brother, a certain Captain John, had an office in port, those journeys concentrating on the sugar and tobacco trade and Havana cigars, for which, in New Orleans, Mr. Stanley was a noted supplier.

Apparently Mr. Stanley lived well—in a fine house on St. Charles Avenue, and had a wife and, it was said, a commendable education as befitting a proper southern gentleman. As for his relationship with my employer, as he had frequent dealings with him and other merchants along that street, he paid Mr. Speake a small fee to keep him a desk in the back of the store, which he visited from time to time during his days back in that strange city.

DURING MY FIRST WEEKS THERE I got to know the slaves quite well. I would say I knew them better than I did any of the white clerks, for in the many hours that we spent loading up the drays, or when we would take a break and sit in front of the store just watching the processions of passersby and carriages on the street, they spoke kindly of their own families and seemed, on the whole, aware of the fact that even if they were slaves, their jobs in the store, lasting some six days a week, weren't so bad

when compared to the very hard labors of the plantation workers upriver. No Simon Legree, Mr. Speake paid them some small
wage so that they might live in their own little sheds, and he
allowed them to hire themselves out to other merchants, on their
own time.

Materially poor, they seemed to derive their happiness out of
small pleasures—at lunch Dan liked to play a harmonica, while
Samuel stuck a Jew's harp in his mouth to twang along with him.
Even a smallish gift of a handful of candies, which the clerks
sometimes gave them, they treated like a treasure. They seemed
to know every other slave on the street—their lunch hours passed
with a litany of "How're yuh" and greetings to various friends,
and all manner of social exchange, such as invitations to dance
parties or birthday celebrations. Most of their friends were slaves,
like themselves, but the most important black man on the street
was a freed Negro—New Orleans had more freed slaves than any
other city in the South—a certain Dr. Brown, a thin, well-dressed
man of an erect posture and serious bearing, elegant as any physician, who mainly treated the slaves working in that district, as
many a white doctor refused to. He'd come down Tchoupitoulas
making his calls, politely tipping his hat whenever Dan and Samuel greeted him; upon occasion he nodded at me in a friendly way.

If they lived in fear of any of the clerks, it was Mr. McKinney,
who sometimes stood sternly by watching them work, a switch in
his hand, as if he were some kind of slave driver; and they always
piped down whenever the burly local constable, Mr. McPhearson,
passed by, giving them a contemptuous glance.

I had been sleeping in that back room for several weeks, an
infelicitous situation, when one evening, as I was helping sweep
out the shop, the slave Dan, perhaps feeling sorry for me, told
me that he knew of a refined black woman, a certain Mrs. Williams, who ran a decent and clean boardinghouse with cheap rates
on St. Thomas Street. And so he arranged to take me there to
find a room. At dusk one evening, as I walked beside them along

Tchoupitoulas Street, on my way to Mrs. Williams's, we fell into conversation.

"Where's that place you say you come from again, Little Boss?" Dan, the more cheerful of the two, asked me.

"A village in north Wales called Denbigh."

"What'd he say?"

"In north Wales, over in England!"

"Oh, the queen's country, is that right?"

"They've got castles and dragons over there, I hear," said Samuel. "Don't they have castles, Mr. John?"

"Denbigh has a castle," I said. "Put up by a very evil English king, a fellow named Edward Longshanks."

They howled at both my Welsh accent and the image of a man with such a name.

"You live around here?" I asked Dan.

"Yes, suh, not too far away, in a little shack, behind a slaughterhouse. It's not much, but it's a home; my wife, she works, too, as a laundress; and my children work, too, plucking feathers for a chicken farmer."

Ever curious about the slave's life, in my ignorance, I asked: "And how did you end up a slave?"

He laughed. "There was no 'end up.' My father was brought here as a slave, through Natchez: and I was born so. It's all I know, suh."

"And your father, Samuel?"

"My pappy, he died a long time ago. Up in one of the plantations. Me, I was the lucky one, being traded by a planter to Mr. Speake for some two hundred dollars' worth of dry goods, when I was a boy."

"'Tis is a sad thing, not having a father."

"Oh, I've heard of a whole lot worse, Little Boss; all kinds of families broken up all the time. Little ones never seeing their folks; husbands took from their wives. At least I got my own family—and Mr. Speake said that maybe one day he give us all our freedoms. When he dies, anyway—and I'm sure he's in no hurry. Anyway, this is Mrs. Williams's boardinghouse."

Then, standing on its porch, he called in: "Mrs. Williams, I'm here with the white fella I told you about."

⁂

ENTERING HER BOARDINGHOUSE, I WAS much taken by Mrs. Williams's amicable presence. Maternal in her manner, she was apologetic that I would have to make do with the highest and therefore warmest room in her house, in the attic, as all the other rooms were rented. But I found the accommodations, at one dollar and fifty cents per week, with meals, more than adequate. The room was small, with an arched ceiling, and had a shuttered window that opened out over the back garden and some magnolia trees—it pleased me that it faced north, for then I would be able to see the moon and stars rise. It had a bed, a chamber pot (several outhouses being in the backyard), a small table, a chair, a washbasin with a pot of water, a speckled mirror that hung off a nail on a wall beam; a little rack for hanging clothes, a kerosene lamp, and, in the corner, a small framed picture of Jesus: my first American home.

That very night, just as I was to turn in, she offered to wash and iron my clothes before morning; and though I protested, she insisted that she knew better. Such treatment, like so many other things, came as an unexpected blessing to me.

Even though she was a Mrs., I never saw her husband around: Perhaps she was widowed—I did not know and never thought to ask her, but in any case she seemed quite self-sufficient. Often as her last act of the day, around ten at night, after she'd served supper and cleared off the dining table, Mrs. Williams took out a money box, and, figuring out her expenses, put a few dollars into a envelope—I supposed to send to relatives. Altogether, aside from liking her, I was very impressed by what she had done with her "free" status in that city known for its commerce in slaves, as her humble prosperity seemed to me further evidence of the equity of American life.

 ☆

WITHIN A SHORT TIME AT the firm, my trial period passed, and I was hired permanently at the rate of twenty-five dollars a month. Evidently my efforts to reorganize the warehouse had impressed Mr. Speake, who day by day began to notice the subtle changes and new order of the place. Shortly my direct dealings with Dan and Samuel ended, which is to say I no longer loaded drays with them. And while I remained just a junior clerk, I had been given, with my promotion, many other duties, including bookkeeping. Few things escaped my attention: A leaking coffee sack I sewed shut myself; or if a bottle of wine shattered on the floor, I thought nothing about mopping it up.

Certain of my fellow clerks began to fear me, or, I should say, they became wary of my alert presence. A few, such as the bookkeeper, Mr. Kennicy, were secret drinkers. He was also disdainful of my friendliness with the slaves. About his drinking addiction I did not care, though some sloppy, miscalculated invoices I attributed to his inebriation. But as to my doings with Dan and Samuel, I thought him clearly wrong. After all, this was America, the land of free speech, of a Constitution that protected personal rights, a country founded on the aspirations of men seeking a society that would be free of the class restrictions of a monarchy like England. The soundness of the slave system itself I did not, in my youthful ignorance of slaves' sufferings, question: I believed it was part of a greater design, and surely, supernatural reasoning aside, it was of indeterminable practical value to the economy of the South. What I objected to was the unfair treatment of such slaves and the cruelties I had heard were rendered to them. Needless to say, a strained relationship, if not an enmity, existed between me and the bookkeeper, but I was not worried, as Mr. Kennicy, in his pickled state, could do little more than insult me behind my back.

∾

AS I HAD A WAY of quickly forming attachments to a place, my attic room at Mrs. Williams's became my refuge. With my monthly upkeep at ten dollars or so, out of my surplus of fifteen—minus what I would pay in increments to Mr. Speake for the loan—I put a certain portion, fifteen percent, into the purchase of books. What I had already read I wanted to expand upon, particularly in the realm of imaginary writings, that of novels and poetry, in which I was greatly wanting. My initial purchase, I remember, was a crumbling copy of Milton's *Paradise Lost*, the opening lines of which—

> *Of man's first disobedience, and the fruit*
> *Of that forbidden tree, whose mortal taste*
> *Brought death into the world, and all our woe . . .*

—I strongly took as the essential truth of our fleeting existence. Enthralled by my elevation into the poet's mind, much greater than my own, I spent one entire evening reading that volume by the light of a kerosene lamp from beginning to end, until my eyes ached: I did not care if I felt a little tired in the morning—I had endless amounts of energy then, and no illnesses had laid me low. Besides, I did not like to sleep; or, to put it differently, I did not like the nightmares that often came to me. Nonetheless I had the solace of my books: If some men went after women or became rhapsodic with alcohol, my addictions, I discovered, were to work and to read what I construed as literature.

It wasn't long, flush with surplus funds, before I acquired other volumes: Gibbon's *Decline and Fall*, Spenser's *Faerie Queene*, Pope's translation of Homer, Plutarch's *Lives*, and Simplicius on Epictetus, among others: and as I was very ignorant about America, a great many volumes on its history as well. (As a matter of interest to my readers, regarding my future African exploits, I also happened upon a copy of David Livingstone's *Missionary Travels and Researches in South Africa*, which I read over a period of several days, little knowing how this man, the so-called apostle of Africa, would later figure in my own life.)

Soon, within that little attic room, my world was contained—I had no need for anything else. During such evenings I forgot myself and became a creature of words. I, who had always learned by mimicry and observation, found myself dreaming of sonnets, couplets, and of great histories of my own. If only I could have remembered them in the morning. Sad to say, in the soberness of my present years, it has been borne out that my greatest gifts would not be in such elevated realms but in the more ordinary precincts of word muscling, detail mongering, and factual reportage.

꙰

AT THE END OF THAT first month, Mr. Stanley returned to the warehouse from his travels, and, learning of my contributions to the running of that place, was deeply pleased.

One afternoon, a small crisis—a discrepancy involving some jugs of sweet white Malmsey wine—arose. It was a Saturday. I had overheard Dan speaking about a birthday party for his little girl, to be held at his place the next day.

During his lunch hour, Dan sat in front of the warehouse inviting just about every black man and woman who went by to his party—"It'll be an all-out joy of joys!" he declared. He even invited me, and I planned on going, along with Mrs. Williams.

The day before I had inspected every single jug of Malmsey wine and judged most of them full: My chalked X on the side marked them so. Nevertheless, several jugs were now appreciably depleted. I had no choice but to look around. Knowing the slaves' habits—they tended to linger in the unseen recesses of the upper lofts, where, I already knew, they opened cases of licorices and candies and took a few things now and then—I asked Dan to hold steady a ladder as I climbed up into the lofts to investigate: He seemed somewhat apprehensive at my ascent.

"Why you going up there, Little Boss?" Dan asked. "Ain't nothing there," he kept on saying. But once I set my feet down on the floor of that low-ceilinged loft—you had to crouch to go anywhere—I began to look around. It was in a broom closet that I made the unpleasant discovery of one of their lunch buckets, filled to the brim with the sweet wine. I also found a cache of tinned sardines and biscuits and jellies stashed beside it.

"Dan," I called down to him. "Come here." And when he climbed up and I showed him the evidence of their theft, I asked: "What could you have been thinking?"

"Mr. Kennicy put us up to it at first. He said, 'Give me half— you take the other half.' A lot of Scotch and rye bottles are low, too. I didn't want to, Mr. John, but I swear, we were put up to it."

"Well, then," I asked, "if you were me, what would you do?"

"I don't know. But I'm asking myself, what's a few ounces of such and such a cheap wine to a business with so many thousands of things all around? Heck, they'll make the money anyways— they wouldn't be doing this otherwise—and Mr. Kennicy, he steals more from this place than any poor Negro ever could." Then: "Mr. John, what will you do?"

In their defense, I thought to propose that it was a lapse of judgment that provoked such an action. Finally, seeing how frightened and contrite Dan seemed to be, I resolved to drop the matter, but no sooner did I think this than I heard someone else climbing the ladder: It was Mr. Kennicy himself, who, finding the evidence, slapped poor Dan across the face and, calling out into the store, declared: "I've found the thief!"

Shortly both slaves were called into Mr. Speake's office. By then, Mr. Stanley was standing in the corner, gravely observing the proceedings. On Mr. Speake's desk lay the bucket of Malmsey wine and another of sweet syrup, found stashed in the backyard under a cloth, behind a tree where Samuel often sat. Along the way Mr. Kennicy had produced a number of other goods—candles, cans of sardines, and hard candies that he claimed he found hidden in another corner. Shortly an interrogation of the slaves began.

"How is it," Mr. Speake demanded to know of Dan, "that these items were found hidden in your loft?"

"Seems likely they could have fallen out a box," said Samuel. And Dan added: "I swear I've never seen those things before. Lord knows how they got there."

"Come, now, then—how can you explain this theft?"

They had no answer, though Samuel did his cause good by getting down on his knees and begging for Mr. Speake's forgiveness. Not so with Dan, who showed a bedeviled side of himself that I had never seen before. "I ain't 'pologizing to nobody. I did what I did, that's all."

"Then you shall be instantly dismissed," said Mr. Speake. And with that he took a rod and struck Dan across the face, then hit him in the back as he turned and tried to run away. I wanted to put a stop to the punishment, but Mr. Stanley laid his hand firmly on my shoulder. Looking down at me, he said, "You've done a fine thing today, Mr. Rowlands. But do not concern yourself with what you cannot change." By then, Mr. Kennicy had taken his switch and started beating both slaves. They were curled up on the floor, his blows striking all over their bodies, tearing their clothes and leaving slicks of blood on each. Their cause was not helped by Dan's stubbornness and the curses he put on Mr. Speake: "You been a good boss, but I hope you die, and soon!"

Constable McPhearson soon arrived, and, putting them in chains, he led them away, Dan cursing the white men and Samuel lamenting, "Oh, my po' children, my po', po' children; what will they do?"

Back then I was softer-hearted: For all I had already seen of the abuses that men put upon other men, I could not help but think about Dan's expression whenever he'd sit out front during his lunchtime, eating with delight a piece of biscuit with some jam on it, his innocence and thorough pleasure bringing to mind the joys of a child. Mr. Stanley, seeing my disturbed state, said, "I know what you're thinking, young man—that the punishment awaiting them is far greater than the crime. Feel no grief for them—they brought it on themselves."

The same afternoon they were stripped practically naked, tied to a post, and publicly flogged, after which they were confined to a windowless shed in the constable's yard for a month. Eventually forgiven, Samuel was reinstated in the warehouse, while Dan, sound of body, was put up for auction and sold to an Arkansas planter for four hundred and fifty dollars, his days to be spent upriver working from the early morning to night, picking cotton. For his actions Mr. Kennicy was given a raise of two dollars a week, a fair sum in those days. As for myself, Mr. Stanley, on his way out of the warehouse, gave me his card and invited me to his house on St. Charles Avenue the next Sunday for a breakfast banquet with his wife and some of their friends.

WHEN THAT AUSPICIOUS DAY CAME I put on my newly bought finery and made my way into the prosperous neighborhood where Mr. Stanley and his wife, Frances, resided. Like so many of the other grand domiciles on St. Charles Avenue, it was of a neoclassical construction and finely painted white. It had a wide portico entranceway and a front veranda that looked out over a blossoming garden. Up some grand steps I went, pulling on the rope of a bell: A well-dressed slave let me inside and led me into a small sitting room, much like a library, as it contained many books, where Mr. Stanley and his quaint wife, Frances, were waiting.

"This is the clerk I told you about—John Rowlands, the one who reads the Bible," Mr. Stanley said. And with that, his wife, a frail-seeming but delicately featured little woman who wore an angelic white dress, rich with embroidered silk, extended her little hand toward me and told me to sit beside her.

"My husband tells me you possess a fine character. But I am wondering what you can tell me about yourself, so that I will have something to say to our gathering about you."

"Well, I am eighteen years old, from Wales, and, I think, fairly well educated for my class. And good with numbers and facts. I can read Latin and Greek, and I can speak French fairly well, though I've never been to France, and the Welsh dialect." Then: "I have begun to read Plutarch's *Lives*."

"And of your mother and father, what can you say?"

"I have none, ma'am." I looked away. "But I know the difference between right and wrong, as I was taught so from an early age."

"Then you should know," she told me, "that you are most welcome here; you see, we have no son of our own."

And getting up, with the assistance of Mr. Stanley, she led the way into the dining room, where their guests, about a dozen or so of New Orleans's finest citizens, bejeweled and perfumed, were gathered around a long table and already in the midst of various discourses. Once Mr. Stanley had taken his place at the head of the table and led the group in a prayer, an Irish maid came in to serve the dishes

It was the consensus of the group that the prosperity of the South was built upon the necessity of slavery, that it was no one's right to interfere with such a proven tradition, and that in countries where the slave trade had been reduced, such as the British West Indies, conditions for the slaves and planters only worsened. Besides, to free the slaves would be to court disaster: "Think," someone said, "about the revolt in Haiti fifty years ago, when the slaves rose up and cruelly butchered their white masters, whether man, woman, or child."

The abolitionists had made no provisions to prevent that kind of slaughter, it was said—nor could they see God's hand in that design: For the Africans came from a godless land, without a knowledge of the Bible or of the Savior, and if anything, at least as slaves they had the prospect of salvation before them and greatly improved lives.

And who among them ever mistreated any slaves or punished a slave who did not deserve it?

"I have decided to free my slaves upon my death," said a gallant gentleman. "And to provide each with twenty dollars cash: Now, where is the crime in that?"

"And what of the immorality of abolition?" asked another. "Is it not thought a crime for a man to have money picked from his pocket? Why, then, should the abolitionists think it moral to take from a man his three- and four-hundred-dollar investment in a property?"

"I've seen some abused slaves brought in from Natchez," said another. "Fellows close to being dead, and I purchased them anyway and presided over the restoration of their health."

The room resounded with "Hear, hear."

Then, startling me, he added: "But let us hear a new voice. Master Rowlands, have you, new to this country, yet formed any opinion on this issue?"

I gulped down some juice, and then, stuttering somewhat, spoke of my observations.

"Well, sirs, I don't know much at all of the subject of slaves, except for what I have seen with my own ignorant eyes. In Wales, there wasn't even one about. But here such Africans are everywhere, and sometimes I have spoken to such folks. Are they trustworthy? I cannot say. Are they deserving of their captivity? Sometimes this is a very great mystery to me, for I do not know how I would feel if I were owned by another man."

A silence met my remarks. Perceiving the deadness of expressions around me and the blanching of Mr. Stanley's face, I decided that I had perhaps not spoken in an entirely approving way of a system in which this gathering was strongly invested.

I bowed to my listeners and took my place beside Mrs. Stanley, who had started to fan herself, as if the room had become too warm, and I became convinced that it might have been better had I said nothing at all.

Smiling, Mr. Stanley later said to me: "You are still young and have much to learn about the world. It is one thing to speak of matters based solely on impressions; another to speak from a deeper knowledge. But it is my hope that, in time, you will become more than what you are. Then, thinking that perhaps I really knew nothing about the matter of slavery in that city, I decided to learn something more of it.

AS IT WAS MY CUSTOM to take an occasional walk during my lunch hour, one late morning—it was a Saturday—I decided to visit the slave market on Canal Street. The building was a large, square, two-story edifice surrounded by twelve-foot-high walls, their tops embedded with shards of glass. An odor of an untended outhouse hung in the air, as did the smells of captive humanity. A few dogs roamed about, looking for scraps of food. Entering into an inner courtyard from the street, I could see the many cells in which the slaves were kept, with their heavy oak doors lining the inner courtyard walls. A murmur of voices was audible through their metal gratings. Wandering about, I happened upon the entrance-way of a room, the guard's house, on whose walls hung all kinds of apparatuses: manacles, iron collars, chains, and handcuffs as well as devices like thumbscrews and pincers of an unusual size. Among the other visitors to that place was a crowd of New Orleans citizens, all finely dressed, who had happened by during their strolls to take things in, as the courtyard was visible from the street. Then the clanging of a bell, the signal for the sale to begin.

Quietly I watched as a line of male slaves was marched out and arranged from tallest to shortest, each having been outfitted with shoes, trousers, a shirt, and jacket; some were in the prime of youth, strong-limbed and clear-eyed; the others, very old and weary of life, were to be had at bargain prices if anyone wanted them. The women, some with their children, were lined up on the other side of the courtyard. Wearing bright calico dresses and silken bandannas around their heads, they were arranged in order of their beauty and youth, the first in that line a woman, who could not have been more than seventeen or so, weeping profusely as she stood waiting, with her head bowed, for that proceeding to begin. The eldest was a toothless and anguished-looking woman of perhaps forty, her back bent and right hand shaking from the years she had already spent in the cotton fields, resigned to the fate that she would be likely "thrown in" for nothing as part of a someone's purchase.

Naturally, the strongest males and loveliest of the women were sold quickly—the highest price being one thousand dollars for a young "buck" in such superb condition that his new master must have reckoned he would be good for at least twenty years of fruitful labor.

"You have a name?"

"Yes, sir. Thomas."

"You know how to pick cotton?"

"Yes, sir."

"And you're a good worker?"

"I've been told so, sir, yes."

"Then why is your master selling you?"

"He had to sell everything, on account of his owing."

"How many years was you his slave?"

"Fifteen."

"Did he ever strike you?"

"No, sir."

"Or whip you, for coming up short in your pickings?"

"No, sir."

"And never once did he beat you for disobedience?"

"No, sir."

"How old are you?"

"Twenty-two, come winter."

"And your teeth are good?"

"Yes, sir. I ain't never been sick. 'Cept once."

"Then you will do."

The buyer then turned to the slave trader and said, "I'll take this boy and the pretty girl, too."

Later I walked back to the store, wondering for the life of me how such dealings went on each morning, six days a week.

Though my mind had not been put at ease by what I had seen on that morning, there is some truth to the notion that even the worst things, once absorbed through constant exposure, become matters of acceptance; and while my heart, with its surplus of harsh memories, was injured by such sights, a shell of denial developed around me.

※

IT TURNED OUT THAT, WHATEVER my shortcomings, Mr. Stanley had seen in me the raw materials of a gentleman: Not a week after I had dined with him, I received another invitation to his house for a Sunday breakfast. On that occasion, we went to church and afterward took a carriage ride out to a local resort by Lake Pontchartrain, north of the city center, for lunch, a routine that was repeated on subsequent Sundays whenever he remained in town. In the process, Mr. Stanley, as a former minister, set straightaway to improving my spiritual outlook, for he had noticed that I sometimes dozed off during the Sunday services. His suspicions about my faith aroused, he would make inquiries as to whether I bothered to pray at all. When I confessed that I was lapsed in that regard, he made me promise to get down on my knees each morning and evening to say an "Our Father."

※

THAT NIGHT, I RECITED THE one prayer I knew well—the "Our Father" in Welsh. It goes as follows:

Ein Tad, yr hwn wyt yn y nefoedd. Sancteiddier dy enw. Deled dy deyrnas. Gweneler dy ewyllys, megis yn y nef, felly ar y ddaear hefyd. Dyro i ni heddyiw ein bara beunyddiol. A maddeu i ni ein dyledion, fel y maddeuwn ninnau i'n dyledwyr. Ac nac arwain ni i brofedigaeth; eithr gwared ni rhag y drwg. Canys eiddot ti yw y deyrnas, a'r nerth, a'r gogoniant, yn oe oesoedd. Amen.

I repeated it again and again, waiting to be moved to a stronger faith.

꿀

IN THE MEANTIME, MY POSITION at the firm only strengthened: It became Mr. Speake's custom to call me into the office from time to time to make inquiries about the personnel and whether I had, of late, noticed any new "irregularities" of behavior. During his inquiries, Mr. Kennicy came often to mind. In his successful "discovery" of the slaves' theft, Mr. Kennicy had been rewarded, but he seemed to be more of a drunk than before and increasingly irritable around the clerks. As for the slaves, after spending a month in one of the prison sheds, Samuel, as I mentioned, had been brought back to work, thank God, and a young man named Jim came in to take Dan's place: It was their misfortune to have Mr. Kennicy to contend with.

Despite my dislike for Mr. Kennicy, I had no need to mention his continuing alcoholism to Mr. Speake. Aside from refusing to be a snitch, I agreed with the consensus among the other clerks that he would sooner or later cook in his own juice. One day, during my third month there, Mr. Kennicy come back from his lunch hour so drunk and in a rile over some failed matter of romance that he tumbled headlong into Mr. Speake's office; so apparent was his state that Mr. Speake summarily dismissed him. I was given yet another raise, to thirty dollars a month, and some of Mr. Kennicy's bookkeeping duties as well.

The Summer of 1859

IN THAT SUMMER OF 1859, while Mr. Stanley had gone upriver again, I still made my Sunday visits to his wife. It was this continued contact with her that had perhaps kept me closer to piety than not. For in those days, without such godly influences, I might have well succumbed to the lurid delights of the city.

But I remained careful: The gains I had made, since my days on the *Windermere*, had precipitated in me a great cautiousness about life, one that has served me well. I had few indulgences—food, I am afraid to say, being one of them. And in those days I was greatly tempted to see a play, my interest having been piqued by a production of *Hamlet* put on by Ben DeBar's theatrical troupe, its theme of patricide vaguely interesting me (I did not go, as I was afraid of squandering my money, and besides, Mr. Stanley had given me a copy of the play to read). On the Fourth of July, there had been a spectacular display of pinwheeling fireworks that lasted for hours. Dense, boozy crowds gathered along the squares and sidewalks in awe, as the skies above went ablaze with a bursting conflagration that could be seen from many miles away, but even then I chose to spend the night up in my attic room at Mrs. Williams's, reading my books.

I suppose I believed that I did not want to tempt fate by any departure from routine, for I counted myself very fortunate in those days. But the future, seemingly so secure in one moment, I learned, could be swiftly disrupted.

IN THIS INSTANCE, I MUST recall the newspaper article I had read aloud to Mr. Stanley when we first met. In it, the health officials of the city had warned of the possibility of a yellow fever epidemic, and by midsummer, it had come true, though I was surely among the last to have noticed. Even when I had heard Mr. Richardson declare one morning, with some concern, that an unhealthy time had descended upon New Orleans.

I had observed for some days, that my employer, Mr. Speake, was looking a little more drawn than usual; that his brow was often covered with perspiration, and that he seemed too short of breath for a man so thin of body—just walking across the sales floor seemed to exhaust him. All kinds of worrisome lines had begun to cross his face, which, I surmised, had come from some disappointment, perhaps in business. Though it was not my place to do so, as one of his more valued employees, I had been tempted to suggest to Mr. Speake that he see a doctor. As this had already been suggested by Mr. Richardson—Mr. Speake, refusing to do so, had called his low physical state a "passing thing"—there was not much any of the clerks could do but attend to our usual duties. But then there came a day when Mr. Speake did not arrive at the warehouse, a message having been sent by his wife, Cornelia, that he was resting at home. That was followed by three more days of his absence. Then one morning, as the clerks were just settling down to work, there came a second message: Mr. Speake, like his former partner, Mr. McCreary, was dead.

A crisis within the warehouse ensued. The slaves were sent home, the doors closed, and the clerks and I headed that very morning to Mr. Speake's residence, which was on the corner of Girod and Carondelet Streets, to comfort his grieving widow. We spent most of the day in her company, speculating among ourselves, with some anxiety, about what might happen to the warehouse. When a respectable amount of time had passed and we had prepared to leave, she, by way of according me some special honor, asked that I spend the evening in her company. This I did not refuse. When my fellow clerks had gone off, I remained behind with the widow, who had touched me deeply by weeping in my arms—that I hardly knew her didn't seem to matter.

"The poor dear man had been suffering from nightmares—as if he already knew what awaited him. He was only forty-seven," she added, to my surprise. "And he had often spoken of you as his successor."

I thought about what Mr. Stanley would have done in such circumstances and found myself quoting from the Psalms to soothe her.

"You are very kind," she said. "God bless my husband's soul."

We said some prayers, then she asked me, in the way that grieved persons do, "You do believe in the eternal nature of souls?"

"Of course, ma'am. Surely as Jesus rose, then will he."

That was hardly a comfort to her, given her sadness, but she was greatly touched and, sitting near me, reached for my hand and held it for a long while. Then, as it was getting late, and just when I was beginning to wonder about what kind of accommodations his widow would offer me that night, she, in tears, led me from that room toward a large salon. Through the door we went; it was then that I saw the defunct Mr. Speake resting, at the far end of that salon, in his coffin.

"I cannot bear to do so myself, but as I do not want to leave the poor man alone, would you, Master Rowlands, sit up with the casket tonight?"

What choice had I?

I passed that night uneasily, and in the morning, I joined the funeral procession, along the streets of the city, to St. Roch's for his interment.

☀

IT TURNED OUT THAT WITHIN a few weeks Mrs. Speake decided to move to St. Louis to live with some relations, and the firm was put up and sold at auction. A different partnership, headed by a certain Mr. Ellison and Mr. McMillan, became the new owner. Mr. Richardson and several of the other clerks found work elsewhere, but as the partners had heard about my efficient ways and my reputation as a "walking inventory," I was retained, though, to my discontent, at a lower wage: Far from making me feel that I had a certain future in the warehouse, my new employers made it clear that I was expendable. No one was irreplaceable. Expecting much of me, they doubled my responsibilities: Suddenly I was an inventory man, a bookkeeper, a shipment manager, all at once. My work was so compacted that, despite my youth, I left each evening feeling fairly exhausted.

☀

AFTER I RELATED MY UNPLEASANT situation at the warehouse to Mrs. Stanley, she had written her husband about it, so that he, upon his eventual return, would, on my behalf, and using the weight of his importance in the mercantile district, have a word with these gentlemen, with the aim of improving my circumstance. But it seems that I was to be hounded by bad luck. Not a week after we had spent a most pleasant Sunday, marked by a memorable dinner in the evening, I arrived at her door on St. Charles Avenue to learn from her Irish maid, Margaret, that Mrs. Stanley had herself fallen gravely ill. She had come down with severe dysentery, one of the diseases that, with yellow fever, had proliferated in New Orleans that summer. This great lady had taken to her bed in a state of such dehydration that when I ventured to her bedside, I saw the skeletal form of a sainted woman about to enter into heaven.

By then, Margaret had been tirelessly by her side since Friday and seemed so exhausted that I felt it my duty to offer my assistance. And so it was that I spent that day and night by Mrs. Stanley's door, alerting Margaret whenever Mrs. Stanley, waking from her sleep, cried out, in a weak voice, for those medicines that would relieve her pain.

That Monday morning I reluctantly took my leave but promised to return within the hour, as I thought to solicit a few days off from the warehouse, a request that did not sit well with Mr. Ellison. Ruddy-skinned, and somewhat obese, he had been eating an apple when I entered his office and barely seemed to care about some "old lady in her last throes." Perhaps a spirit of independence, entirely new, had been aroused in me by my days in New Orleans, but I found myself telling Mr. Ellison that, indeed, whether he believed me or not, and whether he wanted me to or not, I would be taking time off, and that no job, however important it may seem to those who rank profits over human life, could keep me there.

"Good. Then go and take your Welsh arse out of here. And don't come back," he told me bluntly.

SUDDENLY WITHOUT EMPLOYMENT, I RETURNED to Mrs. Stanley's house and spent the next three days helping in what ways I could.

I have seen death come in many forms in my years, but never has a person appeared so serene before the mysterious prospect awaiting her as did dear Frances. What death is I then did not know: If it enters as a change of light, a slight mist, or a dim sound in the air, I still cannot say, nor will I know until my own time comes. But back then, being so young and never having witnessed the process so closely, I was filled with more fear than pity and an excruciating sense of helplessness. Quietly I sat beside the broad bed in which she rested, in wonderment over how someone I had only known for some few months seemed so important to my well-being. From the salted air of a ship in the mid-Atlantic I had gone into a death room in New Orleans: How strange did that fact seem to me.

When the hour arrived, Margaret and I gathered by her side. When she recognized me, her pupils widened, and she began to whisper.

"Ah, my boy, oh, the pleasant times we've had," she said. "When I am in the sweet peace...please, do not forget my husband; look after him." Then: "Oh, God bless you, my boy."

I was holding her hand in my own when that faint pulse stopped beating; her eyes were opened tranquilly wide and fixed upon that distant place.

AT FIRST, I THOUGHT THAT the funeral arrangements would fall to me, for Mr. Stanley himself, somewhere upriver, had not yet heard of this tragic event, and, in any case, he was at least a week or so away. But it happened that Mr. Stanley's older brother, Captain John Stanley, had arrived by brig from Havana the previous evening, and coming to that house the next morning, to pay his sister-in-law what he thought would be an ordinary visit, he was grieved to hear the sad news. Looming over me as I explained the situation, he seemed bemused by my presence in that house.

"Who are you, anyway?" he asked me, without so much as a

syllable of condolence in his voice. I explained my friendship with his brother and the story of our days, but to this he was indifferent. Yet in my confused and forlorn state, it relieved me to learn that he, of a more forceful personality than my own, had determined to take care of the funeral arrangements himself. Shortly we shook hands, and he saw me out the door.

Three days later, as I was sitting in my attic room in Mrs. Williams's boardinghouse, bleakly pondering my future, I received a note from Margaret: Mrs. Stanley had been embalmed and shipped upriver in a leaden casket to St. Louis: Mr. Stanley himself, located in Memphis and informed of his wife's death by telegram, would go there for the funeral.

※

MY SUBSEQUENT DAYS WERE DEVOTED to a search for work among the other merchant warehouses in the district, but my last employer, Mr. Ellison, had launched a campaign against me and besmirched my name by accusations of indolence. But as I made my way up and down that strip, speaking with one merchant and the other, I learned that there were no jobs available, even if he had not resorted to such chicanery. I even tracked down Mr. Richardson, whom I had counted as a friend, but he was reduced in circumstances on account of his age, and now, as a lowly clerk himself, could be of no help to me. For a period, I mainly lolled around Mrs. Williams's house reading books—I even managed to finish my Gibbon.

Still, my fortunes changed again. During a dinner at Mrs. Williams's boardinghouse, I heard about a certain elderly captain on a frigate called the *Dido* who had fallen ill from drinking the Mississippi river water. He needed an assistant, a sailor told me, willing to contend with the unpleasant nature of a bilious dysentery; I signed on, meeting the poor man as he lay in his bunk: an old fellow, he had the bearded face of a patriarch, his skin saffron-colored, his features haggard and drawn. And yet, worn out as he seemed, he was coming out of the yellow fever; and though my olfactory senses were at first offended by, as Shakespeare would have put it, a "bottom that hath no bottom," I had dutifully set out to restore to cleanliness both his person and the conditions in his cabin. I was on this frigate for a month, the first three weeks of which had been anxiety-provoking, as he, a pious and kindly man, had seemed perpetually close to death.

But one day he was well enough to take the sea air, and as he stood on the poop deck, tottering beside me—I had to hold him up—the fresh breezes seemed to make him feel better.

At the end of that month, when he was fully himself again and had no further need of me, this captain, having ascertained from my demeanor that I was in a lowly state of mind, sought to counsel me. "You have spoken of your friend Mr. Stanley and of his many kindnesses to you. Should you not," he asked me, "put your life of petty odd jobs behind you and seek him out? If you have been discouraged, think of me: In one moment I was lying about in a filthy state; the next I was on the deck of my frigate taking in the sea air on a bright and sunny day. Take me at my word—seek out your friend and see what will happen. Go to St. Louis."

<hr/>

AFOOT IN THE CITY AGAIN, I returned to Mr. Stanley's house on St. Charles Avenue to inquire as to his whereabouts, but no one was at home, Margaret having departed. Back at Mrs. Williams's, where all my possessions were stored, I had hoped to find some piece of correspondence from Mr. Stanley awaiting me, and, thankfully, a note from him had arrived: It was addressed from the Planters House Hotel in St. Louis and dated November 11, 1859. This is how I recall it:

Dear Master Rowlands,
I have been told of your unflinching kindness during my late wife's sufferings, may God bless her soul. I have also

become aware of certain audacities regarding your tenure with
your new employers. Rest assured, stalwart young man, that
upon my return to New Orleans I will attend to the resolution
of your current discomforts. When that will be I do not know,
as we are settling many matters of estate in St. Louis.

With best wishes,
Henry Stanley

SO I RESOLVED TO BOOK passage to St. Louis, and within a few days I found myself heading north on the Mississippi aboard the *Tuscarora*. In other places I will mention my enthrallment with such craft; but what I will say now is that my first journey upriver, some nine days long, with its ascent into a port that was nearly as glorious and glutted with ships as New Orleans, and much grander than bustling Liverpool, gave me a further indication as to the enormity and boundless resources of America. St. Louis's docks bustled with the same commerce as those in New Orleans— everywhere I looked there were steamers unloading great cargoes of cotton and other goods; endless barrels and crates, boasting of the river economy, were laid along the docks.

Once I had descended onto the levee, I made my way, by hired hack, to the Planters House Hotel, where I approached the front desk clerk and presented myself as a "close acquaintance" of Mr. Stanley and inquired as to his whereabouts.

"He's not here," I was told. "He left last week on a steamer."

I could not, at this point, fully absorb the ramifications of that remark.

"He did?" I asked.

"He has gone south, to New Orleans."

Such a declaration might have alighted upon me with less consequence had I, in my pocket, enough money to book a return passage to New Orleans.

Shortly I took a room in a modest boardinghouse near the

harbor to contemplate the means by which I would earn some money. For some ten days I made my way around the major streets of that city, which I did not know, looking for work.

One afternoon, with my frustrations mounting and my funds running perilously low, I happened to make my way down to the riverside, where many flatboats and barges were docked. One of them was loaded up with a massive shipment of timber. The crew was an agreeable lot. Speaking with one of them, I learned that the flatboat was to set out that very evening for New Orleans, and so I sought out their boss with the idea of offering my services in exchange for passage downriver.

A few hours later, I returned with my carpetbag, and, dressed in a manner practical for such work, I joined the crew as the flat-boat cast off into the current. It took us two weeks to reach New Orleans.

ON THAT VOYAGE, I WELL learned the lure of the river; the quietude of a flatboat's passage as opposed to that of a steamship, with its clanging bells and whistles. The churning of the paddle wheel was quite appealing, our slow progress giving one much time to think and observe the motions of the water. Its currents and eddies and whirlpools, its fluvial volatility, were a source of fascination to me: I learned how the river could be calm one moment and stormy the next; I learned of its depths and shallows; the trickiness of navigating its snags and sandbars; the way it turned silver and gold in the sunlight or suddenly resembled gruel under the gray skies; with these transformations I grew familiar.

One thing was certain: No matter how many times we saw a steamboat speeding past us along the river, its chimney sending up billows of thick, pitch-pine-fed smoke, it always seemed a fanciful event—the calm waters suddenly stirring, the captain blowing the horn to let us know of his approach, as if we could possibly have missed it! Long after such steamboats had vanished from view, we could see their courses marked out, far into the distance, by the lingering trails of dark smoke, a long plume of which hung in the air for hours as the boats disappeared down the Mississippi.

※

IN NEW ORLEANS AGAIN, AFTER the exhilarations and tedium of that journey, I headed straightaway to Mr. Stanley's home on St. Charles Avenue, and, to my good fortune, found him there, in a receptive and grateful mood toward me. To see him again after so many months uplifted my spirits instantly, for his manner, by way of affections, was more than what it had been before—a consequence, I believe, of hearing stories from his maid about my devotion to his late wife during her last days on this earth. He had been so moved by such tales that, in the clearest way possible, he told me my future would be in his charge from this time onward: Moreover, he declared that he would now directly undertake my development into a man of commerce and instruct me in the ways of his profession.

That night, over supper, we spoke of many things as we never had before, and, with a greater curiosity, he pursued those details of my life that I had been too ashamed to tell him before—mainly, that I had been as good as an orphan, having neither mother nor father to claim as my own. Then Mr. Stanley said that he and his wife had always been childless and, wanting their own, had often visited the infant asylum in New Orleans, but they had been too fastidious and careful to make a choice, something they had come to regret. But now he saw that things could unfold differently in his life—for as a widower, he was lonely and longing for a good companion.

Then Mr. Stanley promised to take me up as his own ward: He would make preparations to adopt me and bestow his name upon me.

That night he clarified for me the details of his life, which I had only known before as hearsay. He had been educated for the ministry as a young man, and for some seven years he had traveled the South as an itinerant preacher, but he had found out, through a deep examination of his conscience, that he felt unsuited to that profession. Commerce, with its social intimacies, held a greater attraction for him. Having succeeded in a number of ventures, he established an office in St. Louis and, with his older brother, one in Havana, Cuba, a land he called beautiful.

It was his wish, once he had made a satisfactory fortune, to sever his city connection and return to the storekeeper's trade, perhaps in some tranquil outpost upriver, for he saw that there would come a time when he would be weary of travel; but, in the meantime, he said there would be much to teach me, his son.

☀

SHORTLY I MOVED MOST OF my books and what other possessions I had from Mrs. Williams's boardinghouse and took lodging on St. Charles Avenue with my new father. At first he taught me the essentials of gentlemanly grooming: the use of clippers, so that my nails might not grow so long and dirty; how to clean my teeth with tooth powder and a brush, something I had never known before. He also introduced me to the concept of a daily bath, bidding me to make use of the grand wooden tub that he kept for such purposes.

"Forget all the nonsense you were raised with," Mr. Stanley told me. "Cleanliness is what differentiates the gentleman from the common laborer and slave."

He had guided me further in the selection of clothing and helped me to accrue all manner of stylish suits: He taught me that that a well-ironed shirt and well-tied cravat did much by way of making a good impression, especially with businessmen, a necessity if I wanted a life in commerce. Shoes were important, too.

Then, with the outward aspects of my appearance somewhat rectified, and with my habits becoming more fastidious, he turned to what he saw as the essential flaw of my bearing.

"You have many fine characteristics: You are swift of mind, pensive, and courteous; but you are also far too afraid and timid around things and people; it is as if you feel beneath the others you meet. I have noticed on many occasion a certain awkwardness in your social manner; you are often sullen in your private moments and easily defer to the opinions of others, as if you have none of your own. In short, you do not seem like a person who will stand up for himself: In business—and in life—this will not help your dealings, as the merchants you shall meet are men, and as men they only want to deal with men, not boys uncertain of themselves. What you must do, young man, is adopt the mental attitude that you are in every way *equal if not superior* to those whom you encounter; in the rare cases where this is not true, then you will learn it a useful posture to assume anyway. Your timidity must be forgotten."

Then: "Remember that Napoleon himself was as diminutive as you. Think of all he did and all that he nearly succeeded in, and realize that his fall did not come from any lack of ability but from a lack of humility, which is different from timidity. As for your physical demeanor, do not slouch at any time, and when you are speaking to someone, look him directly in the eye: Listen to what he says with the utmost interest, no matter how dull he may be, and interject your opinions only when he has exhausted himself of his own."

※

ACCOMPANYING MR. STANLEY ON HIS dealings around the city, to make our way up and down the mercantile strip of Tchoupitoulas Street into all the stores, was a joy, for he would remark with some pride that I was now his partner and son and should henceforth be addressed as Master Stanley. Those who had known me, such as Mr. Richardson, were somewhat vexed at this new development, and yet, in a short time, it was accepted. Mr. Richardson congratulated me on my good fortune, but no greater joy did I feel than to enter the old warehouse in my sumptuous wardrobe, with Mr. Stanley by my side, and to hear Mr. Ellison addressing me in a tone of respect.

᠅

IN THOSE DAYS I LEARNED that Mr. Stanley, so corporeally sound, seemed to have a hidden infirmity, a tic of the sinews around his eyes, so that he blinked involuntarily, mainly after reading or standing too long in a place. He would also tap his feet against the floor sometimes, flail his hands, and shake them in the air when he did not think anyone could see him. Once I saw him direct from his coat to his mouth a smallish flask, which he uncapped in his massive hand and sipped of quickly. He had done so in a natural and unapprehensive manner, but his eye had caught mine: I had looked away, but as I turned, he said, "Come here."

Almost inexpressively, taciturnly, he held forth on his activity.

"You may well be wondering why I would have need of this: It is a strong brandy, to be sure, but in the wake of Mrs. Stanley's death, it was the recommendation of my doctors that I partake of such to calm my nerves. For the death of a loved one does such things. Surely you must understand."

I did not. "But is not the imbibing of certain liquors wrong? Why have you this need?" I asked.

Then he offered me his flask.

"Sip from it and see."

I was reluctant to do so, but as he was now my father, I obliged.

The taste of the liquor was thick and metallic, full of wooden flavors and resins, so burning and syrupy that I jumped.

Momentarily a slight elation of mind, such as to suggest that all the world was before me, ensued. Groggily I asked: "So if this is good, what profit do you gain?"

And then he told me his whole notion of how liquors might be useful: When it came to gatherings in the home, he recommended

French wine, sherry, or port. As for the dealings of business, it was his experience that spirits functioned as a congenial lubricant to ease the negotiations. While city men were prone to drink beer and Scotch, not rye, planters preferred bourbon and Havana rum, a case of which he always took with him on his journeys.

⚜

BY THE TIME WE BEGAN our first excursions upriver by steamer—it was in December of 1859—I was pleased to consider myself an asset to Mr. Stanley, for by then I had been put in charge of his accounting, kept track of his orders, and generally eased the burdens of his dealings. As it was part of Mr. Stanley's routine to make several trips per year up to St. Louis, Cincinnati, and Louisville, our early journeys were spent on the lower Mississippi tributaries, where we would mainly deal, and profitably so, with the merchants in small settlements, our route taking us between Harrisburg and Arkadelphia and between Napoleon and Little Rock. I take some pride in stating that my memory served him well in those days: No face, no name, no detail about shipments, purchases, and sales escaped me.

In our portmanteau, we had packed a great number of books—various ancient and modern histories, books of poetry and plays, essays and biographies—so that when we retired to our cabin we could pursue the furthering of my education.

As he wanted to correct the heaviness of my Welsh accent, he often had me read aloud to him, correcting my pronunciation. In this way, I drifted into speaking a neutral English that, while occasionally afflicted with some evidence of my Welsh origins as well as the influence of a southern drawl, depended greatly upon the precise enunciation of the consonants and hard and soft vowels.

"Forget your upbringing in England, your lack of pedigree: Here in America, we treat all men equally and according to the quality of their character."

WE'D RISE AT DAWN, AND he would send me to bed at an early hour, at which time he would often head out of the cabin to take the air and pursue, in private, his conversations with other merchants.

And he impressed upon me his own feelings about religion, which is to say that he sought to correct my rustic and ignorant view of God. Up to that time I imagined God as a personality with human features set in the midst of celestial glory in the Heaven of Heavens. "How did you come to such a fancy?" he asked me. I told him my idea had come from the biblical verses that said God had made man after His own image. To this he gently said:

"By 'image,' it is meant, in the Bible way, that we are a reflection of Him. But He, by His nature, hath no body. God is a spirit, and a spirit is a thing that cannot be seen with human eyes, because it has no figure or form. A man consists of body and spirit, or, as we call it, soul. We cannot see the earth move, and yet it is perpetually whirling through space: We cannot see that which draws the compass needle to the pole, yet we trust our ships to its guidance. No one saw the cause of the fever that killed so many people in New Orleans last summer, but we know it was in the air around the city. If you take a pinch of gunpowder and examine it, you cannot see the force that is in it. So it is with the soul of man.

"Well, then, try and imagine the universe subject to the same invisible but potent intelligence, in the same way that man is subject to God's. It is impossible for your eyes to see the thing itself; but if you cannot see its effects, you must be blind. Day after day, year after year, since the beginning of time, that active and wonderful intelligence has been keeping light and darkness, sun, moon, stars, and earth, each to its course in perfect order. Every living being on earth today is witness to its existence. The intelligence that conceived this order and decreed that it should endure—that still sustains it and will outlast every atom of creation—we describe under the term of God. It is a short word, but it signifies the being that fills the endless universe, a portion of whom is in you and me."

This I took to heart and have never forgotten.

How I Met Samuel Clemens

ONE EVENING, WHEN MR. STANLEY and I were bound from New Orleans to St. Louis on the steamship *Arago*, I was on the boiler deck, having just taken leave of my benefactor, who had, at the moment of our parting, seemed fatigued. Although I had looked forward to dining with Mr. Stanley that evening, he claimed, and rightly so, that he would be better off resting.

It would have been natural for me to have insisted on accompanying Mr. Stanley back to the cabin, but I had noticed in recent days that he seemed particularly on edge. That night I thought it best to keep to myself, which turned out to be a good thing.

So as my adoptive American father withdrew, I passed my time on the boiler deck among the standing passengers—those who did not have cabins—to continue my studies of the ancient texts of my little Geneva Bible.

At dusk a lovely night began unraveling before me. The orange skies were streaked with plumes of smoke from a distant cane-field fire and went melting into the waterline; mists were forming along the shore, and the first fires, as darkness descended, were appearing. There was something infinitely comforting about looking out toward the riverbank and seeing the lamps lighting the houses of the settlements, the occasional church window or dry-goods-store doorway warming with a glow as some preacher or clerk would spark the kerosene lamps, small flashes of brilliance suddenly coming through the darkness. Indeed, the signs of life that flickered out from the plantation-house windows a mile or two inland were also gratifying. I believed that they signaled the happy doings of domestic living. I could not help but reflect

how even God's forgotten creatures knew well the simple pleasures of companionship and the rewards of family, which so many
take for granted. But not I.

There was a fellow stationed by a calliope, which he played all
day from eight in the morning until eight at night, a pipe organ
kind of music that became a signal to those along the shore of our
arrival as we stopped by small and large towns. I much enjoyed
it when the captain let the steam whistles blow as the children
on shore seemed greatly delighted by our approach, the captain
of the boat, leaning over the rail, tossing out handfuls of hard
candies to the little black children, who shouted out their happy
thanks. Such vessels were always filled with agreeable sounds—
the full, round tones of ships' bells ringing the hours; the constant
churning of the side wheel; the calling of the knockabout seamen
dropping their lines into the water to measure the depths in that
ever-changing river: "By the mark twain!" "Quarter less three!"
"Nine and a half!" "Seven feet!"

On that evening of drowsy, still waters, I found myself standing by the steamship railing studying some verses when I fell into
a conversation with the riverboat pilot, who had come down from
his wheelhouse to have a smoke on deck. He was something of
a dandy, in his midtwenties, I supposed, of medium height, perhaps five feet eight, but he seemed taller in his polished boots and
visored cap, a shock of flaming red hair and thick muttonchops
around his leonine face. His was a large head tottering upon what
seemed a somewhat thin body: sparely built, with narrow shoulders and small-boned, he had the most delicate of features. His
gray-green eyes were like an eagle's, I observed, and he seemed
to look out at the world through narrow slits. In the light of a
pine-knot torch I noticed that his hands were finely cared for, his
nails neither black nor brittle like those of his usual cohorts. I had
seen him before, but we had never spoken, because when he came
down on the lower deck, he was often in the company of friends
who'd gather around him as he would hold forth, telling jokes and
sharing anecdotes in a laconic drawl, a cigar always lit in his hand.

But that evening he clopped down the stairs alone and, gazing at the same shore as I, and perhaps amused by the fact that I was studiously reading my verses, inhaled upon his cigar, patted some ashes off the lapels off his smart frock, turned to me, and said: "Not a bad night, is it?" Then: "Care for a smoke?"

"I'm not one for that, but thank you," I said.

"Well, to each his own." Then: "You mind if I ask you a question?"

"No."

"As you're about the only young man I have ever seen on a riverboat reading a Bible in so intent a fashion when there's so much else going on aboard, I have to presume that you have some connection with men of the cloth. Would I be correct in assuming that you are studying to become a preacher?"

"No sir; to the contrary, I am learning the river merchant's trade with my father, Mr. Stanley. Perhaps you have seen me in his company—he's a tall, bearded man, perhaps the tallest man aboard ship. He is a former minister, and as such he has kept me to my verses."

"A minister, was he? And now a river trader?"

"Yes, sir. But he has never kept the Good Book from his heart."

"And what do you get from these verses?"

"Inspiration...and wisdom, mainly."

"Inspiration and wisdom: two fine things, of which there's not enough in this world. You must be the better for it, I will allow, though I've never had much of a taste for Sunday-school tales myself. Do you read other books?"

"By my estimation, sir, even with my mercantile duties, I read several a week: If I were not to become a merchant I have often thought I would like to become a writer of some kind, so influenced am I to dream from what I have read. But it is my father's opinion that I am quite well suited to the trader's life, though it is still very new to me, as are so many other things in this country."

This comment seemed to puzzle him.

"Oh, so you are not from around here?"

"No, sir. I am originally from Wales."

"So that accounts for some of the occasional strange sound-ings of brogue in your voice." Then: "And so you and your father have come here from Wales?"

"No, sir. He's originally from Savannah, Georgia, but you see, it was not so long ago, in fact last February, that I first arrived in New Orleans aboard a packet ship from Liverpool as a cabin boy. I was penniless at the time and alone. Low as I had sunk in those days, it was my good fortune to have made the acquaintance of the gentleman trader, Mr. Stanley: I have since come under his wing, as his adopted son."

"So you're an orphan?"

"As good as one; but now I am not. You see, in his kindness, Mr. Stanley has undertaken my education in the ways of the world and of books: He is a very learned man and so generous and pious that he has made me his own. I have only just recently taken his name."

"And this name?"

"Henry Stanley."

"Ah, Henry, a good name: It was my brother's," he said, seem-ingly laid low by some recollection. But then, extending his hand in friendship, he told me: "I'm Samuel Clemens, first pilot of this ship."

❖

GIVEN THE NATURE OF MY reserved character, I rarely engaged with strangers, the "small talk" and banter of such ships being of little interest to me. But the pilot, a congenial soul, also had a bookish bent of mind, for as we stood by the railing he told me, "I read quite a bit myself. Lately I have been dipping into all the works of Shakespeare and the writings of Goldsmith; but then I'll generally read anything I can get my hands on—you name it, any books whatsoever...history, travel, literature, and the sciences. Such things are blessings as far as I'm concerned: Along with my cigars, they help me get through the slow moments of the night."

Then, as he looked out over the waters, he said that it was in his interest to speak with strangers, as in those days, aside from being a pilot, he was also something of a writer. He told me it was his sideline to compose short and humorous profiles of the river folk he met, and such articles had been published in certain newspapers along the Mississippi since 1853. He had worked for newspapers in St. Louis and other places, but by the time I made his acquaintance that writing vocation had become a diversion rather than a necessity.

As I had been "reborn" in 1859, so had this Mr. Clemens received his pilot's license in the April of that year, after a long apprenticeship. With his high wages and the finery and good life that came with his position, he had many an hour by which to enrich himself with books and to indulge in the keeping of a journal, whose pages he filled with descriptions of life on the Mississippi and with character studies.

"It is not classy stuff that I write," he confided. "It's strictly entertaining; nothing like the higher works of literature—how wonderful it would be to write something out of history, like an epic poem about the Egyptians on their barges or plays with all manner of flowery language, as Shakespeare did. No, what I am, my bookish friend, is a river hack, a profiler of personalities, a gatherer of river tales; nothing more."

Having ascertained that I was a different sort from the usual types who frequented such boats, he commenced to asking me a great many questions about my origins, and though I was loath to look back at my past, I spoke to him that night of my years at St. Asaph's; then of my subsequent experiences in New Orleans as a clerk and my travels upriver, the story of my month aboard a barge seeming of great interest to him.

"I much enjoyed that journey," I told him. "Being a barge hand wasn't hard work, except when we were pulling at the oars or we got stuck on a sandbar in the shallows. From it I learned something about how the Mississippi moves and all the tricks of the water. I could see how a man such as yourself, sir, could take to a life on the river."

"You fancy the river, then?"

"Yes, sir, I do."

"Would like to see the pilothouse?"

"I would."

"I've got to go on watch: Come up with me now."

⁂

WE CLIMBED UP TO THE highest part of the ship and entered the pilothouse, as elegant as any first-class parlor, with polished wood floors, gleaming spittoons, shiny brass railings, and a ship's wheel six feet high: It was entirely surrounded by windows, and its sweeping view of the river, lit by lanterns beaming out over the waters, left one with the feeling of being up in a lighthouse tower.

As he relieved the assistant pilot and took the wheel, he spoke of his profession. Three times a month he made the round-trip between New Orleans and St. Louis, navigating steamships like the *Arago* up along some thirteen hundred miles of the sinuous Mississippi River. He showed me some charts that folded open in about eight different sections and described the course of the river, which hooked and turned off into wild half loops, curving everywhere, so that it resembled a long and writhing serpent or a medical illustration of human intestines.

"So many are the twists and turns of this river that what might be six hundred miles in a straight line turns into a thousand miles by boat: Now, piloting a steamboat is a very high art indeed. To learn, you've got to memorize the river's eddies and shallows until they become as familiar as the back of your hand. Mainly you have to stay alert to its snags, bars, bottoms, and banks. The worst and most unsettling time is at night, particularly when your shift has come on a night of fog. You can go half crazy searching the darkness for some identifiable landmark—the docks of some town, the church steeple of another, the high woods of a cove— for on such nights, sometimes the sky and water meet in a thin, barely distinguishable line; and then you've got your cane-field fires to worry about, too, for their smoke can blow in, blinding the way.

"But I'm happy in my profession: I'm well paid, have no boss above me save for the captain, who leaves me alone," he told me. "Before I became a pilot, my whole life had been about wandering from one place to another: I was about your age when I had gone out East, to Philadelphia and New York City, working for different newspapers as a printer. Spent a few years in those places—I'd never seen so many freed Negroes and foreigners in my life before, nor had I ever felt so entirely alone. Then came a time when I got homesick for the West again: On the way back, having read some government report about the Amazon region, I had hatched a scheme, in those days, of traveling to Brazil, in South America, to corner the market on the cocoa bean, a vegetable product of miraculous powers, the export of which I had thought would make me rich—how I would corner that market with only thirty dollars in my pocket was not of concern to my youthful mind. But as I was traveling downriver aboard a steamer, the *Paul Jones*, from Cincinnati, with New Orleans as my final destination—from there I was to set off for Brazil—I struck up a conversation with the steamboat pilot, a fellow named Horace Bixby, who filled my mind with all manner of possibilities about entering into that profession. I became eagerly interested—for you see, Henry, growing up as I did in a little town along the Mississippi, a place called Hannibal, Missouri, I had a dream: Like many boys at the time, I wanted to work aboard riverboats. Having made a good impression on this man—as you had with Mr. Stanley—this chance encounter changed all my plans, and in exchange for the first five hundred dollars of my wages I entered into a pilot's apprenticeship that required of me the development of a prodigious memory for the river and its many tricks and deceptions. But by and by, I became an assistant pilot on various boats...."

He seemed quite proud of his standing, and told me that he had always taken care to understand the nature of the ships at his command. On such journeys, he would not only know the exact tonnage of the craft itself but also learn the number of passengers and the weight of its cargo from its manifest, such elements being pertinent to many a split-second calculation, such as the amount of time it would take to a avoid a coal or timber barge (such as the one I had been on) suddenly appearing out of the mist.

Mainly he had enjoyed the important responsibility of presiding over the destinies and safety of the rich cargoes and many human lives left in his charge; and he relished the grand respect accorded him on such ships. A luster of youthful accomplishment emanated from his being—a kind of light; his days, unfolding before him in the warmth and promise of youth, counted as the happiest he had experienced in his life once he'd left Hannibal, Missouri.

And, he told me, there were the glories of calm nights, when the stars were clear in the sky and the moon shone over the water and the river seemed to go on forever in its reflected light, such a fine scenario turning one's thoughts to many fanciful speculations about God and destiny and Providence. The mystery of a universe spreading endlessly onward, as if emanating from one's self, making the pilot feel grand and, at the same time, as if he were nothing at all. (The times I have since experienced such thoughts in Africa are innumerable.) I could not help but ask him if he believed in the Deity.

"Can't say that I do, when I think about it. But on the right kind of day, when everything is wonderful, you can't help but wish that you could thank somebody for it all. On the evidence of this river, and this sky, the fact that you and I can more or less think, talk, and walk around with our senses taking in a million things, I would say that you can't help but wonder how it came about. But no, despite my righteous Presbyterian upbringing, the mystery of it all seems to me to have a physical explanation beyond our scope to understand. Though I sincerely wish it were otherwise. Since you are a Bible-reading man, I am assuming that my words do not fall easily on your ears; if so, I render my apologies, but I won't be dishonest with you."

Then he asked me, "How old are you, anyway, Henry?"

"Nineteen."

"That was my brother's age. He was a clerk, like you...Your face is like his—eager for new experiences and wanting no more than a tad's worth of earthly pleasures...He was all innocence, the poor soul."

And then, as if he wanted to unburden himself of some deep agony, he told me the following.

"About a year ago," he began, "my younger brother, Henry, had been living up in Keokuk, Iowa, out of a job. He had been working for my older brother, Orion, who ran a press and published his own little newspaper there, the *Keokuk Journal*, a good-for-nothing operation. As this enterprise had folded, like everything else Orion ever worked on—he wasn't much for business—I told Henry to come down to St. Louis to get into the steamboat business. I got him a job for no wages as a clerk—what we called a mud clerk—on a side-wheeler, the *Pennsylvania*, where I was a second pilot. I figured that starting out as a clerk, Henry, with time, would end up as a purser, a profession that he seemed well suited for. His was drudge work on the ship, but mainly he seemed to enjoy the river life. We'd made a few voyages up the Mississippi when..."

Then he dropped off into silence, the cigar in his mouth sending up clouds of smoke, as if he were meditating on the next thought. It was some minutes before he spoke again.

"We had made a number of trips up- and downriver, but our finest times were spent ashore, enjoying the local attractions—the circuses and theaters and minstrel shows of the major towns we visited; often at night we walked along the levees of such towns speaking quietly about the river life. I'd always inform him of the precautions he should take in the event of emergencies, to never panic and to keep his head at all times. Why I told him this I do not know, Henry, but I had had a premonition one night, in the form of a dream, in my sister's home in St. Louis. I saw him laid out in a lead coffin, in one of my suits, with white and red roses placed upon his chest. Though I had dismissed it as a passing nightmare, I could not, as a brother who'd had such a dream, feel anything but concern for him whenever our steamboat entered into some difficulty—the jostling of the ship sometimes becoming violent with the swell of waves from passing boats or turbulent waters, bringing to mind the possibility of Henry being swept overboard. Often I found myself rushing down to the lower decks to find him. Generally I felt a great discomfort at having him out of my sight.

"One day, we were coming downriver from St. Louis when the steamer hit some very high winds, and the captain sent Henry up to the pilothouse with instructions for the senior pilot, a rough fellow named Brown, to put into shore. But the pilot, being somewhat deaf and disdainful of lowly hands, ignored the order and continued on his way. Shortly the captain came to the pilothouse to accuse the pilot of disobedience, but, denying it all, once the captain left, the pilot took it out on my brother. With a piece of coal in hand he lunged at him: I had come into the wheelhouse at that moment and, seeing Henry thus assaulted, picked up a stool and clacked it over the pilot's head. Then I pounded him with my fists, and very justifiably so. At the end of that unpleasant affair, when the *Pennsylvania* had been put into port in New Orleans, I was transferred to duty on another steamboat, the *Alfred T. Lacy*, which was to follow the *Pennsylvania* on its next journey upriver to St. Louis.

"Though there was in my gut a sense that Henry should have stayed with me, I made no fuss over the matter: Henry already knew the run of the side-wheeler, and, as each ship had it own system, he had not wanted to make a change, which made sense at the time.

"Two days after his steamship left New Orleans, I followed, aboard the *Alfred T. Lacy*. We were at Greenville, Mississippi, when I heard a rumor that the *Pennsylvania*'s boilers had exploded by Ship Island, near Memphis: The side-wheeler had gone down, it was said, and some one hundred and fifty lives were lost. I immediately thought of Henry and despaired, though my apprehensions were somewhat dispelled when we docked in Napoleon, Arkansas, and I read a Memphis newspaper that did not list my brother among the casualties. The next day, however, farther upriver, I read another 'extra' and saw my brother's name among the 'gravely injured and beyond help' list.

"It was not until we arrived at Memphis that I heard the full details of what happened: As the steamship had been racing along, to make good time, four of its boilers had overheated and exploded. It was six in the morning on a hot day, and my brother was asleep in a hammock on the aft deck at the time. Some seven hundred people were aboard, and the explosion lifted the first third of the boat into the air and tossed about all the passengers within the ship; the chimneys collapsed, spewing sparks and causing a fire; and the boilers rose up onto the deck, shooting scalding steam and objects everywhere—a Catholic priest was said to have been impaled upon an iron crowbar that nearly cut him in half. And while the force of the explosion flung my brother and many an injured passenger a considerable distance into the water, Henry, deeply wounded but unaware of it, had chosen to swim back to the disaster to see whom he could save, for many people, blinded and barely able to breathe, were tottering along the deck in agony or else caught under burning debris, miserably crying for help."

Mr. Clemens, who had maintained his composure to that point, paused to draw from a flask.

"Want a swig?" he asked me.

I felt it would have been improper to refuse him; the harsh and musty-tasting liquid burned in my throat, and the room took immediately on a more intimate quality. Then he continued:

"Attempting to help others, my younger brother was rendered senseless by a second steam explosion, his lungs and body scalded. He fell onto the deck, and the wooden parts of the ship burned down around him. Shortly a fire brigade came out by barge to find which persons were still living, Henry among them, and these they gathered on stretchers and carried to their boat. When another steamer came upon the scene, all who survived were taken from the barge by firemen and transferred to a hospital in Memphis, where they were laid out on pallets along the floor of a great hall—by then Henry's injuries had been examined, and he, wrapped all over in a dressing of linseed oil and raw cotton, had been put into a separate section, of the dying."

Then he looked at me again.

"I was there for six days and nights, and of the general misery I will not report. But I had lingered long enough in that gloomy hall to watch my brother's nerveless fingers grasping after an object that was invisible upon his chest, many times over. That I could not speak words to him that he could hear told me most directly that there is no God who answers prayers. What say you to that?"

I had no answer.

"When he went to sleep, for good, he was dressed in one of my suits and put in a lead coffin: As he lay in his repose, some sympathetic locals came along and placed white and red roses upon his chest—my little dream having, sadly, come true."

"You can't understand my misery over the whole affair—I put him on that steamboat, even when I knew the potential for such disasters... It was my fault."

When he was relieved of his post, the river before us was serene. As we descended down into the lower decks, he stopped to ask me: "Would you, judging by what I have said of that situation, find reason to hold me at fault?"

"I would not."

"Do you judge me to have been a good brother to him?"

"Yes."

"For that consoling thought, I thank you," he said before leaving me and retiring to his cabin, somewhere on the deck.

ON THAT VOYAGE, MEETING HIM on several occasions, I told him, in some detail, more about my father's business dealings— he seemed particularly interested by Mr. Stanley's trade in Cuba, for it seemed to him another of those places where an adventurous and resourceful man could do well for himself. The name of that island sparkled in his mind with the allure of other distant places—from Brazil to China—places that he, with his unabated wanderlust, hoped to see one day for himself: "As much as I enjoy the kingly and unfettered position of riverboat pilot, and the good wages, I can't imagine staying put in one place for long when there is so much of the world to be visited." And he would ask me a great many questions about England—another place of legend his mind—home to Shakespeare and Milton.

"With ink in my veins, it would be a surely fine proposition to write of such places, but I've got to get the Mississippi out of my system first—I suppose I will, sooner or later."

In those days I came to respect and admire him, for he was a largely self-taught man—and far more intelligent than most one would ever hope to meet, his memory, like my own, "sharp as tacks," as he would put it. Among the subjects we good-naturedly discussed on such evenings were the origins of chess, which was apparently an Arab innovation passed on to the Europeans during the Crusades. He thought it the best thing to have come out of those conflicts besides the introduction of the orange to the West. In his affable way, he told me that he had once been hit in the head by an orange that had fallen out of a tree—"To think that we have the Crusades to thank for that!" he said. Then, too, in the way that we spoke of many arcane things, he marveled at the invention of the compass and other such intricate objects, including clocks. He always carried a watch, which he kept in his vest pocket, and he loved to look at it. The tiny gears and latches and springs were of such fascination to him that he could not help but pry open the back of the metal shell to show me the mechanisms. He then held forth on the history of clocks, marveling at the leap from sundial to hourglass to water clock, which somehow led to the modern invention. Machinery in general fascinated him, and he wondered aloud whether such clocklike mechanisms could be applied to the process of printing. Before becoming a steamboat pilot, he had experienced firsthand the dreary careers of compositor and typesetter; altogether, it was if he believed that many of mankind's problems could be solved through mechanical techniques. I thought him clearly some kind of natural genius.

Such musings led, by and by—a phrase he often used—to further discussions of theology. It seemed to him that the whole of the heavens functioned under one "inventive" intelligence, in the way that the gears of clocks have their own unwavering patterns. The few times I tried to expound the religious point of view he would snort or snore, as the man had no patience for such ideas; though he allowed that the order of the universe could not be an accident or the result of arbitrary events—"What that amounts to, I cannot say."

It happened that he had recently read portions of a book by someone named Darwin called *The Origin of Species*, which held that modern man was derived from the apes. (Based on his experience with men—no better than apes—he had no trouble believing this.) I often laughed as he held forth, turning every thought into a matter of humor, a skill that intrigued me. He seemed to find it impossible to take his own erudition seriously—I thought him far better cultured and knowledgeable than most men, save for Mr. Stanley, yet he seemed to have a disdain for pretension: "I am just a lucky fellow from Hannibal, Missouri, nurtured by the dreams that come with growing up on the banks of a great river, the Mississippi. If there's a heaven, it's behind us, in early youth...mine was a paradise, to be sure."

On several occasions during the day, he would come looking for me in the general meeting rooms, where I often sat beside Mr. Stanley and some businessmen, drawing up invoices and making entries into our accounting ledger books as my father went about his commerce. Usually, if he saw that I was occupied, Clemens would simply tip his cap at me, but one afternoon, as I had wanted him to make the acquaintance of Mr. Stanley, I asked him to join us. My father was cordial enough, commending Mr. Clemens for his many skills and thanking him for having taken an interest in me.

"Well, sir," Mr. Clemens said, "you have a fine boy on your hands."

"And he has spoken highly of your befriending him."

They shook hands, my father looming over Clemens, who looked him over carefully and seemed to come to some appraisal.

"Well, good day," Clemens said.

Afterward, gentlemanly as he had been with Mr. Clemens, my father looked at me askance, and he shook his head ever so slightly, as if to remind me of the discussions we had had in the cabin about the dangers of assuming friendships with strangers on riverboats.

"Just remember," he told me. "Riverboats are places for commerce and fleeting relations; a hundred other men you will befriend before long, and few, if any, will care for you as I do." It had not helped that I had let drop, in my description of his character, that Mr. Clemens was not one for religious thoughts: "Such men, fine as they may be in many other respects, are lacking in the fundamental virtues. To mingle with such folks can only have a detrimental effect on your own pious thoughts; to be in the company of doubters is to open the door to doubt itself," he told me one night in our cabin.

"Your job," he continued with bite in his voice, "is to care after the books and accounts and to make all the arrangements pertaining to what dealings I undertake: whereas mine is to create a congenial atmosphere for such things to happen."

The very afternoon he met Clemens, my father and his business acquaintances had sat drinking steadily between the hours of noon and five o'clock, at which point I had to escort him from that public room to our cabin. It was a remarkable thing to see how such a profound change of personality could take place because of these liquors, for the very man who, at some riverside settlements, felt the need to gather a crowd around him and speak of the "Word," and who had often mentioned how proud he felt that I was his son, told me that his business was his own and that it would be best for me to keep my objections over "some harmless social tippling" to myself. Mindful of my promise to his wife, as she lay like an angel on her deathbed, I told Mr. Stanley that, as he had saved me from some inglorious fate, I would save him from his own lapses, no matter his objections. For a moment, my words seemed to have a good effect upon him. He sat on his bed.

"Just allow me some peace...leave me alone in my mourning." Then: "Go off and do as you please—and forget all this, for whatever I am now, I will be as sound and good as I have ever been tomorrow."

✻

IN A STATE OF PUZZLEMENT, and in a low spirit, I made my way out onto the boiler deck, my mind too troubled to attend to my usual studies: My hands were shaking. Wandering up to the wheelhouse, I found Clemens at his post, and while I felt too ashamed to mention the momentary disharmony in my life, he was in a lively mood.

"Come and join me, my friend," he said. "And take the wheel, Henry: Hold it steady as we go." Then, as we approached a broadening of the river, he said: "Tug the wheel slightly downward and to your left." As I began to turn the wheel downward—its enormous weight and the force necessary to move it surprising me— the steamer, heading out over clear waters, glided west. I was not long there at that wheel, but my successful operation of the craft, momentary as it had been, proved salutary to my soul.

✻

BY THE TIME WE ARRIVED in St. Louis, some days later, all was mended between me and my father.

As for Clemens, at journey's end, when all the passengers were disembarking, he sought me out on the deck: "I'll be heading back to New Orleans day after tomorrow," he told me. "You can always look for me in the pilots' association rooms of that city, but if you should like to write to me, this is my sister's address in this city."

And he gave me a slip of paper that said:

Mr. Samuel L. Clemens, C/O Mrs. Pamela Moffett, 168
Locust Street, St. Louis

And that was how we left things for the time being.

᠅

FOR SOME NINE MONTHS IN 1860, my father and I traveled up
and down the river, such journeys, of a two-month duration, broken up by month-long interludes in New Orleans, where we carried out the efficient running of Mr. Stanley's various enterprises. I
had gotten over our little differences by then: Whatever may have
happened, I could not forget that Mr. Stanley had taken a boy—
short of figure, poorly clad, and of little interest to the world—and
made him into a gentleman.

᠅

AFTERWARD, EVERY NOW AND THEN I would receive at Mr.
Stanley's residence a letter from Mr. Clemens, some including
clippings of the short and humorous articles he had written under
the name of Sergeant Fathom and several somewhat older ones
written when he was a youth that were credited to a certain W.
Epaminondas Adrastus Blab, which were of a highly imaginative
nature. Among them was an article he'd published in the New
Orleans *Daily True Delta*, a satire about a riverboat pilot named
Captain Sellers, to which he affixed, for the first time, I believe,
the name Mark Twain, the pilot's term meaning the safe depth of
two fathoms, or twelve feet. He even sent me a few pages of what
he considered a preliminary bit of autobiography regarding his
early training and initiation as a pilot—for he thought such things
might be good one day for a book and asked my impression of it.
River gossip regarding the possibility of southern dissent toward
the North he also reported to me; his fellow river pilots shared
his apprehension that the shipping trade might be disrupted in the

event of a war—"unlikely as it would be to have white men fight one another over slaves."

Statistics appealed to him very much: "Henry, did you know that just last June, the packet *City of Louisiana* made the run from St. Louis to Keokuk (214 miles) in sixteen hours and twenty minutes?" Then, too, he wrote to me about the books he was reading—Sir Walter Scott's *Ivanhoe* (which I had known from the little library at St. Asaph's) and other historical romances having recently caught his fancy. And he would ask me to keep my eyes open for tales of interest that I might pass on to him, as he was a collector of Mississippi lore, and he recommended that I carry with me, as was his habit, a vellum notebook. As he put it in one of his missives, "Surely if we are not brothers by relation, we can be brothers of the written word."

For my part, I kept him informed as to which steamers Mr. Stanley and I were to take to which destinations on which days. While I thought we would soon enough encounter one another, he remained aboard the *Arago*, and our paths did not cross on that ship again.

I Go to Arkansas

BY SEPTEMBER, MR. STANLEY, EMBOLDENED by an old idea, began to speak to me about the opening of a store upriver, at a "tactical point where such goods as we could offer would be greatly wanted." He favored a location along the Arkansas River for its rich backcountry and access by steamer to many other points along the greater Mississippi. Often, as we sat eating dinner, he would mention his knowledge of a country store at a place called Cypress Bend, below Pine Bluff on the Arkansas River, owned by a merchant named Mr. Altschul, a Jew who, "though formed by questionable religious proclivities and a natural inward inferiority," was a good and savvy shopkeeper then in need of a capable assistant. Far upriver from New Orleans, and situated on its own island, Mr. Altschul's store was the sole provider of grocery goods

and other necessities in a region that had recently seen the establishment of many new cotton plantations. It was the kind of place
where a bright young man, with numerous skills of the sort I
possessed, could learn the workings of such a trade. Though I
pointed out to Mr. Stanley that I already had a great knowledge
of the running of a store, given my experience at the Speake and
McCreary warehouse, he corrected my false assumption that a
river outpost could be run in the same way as a big-city store. Mr.
Stanley framed the proposition in terms of my learning the river
trade "in a more thorough manner"—from the perspective of a
clerk working directly with the pioneering planters and the other
sorts who frequented those climes.

"What is to be learned from such a place, sir?" I asked him.

"You'll learn every need and want of the local people. Trust
me, young man, should you know their habits, so different from
the city folk, you will have the key to the inhabitants of all the
Mississippi."

"But when will I see you, Father?" I asked.

"In time. There is no hurry. This is the South; and in the South
things are done in a certain fashion." Then he told me on one of
those evenings: "As hard it is for me to part from you, I have
arranged for you to undertake your apprenticeship in Cypress
Bend with the merchant Mr. Altschul. Much will you learn from
this, and by much will you profit. Once you have become aware of
the particular customs of that place, than we can speak of where
we might open our own store, in an advantageous locality. Within
a few months of this learning, we will embark on yet a new enterprise: This I promise you, my son."

☙

TO SOFTEN THE ABRUPTNESS OF my transition, my father
thought it best that I first become acquainted with the region by
staying on the Arkansas plantation of a riverboat acquaintance,
a certain Major Ingham, who happened to be in New Orleans

on business at the time of our discussion. One night, Mr. Stanley invited him to dinner. An aristocratic southerner, tall and gallant in manner, he had some newly acquired forestland of many acres that he hoped to clear to make way for the planting of a cotton crop. Mainly slaves worked the property. He made it clear that my labors were to be of a physical nature, an idea that I was not entirely averse to. In no rush to begin work in some distant country store, and thinking it wise to get a sense of the land, I agreed with Mr. Stanley that it would be good for me to spend some time there. Major Ingham was to remain in New Orleans for another two weeks, at which point we were to depart together upriver by steamer, and upon the seventh day, at a point south of a settlement called Longview, enter the Saline, from whose banks Major Ingham's plantation was a few miles inland. From there I would eventually embark for Cypress Bend, a day's ride away.

No sooner had this plan been made than did Mr. Stanley receive an urgent letter from Havana, Cuba, informing him that his older brother, Captain Stanley, was quite ill with the yellow fever. Shortly he booked passage and, within a day or so, Major Ingham and I accompanied him and his baggage aboard the brig as it was about to depart from the harbor.

We waited beside him as he calmly began to unpack and review the contents of his portmanteau, crammed with ledgers, documents, and books, and though my father did not speak of it, I knew he was greatly preoccupied over the health of his brother. Finally, when the ship's whistle blew and a porter came down the corridors calling out, "Visitors aboard ship must now depart." My father followed us out to the gangplank and promised that he would write me as to his doings.

☀

OF THE NEXT EPISODE, WHEREBY I resided at the estate of Major Ingham, I will speak but briefly. It did not remain, as I had imagined at first, a place congenial to my spirits, for within a short time I was put to the hard work of cutting down timber with a broad ax alongside a gang of slaves: I did not mind the manly labor, and found it a poetic thing to be working in the midst of a forest, with its high trees and mysteriously changing light and shade, as if I had been dropped into a fairy-tale setting. I came to like the smell of burning resin from the large fires that dispensed with the wild branches and brush, and in general I looked forward to those mornings when the sun streamed freshly through the woods and the air had never seemed so sweet.

It was neither those labors that offended me nor my accommodations in the major's large pine-log house, which was staffed by many slaves, mainly females who tended to every domestic service.

No, it was not this that made me come to dislike my brief time in that place; rather, it was the unavoidable and distasteful company of the slave overseer, who, on account of the finery I had worn on my arrival, had taken me as some New Orleans dandy and rode me for it. In short, he struck me as the lowest form of white man, the like of which I hoped was not common to those parts. Like Mr. Kennicy, though in an amplified way, he hated the slaves and carried with him a black snakeskin whip that he cracked at every opportunity.

One morning, while we were clearing a patch of forest, as some fellow was struggling with a heavy piece of log, the overseer gave him an order, and when this fellow did not hear his command, he struck the whip over the boy's bare shoulders with such force as to leave a deep gash in the skin. The log fell from the boy's arms and crushed the foot of another slave nearby. When the injured slave cried out, the overseer beat him, too; then as the slave repeatedly pleaded for mercy, and as a few others tried to intercede, the overseer pulled out a pistol, fired off a few shots overhead, and threatened to shoot them if they did not back away. Later, when I sought out Major Ingham about the matter, he was reclining in an easy chair on his porch and seemed perplexed by my concern.

That same evening, I resolved to leave the plantation, and I sought refuge with one of Major Ingham's neighbors, a certain Mr. Waring, whose own lands were at the other end of a deep wood. I made no mention of why I had abruptly left, putting it to him that I had merely wanted to rest there for the night. In the morning he arranged a carriage to retrieve my trunk from Major Ingham's house and made a further arrangement to send it off to Mr. Altschul's store ahead of me, as I told him, I would be covering the forty miles or so of countryside and forest toward the Arkansas River on foot, so as to acquaint myself with the region.

⁂

AFTER TRAMPING WITHOUT INCIDENT THROUGH various interesting terrain (and the deepest woods I had entered into until I went to Africa), I finally arrived at my destination, at dusk, two days later. Only a crooked sign on a tree had pointed me to the place. From a kind of road of sandy loam, defined by the deep grooves made on hard earth by wagon wheels and a horseshoe trail, I had crossed over a rickety wooden bridge to reach the island, where moss covered every spot on the banks and tree trunks. With the sun just descending on the river, and with dragonflies floating over the waters, I saw the store standing in a spot of great natural splendor, and for that reason it seemed a promising place to be.

The store itself was a long, one-story affair constructed from logs and divided into four separate chambers, with all kinds of goods—guns and anvils; dresses and finery; comestibles and groceries—arranged therein. Mr. Altschul himself was a smallish and thin man, with large, slightly jaundice-rimmed eyes, a balding head, and dark features. He had been in a state of anticipation as to my whereabouts, as no date had ever been set for my arrival. Greeting my presence as a godsend, he called forth his two clerks and some family members to greet me.

It was gratifying to find several letters waiting for me at Mr.

Altschul's store. These were from my father in Havana, the first conveying news of his safe passage and reporting on his brother's condition, the fever having left Captain Stanley in a grievous state. The doctors of Havana were as baffled by such diseases as were the physicians of New Orleans, and yet it was Mr. Stanley's hope that the captain, of a strong constitution, would eventually recover: "I have prayed for such," he wrote, "but as the will of God is a separate thing from the workings of this world, I would hold no grudge at a sad outcome, for there is a natural order to things." The second letter, of general encouragement and practical advice, had been written in a calmer hand, and at this I took heart.

⁂

I HAD BEGUN MY TENURE in that store in November of 1860, and indeed, with time, I slowly became acquainted with the peculiarities of the locals. We had about one hundred or so regular customers, among them wealthy planters whose character and manners were defined by the customs of the "Old South." Beneath them were the planters with smaller estates and tradesmen; then the backwoods farmers working their little plots—and as one went down the social scale, it was my observation that fine manners gave way to ascending heights of crudity and incivility. Being frontier lands, in the sense of having been settled in fairly recent times, during the cotton-boom years of the 1840s, such places upriver, perhaps a day's ride from the nearest constables of law, seemed more like isolated kingdoms, where little news of the outside world crept in to disrupt their provincial ways. The first rule to be followed, I learned, was one of self-protection: Most of the backwoods men carried bowie knives and revolvers, if not shotguns. And they often walked into the store with bloody game slung over their shoulders or with jugs of liquor in hand. The ever-present heat and humidity of those swamplands left many of them irritably disposed, and many, I'd heard, were quick to fight over the slightest provocation: The kinds of arguments that in New Orleans would have been resolved by genteel discourse or through arbitration became, in Arkansas, an insult to a man's "honor," and the fighting of duels, often to the death, was common enough in those parts.

Slaves, I noticed, were treated differently here. In New Orleans I had seen them walking the streets, side by side with the glut of Creoles, freedmen, and whites that were the population of that city, but in this region they were more strictly kept in their plantation compounds.

Then there was the matter of indecorous behavior in regard to the females. Whatever notions of propriety might have tacitly prevailed in New Orleans in relation to slave concubines, these were discarded in Cypress Bend, for occasionally a gentleman entered the store with one or two young and healthy Negro beauties following behind him, such "items," I heard, being regularly won or lost in card games or swapped at a whim among fellow planters. About that easy abandonment of morals (such as I would later see in Africa) I had written to Mr. Stanley, in frank complaint of witnessing such things.

Out of necessity, as a merchant and German Jew in those Christian parts, Mr. Altschul owned a slave, a burly giant named Simon, whom he used as a bodyguard. But otherwise Mr. Altschul kept no slaves in his household—he had a fine house about a quarter mile away from the store on that island—and he said that in his faith, such things, being considered wrong, were not permitted. It was no wonder to me, then, that I saw Mr. Altschul treated wrongly—more than once had I witnessed planters spitting a spur of chewed tobacco down at his shoes. And although the store was necessary to the practical provisioning of the local plantations, one could read a sort of resignation upon the faces of those who had to enter the "Jew's" premises, for to go against local customs seemed to them the mark of the hostile foreigner.

When not attending to my duties, I filled my spare hours not with books (it was often too hot and humid for that) but by learning to shoot a rifle and a pistol, old cans and bottles set out in the yard being my targets. Though I could not have imagined how such skills, honed over many hours, would serve me well in other places, I took to it quickly and, mastering the art of holding a barrel steady with the recoil, became a superb marksman and was able to shoot a sprig off a tree at twenty paces. In time, as was the custom in that place, I carried, as did my fellow clerks, a loaded Smith & Wesson revolver, its pearly white handle evident in a special side pocket. In those swamplands, to have no pistol on one's person would have been the equivalent of a New Orleans clerk turning up to work without his trousers on, as a firearm was considered an indispensable accoutrement to manly attire.

⚜

NOW, IN THAT PLACE, MALARIAL ague was prevalent, a disease for which there was no explanation as to its cause. Local superstition placed its transmission on exposure to miasmic swamp gases, those will-o'-the-wisps that, capturing the moonlight in their swirls, floated in a ghostly way along the banks of the river and across the swamps at night. Though I had asked a local doctor, a boarder in Mr. Altschul's house, if there were any means to avoid this pernicious disease or if there were precautions to be taken against it by way of pills or medicines, he had wanly smiled at me and said: "Yes, there is. Leave as soon as possible." That, however, was not in my makeup.

As I was attending to my duties in the store one morning, my hands began to inexplicably shake, and then my whole body began to violently tremble. With that came the chills. Helped to my room by the clerks, I lay in my bed shivering, as if I had been packed in ice. I remained in that state for several hours, until a spell of burning fever came over me, followed by delirium: I heard voices and saw the disembodied faces of persons I had known in the past floating before me. For a time I had the very strong impression of being somewhere else, as if I were in a cabin aboard a ship or in the room of a house somewhere in England. In my

hallucinations I imagined a visitation from Mr. Stanley, my benefactor sitting by my bedside and reading me verses from the Bible,
but no sooner had I taken heart at his presence than the vision
went away.

The doctor had come to my bedside, administering to me
some grains of quinine, so that within another six hours, around
noon the next day, I had an appetite and was ravenously hungry.
Within another day I went back to my duties in the shop, but
then, as a week or so passed, I was suddenly overcome with the
same sequence of symptoms. It was during my second convalescence that the doctor told me that I should expect such things to
happen again, and the ague did return, at regular intervals, for as
long as I remained in Cypress Bend and for some time thereafter.

※

HAVING BEEN THUS AFFLICTED, I wrote to Mr. Stanley in
Havana, relating the particulars of my illness and my general dis-
satisfaction with my situation. And yet when I had finished writing
down my complaints, I struck a more congenial tone, putting forth
my continuing devotion to and affection for my father, my most
hidden hope being that Mr. Stanley would instruct me to leave that
place and resume my mercantile pursuits by his side in Havana.

But as the weeks passed I heard nothing from him, and though
this had become a matter of concern to me, and even as fevers
seemed to come back every ten days or so, I resolved to await his
final word.

※

UNFORTUNATELY, MY PERSONAL DISTRESS HAD come at a
time of mounting national disharmonies. During those months,
as I lingered with my recurring illnesses in Cypress Bend, the
issue of slavery versus abolition had boiled over, and war talk had
become prevalent among the planters. Then it had become a fact.

By March of 1861, a number of southern states, among them Alabama, Georgia, and Louisiana, had formed a government separate from the Union, its newly appointed president being one Jefferson Davis. Several of these states had seized federal arsenals, forts, and men-of-war. Even the fortresses below New Orleans had been commandeered by Louisiana. Dan Goree—a planter—said that the whole thing had come to a head the past November with the election of Abraham Lincoln, who'd promised, upon taking office, to free all the slaves, whereupon the planters and therefore the economy of the South would be ruined.

In the meantime, the local inhabitants of Cypress Bend, expecting that Arkansas would soon be joining the other states, had begun to form their own militias.

Upon hearing such news, my first thoughts had been to wonder how commerce would be affected by a war. Most river traffic would be disrupted, and, in any event, many of our provisions, ordered from northern cities such as Cincinnati and Chicago, would be cut off. It was already being said that many a steamboat had been either requisitioned by southern forces or was being held in port. Travelers coming into Cypress Bend from the big port towns told us that fewer steamboats were coming up- and down-river. Somehow I felt consoled by believing that this emergency had affected communications with foreign places such as Cuba: I reasoned that somewhere downriver there was a parcel of mail sitting in a postal warehouse and that a new letter from my father, reporting that all was well with him, awaited me: Yet on one of those days, in March, when I finally received a piece of correspondence, it was from Samuel Clemens. This is as I remember it:

> *Dear Henry,*
>
> *These days I am knocking about New Orleans, mainly playing chess and games of whist in the pilots' association rooms and winning more than losing; I have also had the opportunity of showing my mother around the city—but, truth be told, with all the war talk in the air, I am a little wary*

about my future as a steamboat pilot. When I hear the debates about the North versus the South, mainly over the central concern of slavery, I think it seems hardly worth it to go to war over such a thing. But it now seems inevitable. I go all which ways: My older brother, Orion, whom I told you about, is a dignified man who has always been an abolitionist and has his own strong opinion on the subject. He believes the Yankees are in the right. Then I talk to a plantation man who is on the verge of tears about losing his beloved (and profit-making) slaves—and his livelihood—and I am of another opinion. I go back and forth on the subject constantly: Mainly I, and the rest of my cohorts on the river, are afraid of being forced at gunpoint to pilot a ship for the Yankees—all the pilots are wary of that; I am not a Confederate or a Yankee yet. Most of us are cooling our heels and staying put: I do not want to be conscripted by either side—

In the meantime, I have decided to linger a bit in New Orleans, until the war fever has played out.

Yours fondly,
Samuel Clemens

⁂

I CANNOT SAY WHETHER IT was that letter from Samuel Clemens or the ague that prompted me to leave the store and head downriver to New Orleans, but by then, I reasoned that I might not be able to escape Cypress Bend at all once a war broke out. Approaching Mr. Altschul about the situation, I stated my case, and he, being aware of my distracted state of mind in regard to Mr. Stanley, allowed me some six weeks to attend to my business. Wanting to prove myself a good southerner and American, I had thought to eventually join up with one of the local militias upon my return. To become a soldier, fighting for a glorious cause, seemed a romantic idea filled with promise of adventure—and besides, to not do so would have marked me as a coward with a "yellow streak" among the locals.

And so I signed up with a locale brigade, with the proviso that I would begin my duty within a few months' time.

Adrift Again

IT TOOK ME TEN DAYS to go downriver to New Orleans: Of the possessions I carried with me in a carpetbag was a Colt six-shooter, my Bible, and some quinine tablets and calomel potion that the doctor had given me in the event that my fever should return. Of my fineries I packed a suit, a pair of boots, a gentleman's toilet kit, a watch and chain, various undergarments and kerchiefs, and some fifty dollars in two gold eagles that Mr. Altschul had paid me; these I kept in a money belt with some other funds I'd saved and was covetous to protect.

When Louisiana left the Union in January (the twenty-sixth), New Orleans itself had begun its conversion toward military preparations. Along the levee I saw that a recruitment stand for the Louisiana auxiliaries had been set up in front of one of the wharves, and a great number of young men, many of them laid-off sailors from ships that had been stopped in harbor and requisitioned as transport boats, were waiting in lines to sign up, their patriotic fervor aroused by an old officer, dressed splendidly in epaulets and a plumed hat, who held forth in a fine baritone, saying, "Now is the time for brave young men to show their valor." His words were accompanied by a nearby band that had struck up "Dixie," and a festive atmosphere prevailed. Later, in several clothing-shop windows, I saw fine military uniforms on display; and Tchoupitoulas Street itself was busy in a different way from before: Military officers were coming in and out of the grocers' warehouses and making arrangements for such provisions as were needed for training camps upstate. Here and there banners saying

SECESSION NOW and SLAVERY FOREVER were hanging in shop windows and draped over balconies.

The slaves I saw here and there, off in their labors, seemed more quietly disposed than before I left, a sheepish spirit attending them, as if they'd felt some blame for the coming war.

Since Mr. Stanley's whereabouts and condition were foremost in my mind, I made my way to the house on St. Charles Avenue to see if, by some chance, he had returned, sound and well: Mr. Stanley, I was told, had continued to pay for his lodging for several months, but then his payments stopped coming the past December. His former quarters, the delightful rooms where I had spent many happy moments, had been rented out to a family. And had he left any kind of word? None, I was told by the owner. Naturally, I was disappointed to hear such news—or lack of it—and in a disconsolate state I repaired to Mrs. Williams's boardinghouse in the hope of finding a room.

Happy to see me at her door again, Mrs. Williams looked me over, saying that I must have been through some considerable hard times upriver. It turned out that my attic room, being empty, was available, and after supper, somewhat fatigued and having told her and her boarders at dinner about my experiences at Cypress Bend, I retired.

The next morning, I weighed my options regarding Mr. Stanley: I could wait until some undetermined time for his return to New Orleans from Havana; or, before any greater curfews were invoked on the navigational traffic coming in and out of New Orleans because of the war, I could set out to find him in Cuba.

⁂

A DEEP LONELINESS MADE ME seek out my pilot friend that next day: More than a year had passed since we had spoken about books on the deck of the *Arago*, but I cherished his letters and friendship and longed for his advice and blessing.

After some fruitless wanderings, I came to the entranceway of one of the pilots' association rooms, which was tucked off in a side courtyard, in one of those plant-filled Spanish culs-de-sac so common to that city.

I found Clemens sitting by a table in the back of a billiard room where some old salts were gathered. Wearing a fine broadcloth jacket, his pilot's hat set before him, he was the most finely dressed man in the room; the immense trouble he took with his appearance was evident. At the time he seemed deep in thought and was scribbling in a book. When I approached him, saying, "Mr. Clemens," it was if I had appeared like an apparition from the darkness. A great look of surprise came over his face: "I'll be d—d," he said. Then, looking me over: "My God, Henry, what did those backwoods folks do to you?" He knew that I had contracted malaria up in Cypress Bend—I had written him about it—but he seemed surprised to find me so thin. During my bouts with the illness, I had dropped some fifty pounds, and my clothes hung loosely off of me. (I then weighed about ninety-five pounds—within three of seven stone.) In my diminished state I sat with him for a while, describing my trip downriver, but it was approaching the lunch hour, and as he seemed to feel pity for me, our first order of business was to head out for a good meal—one of his favorite pastimes. Shortly we had left the coolness of that place for the balminess of the day and headed over to the French Quarter. He knew of a good restaurant along Toulouse Street, where he had pledged to make sure that I put a little more skin on my bones. As we walked along, he smoked a thin black cigar, and as soldiers passed by, he seemed to take an amused delight in flicking quick salutes at them.

We were sitting on a terrace, and our table, some two stories up, had a view of Bourbon Street in the distance. For our lunch, Clemens, flush with money, ordered a great many courses as well as wines to go with them and snifters of absinthe, of which he was most fond. That afternoon, my belly full and my tongue loosened,

I related my very deep concern as to Mr. Stanley's whereabouts in Cuba and said that I would perhaps book passage there in the next few days. The very mention of it seemed to intrigue him.

"Cuba? And you suppose that your father has encountered some misfortune there?"

"Yes: I am hoping to find him—with luck, I will find him quickly; if he is ill, I will stay with him until he is better."

"And you've heard nothing from him?"

"Not for several months."

"And you intend to leave in a few days?"

"Yes, as soon as I can book passage."

"Cuba: Well, it seems a likely interesting place. I know a great number of captains who have been there, hauling to and fro across the gulf out of New Orleans, and they speak sweetly of it. Not so much for the usual harborside bawdiness of such places but for more dulcet reasons—mainly climatic—but you've got a lot of fever there, too. Seeing as how you've gotten the ague, what on earth makes you want to tempt fate again?"

"He is my father. If not for him, I would have come to nothing."

"I doubt that, my friend. But I reckon that you're determined enough; and to tell you the truth, Henry, I have thought of journeying there myself."

Then: "Some time ago, as I was coming downriver, my interest in that place was piqued by an old Spanish gentleman, a fine chess player—that's how we met, over a game of chess in one of the public rooms. His name was García, a fellow from Alicante, Spain, and he told me that he had in his possession the deed to a small parcel of Cuban land somewhere outside Havana and that he would be willing to sell it to me for the sum of two hundred dollars. 'A piece of land with a view of the beautiful Cuban sea' is how he put it. As I was financially comfortable and felt sorry for the man, I thought to buy this deed from him, sight unseen, considering it an act of charity. But my practical side prevailed. Still, he had filled my head with the idea that Cuba was worth a look: I mean, Henry, there were tears in his eyes as he described it to me—by his lights it was as beautiful, in parts, as any locale he had ever visited. And as any woman...Even if I don't care for their cigars, I have kept that country in mind; I have also often wondered if I'd passed up something good or whether I might have been gypped. So Cuba?"

Then he said: "And, to tell you the truth, Henry, on one of my journeys downriver, not so long ago, I made the acquaintance of a charming young lady, one Priscilla Hatcher, who is the daughter of a prominent southern gentleman, some kind of businessman, in Havana. I was most attracted to her, I must say; and I have often thought of visiting her."

"Well, then, Samuel, if you would consider it, I would be honored if you accompanied me."

When he made no immediate response, I felt gloomy and wished I had not brought up such nonsense, and soon we were speaking of other things. The afternoon passed, the tables around us emptying of people, and then the tables began to fill again with the dinner crowd. As the sun moved from east to west, a shadow slowly descended over the cobblestones and the shop facades turned gray, but when the sun began to set, all turned golden again, only to be overtaken by a shifting arc of darkness, which inched its way along the street below us bit by bit. Slowly gas lamps began to light. A great fraternity of birds chattered wildly in the trees, then quieted down, the sidewalks below that high patio suddenly jammed with pedestrians taking their evening constitutionals.

We were speaking about the coming war, and as Clemens was holding forth on the recruitment rallies being held each afternoon in the plaza of Jackson Square—and about the "great crowds of young men turning up, for the glamour of the uniforms, as the young ladies swoon over such things"—some residual of the ague came over me, and, deeply weakened suddenly, my hands shaking, my body trembling, and sweat forming on my brow, I slumped forward onto the table, in a poor state.

Helped by Clemens to the street, I was taken by a hack carriage to Mr. Clemens's boardinghouse, near Annunciation Square.

I believe that a day, perhaps two, had passed, before I could make out my surroundings with some clarity: I saw a window and the foliage of a magnolia tree without, and as I looked about the room and its furnishings I saw Mr. Clemens sitting in a chair in a corner, waiting, his worried expression turning into one of relief when I awakened. "You had me scared half to death, my friend," he said. "You were a dead man, as far as I could make of you. It put me in quite a state—so that's malaria, is it?"

"Yes, that's it—sorry for the trouble."

"It was no trouble for me—one of the boardinghouse slaves looked after you: I was just a little concerned, that's all. As I said, you could've been a dead man until you started to talk for a spell. And much about your father...well, for what's its worth to you, Henry, I had some plans to head north to join my brother, Orion, but I've since decided to go with you to Havana instead, if you're still intending to." Then: "Only thing is that I've got to convince Mother Clemens that it will be a safe thing. When you are up and about, come downstairs to meet her."

☀

AT ABOUT ELEVEN THE NEXT morning, I was feeling well enough to bathe and clean myself up, the ague spell having largely passed. Shortly I ventured down to the hotel parlor, where Clemens, dressed entirely in white, sat beside his mother, Jane Lampton Clemens, over tea. Mother Clemens was a congenial woman of about sixty and wore mourning dress: A lacy blouse whose collar was a succession of ruffles was the only touch of adornment about her person. When I walked in, Clemens got up and confided to me that, in regard to Cuba, he would do all the talking. Then he introduced me to her as Mr. Henry Stanley, a dear friend. I joined them for a cup of tea. And as Clemens lit a cigar, which made his mother frown, he spoke of the circumstances that brought her to the city. She had come down from St. Louis on holiday for Mardi Gras and had been left stranded in New Orleans awaiting passage back, as so many of the steamboats had been pulled into other service on account of the coming war. By then, Clemens had found her a place on one of the few ships going upriver a few days hence. Which is to say that at the time I made her acquaintance she had passed many a day in that boardinghouse and was anxious to return home.

"Mother, this young man and I have agreed to undertake an excursion to the island of Cuba, where many southerners frequently go. My friend here has some pressing business there, and I thought to avail myself of the opportunity to see that foreign land. What's more, as he is in poor health, I thought it best to help him along—he is determined to go anyway. We won't be gone for long—I'm going stir-crazy hanging around here—but I would never make this journey without your blessing."

"Cuba?" she said. "What on earth are you thinking, son?" Then: "Samuel, you're a grown man, and you'll do what you want to do, so of course you have my blessing; but if it's true that you'll be most likely leaving the river trade shortly, I would think you'd be better off joining up with Orion again. And besides, you've never traveled to a strange country before." She sighed. "But I suppose if it won't be one thing, it would be the other. Yes, you have my blessing—but don't be a young fool about it."

"Now, Mother, don't be worried. And remember that a month or so passes quickly; maybe by the time we get back, the war fever in these parts will be over, though I admit it isn't likely."

He waited for her summary judgment. Then, with a flick of a hand, she said, "But do be careful, son. Mercy me if something were to happen to you." Like all good mothers, she had said her piece.

᠅

A FEW DAYS LATER, AFTER Mother Clemens had embarked north to St. Louis on *The Crescent City*, its decks overflowing with anxious passengers and soldier recruits, Clemens and I made our way to the harbor to book tickets to Havana. It took us an hour to reach the sales window of the Hamburg–New Orleans–Cuba line, as there was a glut of southerners, their faces drained of color, waiting in a long queue to secure their own passage, an air of impatience about them, apprehensive as they were over the prospect of Yankee blockades sealing them off from their concerns on the island. It seemed to us as well that some of them simply wanted to get out of New Orleans before the war started. Within a few hours we booked passage out: It cost thirty-two dollars for the round-trip, and, at dawn, a few days later, we boarded the steamer *Malta* en route to Havana.

We Arrive in Cuba

ON THE MORNING OF OUR seventh day at sea, after sailing some six hundred nautical miles, we steamed into Havana Bay through its narrow entrance, with fortresses, hooking out on elongated shoals, to either side. Though the tideless waters were sparkling blue and the air was clear as glass, the harbor had the smell of the stagnant and offal-ridden drainage from the city. Diamonds of light quivered in the water alongside shreds of timber and flowing clouds of filth that made the fish scatter. Still, the sun shone brightly, and along all the outcroppings of shore stood tall coconut palms and clusters of other tropical fruit trees that made for hedges of pleasing foliage. Church spires and Moorish minarets rose in the distance, as did a great hill on which stood several neoclassical buildings. The air sometimes became sweet, as if we had come to a city of gardens.

The harbor itself was protected by a large castle that stood on a rocky outcropping, its parapets fitted with cannons that, as we came in, were firing off a volley into the air to summon the day. Church bells were ringing from the interior of the city, and all along the shore were a hundred majestic buildings with yellow and red and blue facades, most of them ornately designed, with parapets and twisting balconies, some being private residences and others warehouses and places of commerce. Spanish flags flew everywhere, but then the flags of many other nations, from every clime, were fluttering off the forest of masts before us, as there were frigates, brigs, schooners, and steamers from all over the world jammed along the docks. Altogether the city seemed booming and in decline; beautiful but aging; a gem and a rough stone; florid with scents and repugnant with rot at the same time.

Clemens remained busy with his notebook, scribbling down some impressions, when we dropped anchor at a place called Regla, which was across the bay from the city proper. Because the yellow fever had come to Cuba from New Orleans that past year, our ship was boarded by a health official, who conducted an interminably slow appraisal of all the passengers, whom he looked over for signs of that illness. This took up most of the morning. Then another official, accompanied by several soldiers, set up a table and chair on deck to check our credentials against the names he had from a passenger list. I still had my old English passport, wherein I was still listed as John Rowlands, and it was in that name that I was given a visitor's permit—what was called a *cédula*: Clemens had a Missouri passport, a holdover from the days when he had planned a journey to Brazil some years before. Altogether he had seemed very pleased that at long last, after so many travels out East, and up- and downriver, he was finally about to set foot in a foreign land.

During the transfer of documents he noticed the name written in my passport and said to me:

"So your birth name is John?"

"It was."

"Well, then, how is it that you've never mentioned it to me?"

"I thought I had. But the truth is, Samuel, as far as I'm concerned John Rowlands no longer exists."

"No matter: I prefer Henry, at any rate; but it is strange to think that happenstance has given you a name most special to me."

Disembarking on a small lighter, we were taken to shore by

locals so thin and emaciated that we thought they'd certainly suffered from the fever, for their limbs were shrunken and their feet
were shriveled down to the bone. As happens in any port, after
we had passed through the customhouse—I had hidden away my
Bible, as I'd heard from a passenger aboard ship that Bibles were
contraband in that country—we were assailed by persons anxious
to sell every service. Were we of a different bent of mind we could
have gone off with some very friendly ladies or taken up residence
in some private home, for there were several poor-looking persons
soliciting passengers to stay with them, cheaply. Availing myself
of my few phrases of Spanish—I would learn the language well
in Spain years later—we hired a carriage and driver to take us
around to the city.

Within the hour we were making our way along the densely
packed streets of Havana, a city unlike any I had ever seen before:
New Orleans, for all its mazes, had many a street that opened wide
to the sky and air, but here the buildings seemed narrowly separated from one another, the passageways between them barely
wide enough for two carts to pass side by side. Where movement
was not slow it had stopped completely, for those streets were congested with carriages and donkey-drawn carts and poor farmers
pulling along their mules, their woven cane panniers filled with
bunches of bananas, oranges, and the local favorite, a tuber called
plantain. And many of them were on foot, hauling chickens tied
by their feet and hung off sticks on their backs. There were slaves
here, too, none rushed in his labors and all of a generally poorer
condition than the slaves of New Orleans. Many of them, steeped
in misery, were going shoeless or were huddled off, sickly and
malnourished, in some shady cubbyhole with their loads at their
sides. Occasionally we saw a fancier kind of slave, usually a postil-
ion in attendance of an expensive silver-rimmed carriage, dressed
in white leggings, long spurs, and a bright red jacket (but that
was more the exception than the rule). Beggars, deformed and
diseased, were everywhere, and lepers, too, their hands wrapped
in rags or covered in worn mittens.

Striking as well was the abundance of Chinese—many of them, Clemens noticed, missing their right ears—conscripted former criminals, we would later learn, brought to Cuba under strict seven-year contracts as indentured servants. These Chinamen were valued by the planters for their resourcefulness and tenacity at labor (and because they were cheaper to keep than slaves). Their imprint on the city was evident in the peculiar flavor of their shops and restaurants, for alongside the Spanish stores called *bodegas* and the usual haberdashery and ladies' dress establishments—my clerk's eye could not fail to notice such places of commerce—there would be a window scrawled with Chinese characters, a dim doorway, and, in the half-light of day, one could see high shelves stocked with all manner of exotic-looking goods. These shopkeepers wore their hair in long black braided pigtails, or they shaved their heads completely, their white pantaloons and coolie hats common among the Chinese of that city.

Clemens was generally delighted with the colorful attractions of the place, whereas I, having seen both the highs and lows of what it offered, remained somewhat mystified by Mr. Stanley's attraction to the city, for from what I could observe, the first impressions I had of impending decline and neglect were reinforced at nearly every turn. Still, despite its apparent chaos, there seemed some promise to Havana—for there were many fine buildings to be admired, some of them tranquil-looking places set back behind palm-filled, marble-floored courtyards, off the street. There were bars and billiard halls, and we noticed that virtually every Cuban man of commerce was quite well—if not practically—dressed, in dark suits with cravats and heavy French hats. And all the Cubans we saw—whether lowly peasant or high-born aristocrat—smoked, either small cigarillos or the Cuban cigars for which the island was famous.

꙳

WE ENDED UP AT A hotel owned by an American woman in the old city, not far from the city's Plaza de Armas, where the gardens were in bloom. It was called the Hotel Cubano, and it was where Mr. Stanley had occasionally stayed while visiting that city, as its guests were mainly southerners like himself. Indeed, when Clemens and I finally arrived—in midafternoon, in the extreme heat of the day—a group of southern gentlemen was shooting billiards in a room off the reception area. The owner, a certain Mrs. Rosedale, late of Savannah, Georgia, was the sort of lady in perpetual bloom despite her middle-aged years, gracious of manner and friendly. When I signed the register, she asked me if I was a relation of Mr. Stanley. When I said that I was, she chanced to remark: "Oh, how is he?"

"I imagine that he is well, ma'am—it is my hope, anyway; you see, we have had some difficulty in communications. But I hope to find him. Surely he is known around here?"

"He is. Last I saw of him, he was in that very bar conducting some business—a few months ago, I believe it was. I spoke to him then: It seemed he was in attendance of some urgent matter involving his brother." Then: "But I am sure you will find him shortly if he is in Havana. Here the community of southern folk find each other, and quickly, especially now, with the probability of war."

And then she turned to Clemens and, reading the entry he had made in the guest book, declared: "A riverboat pilot! And one who dresses so elegantly! Goodness! What a romantic and courageous profession!" Then: "Rest assured, my dear friends, for as long as you are here at my hotel, you will not go wanting for anything."

As we followed her down a corridor to a broad marble staircase leading to the upper floors, we could see that the hotel was a grand and cavernous affair. Behind a grillwork gate, along an inner hall, was a palm courtyard and fountain, and a choir of parrots chortling in an immense cage. Somewhere upstairs an opera company was rehearsing—their voices, ringing through the halls and echoing throughout the place, attested to its scale.

"This was once the residence of a very highly placed Spanish lord," she told us. "Over a hundred years ago, he was poisoned by one of his sons in a dispute over a woman, and so, as is very common in these parts, his ghost dwells in this place. Now and then he is known to come around to greet the guests; but do not be alarmed. He is mainly a sad ghost, and not as vengeful or malicious as one would think."

"And you've seen this gentleman yourself?" Clemens asked her.

"Oh, I have. His English is not very good—you would think it would be, after he's spent so much time around my guests—but my Spanish is very fine, and we do communicate, though I find some of his antique words hard to understand."

"And what do you speak about, ma'am?" Clemens inquired.

"Well"—she seemed amused at the question—"just 'cause he's dead doesn't mean he can't fall in love! As my late husband has told me, there is no end of emotions on the other side. No, gentlemen, he has often confessed to me that I am the very sight that makes his spirit heart tremble with joy! He calls me his beautiful angel and regales me with sonnets. I am flattered, of course, but my one loyalty is to my late husband. As you can imagine, my Spanish lord—el Conde Miguel Asturiano is his name—is none too happy about the situation. Nevertheless, he persists."

She led us to our room, up on the third floor. The accommodations consisted of two hard beds, each with its own canopy of mosquito netting and separated from the other by a Chinese-style screen; a common sitting area, a dresser, and large closet. The airy chamber's finest feature was a broad balcony opening out to the inner courtyard.

"Gentlemen, as you can see, you have a sink, but as the water piped in through the city is fetid, use it only for washing. Each morning you will find several pitchers of clear drinking water outside your door. It is brought in from a place about nine miles north of here called Marianao; this will cost you each ten cents a day. I would also caution you to wear slippers and to never walk barefoot on the floors, as there are, in this city, tiny mites that will bore their way into your toes and settle there with an infection. We have a fine restaurant below us, facing the street, and a billiard room next to it. Just a few doors down from us is a public bathhouse; and above, on our roof, there is a promenade from which you will see the harbor and the ocean beyond, an especially delightful view at sunset."

Then, as she parted:

"But do avoid drinking the water. And if you see the count, do not be alarmed. Now, good day, gentlemen."

THAT FIRST EVENING, AFTER CLEANING ourselves up, we went downstairs to the hotel restaurant, where we partook of a large meal of all kinds of freshly caught fish in a stew, consumed with a sizable quantity of claret and local staples, among them some tasty plantain fritters that were heavily doused in lemon and salt.

Soon enough, we made the acquaintance of several southern gentlemen who invited us to join them after our meal for some billiards. Because I did not know how to play, I remained content to watch Clemens, who seemed to have an endless capacity for the game. Occasionally he would sit down beside me and thusly apprise me of the personalities he encountered.

"A lot of these gentlemen," Clemens told me, "own various and many businesses in Havana and elsewhere on the island. That old gentleman with the silver beard, Henry, is ninety years old—but he doesn't look it, does he? He claims that his mingling with the Cuban ladies of ill repute has been an elixir of youth. He owns six hundred acres of a sugar enterprise. That gent, a retired politician named Morgan, was greatly involved, in the 1850s, in some kind of movement in the South to invade and annex the island of Cuba as a state. And that gentleman runs one of the biggest banking concerns in Havana. Owns fifty thousand acres of timberland somewhere in the East. These businessmen are so many in number that there are several southern commercial associations in Havana—along with lodges and clubs and cultural groups, all distinct from the Spanish variety. Among these, I was pleased to find out, dear Henry, is a literary society situated in the mansion of a gentleman who lives in a verdant neighborhood in the heights of the city, an area known as the Cerro, where the embassies of foreign nations are located. Apparently this man has one of the largest English-language libraries on the island, one at which strangers are welcome. And I've eavesdropped on much talk about the presumed southern victory in the event of a war, which they can't see lasting much longer than a year. And once that happens, Henry, in regard to Cuba itself, it is said that the South will take upon itself what the federal government hasn't been able to do in years past, which is to annex Cuba as a southern state—to buy it from Spain outright.

"It seems that there are already several thousand well-armed American soldiers from southern regiments already here; troops brought in to protect southern interests and help fight rebel insurgencies in the eastern part of the island. These fellows, I was told, are ready to declare themselves for the South should the war come." Then, as he was pleased with himself: "I should teach you billiards, as there is much to learn over such a game."

As he told me such stories, his words brought to mind something else that Mr. Stanley had told me about Cuba: Given southern ownership of its greatest estates and concerns, Cuba might as well have been an extension of the South. (In fact, some months later, the Spanish-controlled government of Cuba, much under the sway of the southern diplomatic corps there, would declare war on the North.)

But the behavior of these gentlemen struck even a youth such as I as somewhere paradoxical, for while it would seem that they should have been wary of strangers (as if Yankee spies might be afoot) they made no secret of the fact that a fleet of ships out of New Orleans and other ports along the gulf—from Brownsville, Texas to St. Marks, Florida—was heading to Havana to fill the city's warehouses with supplies that would, in the unlikely event of a future southern reversal, be vital to the continuation of the war. As a merchant, hearing their boasts, I was fascinated by the difficult logistics of such a feat, and I found myself admiring the confidence and organization of such men. I need not further pursue the theme other than to say that as that evening and others like it unfolded, Clemens and I found ourselves among the converted when it came to the belief that the South would easily win the war.

⚜

AT SOME LATE HOUR WE retired to the discomforts of our beds and tried to sleep. But sleep was somewhat of an impossibility, for even under the best of circumstances, both Clemens and I were prone to insomnia. As I remained awake, in speculation over Mr. Stanley, Clemens, giving up the fight, had gotten up for a smoke or two by the open window. It was his way. When, at some later hour, we finally managed to doze off, what rest we took was brief enough, for at six-thirty in the morning we were awakened by bells and cock crows, and by the loud conversation of some cleaning women mopping the dust off the marble floors outside our door and carrying on a discussion about a woman of their acquaintance named Maria Josefina. Hearing the clipped locutions of their Spanish, of which I had only a fledgling knowledge, and with the sun beginning to stream in through the shutters, and with a great feeling of the strangeness of that place, I finally realized that we had indeed arrived in Mr. Stanley's Cuba.

⚜

I WILL NOW SPEAK OF my search for my father. We had, on the first day, visited his office, which, I remembered from his correspondence, was located on a street called O'Reilly. Along that commercial stretch of warehouses and stores, much like Tchoupitoulas Street in New Orleans, hung many signs in the English language. When we arrived on foot, around ten in the morning, after having partaken (at Clemens' insistence) of a large and fortifying breakfast at the hotel, I was heartened to see that there was much activity along its street and pavements—all manner of carts being emptied and loaded from a countless succession of doorways; a strong smell of manure, coffee, and raw tobacco permeated the air; and there were the usual contingents of blacks at work and Cuban gentlemen to give them orders, while others were lying low in the shadows, a sight typical to that city. There were also some military constables milling about. Then, as we looked for the building numbered 7A, my heart quickened, for I saw a sight that was gratifyingly familiar, that of a tallish and bearded man sitting in front of one of the warehouses reading a newspaper. Believing that this man was Mr. Stanley, I rushed ahead to greet him, but I was sadly mistaken: "If you are looking for Mr. Stanley," he told me, "you will find his offices over there." And he pointed to a darkened doorway across the way: This was apparently the aforementioned 7A, though there would have been no way of telling, for it had no marking. Entering the premises through a long passageway, we found ourselves in the recesses of a warehouse.

Appearing out of the shadows, a Cuban fellow who had seen us come in barked out to us that the *oficinas* were above. A wide stairway at the back led us up to the second floor, where I was immediately elated by the sight of a doorway, alongside which were several signs, among them one that said: STANLEY BROS. & CO. IMPORTERS. Off an inner hallway were about six offices: In the first sat a corpulent Cuban man, his head glistening with sweat, some ledger books opened on the desk before him. He was drafting a letter or some poetry (a national pastime), a plume in hand. When I ventured in and made my introduction, it became quickly apparent that he knew little of the English language: I then tried to explain in my pidgin Spanish that we were looking for Señor Stanley. Shortly he got up, and with some great effort, made his way into another office, then came back with an English-speaking gentleman.

He was a fellow southerner, an accountant who had his clientele among the American businessmen of the city and to whom had been entrusted the management of such offices. I remember that his name was Mr. Johnson; and this Mr. Johnson, having known Mr. Stanley and his brother in passing, had information that was both helpful and discouraging to me:

"I last saw Captain Stanley here four months ago," he said. "But he stopped coming by about then. One of his boys told me he'd caught the yellow fever—or typhoid, I cannot say which. I made nothing of his absence, as he only spent a few days a week here and mainly used this address to receive his mail and to conduct some business. He had another office down by the waterfront. I did see his brother, Mr. Henry Stanley, on one occasion after that. He seemed in some kind of rush to gather up their books, which they kept in a safe, along with some money, I guess. When I asked him about Captain Stanley, he told me that he was still laid low, but that was all. He left one afternoon with a portmanteau, and since then he hasn't been back. But if he's still in the city, I would imagine that the best way to find him would be to inquire after him with the American shippers down by the harbor, or you could locate the Yankee counsel, though I cannot say that you've come at the best of times to do so."

"And Mr. Stanley's office? Where is it?" I asked.

"Just there, at the end of the hall."

The Stanley Bros. & Co. office was but a largish room, smelling still of lingering pipe and cigar smoke, its walls stained with threadlike trails of oil-lamp fumes. Piles of newspapers—old copies of the *Daily Picayune* and a local English-language Havana newspaper—were stacked in a corner. All manner of documents—bills of lading and such—were scattered about on the floor: Indeed there was a safe, its door still open, as were the drawers of a correspondence cabinet; and there was a big oak desk, and on the desk's blotter were several crumpled letters written in Spanish, apparently (from what I could tell) regarding some transaction. These Mr. Stanley or his brother had apparently thought were of little importance. The general impression was that Mr. Stanley had left the premises in haste. Thinking myself in the midst of some kind of dream, I could barely speak, but Clemens, coolheaded and curious, decided to ask Mr. Johnson several questions:

"When you last saw Mr. Stanley, did he seem ill?"

"I saw him at a distance, and he seemed well."

"Did he carry the portmanteau out himself?"

"I think he had a hand—some black boy, anxious for a wage, assisting him."

"We thank you, sir," Mr. Clemens said, and with that Mr. Johnson accompanied us to the head of the stairs. As we went down, he shouted after us: "Good luck to you both," and, as an afterthought, "Long live the South!"

※

WE WERE INTENT ON MAKING our way to the harbor: If this failed to render useful information, we would inquire after him at the hospitals—there were two in the city—and if that bore no result, we would approach the American counsel for help. But in any event, we were briefly detained by a sudden downpour, what the Cubans call an *aguacero*, according to Clemens's guidebook, which he had brought along from New Orleans. It was a rain so profound that we were forced to take shelter in a bar at the end of the street. Though it was still before noon, we ordered several glasses of the local beer, and there we remained for about half an hour.

The downpour, like the torrents of a cataract, cooled things off for a while, but soon a steamy heat followed: Such was the tropical clime. We found a carriage parked out in the street, its driver, in a broad straw hat and rags, hunched over, with his stick in hand, dozing. My Spanish was sufficient to communicate that we wished to be taken to "los barcos americanos del puerto." This he took to mean the sector of wharves along the seafront dominated by the warehouses and docks of various North American shipping companies, toward the southern end of the harbor. Taken down the paseo to the waterside and south along the ship-glutted docks, we came upon a scene reminiscent of bustling

New Orleans, except that few of the frigates we saw were taking freight. Most, in from gulf ports, were being unloaded by fiercely worked slave gangs. Bales of processed cotton and crates lay out along the piers; and while the overseers barked out commands, a group of well-dressed Americans was gathered on the pier and engaged in heated discussion with some Cuban customs officials.

We approached one of these Americans, a tall and lanky man in a stovepipe hat, as to the whereabouts of the Stanley Bros. & Co. concern, but he seemed to have never heard of them, being new to the island. A second gentleman, however, directed us to the offices of the Ward Line company, and there we spoke to an official who knew something of the Stanley brothers' business, the Ward Line being their landlords. He then instructed one of his underlings to take us to a man named Jacob, who sometimes worked for the Stanleys. We passed through several warehouses and long, slop-filled alleys to reach the smallish room at the back of a loading dock that had apparently served as Mr. Stanley's place of business in the harbor. Jacob, a somewhat dissipated-looking man, had been asleep on a cot: The room smelled vilely of urine and liquor. When roused, he was at first annoyed and unfriendly, his cantankerous manner no doubt influenced by the fact that he was jaundiced and probably not long for this world. But once I explained the purpose of our visit there, he told us, with the gleam of self-interest in his rheumy eyes, "Yes, there are ways that I can help you and things that I can relate, but I won't do it here. First you must buy me some drinks, for I have a horrid headache and ain't in no mood to speak to strangers otherwise."

And so it was that we spent the remainder of that afternoon in a dingy harborside saloon, drinking from dirty glasses, and tolerating for several hours what seemed the incoherent ramblings of Jacob.

"What of Mr. Stanley?" I would ask, but he would go on, toothless and with gums swollen, speaking of his own fatherless childhood and of beatings at the hands of ruffian urchins when he was a young boy; of jails and a long stint as a sailor and of somehow ending up in this sorry state in Cuba.

"But what of Mr. Stanley?" I asked again.

Finally—just when the saloon had filled up with a great number of unsavory types who had begun to regard our nice clothes and good shoes, and Clemens's gold watch chain, with menacing interest—he spoke of my father.

"Mr. Stanley was my one saving grace," he said with sadness. "Worked for him and his brother, the captain, for nearly ten years. The captain was not a kindly man; he never understood why Mr. Stanley—who had a soft spot for lost souls—would give a drunk like me a job. I worked hard for them, looking after their shipments out of port—that little office, that hovel, was my only home—and it is only through the indifference of the managers that I keep it even now."

"But do you know where Mr. Stanley is?"

"The captain liked to give me a good beating for no good reason from time to time. Heaven help me if he whiffed a drink on my breath. Down would come the cane. So I was very happy that he caught the fever and died. Yes, he is dead. But then Mr. Stanley himself got the fever, and in his sickness he became a different sort of man—or maybe he was all grieved over his wife's death, but I know that when I last saw him, a few months ago, he didn't have much concern for me. Just gave me a few gold coins and told me that he was done with Havana and with many other things. But first he said that he would have to tidy up after some of his business affairs: You know, he and the captain had traveled all over this island. The very day he set out, I had the feeling I wouldn't see him again, but I know where you will probably find him, if he's still alive."

"Where?"

"Buy me two more bottles of rum to take home, and I will tell you."

To this I reluctantly agreed.

"Well, I know he took off to various parts to collect on debts and settle up accounts with his planters. I know he went out west to Pinar del Río for a spell; the best tobacco growers are there.

Then he came back here for a few days, but soon left by schooner to the city of Santiago de Cuba, at the far southern end of the island, on account of his wanting to sell off his share in some business. Where else he's gone I can't say, but my guess is that he went out to Matanzas. He's owned a share in a sugar plantation there for quite some time—owned it with his brother and an Englishman named Mr. Davis, who has the biggest stake. Used to talk about it as a place he was fond of. But it's only a guess that he's there. More than that, I cannot say."

"And this plantation, Jacob. Where is it?"

"I've never seen it myself, but it's about sixty-five, seventy miles southeast of Havana as the crow flies, somewhere near a town—really just a little settlement—called Limonar, maybe a half day's ride out from there, through bandit country. And I can tell you something else: The plantation is called the Esperanza."

And then, asking our pardon, Jacob took another drink and smacked his lips in savory delight. Leaving him, Clemens and I headed back to our hotel.

BEFORE WE SET OUT FOR Matanzas, Clemens, having come such a long way, wanted to spend a few days in Havana sightseeing. For several mornings, with his guidebook in hand, Clemens would, with some vague itinerary in mind, lead our somewhat haphazard excursions through the city, the main points of interest being the architectural grandeur of the main boulevard of Havana, el Paseo Tacón, named after a past governor of the island; several old convents; and several churches. Foremost of these was the cathedral near our hotel, in the old colonial quarter. The bones of Christopher Columbus were said to be interred there, and Clemens, reading of this, had been most anxious to see the supposed crypt. In that somewhat gloomy place, we had stood for some time facing Columbus's mortal remains. This comprised the only instance when I had seen Clemens possess a sense of wonder and nearly religious awe for anything: "To be a great explorer who finds a new world," I heard him say. "Now, that would be worth a thousand years of living." But on the whole, he remained unmoved by the atmosphere in that church. In this regard, his Presbyterian upbringing notwithstanding, he remained curiously coldhearted about religion and matters such as the afterlife, dismissing them as the wishful fantasies of people trying to make sense of this world.

"Even at my young age," he told me, "I can see there's no rhyme or reason to the way things go, or any fairness about it. I've only to think of my younger brother to see that." Then: "As for this 'Father in Heaven' business, as far as I am concerned we may as well revert to being cavemen and worshipping the trees."

Nevertheless he remained particularly interested in the occasional mendicant we encountered—religious folk who preached on the sidewalks and, for a small fee, gave a personal blessing. Whenever we passed such a person, Clemens had to stop and watch the incantations of prayer; in general he seemed quite skeptical—but fascinated just the same—in things supernatural, which were in evidence everywhere. It was unavoidable, as the city had an undercurrent of animistic beliefs.

This was particularly evident at night, when, in alleys and hidden courtyards, groups of Negroes gathered to sing—not church hymns but strange Yoruban chants evoking the African gods, such activities being accompanied by the beating of drums and wild dances. Twice in the course of our nightly wanderings did we see such things—these rituals, I should add, were conducted on streets that the Spanish guards purposely ignored, for, as Mrs. Rosedale informed us, such practices, though against the law, were impossible to repress, so much were they a part of the slave culture.

꙳

ON OUR THIRD DAY IN Havana, Clemens decided to look up the young lady of his passing acquaintance, Miss Priscilla Hatcher, whose father was doing business in Havana. We went to visit her at her home up on the great hill over the city, where many of the consulates were to be found, and had arranged to do so through Mrs. Rosedale, who had some acquaintance with her family.

Earlier he had confessed to me that he had, some time back, sent her several gushing notes of a somewhat romantic nature, and that she had responded in kind. Though he doubted that he was ready to take any kind of leap, in the morning he had spent an inordinate amount of time in our hotel room, shaving and trimming his muttonchops and mustache, before putting on his white linen suit and polishing his shoes so that he would appear before her as the image of sartorial splendor.

I should add here that Clemens was, in some ways, a sentimentalist: Among the possessions he had brought along with him on our journey, aside from certain practical items, were a cameo of his mother, a small oval photograph of his departed brother Henry, and, in a pouch, a lock of hair from, as he told me, "a girl I once loved in Hannibal, Missouri." Such an admission aside, he was otherwise circumspect about his dealings with the female sex, his interest in romantic involvements, as he once told me, limited to occasional flirtations and fleeting infatuations that he viewed as pleasant enough ways to pass the time while spending a few days here and there in various towns. Whatever his ultimate intentions—in this instance, to pay the young lady a "courtesy call"—he was in no rush to become involved.

We turned up sometime past noon, and after an introduction to several other family members, and after answering numerous questions pertaining to the reasons we had come to Havana— Mr. Hatcher had indeed heard of Mr. Stanley, without knowing him—and after a discussion about the prospects of war, we dined in a shuttered salon and were then treated to a performance of Chopin by the young lady herself. After this, she and Clemens, in the company of her aunt, sat together for some time on a love seat, Clemens charming her with his stories about the Mississippi. Though I was engaged in conversation with Mr. Hatcher about Arkansas, from where he hailed, I overheard much laughter; then, apparently, they entered into some more serious discussions, for their voices quieted. Finally it was time for us to go, and while Clemens had been quite taken by Miss Hatcher's personality and was glad to have visited her, in the end, as we later retreated back down into the city proper, he seemed somewhat relieved to have concluded his fanciful romantic speculation.

"I like her, Henry," he told me. "And I'm glad to have seen her again; but she would clearly do better with a practical businessman like her father. For all her refinements, she doesn't like to read books, which she finds too troublesome, and her lack of interest in literature holds no appeal for me. And something else, which I did not know: She is a Catholic, and Mother would never like that."

Later, around dusk, we visited the Plaza de Armas, where it was congenial to sit on a bench and listen to a military band play waltzes. Clemens remarked: "Life doesn't get much better, does it, Henry?" Then: "This is a curious land. At one in the afternoon, it's hell: at seven in the evening, pure bliss."

We were planning to head for Matanzas the next evening, but it was my misfortune to come down with a renewed attack of the ague—and so it was that we lost three days. During those nights while I was laid low, Clemens began to frequent a large café just outside the old city walls called the Louvre, a haunt favored by the American shipping fraternity. Which is to say that Union and Confederate sailors and their captains and mates gathered uneasily there, for by that first week in April, 1861, the war seemed inevitable.

In that café, Clemens had found a southern captain whom he wanted me to meet: a surly bear of a man named Captain Bailey, who had a dead eye and had apparently known my father well. And so it was, when I had gotten better, that Clemens took me there. Why Clemens thought it important for me to meet Captain Bailey I cannot say, but shortly we found ourselves sitting across a table from the man, his left eye ghostly dull.

"I understand from your friend here that you are close to Mr.

Stanley. Now, before I say my words, I must ask you what you know of him," Bailey said.

It was a curious question.

"Well, sir—He is an old Georgia gentleman of refinement and education, a former minister who had become a commissions trader; he is a pious widower, with no children of his own. I am his adopted son, or will be, when I find him."

"That is all well and good that you think this: But here is what I know of him—and I am telling you this, young man, to correct any mistaken notions you have of him." He finished a glass of rum and filled it again from a bottle.

"I met Mr. Stanley aboard a ship when I was a mate back in the early 1840s; the ship was not from these parts, but had sailed from England. Contrary to what Mr. Stanley may have told you, he is originally from Cheshire, not far from northern Wales. He came to Louisiana to make his fortune as a young man in the cotton trade, and in those days, he met his first wife, a Texas girl named Angela—as pretty a woman as one will ever lay eyes on. They opened a boardinghouse on Dorsiere Street in New Orleans—I had stayed there myself upon occasion. It was a clean place, and she was a good cook who ran the place efficiently while Mr. Stanley went about his business as a trader. Now, upon his return from one of those trips, it was his misfortune to find the house locked up and deserted on account of the fact that his dear wife had died of the yellow fever in his absence. I think he may have made some Bible studies then—for such tragedies bring all men closer to God—but if he was a minister, it was a profession that...how shall I put it?...facilitated an intimate knowledge of many a widow and neglected wife in the counties of the South through which he'd traveled.

"But even of these activities does a man soon tire, and so it was that Mr. Stanley returned to New Orleans to resume his life as a trader. I knew him—and his brother—well then, for we encountered each other in many a lively saloon; but as it is natural for a man to put down roots, Mr. Stanley wanted to marry again, and his intended was a young woman by the name of Frances Mellor—also English by birth, I should add. I believe it was in 1847 that they were wed, and a happier, more genteel couple one would be hard put to find. The only problem was that Mrs. Stanley was a frail sort of lady, aging quickly beyond her years, and because of some infirmities she could bear no children, and this, alas, did not please Mr. Stanley, who took to traveling far and wide, which is what first brought him and his brother, Captain Stanley, to Cuba. Now, aside from setting up some profitable business relations here, he, away from the wife, availed himself of . . . certain pleasure-making opportunities," he said, winking with his one good eye. "But not to say that Mr. Stanley is not a gentleman. One could not find a better man than he in New Orleans; and, indeed, he cared enough for the wife to provide for her a small family of sorts—two young girls whom they adopted from an orphanage. They live in St. Louis. Surely you know these things." Then: "Now, as for Mr. Stanley's life here on this island, I'll ask you a question: Aside from business, what would a man find for himself in this place?"

And when I did not answer him, not knowing what to say, he pounded his fist against the table and said: "Freedom, pure and unencumbered, young man." Then: "As much as you might want to find him, has it occurred to you that Mr. Stanley might not want to be found?"

I had listened to his words with as much patience as I could muster, as Clemens had so kindly thought that this man would be of help to us, but looking at this Captain Bailey and knowing just how low men can sink, I paid him no heed.

"Did you notice how he made no mention of my father's great knowledge of books?" I mentioned to Clemens afterward. "How can a man speak of him without mentioning it, unless he does not really know him? And who was this captain to tell me that Mr. Stanley had adopted two daughters—what proof has he? I am almost admiring of the flourishes of his invention, Samuel, but I refuse to take them as nothing more than that: an invention born of twisted self-amusement."

"Don't get riled up," Clemens told me consolingly. "I had thought the fellow's words might have made you happy—I did not know what he'd say." Then: "Anyway, I've made inquiries at the harbor: There's a steamer leaving for Matanzas at ten tomorrow night."

Finding Mr. Stanley, at Last

NOW, IF YOU LOOK AT a map of Cuba, you will see that it is an elongated country, and in square miles the approximate size of the state of Pennsylvania. Just south of the Tropic of Cancer, it is shaped somewhat like a crocodile, its snout dipping down to the far southeast and its coiling tail, in the west, bounded to the south by the Caribbean Sea and to the north by the Gulf of Mexico, that end comprising the provinces of Pinar Del Río, Havana, and Matanzas. The coastlines to the north are, at any rate, indented with numerous coves and inlets and small bays, the largest ones being those at Havana, Matanzas, and, farther east, toward the torso, the Bay of Cárdenas, beyond which that scaly tract is topped with countless islands of various sizes. And while looking at the northern coast, you will see that although the distance between Havana and the city of Matanzas is not very great, few places of consequence dot that verdant passage. But when one stands on the deck of a small steamer coursing through such waters at night—as Clemens and I did once we left Havana's harbor, where ship after ship, including many a man-of-war, was anchored densely and in every direction around us—the very nature of the sea and the life within it seems to be of a more or less magical nature. For in our steamship's wake, numerous phosphorescent eels and translucent medusas seemed to follow, something one would never see on the Mississippi (or in the Congo); and the sight of such things, which left a flickering silver trail behind us continually, had, along with the brilliant moonlight triangulating on the rolling sea, a rhapsodic effect upon Clemens. Having caught the sailor's madness, he wanted to remain on deck for a large part of that brief voyage, which was only of five hours' duration.

"Think of the pirates, Henry, who marauded in these very waters and lay waiting in hidden coves—what glorious times they must have had, plundering ships of the Spanish Main! Brings to mind my boyish days in Hannibal, Missouri, when I read of such tales—Captain Kidd, Blackbeard, Henry Morgan: pirates all. Back then, my best friend, a fellow named Tom Blankenship, and I pretended we were pirates in the woods, and we prowled about caves in search of imaginary treasures. Could be a rusted can or a few nails or some beer bottles that we'd dig up, but they all sparkled like jewels. Our pirates' headquarters was a rotted shack on a little island, where we would plot, as only boys can, pranks to pull on our friends. We made raids on chicken coops; we attacked trees; we pushed each other around on wheelbarrows; we hoisted wooden swords as though they were cutlasses. Friends, and sometimes a slave, became our captives, and we held them for ransoms of rabbits' feet and useless bottle caps, or sometimes for berries and a handful of walnuts, but that didn't matter. Poor as were—and we didn't know that we were poor, anyway—we were the richest buccaneers in the world. What times I had, Henry! Such days being quiet and lazy, each more glorious than the last." Then: "It's a pity that such Edens have to pass, isn't it?"

"Yes," I allowed, wondering what it would have been like to have experienced so happy a boyhood.

SETTLING INTO OUR BERTHS SOMETIME past midnight, we hadn't bothered to change our clothes, for the voyage was brief enough, the ship coming into Matanzas harbor and dropping anchor about three that morning. As we had in Havana, we waited for smaller craft to transport us to shore, then groggily paid the fees, some two *reales* each—a *reale* was equivalent to six and a half cents, the price of an *aguardiente*. When we landed, in the bright moonlight, we were taken to a waterside inn near the quay.

The next morning we were awakened by a burning heat that made the prospect of sightseeing, which Clemens was always intent upon, a dispiriting possibility. Still, after breakfast, as we had some hours to kill before catching the only train to Limonar, at 2:30, we left the inn for the center of the city, which, without the high temperature, would have been a quite pleasant place, as it was quieter and less hectic than Havana, with no beggars, lepers, drunken sailors, and few soldiers about. In general, it citizens had a less debauched character; the planters we saw—for this was that province's commercial center, sugar and tobacco flowing into it from the interior—were of a more elegant and unhurried nature, and seemed healthier for it. They were usually clad in white linen suits (as opposed to the French-style dark suits of the businessmen of Havana) and wore broad felt hats, boots, and spurs, most of them riding through town on horses. I noticed they were an unusually handsome lot—"tropical Apollos," Clemens called them—their skin sun-bronzed, their bodies strong and sinewy, their manner serene.

And the town was beautiful: Many of its houses seemed ancient, a result, I think, of the play of the sea upon the porous nature of the stones used in their building. As we traipsed about, without any idea of where we were going, Clemens delighted in the facts of his guidebook.

"Says here that the word *matanzas* means 'slaughter' in Spanish. Here is the site where the local Indians slaughtered a party of conquistadors long ago. Also, it says that the name commemorates a 'sanguinary encounter between the Moors and Christians in Castile, Spain, centuries before, at a battleground called El Campo de Matanzas, just at the time when Columbus was about to embark for his American adventure.'"

Despite the blinding whiteness of the day, we were charmed by our surroundings, as the city had a quaint and unspoiled antiquity about it: Mules pulling high-wheeled carts plied its cobblestone streets; Spanish ceramic tiles, instead of street signs, were embedded into walls to mark a location; citizens moved quietly along. We came across a bullfighting arena, and the public buildings we saw were of a neoclassical architecture, with Doric columns adorning their facades: "Hence," Clemens told me, "it's also known as the Cuban Athens."

From the distant terraces of wooded hills that rose behind Matanzas two small rivers flowed, and these divided the city into three or so sectors, each joined by a fine stone bridge: I had never been to Venice, but as we traversed such spaces, that is what came to mind. Indeed, more so than we had in Havana, we seemed in a foreign place.

Thirsty and overheated, and after taking in what we could of the city of Matanzas in so brief a time, we rode a carriage into the district south of the Río San Juan to the rail station: I should mention that east beyond Matanzas, railroads were practically nonexistent, only some fifteen hundred miles of American-style gauge having been put down, during the 1850s, to serve as transport for the most productive and fertile regions around Havana, mainly the large sugar plantations. These trains plied a route along a sparsely populated region, apparently of great beauty: Limonar itself was in the heart of the countryside to the southeast, some thirty miles away over the highlands from Matanzas. The train, to our reassurance, was of American manufacture, and the siding of our second-class car had markings that said it had been built by Eaton, Gilbert & Co., of Troy, New York—a long way, to be sure, from the remoteness of that place. Shortly, taking our seats among a handful of passengers, we left Matanzas.

As our train rose along an ascending grade into the hills, the harbor below became a pond of Mediterranean blue water, its houses cubes of dice, the land falling away beneath us in a succession of natural terraces, stately palm trees rising as far as the eye could see. And then, in the time it took Clemens to smoke six cigarillos, after our train slowly rose upon what seemed like an endless succession of curving track, the land began to flatten again, and we saw clusters of weepy, sad-looking trees with fronds that dropped to the ground and bore green melons; then countless banana trees and orange groves, neatly divided by avenues. Such farms were separated from each other by miles of dense jungle, the foliage so thick and livid with bright tropical flowers that it was impossible to imagine how its birds, of bright plumage, passed through such woods. What fences or stone walls we saw were overgrown with lianas and creepers and blossoms. The air of that place was so pure and delightful that we began to doze; first Clemens, his head slumped against the window, then myself.

Whatever else I knew, I was far away from Wales.

We awakened when the train stopped to take on some produce at a way station in what seemed to be the middle of a sugarcane field; here, the Negroes and Chinese coolies who worked as brakemen and porters got off and, with machetes—cane knives—*how well I would come to know them in Africa!*—made their way among the high stalks, each cutting off a piece and stripping it of its rind to suck happily upon its pulp. The train would make four more stops along the way, each taking some twenty minutes or so, to load or unload whatever goods were coming from and going to the plantations, much as the riverboats did on the Mississippi, but here, in Cuba, there seemed to be no hurry about anything. Seeing as how some things were being unloaded, we decided to stretch our legs. Perhaps Clemens was just tired, as we had not slept well the night before, but he had said little to me that morning, and I had feared, as I sometimes had with Mr. Stanley, that in my youthfulness I had been too enthusiastic in my gratitude for his friendship. I had made it my habit to express such sentiments to Clemens each and every day we were together. I should have remembered that he was not one for demonstrations of feeling, and I had resolved to stay mum about such declarations, though it was difficult. But as we stood there waiting, for all my intention to restrain myself, I told him: "Samuel, that I have you here makes a big difference to me. Surely you have chosen to accompany me out of concern for my safety—and if you hadn't, who knows where I would be right now; surely not so close as I am to finding Mr. Stanley. Indeed, though you may feel some dismay at the foreignness of this place, know well that you have made me your lifelong friend."

Clemens considered my words and said: "Look, Henry, I don't mind tagging along with you, and I don't mind that things seem a little different here: And in a way I'm kind of fascinated with this country; from what I can see this is one very interesting place, and it's beautiful. But you've got to promise me something. Please don't forget that some folks—namely, myself—don't need to be reminded of their good deeds, or friendship, for that matter. It's just something that happens between people sometimes. You understand?"

Funny what memories are: The steep grades of a provincial hillside, the colors of a blossom, the florid plumage of a bird—all such come back to one, even years later, in a dream of idealized perfection; but words, such as which can be recalled, shift about— some more vividly remembered than others, some completely lost. In this instance, concerning my friendship with Clemens, my approximation of what he said may not be entirely accurate to the word, but the sentiment of this and other moments, at their heart, remains true.

☄

IT TURNED OUT THAT THE "town" of Limonar was just another two-building stop in service of a large nearby sugar plantation. A tall Negro was napping in a chair as we came into an office with our valises; a second man, a white Cuban, was sitting by a desk and seemed well disposed to helping us, but as he spoke only Spanish, the matters of where we would spend the night, how we would find directions to Esperanza—a half day's ride from Limonar, I remembered—and how we would arrange for a carriage and horses seemed in those moments a daunting proposition.

Though I have since learned in my subsequent travels that such problems can always be overcome—money and force being the magical expediters of all things—in my inexperience, I considered it a small victory to have negotiated with this station clerk the use of a room in the back of the station and several blankets for the night, a prospect that left Clemens gloomy and pacing the floor.

Having ascertained that we were *americanos*, and intending to help us, this man roused the dozing Negro and instructed him to find someone who could speak English at the nearby plantation, about half a mile down the road. To our relief, within half an hour, there arrived, on an English-saddled white stallion, a majestically dressed gentleman who dismounted and entered the station house. It was the plantation owner himself, Mr. Bertrand, a French man.

"So," he said in impeccable English. "I take it that you are in need of assistance."

"Indeed we are," said Clemens.

Shortly we had made our introductions and explained our situation; as to our concerns, he was immediately helpful. He would rent us two horses the next day and would inquire after the location of Esperanza, apparently a mill of small import in those parts.

"Come to my plantation for the night," he said. "You will be better refreshed then, in the morning."

Later we were accompanied by the drowsy Negro to the gates of the plantation; then we made our way along a road of what seemed to be pulverized red brick, the color of the clay in that region, and entered into an orange grove, which was another quarter mile in length. The trees in every direction around us were alive with birdsong; wildflowers were flowing over the ground and covering every thicket—all such things having a pleasing effect, for we had in those moments passed into a quite peaceful-seeming place. That dream of tranquillity, however, abruptly dispersed after our idyllic entry. Shortly we came out onto the grounds of the plantation proper. In the distance stood a group of white buildings. One was a barracks; the other a sugar mill, its furnace sending up great volumes of black, billowy smoke; a third was a warehouse; a fourth a stable for the oxen: Surrounding these buildings were endless acres of sugarcane—the stalks, some ten feet high, as densely packed as fields of corn—and hundreds of slaves, whether man, woman, or child, at work cutting cane or loading it onto oxen-driven carts. Other slaves, further on, were busily feeding cane stalks into the mouth of a furnace.

Then, too, there was a separate enclave of some three buildings, at whose center stood a fine mansion, but not in the southern style, with porticoes and columns, but in the Spanish style—a massive house with Moorish flourishes. Our Negro, taking us that far, then stopped in his tracks, like a serf before a lord's castle—he pointed the way and, tipping his hat, turned back, but not before Clemens gave him a few reales for his troubles, which made him smile. At the door waited our host and his wife; a southern lady, as it turned out. Inside, the planter's wealth was evident: a Frenchmen by birth, a Cuban planter by way of successes in Santo Domingo, Monsieur Bertrand had filled his mansion with the ornate gilded furnishings associated with the glory of the French Empire. We were each given a small room, and even these were of a luxurious nature such as I had never experienced before—a canopied bed, a writing desk, a closet; even an Italianate chamber-pot holder, its shelves of marble as well.

From my window I could see the fields, the slaves laboring into the night. A servant had come to escort me to a bathing room containing a toilet, its drainage abetted by a copper barrel whose spigot flowed with water into the convenience. We each took our turns in the bathing room, and by nine, cleaned up and refreshed, Clemens and I joined Mr. Bertrand and his wife for dinner.

THE MEAL WAS TYPICALLY CUBAN: fried plantains, rice cooked with eggs, sweet potatoes, boiled cassava, and dishes of fowl and vegetables, all drowned in oil and salt and garlic—"Just like breakfast in Havana," Clemens had said. These dishes we consumed with a lordly quantity of Catalan wine, popular on the island, followed by goblets of French sherry.

"So what do you hear of the war?" Mr. Bertrand asked. "Are the rumors true?"

"Yes, sir," Clemens said. "I'm afraid it seems likely. When we left Louisiana, a few weeks back, the city was all up for it: For someone like myself—I am a riverboat pilot—it means having to sit the whole thing out. See, much of the Mississippi river traffic has been turned on its head. Anyway, I'd almost forgotten about it 'til you mentioned it, but even in Havana—well sir, that's all the southerners talk about there."

"And would you fight? And for whom, Mr. Clemens?"

"I suppose if I had to, I would, on the southern side; I am from Missouri."

"And you, Mr. Stanley?"

"It's my intention, sir, when I leave this island, to head back up to Arkansas to join up with a regiment called the Dixie Grays."

"And do you gentlemen believe it is worthwhile going to war over slaves? Even if they are freed, it will make for many difficulties: Here in Cuba, we are not allowed to buy slaves—we must import them from Africa, at great expense. And then there are laws that require us to free them after so many years: Some slave owners use that as an excuse to work the slaves even harder. And then, even if they are freed, they have no work, most of them—they do nothing but beg, or they become bandits and criminals. I am personally against the war for those very humane reasons." Then: "Look at my slaves and you will see they are well provided for."

Mrs. Bertrand had mainly listened in silence, but at this point in the conversation, she said: "I don't understand it at all. We, of the South, are peaceable: I am mainly worried about our travels back to Georgia, which we undertake once a year." Then: "Well, it seems stupid to start something up over the slave issue."

"Then let us make a toast," Mr. Bertrand said. "To peace, and that there will be no war."

That same evening, as we dined, an alarm had been raised—the plantation bell, weighing nine hundred pounds and mounted on a high frame, tolled rapidly, the signal for danger, as someone had apparently been caught attempting to steal a horse. An overseer had come in with the news, and Mr. Bertrand, excusing himself, went off to see to the matter, which was later apparently resolved, with the thief bound in chains and quarantined in the plantation jail.

Afterward Clemens and I retired to this gentleman's veranda to smoke some cigars. Despite the reputation of Cuban cigars—*cohibas*, the indigenous word for "tobacco"—which were said to be the finest in the world, Clemens preferred the two-cent cigars he had brought with him from the South, the burned-cord taste reminding him of home. Even at that hour—it was well past eleven—the great mill continued in operation, shadowy figures in the distance barely illuminated in the furnace's glow; and we saw that a few slaves were still out in the fields, some of them singing Yoruban chants, which would ring out at all hours of the night.

☙

THAT NEXT MORNING MR. BERTRAND had two horses saddled and ready for us. Through inquiries with various of his overseers, he had ascertained some notion as to where Esperanza was located.

"It is my understanding, gentlemen, that it is in the vicinity of a natural spring called San Miguel de los Baños, some twelve miles southeast of here. One of my men will bring you to a crossroad that will take you in that direction; but mind you, part of the route is through the *selva*—the jungle—and there you will not find any *guardes civiles* to keep the law. Not to frighten you, but it would be a good idea to bring some arms—have you any?"

"I have a revolver," I told him.

"Good—if you are harassed by anyone, show the gun and you will be left alone." We thanked him for his hospitality, mounted our horses and, following our guide, left the plantation.

ABOUT TWO MILES SOUTH ALONG a red clay road, we came to
a civil guard post, a shed attended by two soldiers in striped blue
linen uniforms with scarlet trimming, to whom we had to present
our traveler's passes (the *cédulas*). The main road then continued
on toward several large plantations. Another road turned to follow along some river, and a third, to which we were led, seemed
a less traveled course, as it was not so tidily attended or tramped
upon, for the forest surrounding it had encroached on much of it,
vines and shrubbery and lianas and the fronds of densely packed
trees, and all their undergrowth, having flourished without much
interruption. At best one could call it a narrow trail, not so much
different from the two-foot-wide paths I would encounter in the
Congo years later, in the Ituri Forest. In all honesty, it did not
seem an appealing tract to cross, but our escort, in parting, told
us in broken English that it was not so very long, perhaps nine or
ten miles in length; after following this trail we would come to
una cascada—a waterfall—then, within a short distance of that, a
trading post and another road, where we would find several other
plantations.

"But" he warned, "there will be no town, only the countryside."

So we proceeded into the tropical forest, with uncertainty at
first. I had learned to ride horses as a child from my grandfather
Moses, and what practice I lacked in the intervening years had
been made up for at Cypress Bend, where I had the occasional
use of one of Mr. Altschul's mares; Clemens had learned to ride
as a boy on his uncle John's farm in Missouri during his idyllic
summers, he told me.

And as we rode farther into the wood, the journey began
to seem like a youthful adventure. That we were riding into an
unknown territory, with the possibility of danger facing us, for we
had been warned to be wary of bandits, was both a little frightening and exhilarating at the same time.

∾

EVENTUALLY WE CAME TO THE waterfall—which flowed suddenly from a high outcropping of rocks to our right: An early
morning rain had sent the current rushing swiftly, and some over-
flow had flooded the road there, so that we were riding in about
a foot of water for some distance, the trail muddy; but shortly,
once we had made our way onto the dry tract again, we could
see the forest's end and a dirt road crossing in front of cane field.
As we approached that road we came to a clearing, on our right,
where stood the trading post, which Mr. Bertrand had described
to us. A few mules stood outside by a trough, and the long, tile-
roofed shed that was the store lay underneath the shade of a great
tree. Tethering our horses, we went inside. A heavy woman was
sitting behind the counter, a cigar in one hand, a fan in the other.

I asked her if she knew of a sugar plantation called Esperanza,
and without any hesitation, she said that she did. From what I
could decipher, it was some two miles east down the road.

∾

WHAT DAY IT WAS I cannot say—maybe a Tuesday or a Wednesday; I cannot remember—but it was about four o'clock when, as
we rode along on our horses, a local peasant pointed us to the dirt
road leading to the Esperanza plantation. When we came upon
the property, an orange grove—like the one at Bertrand's, but on
a smaller scale—first met the eye. Natural gardens were flourishing all around—ceiba, tamarind, and mango trees, mainly. Beyond
were the cane field, the processing mill, barns, and a corral for
oxen. Slaves were working in teams to harvest the sugar, their
ebony backs glistening with sweat. We saw only one overseer
among them, but he seemed to have neither a pistol nor a whip.
And unlike the slaves we had seen at Bertrand's plantation, these
slaves seemed unafraid to speak to white men before being spoken

to, for as we approached, within sight of the owner's residence, an old black female slave greeted us.

I asked to see Señor Stanley.

As she made her way into the house, a fine-looking dwelling with a wide veranda, we dismounted, and another slave of about twenty, with a most agreeable smile, took our horses away to a trough. Soon at the veranda railing appeared a well-dressed white gentleman of about fifty. In his right hand he was holding a pearl-handled revolver.

"You are Mr. Davis, I presume?" I asked, and he answered: "I am. And who are you?"

"This is Mr. Samuel Clemens, sir. And I am Henry Stanley, Mr. Henry Hope Stanley's son. We've journeyed here from New Orleans."

"Ah, he has spoken of you. Forgive the gun—we sometimes have interlopers in these parts. Come, and I will take you to him."

We followed Mr. Davis inside and found that the interior of this plantation house was much larger than we had assumed from its facade. For when entered, we were standing in a parlor some forty feet deep, its ceilings, some twenty feet above us, supported by immense cedar beams. There was a dining room directly adjoining it, all its windows shuttered against the light, and behind that were several other rooms off a hallway lined with potted flowers that led to an inner courtyard in the Spanish style, which was a garden at whose center was a trickling fountain, like one would find in a cloister. Off this honeycomb was an old family chapel, dim, with dark stone walls and an immense statue of an angel looming over a small altar, surely a place for prayers and meditation.

Mr. Davis then led us down an interior hallway to Mr. Stanley's chamber; as we waited, I heard some words—Mr. Davis saying: "Henry, someone is here to see you." I entered, Clemens behind me, and found Mr. Stanley resting in bed, two young female slaves attending to him, a book on his lap and a weariness about his person that I did not recall. At first he did not seem to know me, but when I called out to him—"Father?"—he took another look, no doubt confused by my appearance, for I was still drawn and terribly thin from my bouts with the Arkansas ague. But as soon as he recognized my familiar and friendly face, then brimming over with many emotions, his spirit suddenly brightened, as if he were a man come back from the dead.

"Is it you, Henry?" he asked. "My God, it is!" Of course he was surprised to see me in Cuba. "You've come so far. How could I have imagined that it could be so?"

To convey the magnitude of this moment is beyond my powers; but at once, I rushed forward and gave him an embrace, repeating the words, "Oh, Father; my father!" My forwardness surprised him, and gently patting me on the back and sitting up, he said, "Now, Henry, be calm. Now that you are here, all will be well again." Then: "Tell me of your journey."

I related my travels from Arkansas and my good fortune of having a friend like Samuel Clemens to accompany me. I told him that I had been driven to find him for reasons of concern for his well-being.

"To learn that someone cares so much for me," he declared, "does my soul much good; your devotion touches me greatly."

Taking in the scene of our reunion, and seeing my need for privacy in such a moment, Clemens went off with Mr. Davis to have a drink and discuss plantation life there. My father instructed a female slave to bring us refreshments. When I then asked my father why I had not heard from him, his answer was forthright and earnest.

"If you have found me resting in my bed during the hours of siesta, it is for a good reason," Mr. Stanley told me. "For you see, I was gravely ill for several months, and my strength never completely returned: At best I am good for some six or seven hours a day, and then I am left greatly fatigued. This is because of my brother's illness. When I arrived in Havana this November past, I found my brother in a sorry state with the yellow fever; enormous and hearty and fearless of spirit as he had been, my brother could not defend against his final calling, and early one morning, while I attended to him in his little house by the sea, he said some last few words and expired. By his request, his body was laid to rest in the waters. That he died was in and of itself a great blow to my spirit. But what my brother had—the yellow fever—I soon contracted; and it brought me close to death. My survival I owed to God. Upon my recovery, in a weakened state, I traveled across the island to settle up some accounts, but through all my journeys, I could barely maintain my interest in such things, so greatly despondent and dispirited was I by the recent turn of events."

Indeed he seemed to have been aged by his troubles: His black beard had become streaked with white, and many lines, as would come from weeping, had accrued around his intelligent eyes.

"I came here in late February, to see my friend and partner in this enterprise, Mr. Davis. I was not completely well and still hindered by weaknesses, but once I arrived, my heart so weary, I found that I was much calmed by the beauty of these surroundings. I began to succumb to its many soothing qualities, and I decided to give my life here a chance—what remains of it, anyway. And as there was work to do here, I set myself to those tasks and thereby began to forget my troubles—but never have I forgotten you. Once I had settled things here, I had planned to visit New Orleans, and then it was my intention to find you in Arkansas and bring you back here, if you would have so liked. Yet because of the coming war, I knew that it would not have been the best of times to journey there, and so I have remained."

"But why could you not have written to me? It would have relieved me greatly." I asked.

"When I heard that you had come down with the ague, some months ago, I was ready to advise you to leave that place. But then my own pressing matters overwhelmed me, and, in any case, knowing Mr. Altschul as an honorable man, I feared not for your safety.

"And there's something else you must understand, Henry. At my age—I am pressing fifty-eight—the wild rush to get things done quickly does not seem so important. As the days go by more swiftly than in earlier years, it is easy to watch slip by two or three months—for they come now as weeks used to. In other words, my boy, what with my obligations here and the restful nature of these surroundings, I have slowed down considerably, and my mental resources are not what they were even a year ago: Surely you must understand."

THEN, AS I WAS SOMEWHAT vexed by certain things I had heard about him, I said: "Not so long ago in Havana, my friend Clemens had struck up an acquaintance with a man who claimed to have known you—a certain Captain Bailey, whom I met one night at a saloon called the Louvre. Do you know of such a person?"

"Yes, for some years."

"Well, he told me of some matters regarding you that, I am certain, are wrong."

"What kind of matters?" Mr. Stanley asked.

"He told me that you are originally from Cheshire in England."

"A fantasy. We had met on a ship out of England. I had been visiting some distant relatives there, that's all. What have I of any accent, other than southern? Why would I pretend to be something I am not?"

"Then he said that you were married once before you met your late wife."

"Yes, that is so. Her name was Angela. She died of the fever. As did Frances, and Mr. Speake, and my own brother—as I almost did. What of it?"

"He also said that during your ministry you exercised a bachelor's whims to excess."

He laughed.

"Bailey said that? It figures. You see, Captain Bailey is not the most virtuous of men. And as with such men, he, whatever his reasons, takes pleasure in spreading rumors about the righteous. Why he would choose to tell you this I cannot say. But that is not the truth."

"And do you, as Captain Bailey told me, have two adopted daughters in St. Louis?"

"Years ago I became the sponsor of two girls who had come from one of the Catholic orphanages there. We paid for their schooling and board—it is something Mrs. Stanley always wanted to do. In the same way that I have been your benefactor, I have been theirs. As to whether they are adopted, no, they are not—no more than you are."

I felt discomforted by those words.

"But do you still intend to adopt me?"

"I have told you that it was my intention to do so, but as you can well imagine, the question has slipped from my mind in recent times. Surely you know that these matters require certain legalities. Being that there is a war looming, and as such legalities require the assistance of attorneys, and as you are truly not of my blood and yet would inherit what funds and properties I have, it remains something that I must closely consider, for I do not believe it would be so easy a thing to do here in Cuba."

"Then have I dreamed of your promise to adopt me?"

"You were not dreaming, but I think that perhaps in your fevers, you have exaggerated the urgency of the matter."

"But did you not say that you would sign a proper letter attesting to my adoption? And have you not sworn, through your promises, to assist me in any way possible?"

"I did—and forgive me if this matter has been absent from my thoughts, as I forgive you for your manner with me now. No doubt you are tired from your travels and, if what you say about the recurring ague is true and you are somewhat strained at your seams from such an illness, I will overlook your hot-headedness, for I have always known you as a far more humble and reasonable person than the angry fellow standing before me. Of course you are expecting much from me, by way of adoption, but I must ask you to convince me that this is not the only reason for your coming here. Is it?"

"No, Father."

"Why, then, do you not exercise some restraint in regard to the legalities of it all? For in the eyes of God, such a promise is a fact. Your sanctified name is Henry Stanley now. Is that not enough?"

I could not answer him. The truth is that I wanted the legal paper, but his words had humbled me, and I felt ashamed of my behavior. And then, just as I turned my head away in a downcast fashion, and could no longer look him in the eye, he softened.

"You will have your paper, but I should let you know that I intend to be around for many years. Just the same, in the coming days I will make my letter regarding your adoption, since it is of such urgency to you; but do not mention it to me again, as I am weary of such things."

⚜

OVER THE NEXT SEVERAL DAYS, despite our momentary misunderstanding, my father and I enjoyed a felicitous and tranquil existence, such as we had known before in New Orleans. Since he knew my love for books, what modest library he possessed he shared with me.

Reminded of Mr. Stanley's literate side, I had noticed in him a tendency to spend several hours each afternoon, after lunch, sitting under the shade of a banyan tree, recording his thoughts in a ledger book—the type that, in days past, he had once used for jotting down, in pencil, the details of his business. But there, in Cuba, in the remoteness of his plantation, and with a dulcet orange-and-lemon-scented breeze blowing often, he would lose himself in some absorbing composition.

Clemens, I should say, had the same proclivity. Back in Havana, he had continually made notes, and he could not look at anything of interest without feeling a compulsion to write his impressions down: the unusual names of shops—calling to mind planets, jewels, animals, and mythical characters; the oddities of a city where there were no glass windows, carpets, or fireplaces; and all manner of character portraits. He took such relish in their composition that, even then, I doubted he would long remain a riverboat pilot. At Esperanza, nothing of this inclination had changed. A loner at heart, he, with notebook in hand, tended to wander off early in the morning to watch the slaves milk the cows, tend to the chicken coops, and harness the oxen for the fields. Once their harder labors had begun in the cane fields, he withdrew, feeling some shame at his leisure, and he would return to the main house to sit on the porch, smoke his black cigars, put his boots up on the railing, and take in the enormity of the enterprise. But toward dusk, he was drawn back to the slave barracks, especially when he heard drums or chants being sung. However he presented himself to the slaves, with his few rudimentary Spanish phrases, he won them over, especially the children, who would follow him around in packs. Playing among them, he had learned their spirituals and ways of telling stories, even the manner in which they would speak; in describing such things to me, he had such affection in his voice that I doubted he approved of slavery at all.

"What do you write of these Cuban slaves?" I asked him.

"Aside from having no idea what they say to me, beyond general welcomes and good-byes, I just look at their meager surroundings and try to understand the meanings of the objects they surround themselves with: a drum that barks what to them are meaningful phrases; a gourd that is scraped in a certain way as they sing incantations to their gods—Obatalá and Changó are two that have registered on my dim brain. No crucifixes anywhere. Above all, Henry, at a white man's kindness, they smile—despite the fact they are slaves." Then: "I suppose they saw that I am used to their kind, even if they speak a different language."

For my part, while spending time with Mr. Stanley, I took every opportunity to offer him my services: He seemed to have taken on the role of bookkeeper for the estate, though from what I could observe, their "office" consisted of a single desk set out in the cool inner courtyard, on which were stacked several ledger books.

"If you would like to me to go over your books, it would be a pleasure to do so," I told him. But of this he felt no need: "Why should you, when you might well decide to leave this place for good?" Then: "In any case, there is not very much to do right now: As you can see, even though I am not what I once was, I don't mind these little chores."

It disappointed me that despite my friendliness toward my father and the outward signs of his paternity toward me, he seemed most content to be left alone. News from the outside world came only by means of passersby and from a postal courier who was said to arrive only once every ten days or so: What newspapers came to that place were weeks old, and we did not see any visitors. Which is to say that within a short time, both Clemens and I were becoming somewhat restless, especially at night. After dinner, at around nine, when Mr. Stanley and Mr. Davis would retire, Clemens and I were left, in somewhat dimly lit rooms, to amuse ourselves. But playing cards had never been a favorite pastime of mine; and while games of checkers helped to pass the hours, we inevitably ended up on the veranda, under the stars—the Southern Cross being the most prominent constellation—watching the mill's steam-driven furnaces glowing in the distance, and generally lamenting the absence of town life.

Of the plantation itself I will now speak, for Clemens and I rode around it one morning with Mr. Davis and my father.

It was at least several square miles in size, I would judge, given its distance from the forest surrounding it on all sides. To run it, the partners had about one hundred or so working slaves—not counting the children, who seemed to be everywhere; one white overseer, a Cuban; and several old, experienced slaves also acted as bosses. Two dozen slaves worked in the fields, slashing away at the cane stalks. They moved in unison, in one direction, much like a line of infantry, harvesting yard by yard the seemingly endless forest of cane. Afterward, they gathered the stalks up and loaded them into the oxcarts, and these were pulled to the sugar mill, where the raw cane was laid out in big piles on a platform and fed lengthwise through the trough of a machine whose steam-driven rollers crushed them into a pulp, their juices dripping down into enormous vats. Their residue of leftover bark and fibers was then carried out to dry in a field and stored as fuel for the mill's furnace. All during the process there was a constant grinding of machinery, the cries of the slaves giving one another instructions—"*Dale candela*"—and chanting and sometimes singing. The air in that place was so intensely sweet and thick, I imagined it would take a long time to get used to it.

"Our problem here," said Mr. Davis that day, "is not the production itself. Aside from the machinery, the slaves comprise our greatest expense. But they are good and hard workers—we try not to use force against them. Isn't that so, Mr. Stanley? In general, we have found that, while this is not a paradise for them, they have it better here than they would in many other plantations; certainly better than what I have seen in your American South.

"Now, as you two have come here through that wood, you can well imagine that our biggest problem is transport, for it is not an accommodating route. For some time now we have been attempting to build a new road through the woods between here and the train station at Limonar; a road we hope to get under way with the help of monies and slaves from other plantations, as such a road would benefit us all. Having ridden here through the jungle tract, you know that such a road is barely sufficient for two riders abreast, let alone wide enough for the easy passage of oxen and a cart loaded with hogsheads and casks, and in any case it is always quite slow going. With such matters, it always takes some cajoling, and so Mr. Stanley and I have been riding out to various plantations to arouse an interest—no easy task." Then, to Mr. Stanley, he said, "We are planning to visit with a plantation owner tomorrow morning to discuss the matter. Perhaps these lads would like to accompany us."

"Why not?" said Mr. Stanley.

◦〃◦

SINCE OUR DAYS HAD BEEN largely uneventful, we welcomed the diversion, but oddly, as Clemens and I retired to our rooms that night, I was overcome by a strange misgiving about it. Where such impressions or manifestations of dread come from, I do not know, but as I attempted, somewhat restlessly, to fathom the source of my intuition, I became convinced that Mr. Stanley should not make that journey. Such was my alarm that I could not sleep, and in an agitated state I went to Clemens's room, knocking fiercely on his door. Fortunately the strong smell of tobacco smoke met my nostrils, for he, too, had remained awake and had been restless, but for other reasons, I suppose. "What is it, Henry?" he asked, and in that moment I poured out my apprehensions.

While sympathetic to my fears, he remained cautious. "Come, now," he told me. "As you know, I once had a dream about my brother that came true. But that was a mere coincidence: a coincidence that I have never been happy about, but a coincidence all the same. No doubt you are just feeling anxious about your father."

Shortly I went back to my room, but I was again unable to sleep. Quietly I made my way out from one hall into another, my path lit by a candle, and, coming to my father's chamber door, I knocked. And when I heard no response, I knocked again.

My father, Mr. Stanley, a grave expression upon his face, opened the door.

"What on earth can you want at this late hour?"

"Father, do not make that journey tomorrow."

"What?"

"You will be in danger. Do not question me—I know it to be true."

He sighed. "It is a late hour; you have been dreaming; and perhaps you are somewhat out of sorts." Then: "If it is the business

with the adoption, rest assured, my boy, that I will attend to it."
And he closed the door.

That night, when I finally fell asleep, I dreamed of many wishful things. I saw that I lived in a magnificent house surrounded by
a garden, and I had wife to love me, and three children. I saw Mr.
Stanley coming to visit us, and with his enormous frame settled
down upon a chair, jostling an infant on his lap; but then that
soon turned to air, and I awoke early that morning, hearing the
plantation bells summoning the day.

꙰

AFTER BREAKFAST, CLEMENS, MR. DAVIS, Mr. Stanley, and I
saddled up and rode out to the edge of the fields, about a mile
from the house. For part of the way, as I remember, Clemens—or
Sam, as he preferred to be called—had engaged my father in a discussion that veered somewhere between literature and religion,
for they came, in that Cuban clime, to talk about the Bible.

To Clemens's inquiry "What, in your opinion, is the Bible?"
my father, with his effortless genius, summarized his feelings about it in a single phrase: "The Bible is a book of allego-
ries made to instruct man in the higher principles that should
guide life."

"And would you consider it a true history of those times?"
Clemens asked.

"Yes—a history in the sense of reflecting general ancient
events. But mainly they are attractive myths, to console men and
guide them."

"And the word of God?"

My father exhaled a deep breath.

"The awareness of God, the speculations about Him, surely
fired up the imaginations of the holy thinking men who accu-
mulated such stories, all of them glorious in the Decalogue. But
after so many years of study, I have come to consider it more as a
literary creation than anything else."

"You know, Mr. Stanley," Clemens said, "you would get lynched in some parts of the South for saying that."

"And for that reason," my father said, "I was never a very good minister."

"Well," said Clemens, "I was raised hearing such tales, but retold by the colored folks, in a human way. Sweet and tender do I remember their accounts."

"Yes," allowed Mr. Stanley. "As much as I look down on slaves—or, to put it differently, as much as I find them simpleminded—I envy their uncomplicated connection to such tales. They see them as not something that happened a few thousand years ago but as the kind of thing that could have happened yesterday, to a close relation."

"And Jesus? What make you of him?" Clemens asked.

"A very holy man, I figure. A man who spoke—and speaks to this day—to the hearts of slaves. Much of his world was composed of them back then, but what his promised salvation from their hard lives—his paradise—might well be, I cannot say."

We moved along that narrow trail, in a remote part of that plantation, under an arcade of high trees, whose bending foliage ensconced us in shade for much of our passage. Just as I, riding beside my father, had been looking cautiously in all directions, we heard horses. Then some hushed voices. Suddenly six mounted men astride palominos emerged from the surrounding brush, accompanied by a great clopping of hooves and several gunshots. The first I saw on his mount was a large black man with a machete by his side; the next a Cuban, I supposed, most stern and severe of expression. Three others were also Negroes, their faces covered with scars, one as fierce-looking as the next. Then a second Cuban followed from behind: He had a blood-red kerchief around his neck, and two fingers were missing from his left hand. They had converged upon us, smiling at our sudden consternation.

As they began to surround us, Mr. Davis muttered: "Turn now—whatever you do, turn back toward the house."

But no sooner did we try to turn our mounts around than

one of these men reeled his horse out behind us to block the road. Now, as Mr. Stanley wore a gold watch off a chain in plain sight on his vest, and as it glowed as a precious object, the horseman with three fingers came forward and, coveting this watch, slyly asked for the time of day. Suspecting his unfriendly intent, Mr. Stanley, being a foreigner, pretended that he did not understand the language. "No comprendo," Mr. Stanley told him. But the fellow continued to circle around, and when we attempted to move on, that same Cuban leaned forward and took hold of Mr. Stanley's bridle. And then he pulled from a holster below his saddle a machete, the variety that was most often used to chop sugarcane, and, jabbing it menacingly into Mr. Stanley's coat, forcefully demanded his watch. At this point, Mr. Davis, who spoke Spanish well, explained that we were local landowners and that they were, in fact, trespassing upon the outer fringes of our plantation. But this made no impression on the Cuban brigand, for at this point, he became blunt and said: "Muy bien. Dame todo lo que tienen!" ("Hand over everything.")

With this, Mr. Davis pulled out his ivory-handled pistol and pointed its muzzle back at him. Frightened, with good reason, the man with three fingers moved off; and when Mr. Davis turned to the large Negro who had taken hold of Mr. Stanley's horse, he, too, backed away. Then Mr. Davis said, "Come on!" And we began to gallop back toward the plantation, Clemens and I in the lead. But as it was not so easy for so many horses to advance along so narrow a path, Mr. Davis himself, a superb horseman, was jostled after some seventy yards by Mr. Stanley's horse and thrown onto the road. Having advanced forward, I looked back and saw that Mr. Stanley had stopped to help him. But by then the Cubans had produced their own pistols and were charging toward us—I can remember that Clemens tried to halt his mount, but had gone some distance before he could turn around. In the meantime, my father, having helped Mr. Davis onto his horse, was about to ride off himself when some shots were fired. I responded with my own pistol, aimed at the Cuban with three fingers, but my horse, frightened by the noise, bucked, and I hit nothing. Eventually the brigands dispersed, though not before firing more shots after us. It was then, I am afraid to say, that Mr. Stanley, galloping toward us on that road, received a bullet in the side of his neck.

All this occurred so quickly that I was hardly aware that Mr. Stanley had been wounded, until he, riding wildly and grasping his neck, began to sway from side to side. By then, the plantation slaves, hearing the shots as they worked in the fields, were waiting by the road to help us. Bleeding badly, Mr. Stanley slumped off his saddle into the arms of two slaves, and they carried him into the house, where he lay stretched out on a chair in the parlor.

Gasping for air, and with a gurgling sound coming from his dressing-wrapped, swollen neck, Mr. Stanley seemed, in those moments, as good as dead. I could only pray for his recovery.

After a few hours Mr. Stanley began to suffer from a high fever, and in the delirium that followed, he asked several times to see his dead wife. By then, Mr. Davis had instructed one of his overseers to head out to one of the bigger plantations to look for a doctor (and to inform the civil guard about the bandits so they might round up a posse), but at some late hour, as it seemed that Mr. Stanley would surely die without immediate medical assistance, Mr. Davis, having some knowledge of surgery, loosened the wrapping and decided that it would be best to extricate the bullet. A large black-and-blue lump had risen along the right side of Mr. Stanley's neck, and discerning that the bullet was lodged there, Mr. Davis, pressing against that swelling and manipulating the hardness within, gradually brought the round dark pellet out, along with much blood and an ooze of pus. Dousing it with a cup of brandy, he then instructed one of his slaves to pour pitcher after pitcher of cold water over the wound until the swelling gradually subsided; then he dressed the wound again, and all of us, somewhat exhausted by the ordeal, retired to the veranda to drink.

✳

A CUBAN DOCTOR DID ARRIVE—TWO days later—and when he examined Mr. Stanley, he saw that while the wound itself was in a process of healing, an infection of a septic nature had begun to spread through his system. Blunt in his appraisal, he could only recommend rest, but he thought it not a bad idea for us to summon a priest to give him the last rites, "in the event he believes in such things." Despite our obvious despair—I was inconsolable in those days—the doctor took legal issue with the fact that Mr. Davis had attended to the wound himself, and he threatened to report him to the authorities. At heart, even if he knew that Mr. Stanley would have surely died without Mr. Davis's assistance, this physician, a somewhat bitter and gloomy man, argued for several hours with Mr. Davis about it, until Mr. Davis, getting the drift of the doctor's threat, agreed to pay him a fee so substantial that it amounted to a bribe.

And so the doctor, having made his point and profited by it, rode away.

✳

HERE I CAN HARDLY CAJOLE my own hand to write more of those days: I cannot say whether a recent fever has weakened my resolve or whether it is always painful to continue with the remembrance of sad things as one treads on a march of words toward a resolution. Beginnings are exhilarating; middles are comforting; but the final chapters of such memories are fearsome and resist easy summary. But here, as I squeeze out the words, is what happened:

Because he slept through many of the hours of the day, I had made it my habit to look in on Mr. Stanley, to find if he had awakened. He was dressed in a long white shirt that reached to his

ankles and was laid out in bed; his beard had been shorn, expos-
ing his fine chin, and the scab on his neck, I could see, was the
size of a silver dollar. In his company were two female slaves, one
of whom stood beside his bed moving the air with a feather fan;
the other attended to him with a casual familiarity that I found
dismaying.

On the fourth morning of my father's illness, with little progress by way of his recovery to report, Clemens accompanied
me into his room and witnessed a remarkable thing. For a few
hours my father seemed to take a turn for the better: As when we
entered, he was sitting up, and though by no means cured, he had
apparently regained some strength.

"Come close to me," he said to me in a hoarse and low voice.
"There is something I must tell you."

"What is it, Father?"

"As you can see, you have journeyed far to look upon the face
of a dying man."

"Think not of such things," I said. "I know in my heart that
you will get better, and when you do, there will be much awaiting us! And if you must stay in this place, then I will be by your
side."

"Oh, my boy, just wanting something does not make it so: I
can no more wish myself to good health than I can command the
furniture to rise off the floor. But take heart: Though I am a dying
man, I am not bothered by it, for I know that I will soon find the
answer to many things." Then, as if he could read my thoughts,
he said: "As to more practical matters, regarding your adoption:
I have promised to make you my legal heir, and I am now ready
to do so. But I have no such paper, and so you, my dear young
gentleman, must compose one for me to sign while I can still hold
a pen."

This I agreed to do, but thinking it unsavory to hurry the
matter, I remained by his side. Within a few hours Mr. Stanley's
condition worsened to the point where he could barely open his

eyes or even move his head: His breathing had become forced, and all manner of aches overwhelmed him. But Death was merciful, for there came over Mr. Stanley's face a change of expression. Shortly whatever anxieties and sadnesses were going through his mind departed, and with a sigh, and with his pulse slowing, he took my hand into his own and was about to say something, when all at once, he faintly smiled and closed his eyes and settled into a sleep from which he would not awaken. Later that night, as I stood by his side in misery and with a feeling of an impending and irretrievable loss, he breathed his last.

MR. DAVIS HAD THOUGHT TO arrange the transport of his body back to America, so that Mr. Stanley might be buried alongside his wife in St. Louis, but the logistics and the matter of preservation made it impossible, for there was no ice in that place, nor was there a nearby mortician to do the work; and he had thought of instructing his blacksmith to build a lead coffin, but such materials were not at hand. And so it was that on the morning of April 12, 1861, after a brief ceremony, during which Mr. Davis and I said some words, Mr. Stanley was laid to rest in a grave under a banyan tree on that plantation.

The next day, Clemens and I began our journey back to Havana. What I had left of the late Mr. Stanley, aside from an indelible memory of his last moments, were a lock of his hair, which I had cut from his head as he had lain still in his bed, some few letters, and a watch of his that Mr. Davis had given me as a keepsake. Naturally my spirits were low, and my body was soon again racked by illness, my recurring malaria coming back to me: I was so grieved and upset that my constitution suffered for it. But hardly anyone would have noticed my state, for when we finally arrived in Havana, the city was in an uproar over the latest news brought in on ships from Florida. A few days before, on April 12, 1861, the same day that my father was buried, Fort Sumter had been bombed, beginning the armed hostilities of the Civil War. It took us another nine days before we reached New Orleans, and from there, we parted in the harbor, Clemens heading north up to St. Louis to join his family; and I, some hours afterward, setting off upriver to Cypress Bend, mainly to retrieve my possessions. But upon my arrival, like most young men from those parts, I was quickly swept up by the war fever, and, wishing to take my mind off Cuba and Mr. Stanley's death, I decided to honor my promise to join the Dixie Grays, under the command of a certain Colonel Lyon, thereupon beginning my life as a Confederate soldier.

I did not see my dear friend Clemens again for six years.

Here the manuscript ends.

In September of 1964, during a gathering of the ever-dwindling membership of the Stanley Society in London, the issue of the "cabinet" manuscript's pedigree became a matter for authentication. While members agreed that Mrs. Stanley had sent it to Samuel Clemens (for the manuscript had been found among Clemens's own papers), experts were brought in to verify that it was indeed written in Stanley's hand. After it was submitted to the modern analytical technique called stylometry, it was determined that the manuscript seemed to contain the mixed utterances of two or more people. Moreover, while most of the sentences seemed to be by the same person, it was the expert consensus that in the editing of said manuscript the stylistic imprint of another writer, possibly Lady Stanley, may be responsible for the occasional mixed utterances and the toned-down nature of the narrative. "The number of sentences that appear to be by another hand, however," the society concluded, "are too few for an identification to be made without further extensive and tedious effort."

READING THE "CABINET" MANUSCRIPT OVER several evenings, Samuel Clemens gathered his own recollections regarding those days with Stanley, distant though they were to the seventy-one-year-old writer. Though he well understood the improvisational nature of memory, he found the latter part of Stanley's account a mostly imaginative interpretation of what, so many years before, had transpired in Cuba. Clemens also thought his old friend had taken liberties in his portrait of his American "father." Having read it over, with one or another of his half a dozen cats purring on his lap, at a time when his own writings seemed hopelessly beyond achieving the continuity of memoir—or, for that matter, the concentrated expression of the self required in novels— Clemens, who knew how difficult such writings were, deliberated endlessly about his response to Lady Stanley, "an aristocrat as nice as any he had ever known."

In the end, Clemens wrote a gentle note back:

May 27, 1907
21 Fifth Avenue, New York City

Dear Dorothy—
I must thank you for Stanley's manuscript, and therefore thank you as well for the opportunity to comment upon it. It does, indeed, cover some terrain of my life—and opening such old doors brings to mind how much I miss your late husband. However, although I would like to fill you in, I can't right now, on account of the fact that I am getting ready to leave for England next week. I would prefer to wait and discuss it with you in person when I come to London. In the meantime, as always, on behalf of myself and my daughters, I send you our love.
Samuel

ON TWAIN AND STANLEY MEETING AGAIN

I'd seen Stanley's anger before, going back to the days when I first came to England, in 1872, during the blossoming of our mutual fame. He was maltempered, indignant, and thought nothing about lashing out publicly at his detractors, who had dared to doubt, and rather viciously so, the truth of his Livingstone expedition. I had seen him conversing with persons and storming off in the middle of a sentence and muttering, "I have seen baboons smarter than you!" I had seen Stanley pacing frantically in a room, after a reception in his honor, denouncing one person after the other, to the point where I would have to say to him: "Henry, calm yourself, you're doing your reputation harm." I understood him in that regard, having a temper myself. And I knew him well enough to stand off on certain subjects; and I understood just how he, who had come up from nothing and made something of himself, had been mocked (our own friendship had suffered for several years when he had happened upon a false rumor that had me accusing him of being a "rancorous puppy," a remark that was taken out of context). I sympathized with his feelings about the aristocracy, to whom he sometimes referred as the "upper asses." And I suspected that the Africa business had left him thin-skinned, but my God, did he always remain bitter about those days.

—SAMUEL CLEMENS, IN A LETTER TO

WILLIAM DEAN HOWELLS, CIRCA 1892

✲

FOR THOSE WHO KNEW NOTHING of their Cuban journey, it was assumed that Twain and Stanley's first meeting had taken place one evening at the Mercantile Library in St. Louis in 1867. By then, in one of the more satisfying symmetries of their friendship, each had entered into the profession of writing, though by that time, Samuel Clemens, as Mark Twain, was by far the more successful and better known. while the years of the Civil War had found him attempting other occupations—as a miner, as a printer, and as a typesetter—he, with his love for colorful yarns and sharp eye for details, had gravitated to a life as a wandering "cowpoke" journalist. He plied this trade for various Western newspapers—the *Missouri Democrat*, the *Territorial Enterprise* out of Virginia City, and the *Morning Call* in San Francisco, where his colleagues included the likes of Ambrose Bierce and Bret Harte. Aside from a brief period of unemployment (he had been fired from his staff position in San Francisco for reporting too faithfully on the corrupt doings of the local police and other officials), his journey had been altogether easier than Stanley's, whose route had been far more circuitous and filled with danger.

STANLEY'S OWN CAREER SEEMED TO have started at a Confederate camp at Corinth, Mississippi, as a private with the Sixth Arkansas Volunteer Infantry, under the command of Generals Pierre Beauregard and Albert Sidney Johnston, awaiting deployment into the Battle of Shiloh. Even though he worked as a provisions clerk and was known for his sharp marksmanship on the firing range, he was most valued for his informal role as an amanuensis for the illiterate soldiers of Company E, who were mainly veterans of the Mexican-American War of 1847. On their behalf, Stanley wrote what in many cases would turn out to be farewell letters to loved ones and family.

AND SO IT WAS THAT Stanley, wishing to leave some word of his whereabouts, drafted several letters for himself to the only "loved ones" he knew: his Uncle Thomas and Aunt Maria Morris in Liverpool, with whom he was in occasional correspondence. In one missive, he sent his regards and assurances that all was well; in another, he wrote to a young woman he had known at Cypress Bend, expressing some exaggerated feelings of impending glory or doom:

> Either I will rise one morning after the coming battle,
> ablaze with dignity like the sun, or I will perhaps be dead, like
> a moon dropping into the sea.

And he wrote to his friend Samuel Clemens—whom, at this point, he had not seen or heard from in more than a year—in care of his sister in St. Louis.

> *March 22, 1862*
>
> *My dear friend, Samuel—wherever you may be—I imagine you are with your brother Orion somewhere West—I just wished to tell you of my kindly thoughts, regarding our friendship, for the clerk you put up with is now about to go off with his regiment into a very great battle. Should this be the last you ever hear of me, I want to let you know that I am hoping that every good wish you have comes true, and that yours will be a long and happy life. Should we find one another at some distant point in the future—and even if we do not—I have valued your kindness and sage advice. I do miss our conversations about books, and your funny tales as well, the memories of which, in the dreariness of these days, with their incessant drills and pointless mustering of the ranks, has relieved me from the melancholic state I often find myself in. This is nothing more, then, than a simple note of gratitude, and it would be longer, except for the fact that I do not know if you will ever*

receive it. Should that be the case and you wish to let me know
of your doings, a letter addressed to the Confederate camp in
Corinth, Mississippi, Company E, Sixth Arkansas Volunteer
Infantry, in my name, should suffice to reach me, though by
then I may well be in some other unearthly locale.

Henry Stanley

And before he set out with his regiment toward the banks
of the Tennessee River to fight against the forces of one General
Grant, Stanley, by then much exposed to the florid and heartfelt
sentiments of other soldiers toward their families, came to reflect
upon the elusive presence of his own. He'd heard from Liverpool
that his mother had married a certain Robert Jones, by whom she
had several children; they ran a small inn called the Cross Foxes
in the village of Glascoed, in Monmouthshire, not far from where
he'd been born—that was all he knew.

While sitting under a spreading oak tree in a field at Corinth,
Stanley, in a lonely frame of mind, allowed his fertile imagination
to take prominence over an awareness of his feeble relations with
her. And so he sent this tender note:

Dearest Mother,

Though you have been absent from my life for a very long
time, I am writing you with the aim of tearing down the wall
that circumstances have put between us; yours has not been an
easy life, nor has mine. Fortune, that curious thing, has sepa-
rated us, and though I believe that, deep down, you truly care
for me, I know that you have been struggling long to find your
own comfortable place in this world, the distractions of which,
to my mind, account for your distance from me, and rightfully
so, for what would I have ever been to you but yet another
burden in your already burdened state? I have sometimes won-
dered if you know how to write and read. I imagine that you
can—but if you do not, I am trusting that someone will read
these words to you, even if I would prefer they be kept private.

So if it is a matter of personal shame that has kept you from writing me in the past, please understand, dear Mother, that whatever you should say to me would be received with a happy and open heart by a son who with sincerity holds a great affection for you.

I have been told by cousins Tom and Maria that you were recently married at the St. Asaph's chapel and that you have two small children by your new husband. This strikes me as a wonderful development, for it speaks to me to your worthiness as a mother, and it is my hope that you will have some maternal affections left over for me. I do not blame you for your lapses—what I have been, as a lowly charge of the state and parish of St. Asaph's, could never be a source of pride to a woman such as yourself, with her own past bereavements to contend with: I am speaking of the early death of my father, John Rowlands, whom I have never known. But I should let you know that the miserable boy you last saw at St. Asaph's has since blossomed into a person of promise: If you recall, I have written you before of my journey to America, some scant four years before, and of my brief but educational sojourn as a merchant trader. But of other things, which you do not perhaps know, I will tell you now: My employer and dearest friend in those years was a New Orleans merchant named Henry Stanley, and as he regarded me as closely as he would a son, I have taken his name. I have done so not out of disrespect for the man who had been my Welsh father, but to clear my mind and soul of the lowly state I had once been in; and never have I forgotten that you are my mother, a fact I hold close and dear to my heart.

My life has been spent with some travels: As a clerk in Mr. Stanley's company I learned much about the region of the American South and its ways; things were going so well I had thought to go into business with Mr. Stanley, as his son and partner, but I am afraid to say, he died in my company on a plantation in Cuba, where I had gone to join him in his work.

*When I returned from that journey to the place where I had
made a recent home, a state called Arkansas, I joined a regiment of the Confederate army, my rank being that of a private,
but with the promise of further promotions awaiting me, as I
have been singled out by certain officers for my very good abilities as a provisions clerk and marksman. There is so much
more I would like to tell you, but as my regiment is just now
making ready to engage the enemy in the coming days, I have
mainly wished to express to you the sentiments of a son who,
going to war, regards the dear lady who begot him with many
wonderful feelings, despite our long separation.*

*It is my wish, then, to plant the idea in your mind—and
heart—that should I get through all this, I will be looking
forward to the day when I will see you and your family in
England again, and that you will find me as suitable a son as
any fine lady might ever want. Please write me, if you can; but
if you cannot, rest assured that I remain your son, always, in
this world or in the next.*

With my dearest affections,
Henry Stanley

AT AN EARLY HOUR ON the morning of April 6, 1862, a Sunday,
just before the sun had begun to rise, while Clemens was still
asleep somewhere out West, Stanley's regiment, bivouacked in a
damp and miserable field, had been mustered into battle forma-
tion, the Confederate army creeping through the misty gloom
of a forest to sweep down and overrun the Union lines, which
they had hoped to slaughter, or at least push into the Tennessee
River. Equipped with a muzzle-loading rifle, tedious and time-
consuming to load, Stanley had been among the troops who, with
whoops and rebel yells, had come charging out with fixed bayo-
nets in a frantic run out of the woods. Their volleys cut down the
Yankees as they, just stirring awake, half-dressed and unarmed,

were completely caught by surprise in their encampments; and it seemed as if the many Yankee dead and wounded lying in the field augured for a quick Confederate victory, despite the length of time it took them to load ball, buckshot, and paper charges into their muskets.

Shortly, however, once the Union forces had been mustered and had formed their own lines, the Confederate advantage was quickly nullified. Confederate soldiers, under a furious fusillade of bullets and shells, fell everywhere around him. Then the Yankee artillery came into play: men and horses were blown to pieces, and many a torn-open gut, entrails exposed, sent swirls of steam into the cool morning air. Taking refuge with some dozen of his fellow soldiers behind the trunk of a fallen tree, Stanley turned to see one of the men he had written a tender letter home for, a young lieutenant, shot between the eyes, his pupils wide open and dreaming—of who knows what: then he saw the soldier known as John Bull, his face blown off, collapsed on the ground. Stanley's remarkable ability to feel detached from himself in the most troubling of circumstances served him well in those moments, for, later, keeping his calm, he survived to join a line of troops advancing toward a second Yankee encampment. It was while he had been charging across a field, behind enemy lines, that he was knocked over—a piece of shrapnel having hit the buckle of his belt; stunned, but spared mortal injury, he lay quietly for a long time before managing to crawl, exhausted, behind a tree.

Just as it seemed as if all were lost, he heard the command for his regiment to regroup. Night was falling. He ate some rations and tried to sleep—"Oh, Mother; oh, Father," he muttered to himself again and again—sharing with his fellow soldiers the widespread fear that the Yankees might be upon them come dawn. But by the morning, he had recovered his nerves enough not only to join a line of infantrymen who were ordered to advance toward the Yankee lines in "good order," but also to do so with great valor and enthusiasm, outpacing his fellow soldiers and penetrating so deeply into the enemy campgrounds that soon no gray

Confederate uniforms were to be seen. Searching for a place to hide, he ran toward some trees, only to find himself in an exposed clearing, Yankee uniforms everywhere surrounding him: And, just like that, with half a dozen soldiers converging upon him, their pistols drawn, he found himself in ankle chains and taken as a prisoner of war.

He was sent upriver by steamboat to St. Louis, then by rail to Illinois. A few weeks later, he arrived at Camp Douglas, outside of Chicago, the long huts of this federal prison abundant with vermin, its trench latrines overflowing with human ordure, and the men, clustered two and three to a wooden bunk (in dense rows, like small boats), suffering from dysentery or typhus or their own septic wounds, dying in their own filth, their bodies carried away to the death wagons each morning, like "loads of New Zealand mutton," as he would later write in his journal. Ill himself with a very bad case of dysentery, Stanley, brooding and weary, supposed that sooner or later his would soon be among the bodies carted out of that place.

But in those days, his orderly manner attracted the attention of the Union commanders: His achievements—keeping inventory of the meager food rations that were appropriated for his barracks, a list of which he maintained in neat columns in his careful script (he was, after all, a clerk)—impressed them very much, as did his skills as a marksman. Such officers, thinking that he might be of some use to the Union cause, and reviewing his status as a British national, offered him a way out, which was to enlist as a soldier on the Union side. And while his sympathies for the South were mainly a matter of geography—it had been four years since he had arrived in New Orleans—and because he feared for his own life, he, after some six weeks in that hellish place, took the Union oath of allegiance and signed on with the Illinois Light Artillery. Sent south to a camp near Harpers Ferry, West Virginia, he had a short-lived stint in a blue uniform: Collapsing during a drill, he was deemed unfit for service. For two weeks he lingered in a Union hospital, and, released from his duties, wandered, deathly ill, on foot, traveling some twenty-four miles over the course of a week into peaceful Maryland, where, finding refuge at a farm, he recovered well enough to partake, with some gratitude, in the apple harvest.

(How beautiful that was, so long ago, he thought, to be walking in the shady groves of those trees, a patch of blue to be glimpsed now and then through the briary cross-hatching of branches, as he serenely went about practicing the peaceful activity of picking apples and dropping them into a basket in the spring sun.)

In that time a terrible homesickness for Wales came over him, a longing for the quietude of dulcet vales, and so upon his recovery (and with the help of the kindly family he stayed with) he left for Baltimore, finding work on an oyster schooner in Chesapeake Bay. Later, as a hand on a ship bound for England, he spent a month in the crossing, then walked some forty miles from Liverpool to north Wales to Denbigh. There he sought out the company and welcoming embrace of the mother who had long ago abandoned him: Seeing him in rags, she—Mrs. Robert Jones, née Betsy Parry—put him up for a night, and then sent him away from her door the next morning.

Then followed a year of further travels as a hand on various ships—water, like paper and disease, always playing a part in his life: Girgenti, Italy; Marseille, France; and Athens, Greece, being among his ports of call. On one of his journeys, he was shipwrecked in the seas off Barcelona. October of 1863 found him in New York City, working as a clerk in a legal office on Cedar Street, in lower Manhattan, his employer an alcoholic judge with whom he boarded in Brooklyn. Some six months later, young Stanley, at twenty-three, cooped up in an office and craving further adventure, enlisted again, this time in the Union Navy, as a clerk and admiral's secretary on the warship *Minnesota*. It happened that he had been aboard the *Minnesota* on December 24, 1864, during the Union fleet's bombardment of Fort Fisher, a Confederate stronghold on the coast of North Carolina, one of the last great naval engagements of the Civil War. Witnessing this conflagration. Deciding to write some news dispatches, he later sold several of his descriptions of the battle to notable newspapers, among them the *New York Herald*. By the following February, bored again and judging the record-keeping facilities of the Union forces haphazard enough to risk taking an unauthorized leave, Stanley shed his uniform and, in the company of a fellow mate, slipped off the war brig as it lay in harbor one night at Portsmouth, New Hampshire, awaiting repairs. For a time he lingered in New York; by May of 1865, hearing much about the frontier lands and thinking that he might become a journalist, he headed west.

On that journey, recalling that Samuel Clemens had once worked at the *Missouri Democrat*, he turned up those offices, in St. Louis, and offered his services. At the time he brought along several of the dispatches he had written during the war, and these, along with a mention of his friend Clemens, who had by then, writing under the name of Mark Twain, become something of a legend to the Western newspaper community, helped the young Stanley procure a position as an attaché (or freelance stringer).

Leaving St. Louis for the frontier, he, without knowing it at the time, followed in the footsteps of Samuel Clemens, his travels taking him to St. Joseph, then by stagecoach across the Rocky Mountains and onward to San Francisco, California. Eventually, he based himself in Denver, but because his earnings as a journalist were not guaranteed, he found work as a part-time bookkeeper in Central City, a mining town where he entertained (like Clemens and many others before him) the notion of striking it rich by prospecting for gold. But as money to buy the needed supplies was scarce, he became an employee of the *Daily Miners' Register*, not as a journalist but as an apprentice typesetter—as if Samuel Clemens's own past had come to shadow him. Finding no gold in the hills around that city, he returned to his fledgling skills as a writer, keeping notebooks filled with observations and successfully selling many an article on the doings of the rugged cowboys and miners he encountered on his travels.

In those days, while on a trip down the Platte River to the Missouri, through hostile Indian Territory (this never bothered

Stanley, for he was handy with a Colt revolver and loved to practice his aim, shooting birds out of the sky), he, with his own great ambitions, hatched a scheme to travel the world. Confident that he could recoup his expenses by writing an account of it, he arranged to set out with several companions by way of Omaha and St. Louis to New York, then to Boston, toward Asia Minor. Paying for his passage to Smyrna (modern Izmir), in western Turkey, as a hand aboard the ship, he planned his route during the fifty-one-day voyage: He would cross the expanses of Anatolia into Georgia, then go through Kashmir toward China and ultimately Tibet, where few foreigners had ever traveled.

Unfortunately, not some few days out from Smyrna, as this small party—a seventeen-year-old former shipmate of Stanley's aboard the *Minnesota* named Louis Noe; a journalist whom Stanley had met during his Central City days, William Cook; and Stanley himself—was crossing the mountains east of that city they were waylaid and taken captive by a band of twelve Turkish brigands. They might have lingered in that place indefinitely or been killed were it were not for the intercession of a Turkish banker sympathetic to their plight who secured their release and safe passage to Constantinople.

Some months afterward, in mid-February, Stanley, late of Constantinople, Athens, Marseille, Liverpool, and Denbigh, Wales, arrived at the offices of the *Missouri Democrat* in St. Louis. Received gladly by the editors, and put on a staff salary of fifteen dollars a week, he counted among his first duties, during his renewed tenure with the newspaper, an assignment to report upon some dreary legislative proceedings in Jefferson City. Later on in that early April of 1867, he was on hand at the Mercantile Library in St. Louis to cover a lecture by the latest literary sensation, Mark Twain—whom Stanley remembered, as he always would, as Samuel Clemens.

BY THEN, IN THAT CLIMATE of a recovering post–Civil War America whose public was hungry for amusement, Clemens had achieved much renown for his humorous, homespun writings and for his cheerful and rather theatrical public presentations of his works. The first gleanings of his fame came with the publication of a short story called "The Celebrated Jumping Frog of Calaveras County" in the *New-York Saturday Press* in 1865. In much demand, his reputation preceding him, and wildly popular for his travel articles, Clemens, somewhat bemused by his ability to draw a crowd, had packed the auditorium. For several hours, Clemens, as Mark Twain, ever resplendent and dapper, held forth from the stage about his recent six-month stay in the Sandwich Islands— Hawaii. His written lecture and improvised asides filled the premises with laughter, and the fine quality and detail of his prose much impressed Stanley, who stood quietly in the back observing him. While dutifully recording in his notebooks the contents of Twain's lecture, Stanley had somewhat jealously studied his friend's techniques at stagecraft, for, upon his own initial return from Turkey some months before, Stanley himself had tried his hand at lecturing. He had rented a hall in Jefferson City, printed flyers and tickets, and advertised the subject as the adventures and perils encountered by the American traveler in Asia Minor. He had promised to recite aloud the Islamic call to prayer, which he had memorized in Constantinople and heard from every mosque, to sing Turkish songs, and to speak of other cultural eccentricities. (When that night arrived, Stanley—dressed in a Turkish naval officer's uniform and with props and souvenirs to display, among them a scimitar and a Saracen coat of chain mail—mounted the stage to find that only four people had shown up, He later burned the box full of remaining tickets in a stove.) So while attending the St. Louis lecture, he had perhaps envied Clemens's popularity with the audience—but he showed no signs of it when he sought out Clemens backstage.

Sipping a glass of warmed whiskey and smoking a cigar to relax before heading out to greet the crowd of well-wishers, Clemens, lounging in a chair, looked up and, through the swirls of smoke, saw a much-changed Stanley approaching. When he got

up, Clemens said, "My God, Henry, is that you?" in apparent surprise over the very fact that Stanley was still alive. They briefly
embraced, neither man prone to overt expressions of affection.
Later, after Clemens had partaken of a salon reception and ful-
filled his duties to the crowd, he and Stanley repaired to a hotel
bar, where, with the abundant enthusiasm of youth—clocks
were irrelevant then—they stayed up until three in the morning
recounting the events of their recent pasts to one another, for they
had been long out of touch.

In the years since they had parted in New Orleans, Stanley,
never knowing of Clemens's meandering whereabouts, had managed to send but two brief letters to him, in care of Clemens's
sister in St. Louis, but these, apparently because of the war, Clemens had never received. For his part, Clemens had never known
Stanley's transient addresses, though he had over the past several
years occasionally read some of Stanley's dispatches in the *Missouri Democrat* (often signed with a simple *S*) and admired them
without knowing their authorship. Mainly, he was grateful that
Stanley had not been killed in the Civil War, and to that sentiment
they toasted.

That same evening, Stanley, in his cups, knowing that Clemens, as Mark Twain, was turning into something of a prolific
memoirist, broached the subject of their journey to Cuba. "What
was it but a disappointing journey for me? Can you, Samuel,
knowing me as your friend, agree to forgo any mention of it in
your prolific writings, simply because it is a friend's request?"

"Well, to be truthful, Henry, I had not thought about it one
way or the other, our journey being so old. Though I much
enjoyed our brief travels there, Henry, and though I found many
a fascinating thing about the place, I have come to know where
my bread and butter comes from. My stock seems to remain
in the presumed charm of an ironically determined small-town
southerner who grew up along the banks of the Mississippi and
happens to describe his surroundings in a humorous way—an endlessly humorous way that does not allow too easily for seriously

intended digressions. Our time in Cuba resulted in my own longing for home, and while I have considered writing about it—*A
Southerner in the Land of Mosquitoes* being a title I considered—I
have long decided against it."

About three in the morning, they, filled with drink, and, practically leaning on one another, parted.

⚘

IT WAS ONLY A FEW days later, however, that Clemens, while
perusing a copy of the *Missouri Democrat*, found that Stanley had
published, nearly word for word, the entire contents of his lecture
on the Sandwich Islands, thereby ruining the freshness of it for the
local public. Clemens was left so peeved that, despite his warm
feelings for Stanley, he withdrew his friendship for a very long
time, choosing not to answer any of Stanley's notes of apology—"I
had been put under much pressure by my editors to report it"—
and forestalling any meaningful continuation of their professional
or private relationship for some five years, when they would be
reunited again in Brighton, England, in 1872.

⚘

ABOUT STANLEY'S PROGRESS IN THE years after that St. Louis
event, we can learn from his own words—an address he gave
before a gathering of the Anti-Slavery Society in 1890:

"My dear and gracious friends," he began, his eyes a little
teary, his voice fluctuating from strength to weakness. "Gathered dignitaries, brothers of the letter, brothers of the cloth, my
fellow explorers, lords and ladies of the realm... For a man like
myself, who's come up in the hard ways of life, to be standing
here before so august a gathering is a very great honor indeed—
and something of a miracle, if you ask me. I stand before you
having already lived enough for several lifetimes. I have known
the life of common Welsh farmers and the loathsome trials of the

workhouse, to which I was remanded as a boy. I have known the life of a butcher's assistant, a schoolteacher, a sailor, a shop clerk. I have lived in America for many years. I have traveled the Mississippi River and have fought in the American Civil War....As a journalist I have traversed the great American plains to report on the Indian Wars—I have even ridden alongside the famous Wild Bill Hickok over plains still brimming with vast herds of buffalo. I have accompanied the very great General William Napier in pursuit of King Theodore during the Abyssinian campaign and witnessed the bloodshed of the antiroyalist insurrections in Spain....I have journeyed up the Nile to Philae, in the ancient land of Kush, then across Persia, where, following the example of many illustrious men before me, I carved my name upon one of the monuments of Persepolis. At Jerusalem, I descended into the excavations of the Temple of Solomon, then walked in the malarial marshes by the Sea of Galilee, in the footsteps of Jesus. I have been no stranger to the Russian realm, nor am I unfamiliar with the vast distances and peculiarities of India. In short, like the proverbial Hebrews of the Bible, I have wandered widely to places that I could never have imagined as a young boy. Along the way, Africa was placed on my plate of experiences.

"My challenges began there with a great task, which was to find the devoted missionary Livingstone. Took me a bloody and arduous year, but I bloody well succeeded where others had not. [Applause] And with Livingstone I undertook an exploration of the northerly reaches of Lake Tanganyika with the aim of determining it as the source of the Nile. We made many good discoveries, but nothing was greater than my contact with that saintly man, who became something of a father to me....Upon my return to England from the company of that gracious soul—whose pious life my efforts had extended by some years, I do believe—I was received with much skepticism by our most prominent geographical and exploratory bodies. That a lowly reporter, sent on assignment by the illustrious James Gordon Bennett of the *New York Herald* to a place he did not know, without any prior exploring experience beyond his morning searches for a comb [laughter], had indeed succeeded, against all odds, seemed, on the face of it, an improbability. And yet because few believed me, the savor and delight of my exertions were so much tainted by petty jealousies that for a very long time it was difficult for this humble servant to bear foremost in his mind the nobler fruits of those travels. And these, as I think must be by now well known, were in regard to my revulsion over the evil practice of slavery....

"It was during the flourishing of this ravishing and immoral practice that Dr. Livingstone first undertook his meandering missionary wanderings through the region. Mind you, he witnessed much of these natives' sufferings—for the Arabs at that time were putting in neck and ankle chains some eighty thousand or one hundred thousand Africans a year, and that is counting only the ones who survived. By the time I reached Ujiji on my historic encounter, Livingstone, after more than a decade of witnessing such evils, emaciated and forlorn as he was, thought first of only two things: the glory and immanence of God and the deliverance of the poor souls thusly afflicted. He was a saint, I should say again. [Applause]

"It is an irony that I found him in an Arab slave-trading town, Ujiji, along the shores of Lake Tanganyika, but however he had settled there, it was surely from desperation. He was nearly dead then, suffering much from malnutrition and malaria: He had very little food, other than the scraps the slave traders would throw him, but his lack of medicine, particularly quinine, a box of which had been lost or stolen by one of his porters during his travels, was worse. We had marched in, my armed Zanzibaris sending off a fifty-gun salute; we had a drummer beating on a snare, another bloke blowing on a trumpet; we held up two flags—the Stars and Stripes and the Union Jack—and, as for myself, though I had barely survived the great march, I appeared in a clean white uniform and sparkling boots, a pith helmet upon my head. That I take relish in reciting this to you, please forgive me, but on that day, November tenth, 1871, as I moved through a tumultuous crowd of Ujiji inhabitants to reach him, at my first sight of Livingstone—thin and feeble, with gray whiskers on his haggard face—I had my first moment of encountering true greatness.

"In a trunk I had brought along three pint bottles of Champagne for the occasion, and though he was weak from some six years of travels and from illness, after his first civilized meal in a long time—we had cooked a hen and other victuals—we sat drinking for a bit in his hut. Faces were always peering in at us through the mosquito-netted windows. He nearly fainted a few times, but then, with nourishment, he revived, and on that first night he recounted to me the many sad things he had seen in his travels—the slaves' solemn marches through the jungles, their burned villages, their rotting corpses lining the trails. And, I should say, he seemed to appreciate my efforts to reach him, for few white men had traversed the climes I had (Burton and Speke were the only two I knew of, and they had stopped short of that place). But mainly he spoke of his gratitude at the thought that he was the object of such universal concern.... Then, after he shared his thoughts about the Bible and the solace it had brought him in the most desolate places, we spent the evening discussing the criminal disregard for human life that the slave trade represents.

"'Either you are the sort who truly believes in the Good Book, or you are helplessly entangled with the avaricious mind of the devil,'" he told me.

"I could go on...but as I am here to introduce a greater program of speakers, far more informed about the history of that trade and, perhaps, more dedicated than I, I should end my brief statement with this. Even though I was once perceived by the preeminent geographical bodies of this land as a self-serving adventurer, the five months I spent with Livingstone not only made me feel a great personal affection for the man, they also strongly amplified my religious beliefs. And regardless of the passing indifference I previously had to the slave trade in Africa, the practice of which I first witnessed in America (and over which that war was fought), my travels with Livingstone stirred me awake—not just to the geographical mysteries of the region but also to a greater concern: the betterment and freedom of our fellow man."

❧

THAT STANLEY, INEXPERIENCED IN AFRICAN travels and a mere American "penny-a-liner," had overcome the dangers of that tropical clime to find Livingstone—tall, pale, thin-limbed, and sickly (from malaria), but still alive—in a remote village called Ujiji before other expeditions could do so had inspired not only much jealously among the members of the Royal Geographical Society, but their professional skepticism as well. Even if Stanley had gone on to spend five months in the company of the saintly and kindly Livingstone, exploring by small boat the upper reaches of Lake Tanganyika, which Livingstone believed to be a possible source of the Nile, and even if he had endured many bouts of malaria along the way and could speak with much affection and intimate personal knowledge about the man who, in those months, had, by his lights, become a second father to him. After Mr. Stanley of New Orleans, and despite the compelling changes that had taken place within his own soul—Stanley, as Livingstone's disciple, became a full-fledged antislavist then, and his hunger for exploration, with Livingstone's geographical passions aflame within, had been aroused from the moment his first dispatches were carried by native runners to the coast and then sent onward to Zanzibar and Europe to be published.

While Stanley had been making his way back to England, most of the Fleet Street press was publishing articles that called into question the veracity of his stories. At hearings held by the Royal Geographical Society, a parcel of letters written in Livingstone's hand for publication in the *New York Herald*, which Stanley had sent off before him from Zanzibar as proof of his achievement, were called forgeries; and his own detailed descriptions of his travels with Livingstone and of the man himself, also published in the *Herald*, were dismissed as the wishful inventions of a glory-seeking, ambitious journalist.

By the time certain members of Livingstone's family—his son Tom and his daughter Agnes—had come forward to authenticate the letters, Stanley, arriving in England, was already put off and full of resentment by the way he had been treated. The Royal Geographical Society had, as a way of reticently recognizing his achievements, invited Stanley to address a conference held by the British Association that August. But instead of taking the opportunity to ingratiate himself to his hosts—among them Sir Henry Rawlinson, head of the RGS, and Francis Galton, president of the British Association's geographical section—Stanley, incensed that no formal public apology had been made, took to the stage and in two separate speeches made his lack of respect for those bodies clear to all.

IT HAPPENED THAT SAMUEL CLEMENS, newly famous as Mark Twain by then, and in Britain on a lecture tour, had been among the three thousand people who had packed the hall that morning. Despite not having seen Stanley since their last meeting back in St. Louis in 1867, and even though, like many an American and Englishman, he had followed with admiration Stanley's much-publicized exploits, despite the controversies surrounding them, and was quite anxious for Stanley to do well, he was disappointed by his friend's performance that day.

From Clemens's notebook:

> Watching him floating further adrift from the good
> graces of the audience, I had to remind myself that Stan-
> ley was still a reasonably young man of thirty-three,
> though a quite different sort from the boy I once knew
> in New Orleans—somewhat more high-strung than I
> remembered and, in those days, way too bitter for his
> own good. As his friend I resolved to sit him down and
> have a good chat with him before he did himself more
> harm. Unfortunately, I only had a few moments to
> speak to him that morning, as he was in the company of

the very miffed Galton; but when I greeted Stanley, he seemed genuinely relieved to see me, as I was glad to see him, my own annoyances with him, going back to 1867, having passed.

"How did I do?" he asked me, and I, of course, told him that he had performed splendidly, though given Stanley's skeptical expression he seemed to know otherwise. Parting, we made an arrangement to meet a few days later in London.

THEN THIS, ANOTHER ENTRY:

Tonight dined with Stanley at the Langham hotel, where we are both staying, and while I was happy to see that Stanley, with his hair let down, was quite affable and full of wonderful travel stories, once the subject of the conference came up, he became as bitter as any man. "Why should I, a person with a miserable, unfortunate past, have to bow down before people who have wined and eaten to the full all their lives? They have no idea what it took for someone like me to have lifted himself from poverty. I have no interest in humoring such fools."

While I then tried to convince him otherwise, he at one point looked at me in such a way as to suggest that such sentiments would never leave him. Fortunately, while sitting up late and drinking beer, the felicitous effects of imbibing cheered him up, and we were together until nearly four in Stanley's suite, reminiscing about the past. I am glad to say that the old Stanley I knew turned up again that night, pleasant and very interesting. We only gave up when we ran out of beer and tobacco. We then made a date to visit some antiquarian bookshops the next day.

꙳

IN FACT, THEY VISITED WESTMINSTER Abbey and St. Paul's Cathedral together, then went out to see Stratford-upon-Avon, Shakespeare's old haunt, and made a brief stop at Oxford to look at the library. Three days of travel that neither recorded.

Thereafter they only met occasionally over the years, mainly in England, the two often sitting up until the late hours smoking and drinking beer. Since Stanley was often away in Africa over the next decade and a half, their friendship was mainly conducted by mail.

STANLEY IN LOVE

160 New Bond Street, London
December 20, 1885

Dear Samuel,

I hope this missive finds you in good spirits and good health; since I last wrote to you from Zanzibar, much that is new and much that is not very new has transpired; of my accomplishments in the Congo I will not speak—I know just how wary and contrary in opinion you are about that subject. Thankfully, you and I, going back so many years, can speak of other things, as, dare I say, brothers of different opinions might. If I presume to put you in such a category, please forgive me: But few are the men I respect; even fewer are the men I trust; and you are one of them, having always kept "our little secret" (about our travels together) so faithfully and for so long.

But on to the subject of this letter: What has transpired in my life as of late has occurred in the area of romance, a realm as dangerous and foreign to this long-solitary life as any jungle I have trod. The lady in question, with whom I have been in frequent company over the past months and with whom I have corresponded nearly daily, is one Dorothy Tennant. She is about thirty-five, but well preserved, tall and statuesque, and with the lively attitude and bright spirit of a young girl. She is something of a society dame. A friend to royalty and the artistic set alike, she comes from a Welsh family of wealth and great estates—they have in their household staff eight servants and housekeepers, a head butler, a cook, and a carriage driver—and yet, though she lives in a mansion on Richmond Terrace, on the east end of Whitehall, and has an acquaintance with the Prince of Wales, among other persons of note and fame, Miss Tennant is no ordinary coddled aristocrat; on the contrary, she has an interest in many things that one would not expect of such a personage. Her mother is an old bat, a snob of the old school, with whom I do not particularly get along (and in truth I do not like being in a room with her, as she has the manner of a strict schoolmarm and has not once looked me in the eye when speaking—aloof, I would call her). But she is an aesthetic sort, having once been an artist, and her daughter has followed suit, being a painter of some reputation, trained here at the Slade School and in Paris (she speaks very good French and dresses with impeccable taste). She has, to my eye, a remarkable ability for miniature paintings, no more than a foot high and wide, which she showed me one day: They are little fantasies of a neoclassical theme, set in places like old Greek temples, with all manner of buxom nude maidens (at first I was shocked, I should tell you) and scantily clad nymphs and sprites cavorting about placid Arcadian woods, after the style of the popular Lawrence Alma-Tadema. Her highly developed imagination for such scenes is fueled by her considerable reading of the classical myths.

In the main, however, her most prolific works have depicted common London street children—her "beloved ragamuffins," she calls them, her métier being the very poorest of the poor: chimney sweeps, flower girls, little beggars whom she finds here and there during her rambles through the city. She brings them back home to her mansion, where they are given a good meal before going into her studio to pose. For their troubles she allows them to play her piano, a great luxury to such children (her piano's ivories are always smudged with black fingerprints and darkened by soot), and finally she gives them sixpence.

Because you know about my own upbringing, I need not tell you how deeply her benevolent and somewhat maternal attitude toward these poor children touches me. Certainly I do not believe that painting a smiling chimney sweep or a vagabond waif makes any great difference to their lives, but there is some truth to her assertion that such children will be remembered—immortalized, as it were—and perhaps helped because of what she does. (She publishes articles about such children's poverty in several newspapers.)

Now, as to the details: We met last June at a poetry reading by our mutual friend Edwin Arnold held at the Athenaeum Club, and in the months of July and August, when I had mainly remained in London, I would see her at least twice a week for lunch at first, and always in the company of her mother. But as she wanted to know me better, she devised a means by which we would have some privacy, and so since those months, Samuel, I have been going to her studio to pose for her. She wants to make a "proper portrait" of me—not of the tired and world-weary and solitary Henry Stanley but of the triumphant and virtuous and "very charming" Stanley, or so she has put it. And, as we have begun to know each other a little better, she has even gotten me to talk openly—not about my African exploits (a tiring business to me) but about the ways I came to be, particularly my childhood (of great interest to her, it seems).

But even as I have been hopeful, I have been suspicious of her motivations. I have wondered if I am some glorified vision of a chimney sweep who's done well, in her eyes, or if I am a simple diversion from the haughty and bloodless folk of her normal acquaintance. My doubts in this regard are further heightened by my still painful memories of past affaires de coeur *gone bad. To this day I think about Alice Pike, the young American girl I met here in London before my expedition of 1874 and to whom I thought I had been engaged. During the loneliest and most solemn Christmas I have ever spent, in a place called Ugogo, laid low with fever in a rain-soaked tent, it was the simple idea of being with her one day that kept me from taking my own life. (Samuel, I am describing an extreme state: Have we not talked about life and the sheer abstraction of the idea? However we may feel, have we not asked if our lives really mean much to the world one way or the other?) That I returned from the wild to find that she, a fickle girl, impatient to wait three years, had married someone else—a soft fellow named Barney—left me rather soured on the idea of love.*

I do not know if you can understand this, having been wedded to Livy so long, but no matter how I tried to remove from my thoughts the memories of that experience with Alice, the deep wound she inflicted upon me has remained. One day, being forthright and earnest, I related this undeniable fact to Miss Tennant, who seemed, at the mention of that past affair, I am selfishly happy to say, rather jealous of my strong recollection of that woman. Though I have been feeling greatly distracted by her I remain hesitant to commit myself to what may well be another folly and disappointment.

Miss Tennant seems to feel otherwise. Nearly daily, during July and August, I received notes from her: "Come tomorrow"; "Do say you will dine with us"; "Can you arrive at three in the afternoon?" "I have read your latest letter to the London Times and found it most interesting—please, come tomorrow, I must see you so we might discuss it"; and on and on. We have been seen at the theater and attending charity balls together; one of our appearances, at a reception at the US embassy for a July Fourth celebration, created a rouse of unwanted speculation in the newspapers. I have lately heard much gossip about us, implying a possible romance, but we have always regarded each other as friends, and platonically so. While we have often sat on the couch speaking intimately, even holding hands, I have been reluctant to physically express my admiration—and attraction—to her.

Only once have we crossed that line, in July—as a gentleman, I did not initiate it. We had finished one of the painting sessions. She had been cleaning a brush with turpentine when, as I was about to take my leave, she told me, "Mr. Stanley, you have something on your cheek." What kind of speck it might have been I cannot say, but she touched my face to remove it, and then, quite forwardly, she suddenly chose to kiss me. It was an innocent enough act, lasting no more than a few moments—but it was one that, to an observer, would have seemed more than it was. Certainly it appeared so to her mother, who had happened into the studio at that very moment.

I mention this because shortly thereafter, I learned that mother (of whom I am very wary) and daughter were to suddenly embark on a two-month tour of Europe; and though Miss Tennant later told me that this journey had been planned for quite a long time (I had heard nothing of it before), I am convinced that her mother quickly contrived it to keep Miss Tennant and me apart. (In my gut, I believe her mother thinks I am not good enough for her.)

So we did not see one another for two months. Miss Tennant and her mother left in August for a grand tour of Europe and other places in England that lasted until early November. In that time, we wrote one another constantly, looking forward in anticipation to the very day when we would see each other again. Over those months, for all the busyness of my life, and

*even during a thankfully brief and mild bout of my recur-
ring malaria (early September), in which I had a very strange
dream about Miss Tennant coming to my New Bond Street
flat as the goddess Demeter (whom I have always thought she
resembles anyway), I had begun to wonder if I should be so
bold as to find a means to broach the subject of matrimony
with her. (When I mentioned this to King Leopold, he, true to
his rakish form, told me: "Why not, Monsieur Stanley? After
all, if you get bored with her, you can always find yourself a
mistress.")*

    *I had become so obsessed with the subject as to experiment
with an old wives' superstition, recommended to me by Baron-
ess Von Donop, which is to sleep for many nights with a piece
of wedding cake, wrapped in wax paper, under my pillow, so
as to better ascertain my truest feelings about Dorothy. The
cake did not work, however, because no revelations came to
me, though I wished it otherwise.*

    *We took up again upon her return, and, to her mother's
unhappiness, there came to us a renewed sense of purpose
about our courtship. But the fly in the ointment remains: Her
mother exerts so great a control and hold over her daughter's
life (Miss Tennant has confided in me that she sleeps in the
same bedroom with her at night) that her dislike for me and
what I seem to represent—i.e., a lowly born person of nonar-
istocratic pedigree—does not bode well for my future with her
daughter, and for that reason alone, I am somewhat afraid of
her. Though we have not yet spoken of marriage, and I remain
wary of her mother's interference, I am bracing myself to propose, to what outcome I do not know. Still, I am afraid of a
possible rejection. Perhaps I am being a fool to say this, but I
feel that to propose and be refused would be my death. What,
old companion, do you, with your great success in domestic
matters, advise?*

    *As for my immediate future, I seem to spend month upon
month cooling my heels while awaiting a new assignment in*

Africa, though what it might entail I have no idea. King Leopold, whom I know you do not care for, has been promising me the directorship of the Congo Free State, though he has been agonizingly slow in making the appointment. Further, I have heard some rumblings in regard to my involvement as a possible commander of an expedition to bring supplies and armed men to one Emin Pasha, General Gordon's successor and governor of Equatoria in the southern Sudan; he is holed up in a stronghold in the Lake Albert region, besieged by the forces of the Mahdists, those same Islamic fanatics who had cut off General Gordon's head at Khartoum. It is being said that I am the most qualified man in Europe to lead such a mission—though if the truth be told, Samuel, I am getting tired of such exertions and would now prefer a quieter and more tranquil existence.

I go on too long. It's now snowing here in London: I imagine it could well be so in Connecticut—it is that time of year; Christmas is not far off. May yours go well—for I always keep good wishes for you and your family close to my heart.

Most faithfully yours,
Henry M. Stanley

❉

January 2, 1886
Farmington Avenue
Hartford, Connecticut

Dear Stanley,

I received your welcome letter on Christmas Eve, and to be truthful, as I am always happy to hear from you, I was doubly delighted byl news of this promising lady in your life, no matter how difficult the mother situation may appear to be. From your description of her, it seems to me that you have come across the rare creature who combines intelligence, grace,

*abilities, and a good heart—my own Livy, putting up with
me endlessly, is also of that category. (Let me remind you
that when I first courted Livy, her parents wanted nothing to
do with me.) But as for your reluctance, stemming from past
disappointments—the Alice episodes, of which you reminded
me (you had written to me about her before)—my God, dear
Stanley, what could you have expected from such a child of
seventeen? And you should ask yourself if you, as a man of the
world, would have been able to put up with the supercilious
prattling of a young spoiled society dame for very long. What
by way of intellectual fulfillment would she have brought you?
Or what assistance, of any kind, to the constant process of
your writing? Seems to me that you were spared an intermi-
nable boredom with that one. As for Miss Tennant—though
I am not a lonely hearts columnist—I say that you should
exercise more patience and less suspicion, as you are of an age
and position in this world where you should not be scrounging
around for companionship of the female kind.*

*As for me and my family, we, including nine cats, remain
happily intact, and have in recent weeks, around the holidays,
been mainly at home entertaining numerous visitors, among
them my old friends Dean Howells and the Reverend Twichell,
who as a preacher continues to try to put me on the righteous
(ergo, God-believing, prayerful) path. We had a fairly grand
Christmas tree, a New Hampshire fir, burning with candles in
our salon (until the tree dried up), but happily the house did
not burn down and all of us are in one piece, though the usual
ailments (rheumatism, mainly) bother Livy and me.*

*By the way, Stanley, I've been asked by my lecture repre-
sentative and friend Major J. B. Pond if you would have any
interest in meeting with him at some point in London; he has
plans to travel there this summer with Henry Beecher and
seems to have an interest in bringing you back to your old digs
in the States for some kind of tour, given that you are so much
a household word over here. Should you make your way across*

*the Atlantic, you will have, as always, a friendly room and
bed, and a cat or two, awaiting your comfort in my home.*

*Forge onward, great explorer! Be not afraid! (Especially of
the mother, for it is in their makeup to be contrary to the men
who come along to steal their little girls away.)*

Livy and the girls send you their best.

Yours,
Sam Clemens

⁂

London, 1885

AS STANLEY WOULD CONFESS TO his old friend, when it came
to matters of the heart and dealings with the gentler sex, his past
was littered with rejections. Though he could not walk down a
London street without passersby stopping to shake his hand or
stroll along Piccadilly without coming across a tourist-shop window that sold brass Stanley busts or plates bearing his image, and
though he knew himself to be something of a hero to the people
of England (and to Americans, too), he remained a solitary bachelor whose best companions, as he would say, were books, dogs,
and the abstract ideal that he called the "freedom of the wilds."
For all the many honors he received over a decade and a half in
recognition of his three arduous missions to Africa, the simple
caress of a woman's hand across his brow eluded him.

HE HAD AT THIS POINT in his life changed the face of Africa, his
mark having been made through various explorations into previously unknown regions: Among his most notable achievements
were the circumnavigation of Lakes Tanganyika, Victoria, and
Albert and the discovery of the location of the Mountains of the
Moon. He followed the course of three of central Africa's greatest
rivers, the mysterious Lualaba, the Aruwimi, and, most epically,
the treacherous Congo, the second-longest river in the world. He
was the first man to have navigated and mapped that body of

water from its source at Lake Tanganyika to its outflow on the Atlantic Ocean.

Such a summary cannot even begin to convey the extent of what Stanley and his men suffered on those journeys—countless attacks by natives, episodes of starvation, various mutinies, and repeated bouts of malaria, contracted in the leech-, crocodile-, and snake-infested swamps through which his expeditions often waded. An endless purgatorial darkness, too, had he endured, spending months at a time forging a path through the great and lightless forests of the Congo (a woods the size of France and Spain combined). Stanley's sometimes harsh discipline, his relentless drive, his extraordinary luck ("the Providence of God," he called it), and his stoicism in the face of physical pain and adversity made such feats possible.

Of course, he had been changed greatly by his travels. While he had looked like a lad of fifteen during the Civil War, Stanley was, at forty-four, somewhat prematurely aged; he resembled a man in his late fifties. His hair was gray, his pockmarked face, tightened by years of exposure to the tropical sun and an addiction to tobacco—thank you, Samuel Clemens—was lined with wrinkles, and his gray-blue eyes were often slightly yellow from jaundice. By then his formerly trusting countenance had been overtaken by a somewhat stern and solemn air, his gaze regarding the world with suspicion. Beset by episodic bouts of sudden illness, he passed through life awakening each morning without knowing if, by nightfall, he might be doubled over in agony from the torments of his chronic gastritis or, worse, find himself enduring the fevers, chills, and waking hallucinations of malaria, which by his own count had already struck him more than one hundred times. Never taking any imposition upon his health lightly, for he felt that he had a ticking bomb of blood- and bowel-feasting parasites inside him, he was most wary about cleanliness, rarely shaking hands without a glove; and when it came to food, he would only eat in the finest and most well-scrubbed establishments, for he knew that once he got sick, he would lose days, if not weeks or months, of his life.

But sometimes, too, when he was in the pink of health—as he was, fresh from a month's rest in the Swiss Alps, in 1885—there was about him a general robustness, his cheeks bright red, his eyes wildly alert, and his physique sturdy. Despite the man's diminutive stature—five feet five—to shake Stanley's hand with one's eyes closed was to feel the powerful grip of a blacksmith or a quarryman, more akin to stone than flesh. He had a broad chest, wide shoulders, and strong and well-muscled limbs. Which is to say there were two Stanleys—one, helpless as a baby, eased his gastric pains by chewing a mild opiate called "dream gum"; the other, according to the popular imagination of England, was a "modern Hercules."

By his own account—his newspaper dispatches and the pica-resque narratives that made up his books—he had trekked thousands of miles through the great forests and plateaus of central Africa and, along the way, had often wielded machetes and axes to cut a narrow trail through the dense jungle, foot by foot; he had scaled cliffs, hustled over great rock barriers, and had slipped or fallen so many times on rough terrain that his limbs were covered by scars. He wore a mustache whose waxed tips spiraled upward in the manner of a Bikanir sergeant, and his eyes burned with the intensity of a man who, having come close to death on many occasions, sometimes felt himself immortal. Whatever else could be said about him, for all his demureness around the ladies, he was known as a fearless man.

HIS CHARMS WERE MANY, BUT as a social creature he felt far more comfortably disposed around a cannibal chieftain of the Congo than around a woman, and less nervous facing a hail of poison-tipped spears in the African bush than facing Cupid's arrow. During the short periods of time when he was not actively adventuring as a journalist and explorer, what love affairs he had managed to pursue had come to nothing. His courtship of a girl from Greece, whom he encountered in a small village on the island of Syra, in 1868 or so, while he was a reporter at large for the *New York Herald* covering the Cretan rebellion, ended with rejection. His affections for a well-landed Welsh girl, Katie Gough-Roberts, whom he had been introduced to during one of his quick visits to Denbigh in the late 1860s, had also turned to air. His surest romance, however, had been with Alice Pike.

Just remembering the particulars of that affair would depress him, for while she, lively and flirtatious, had loved to parade about the city with him (the celebrity of the day) and had, in a sacred pledge, accepted Stanley's proposal of marriage in the back garden of her Fifth Avenue mansion some months later, during one of his visits back to America—once he had taken off to Zanzibar it was not long afterward that she began to go her own way. While Stanley had been off traveling through equatorial Africa, naming a mountain and then a lake after her—"the shimmering play of light, blue upon blue, upon its surface, glorious as her eyes"— and while the men of his expedition were hauling along, in four heavy sections, the components of a forty-foot wooden boat he had named the *Lady Alice* over all kinds of difficult terrain, she had been in the midst of enjoying a most carefree life as a social flower in New York. By the time Stanley, back in England after three malaria-ridden years of travel in the Congo, had gone to the *Herald*'s London office on Fleet Street to collect his mail, he found awaiting him a letter from Alice: In it he read that, during his absence, his beloved had married someone else.

"If you can forgive me, tell me so; if not, do please remain silent."

From then on, Stanley had acquired the air of a man who had been bitterly disappointed, his fame, to which he had never become accustomed, no assurance of earthly happiness.

⚜

TIME PASSED, HIS MEMORIES OF that false romance still rankling his soul. If he found himself thinking about the prospect of love, he simply preferred to put it from his mind. "If it should enter my life, it will not be forced," he would say. Gossiped about by women in whatever city he happened to meet them, whether in London or Paris or Brussels, he became known for his shyness and for blushing at a lady's first approach; and if he noticed the comeliness of her figure, his ears turned red, so fully did his blood rush; to look at a woman closely was in his mind the same as touching her. A kind of uncontrollable bodily fidgeting followed by many exaggerated arm gestures, as well as a habit of shifting from foot to foot, accompanied a change in the tone of his voice, his baritone rising into a series of squeaky utterances that some took for shouting, as if he thought the woman he was addressing had gone deaf. He was judged as being a sad and remote sort, and his conversations—or so it seemed to the ladies of his passing acquaintance—were somewhat pedantic and dull, reminiscent of a schoolmaster giving a lecture. For around such ladies, he seemed to believe that his own true personality—"that softer side that leads to nothing"—would be of no interest to them. On those occasions, Stanley, to his detriment, took refuge behind the fame and bluster of his life as an explorer.

The irony of it all was that he could be quite personable in private conversation with men, possessing as he did a wide range of interesting anecdotes culled from the many lives he had already lived. In one moment, if he cared to, he could, with some fondness, reminisce about his days riding along the Western plains as a dashing reporter for the *Missouri Democrat*, covering the Indian Wars of 1867 along with the likes of Wild Bill Hickok, icon of the American frontier. He could recall strolling through the bazaars of Cairo with the late General Gordon in the 1870s; or, if one happened to bring up the name of Mark Twain among persons ranging from Queen Victoria to the Prince of Wales, Stanley could speak at length about him, and happily so.

"I have always found him an interesting and amusing character," he was once quoted as saying.

Because Stanley had a photographic memory—after he read a page of a book, its contents remained with him always—he could be many things to many people. With classicists he could recite by heart passages from Ovid and Catullus in Latin, the bawdier aspects of the latter not escaping him; with literary friends he quoted Byron or Browning or Milton; with geographers he could discuss the intricacies of mapping; with navigators he deliberated the uses of the sextant and the difficulties of taking river "soundings." Even his medicinal knowledge was deep: He devoured the contents of various medical books so that he would know just what to do when physical disaster afflicted him or one of his native porters. He could draw quite well: Having won prizes for his renderings at St. Asaph's, he might have followed a career in art in a different life, and he was something of a musician, too, able—like Samuel Clemens—to play the piano and guitar serviceably enough. He was mildly proficient at other instruments as well: Often on his expeditions, he had soothed the gloomy hearts of his native porters and charmed the chieftains he encountered by playing, as he appeared before them in some smart cream-colored outfit, French, English, and Yankee melodies on an accordion (as long as the instrument was not worm-ridden or soaked through with the moisture of the jungle).

Nor did languages elude him. While his own native tongue, Welsh, had slipped with the years into the recesses of memory, he spoke Spanish and French and Arabic fluently, Italian and Portuguese well enough, and German, Russian, and Dutch passably. He could converse in various dialects of the Bantu language and efficiently speak Swahili (to the point that in later years, while under malarial delusions, he would write entire letters in Swahili, regardless of the recipients' knowledge of the language). Holding forth with much erudition about a wide range of subjects, from Ptolemy to the czar, he could be randy as well, having heard during dozens of voyages the filthiest jokes from the sailors—although he rarely pursued this latter talent, and never in mixed company. To preachers he could talk about the Bible; to astronomers he could talk about the charting of the stars. With such diverse folks he could go on and on and hold his own, but never with women.

That he had no lady companion or a family of his own was among the things he had come to regret during his life of adventure. In any event, he was always bound up with his writing. After each of his expeditions, he always had a massive book to produce and speaking tours that took him from city to city, so he had no sure home in which to lay down roots.

꧁

IT WAS ONLY IN THE previous year that he had moved into a many-roomed apartment on New Bond Street, where he lived with his manservant, Hoffman, and with Baruti, a former member of the Basoko tribe, whom Stanley had brought back from the Congo on his last expedition with the aim of "civilizing him" as a kind of social experiment. At heart, his hope was to eventually teach the unruly Baruti, whose name meant "gunpowder" in Bantu, how to read and write and feel comfortable in a gentleman's wardrobe so that he might one day become an upright and sturdy British citizen. To break him in, Stanley had Baruti dress in pantaloons, shirt, and jacket, plus stockings and stiff leather shoes, but as this was a mode of apparel for which Baruti, accustomed to a more unencumbered life in the Ituri Forest of the Congo, had little liking. He tended to shed his clothes, and it was not an uncommon sight for visitors to Stanley's flat to encounter Baruti stripped down to a mere loincloth and climbing over the front parlor's furniture, couches and sturdy club chairs toppling over in his wake. Stanley's nonchalance about the aforementioned behavior contributed to his bachelor's air of distraction.

In his employ was one female: Mrs. Holloway, his cook and housekeeper, who put up endlessly with his attitude that a gentleman should be picked up after. Despite all her efforts, his flat was a disaster of cast-off things. He had four hounds, rescued from the Battersea's home for unwanted animals, one of whom, a Scottie, had recently given birth to a litter of puppies. To the distress of Mrs. Holloway, these creatures peed upon and otherwise disfigured the fine Persian carpets that were laid out on the floors of every room, a state of affairs to which Stanley was indifferent—"As long as they do not eat up my maps, books, or important papers, let them do as they please. After all, it is not as if they are carrying malaria." Two parrots chortled happily away in cages that stood in his front parlor.

In general, Stanley could not have cared less about his cluttered, and sometimes chaotic, surroundings, for he had set aside for himself one orderly area for his work—on the floor below the parlor, under one of windows that looked out onto the traffic of New Bond Street, a humble and orderly space. With an Islamic prayer carpet spread out beneath him, Stanley, replicating the way he made his journal entries in a tent in the African jungle, would sit on a wicker stool about eight inches high and write on a small table just big enough to hold a quire and an ink pot. It was on that table that Stanley composed his lectures and wrote his most important correspondence, the brunt of which was sent to King Leopold, with whom he was in nearly daily contact.

As the king's handsomely paid consultant for Africa, Stanley spent a large part of his day answering Leopold's many queries about further enhancements to the organization of the Congo, wherein Stanley, combing over maps and his own journals, would make suggestions as to the possible locations of future river stations and where new roads might be cut through that territory to expedite the trade and fortification in the region.

RECEIVING MUCH MAIL DAILY, STANLEY also had notes of a personal nature (but no love letters) to attend to, mostly in polite response to the great number of dinner and luncheon invitations he received from various persons and clubs in London—high society always requesting his presence in those days. He got so many invitations that he accepted only a few, generally considering such outings—save for when he had the opportunity to voice his advocacy for greater British involvement in Africa—a waste of time.

Then, too, there was practical correspondence with several people of importance in his life—among them William

Mackinnon, head of the British India Steam Navigation Company, and Edwin Arnold, the poet and "old India hand" who was also the editor of the *Daily Telegraph*.

Though he saw all these gentlemen socially in London, usually at the premises of the Royal Geographical Society in Knightsbridge or at one or another of the famous clubs—the Carlton, the Travellers, the Oxford and Cambridge, the National Liberal Club, and the Garrick—the "public" Stanley, being somewhat formal and privately disposed, was wary about his assignations, for wherever he went, groups of admirers gathered about him. Wanting to be left alone, h felt resentful of the way strangers would press him to hold forth about his past journeys—"as if I were an intimate friend." On the other hand, if he entered a room and people did not turn and notice him instantly, he took it as a personal failing, as if he had been judged and rejected, his mood sinking low. Then he'd sit off in a corner, sulkily, until someone, recognizing him, introduced him around, as "Henry Stanley, the eminent explorer." And all would be well with the world again.

WHAT HE, BORN OUT OF wedlock, mainly wanted, beyond the admiration of others, was a modicum of affection from the public—or from anyone. What family he had on his mother's side were distant cousins and a few aunts and uncles, though he had several half siblings from his mother's marriage to Robert Jones.

Other persons who claimed to be family only came forward after he had achieved his greatest fame—supposed cousins and long-unheard-of brothers and sisters on his father's side who sent the most heartfelt notes, bursting with pride over the Rowlands line, and all, in the end, asking him for money. He sometimes received letters from England and America claiming that such and such a person, whom Stanley had never heard of before, was a relation. One missive, from a woman in Colorado, where Stanley had once roamed as a frontier reporter, went so far to say that she had borne his child and was now ready to take her place by his side (an impossibility, unless it was an instance of what the Catholics call immaculate conception, as Stanley wrote her). Another letter came from a certain Joanna Eastaway, who claimed to be his mother:

> *My dear William Henry [sic]—*
>   *How I've missed and longed for you all these years...*
> *Why it is that I have not be in touch with you is owed to*
> *"curious circumstances." Many years before, I was a wanton*
> *and innocent young lady, working in London, where through*
> *grave necessity I, having fallen under the spell of hunger, made*
> *arrangements with a certain high lord; without spelling out*
> *the obvious I must tell you that scandal and threats to my*
> *livelihood were pressed upon me, and so with my heart broken*
> *I had to convey you, darling infant that you were, into the*
> *hands of strangers—the Parry family, who claimed you as*
> *their own. That you have suffered all these years, without a*
> *mum, weighs heavily upon me, but rest assured I am here to*
> *give you all my love—to hold you is my dream.*

Sometimes gifts arrived at his flat—cakes, articles of hand-stitched clothing, and books, for which he always remained grateful. From several misguided ladies there arrived notes that amounted to marriage proposals: "To have the great Stanley as the father of my child would be all," one said. Some ladies sent a photograph, and, in one instance, he received a pair of perfume-doused bloomers. Most correspondents just asked for his autograph. But it was the children he most enjoyed answering, this grave and serious-minded explorer not only writing back but often embellishing his notes with some outlandish details about Africa, as if to enchant them:

> *My dear little Tom of Cheshire,*
>   *I very much appreciated the note that you took the time*
> *to compose for me: Enclosed you will find a photograph of*
> *me, so pleased was I by the drawing of you that you sent me.*
> *Well done! I imagine you must be a very bright boy, having*

*learned to write at five, you say. That alone tells me—and
say this to your lucky parents—that you will always do well
in this life. My cap is off to you, young Tom. As for your
question—"What are the animals of Africa like?"—I will say
this, and I only tell you the truth. In Africa, there is a breed
of antelopes who fly; and of the flying creatures there are birds
who sing like angels, and there are many very wise and kindly
elephants afoot, some over a thousand years old, but youthful
in their ways, and these elephants, loving children, will lift
them with their trunks onto their backs and take them along
on exciting adventures. It is a place that you should certainly
see, when it is all the more peaceful and its bad people driven
away. This, I assure you, will happen one day.*

With my sincerest best wishes,
Your friend, Stanley

He was no less willing to play the kindly uncle for the children
he met in the homes of friends or out on their country estates. He
took great pains to share with them the amusing things he had seen
during his travels, delighting them with his tales of the pygmies of
the Ituri Forest. Imitating many an animal's growl and utterances,
he was not above getting on his hands and knees to demonstrate
how a lion walked or emulate an elephant's lumbering gait.

Still, as with most things regarding his life, Stanley had
another side, for the man who could be so playful with children
had thought nothing about putting his beloved rifle bearer, Kalulu, in neck and ankle chains during their last expedition together.
And he was quick with a lash, quick to administer proper justice
to those he considered his enemies.

꧁

IN THOSE DAYS, BEFORE HIS eventual fall from public esteem,
he was a heroic figure to the masses, his popularity such that
his image appeared on coffee mugs, on candy boxes, on cigar

wrappers, tea tins, and plates. Even on toys: There were Stanley cork-shooting rifles and tops, a children's marble maze game entitled the Stanley Souvenir, even lead figure sets from Germany with names like Stanley on Safari and Stanley in Darkest Africa. Plays were mounted about his exploits, and for more than a decade, English vaudeville comedians had spun endless skits from his defining moment in Ujiji, the one when he had uttered the words "Dr. Livingstone, I presume?" (That phrase was so much a part of collective English consciousness that Stanley was often greeted, much to his irritation, the same way.) His face appeared in cartoons in magazines like *Punch* and in newspaper advertisements. Songs were written about him: "The Stanley March," "The Stanley Polka," and "The Source of the Nile Waltz" among them.

☀

"DO YOU NOT KNOW YET that you are furiously famous for your exploits?" said Edwin Arnold, editor of the *Daily Telegraph*, one day as he encountered Stanley roaming through Regent's Park with a melancholy mien. Knowing only his bachelor's solitude, Stanley answered him in this way: "I seem to notice it sometimes, but it is not anything I give weight to: So what if you are temporarily 'someone' in the eyes of others? What does that matter if you are never invited openly into someone's home as a true friend, not as an attraction? Fond as I am of such folks, as much as they seem to love me in one moment, they are shortly gone."

"Ah," said Arnold. "If you do feel this way, than something must be done about it."

Doffing their caps, they parted.

A FEW DAYS LATER, IN June of 1885, a note from Arnold, announcing that he was to give a reading from a new book of verses at the Athenaeum Club, arrived at Stanley's flat: "Do come, old boy. I think you will much enjoy my new verses, and if I am not mistaken, I believe there will be someone there, a quite gracious lady, whom I would like you to meet."

At first, he made nothing of the invitation and spent the morning attending to the voluminous correspondence that arrived daily, but Arnold had aroused his curiosity, and eventually, as the day unfolded, Stanley found himself standing before his bedroom mirror in a Harris tweed suit, trimming his mustache and giving his hair a good brushing

"I should be back by seven or so," he said to Hoffman.

THE ATHENAEUM CLUB WAS SITUATED in an old neoclassical building at the intersection of Pall Mall and Waterloo Place, the Grecian-style facade of this palatial edifice graced by a statue of Minerva. It was the kind of cultural organization that Stanley secretly admired but felt excluded from, as, in those days, despite his many admirable accomplishments, he was still looked down upon by the lofty sages of the Victorian establishment as a "penny-a-liner" journalist who had been lucky as an explorer.

Just before five in the evening, Stanley entered its premises.

"And this lady, you mentioned, Arnold, is she here yet?" he asked the poet in the hallway outside the main salon.

"Not quite yet, my dear Stanley," Arnold told him. "But once you are inside, look for the most beautiful woman who comes into the room; I am certain it will be she."

And so it was that Stanley entered the salon—its frieze, copied from the Parthenon, looming above him—and took a seat toward the front, among an audience of some forty other persons. A few people recognized him, and for a time he signed their programs; but then, as Arnold had assumed, just before the poet took to the podium, a majestic-seeming creature of the female sex came into the salon. Tall and buxom, and with a beaming smile and eyes that were droop-lidded but soulful, and with her auburn hair done up with stylishly frizzled bangs after the fashion of the empress Eugenie of France, she brought into Stanley's mind a great excitement:

This lady, who also took a seat near the front, was one Dorothy Tennant, Stanley would learn.

That afternoon, Arnold, with his pallid face and long white beard reaching below his collars, read from his most recent volume, *The Light of Asia*, which told the story of the great Buddha.

Once the recitation of those verses ended, with Buddha achieving serene self-knowledge, Miss Tennant had been among the first to approach Arnold at the rostrum. They knew each other well: In his capacity as an editor of the *Daily Telegraph* he had sometimes retained her services as an illustrator. Her drawings graced the pages of his newspaper, and he had been a frequent guest in her home, where he often recited portions of verses in progress before gatherings of her dinnertime guests. As Stanley saw her standing by Arnold's side, it gave him pause—and he thought to wait until she had left, as they seemed to be engaged in a spirited conversation about reincarnation. But then Arnold himself, with his massive head and savant's beard, called Stanley over, and it was then that he made the introduction.

"This enchantment, my dear friend," he said to Stanley," is one of the finest illustrators and greatest ladies in London, Miss Dorothy Tennant." Then: "And this gentleman, Miss Tennant, is the one and only Henry Stanley."

She wore a velvet French skirt, a floral blouse, a petticoat that seemed a size too small, and a pearl necklace that hung from her collar. About her wrists jangled several bracelets set with odd stones, in the Bohemian mode; on her long and delicate hands were a pair of white gloves. Some three inches taller than the explorer, in her boots of soft black leather, with their two-inch heels, she seemed to tower over him.

"So you are he!" she said. "I cannot begin to tell you the extent of my curiosity about you." Then: "I should let you know that I have been your admirer for the longest time, since the days you found Livingstone. I have always believed your stories to be true. In fact, Mr. Stanley, your exoneration was of such interest to me that I was among the crowd attending that meeting of the British

Association at Brighton in 1872, when the Royal Geographical Society recanted their criticisms and awarded you the medal you justly deserved."

"Well, now," he said, his face reddening. "I feel somewhat honored, but barely deserving to hear such words."

And yes, years later, among the details she would remember about that event in Brighton—where Stanley, once criticized as a fraud and then honored by the Royal Geographical Society, took the stage to make, with much anger and vindictiveness, the speech she would describe as "noble and convincing"—was that in the audience that day was the American writer Samuel Clemens, whom she saw strolling down the aisle and who had traveled from London to see his friend.

AS ARNOLD HAD GONE OFF to meet with his admirers, and tea and crumpets were served for the attendees in one of the club rooms, Stanley, off in a corner with Dorothy Tennant, could only summon up some small talk about his recent visit with King Leopold at his palace at Ostend. But he could have spoken about his shoes, for everything he said seemed to fascinate her. She had read all his books, from his first accounts about finding Dr. Livingstone onward, and she told Stanley that she was looking forward to finishing his latest, the massive two-volume *The Congo and the Founding of Its Free State*, about his most recent expedition.

"Your books have been by my bedside each night," she said. "The many hours I have already passed in your company have made me think that I already know you somewhat."

Such flattery, however, he regarded with suspicion, having the notion that certain members of the aristocracy, when finished with their collecting of country estates, finery, jewelry, and paintings, tended to collect people: Why should this lady, attractive and sincere as she might seem, be any different?

Altogether, for Stanley, it had been a worthwhile encounter, but he made nothing more of it. In parting, they exchanged calling cards, Miss Tennant telling Stanley that they would surely see each other again, that shortly he would receive an invitation to dine at her home on Richmond Terrace.

※

THAT NIGHT, AS HE SAT up in the bedroom of his New Bond Street flat, with a few of the Scotties he adopted from the Battersea home for animals dozing on one of the carpets by his bedside, his heart beat rapidly. He decided to write a note to his friend William Mackinnon to inquire if he had any insights about Dorothy Tennant—"Is she worth the trouble of knowing? Is she serious or really just another frivolous person?" he asked, but while jotting this missive down, by the light of a gas lamp, he decided that such a query was premature. What did he know of women, anyway? He recalled that the furthest he had advanced by way of expressions of affection was a few kisses in the garden behind Alice Pike's Fifth Avenue mansion; well, truthfully, it was she who did the kissing, her soft and moist lips pressing against his neck, his cheek, his ears, and then with the warm bloom of her perfume and hair enveloping him, she had kissed his lips—her tongue, like some small creature, entering his mouth with force.

His thoughts drifted again, women and their physical natures confounding him: Why was it that he thought of himself sitting in his tent in the Congo one early evening during his last expedition? As he was writing in his journal, a young Negress, naked save for a loincloth, entered—the "gift" of the slave trader Tippu Tib, with whom Stanley had had dealings. Why was it that he hardly acknowledged her when she knelt down near him and, with a vacant but somewhat willing expression upon her face, lay back on a mat, lifted her loincloth, spread apart her legs, and awaited him? Why was it that he did not send her away but allowed her to lie there while he made some notes, quickly glancing at her and thinking, "But my God, what a comely and deliciously shaped woman"? Only for a moment did he get carried away and, unable to prevent himself, pass the palm of his hand all along her body.

But even then when he was feeling a physical ardency, he refused to give in and finally sent her happily away. "Please tell your master that I am thankful."

It was the kind of thing that happened to him from time to time: In those wilds, beautiful and nubile women passed from man to man in the way that one would give a book to a friend in England. Although he would always abstain, in such a setting it was not easy. Death traveled with his expeditions, and his native porters, having brought along their wives, would punctuate the loon-cry-filled night with the savage noises of fornications carried out as if there would be no tomorrow. In the end, knowing that with little effort he could have a most beautiful concubine to do with as he pleased, he considered his abstinence a matter of moral fortitude, reading the Bible whenever such temptations came to him.

* * *

TRUE TO HER WORD, A few days afterward, as Stanley sat before his writing desk, a summons to her home for a formal dinner arrived at his residence by courier. At first he thought to politely turn her down, as he did with so many other invitations, but his memory of Miss Tennant's warmth—and forwardness—had given him pause; and so, to test the waters of a potential courtship, he wrote a note of acceptance.

* * *

THOUGH HER FATHER HAD BEEN dead for many years, Dorothy believed that he was ever-present in her life, and nightly she addressed him in her diary.

> *Dear Father,*
> *I am aflutter with anticipation over the dinner party*
> *Mother and I have planned. We have invited, among many*

interesting individuals, no less a figure than the Prime Minis-
ter Gladstone himself, a very brave thing as far as Mother and
I are concerned, particularly given the controversy about the
death of General Gordon back in January: But I feel astonished
to say that we have succeeded, for Gladstone has consented
to come. That is all very well, but now I am wondering if I
was wise in also inviting another most charming man, Henry
Stanley, the explorer, who is known to dislike the prime minis-
ter. Oh, dear God, help me, for I wonder if in my eagerness to
please and impress Mr. Stanley I have made a mistake in judg-
ment. What will I do should these two formidable men meet
and not get along? Yet I am hoping for good things to come of
it anyway. Goodnight, my darling.

The Evening Saved by Samuel Clemens

BY THE EVENING OF JUNE 24, in addition to Stanley, the guest
list, as organized by Dorothy's mother, Gertrude, a longtime
doyenne of London social life, had, to Stanley's eventual dismay,
grown to include Prime Minister William Gladstone, a man Stanley considered a monomaniac, and his cabinet colleague Joseph
Chamberlain, two of the most important and powerful politicians
in England, then electioneering for their next terms. Stanley and
Gladstone disliked each other. Of a liberal cast of mind, the prime
minister held the opinion that Stanley, having done much more
harm than good in Africa, was a ruthless and dangerous fool, and
he had often said so in public. And for his part, Stanley, aside
from being aware of Gladstone's unkind opinion of him, thought
him the worst kind of leader, as he had felt greatly incensed and
grieved over the unnecessary loss of his friend General Gordon,
the governor of the Sudan, who died some six months before at
Khartoum, where he had been besieged by an army of Islamic
fanatics and beheaded. This Stanley blamed on Gladstone's failure
to send in the British army to relieve Gordon in a timely fashion.

Which is to say that when Stanley first entered into the grand parlor of the Tennant mansion, on Richmond Terrace, where cocktails and Champagne were being served by servants in livery, he was not in the best of moods, and he was not looking forward to encountering the prime minister. Neither he nor Gladstone spoke to one another, even though at one point during cocktails they were standing nearly back-to-back. Gladstone, tall, aloof, and imperious in bearing, would not even allow Stanley into his sight, and when he happened to turn his stately and very large, high-browed head in Stanley's direction, the detachment of the prime minister's expression struck Stanley as being typical of the kind of upper-class haughtiness that he, since boyhood, had always strongly despised. And though he had made no overtures to meet the great politician, refusing to give ground and preferring to make conversation with the shipping magnate William Mackinnon, he considered the prime minister's behavior a slight.

But all these feelings gave way when Dorothy Tennant, lovely in a silken French dress, joined the gathering. In that instant, as she moved across the crowded room, his annoyance with Gladstone dissipated and his eyes lit warmly at the sight of her, as she had warmed at the sight of him. Her pleasure at seeing Stanley was so evident that her mother, Gertrude, a former beauty and a society snob down to her deepest molecule—the kind of older woman who would fuss over the most handsome men in the room—puzzled over her daughter's interest in that "long-winded little man." Upon meeting him Gertrude had not been charmed at all by Stanley or particularly impressed by the legend surrounding his exploits. She thought he looked like a bank clerk and had only reluctantly included Stanley on the invitation list because of his fame and her daughter's insistence. Ascribing Dorothy's interest in Stanley to the eccentricity of her artistic spirit, and perhaps because of some vague similarity in appearance between Stanley and her late husband, Charles, whose painted, gold-leaf-framed visage occupied a prominent place in the room. Gertrude, a widow of some twelve years, put Stanley's presence at the dinner in the same category as certain of Dorothy's other seemingly capricious, whim-driven acts.

Still careless and carefree at thirty, Gertrude's "little girl" remained a kind of flighty bohemian aesthete, one for whom, Gertrude hoped, Stanley was nothing more than another street urchin to be painted and cared for—albeit one of great reputation and quite grown up, but still a "common" element brought home and only valuable as an item of fleeting interest.

Despite her mother's opinions, Dorothy fawned over him. For all the fearlessness that surrounded his legend, she found Stanley a man of vulnerability and, at heart, quite lonely-seeming. Fiercely intelligent, he seemed to know much about the world in all its details (how enchanted would she be to tell him about the little street urchins she loved to paint and to show him her portraits of the beautiful Lady Ashburton, a dear friend whom she had depicted as a living Venus, and of Benoit-Constant Coquelin, the famous French actor, for whom the play *Cyrano de Bergerac* would later be written). No matter that he was not very tall; he was formidable all the same, and his presence in a room was felt by everyone around him. And there was something else: She liked the difference in their ages, drew comfort from it, as in many ways Stanley, with his hair gray and aged before his time because of his expeditions and the many illnesses attending them, reminded Miss Tennant of her late father, a landed Welshman and former member of Parliament whose passing she had never gotten over. "How wonderfully smart you look tonight, Mr. Stanley," she said upon seeing him. "I hope you are well—you certainly look so." Then: "Surely you have made the acquaintance of Prime Minister Gladstone?"

"As he has been busily talking, I did not wish to disturb him."

"Well, then, if you have not made his acquaintance, you should know that you will be sitting across from him at dinner."

"I cannot wait for that honor."

Later, with Dorothy's arm hooked into his, Stanley made his way out of the parlor into the dining room: There, two long tables, covered by French lace tablecloths and cluttered with plates, tulip-stemmed glasses, and bouquets in silver vases, glowed white under two hanging gaslight chandeliers. Some thirty or so guests were accommodated.

Once the guests were seated, Gertrude addressed the gathering, her "dear exalted company of London's luminaries." Reciting the names of each, she gave special mention to a few, among them the dashing painter James McNeill Whistler, the Right Reverend Hughes, vicar of St. Paul's, then Stanley himself.

"But as illustrious as these guests are, there is none more notable among us than our prime minister, William Gladstone, who has honored us with his attendance."

As the elderly Gladstone, with his fifty years of public service showing in the many lines on his gaunt and grave face, stood up, bowing, so did the participants of the dinner, clapping and clinking their glasses with their utensils in his honor. Gloomily contemplating his hands, Stanley had been one of the last to get out of his chair. But as he did, Gladstone noticed it, giving Stanley a disdainful sidelong glance; then, asking the gathering to sit, he gave a short speech, in which, among other subjects, he addressed the necessity of establishing an Irish Free State and matters of commerce. Of Africa and his failure to relieve general Gordon at Khartoum some months before, a great national tragedy, he made no mention.

Then, with the disharmony between Stanley and Gladstone evident, the dinner proceeded. Soup, salad, roasted goose; legs of lamb, roast beef, and Brussels sprouts; string beans and boiled potatoes.

During this meal, Gladstone, eating little, did not so much as look over at Stanley. And Stanley, normally a voracious eater, hardly touched his plate, his stomach in knots. Worse was the continued silence between them. As much as Dorothy attempted to provoke a lively conversation, Gladstone remained rather uncommunicative, answering most queries with one- or two-word responses. ("And how is your campaign proceeding, sir?" "Well enough.")

But then Dorothy asked Mr. Stanley if he might not mind making some remarks about his recent expedition, and though Stanley felt somewhat reluctant to do so, he addressed the gathering, somewhat timidly at first. Then, taking a deep breath and sipping from a glass of brandy, he continued:

"Even now, great numbers of managers and officers of the African Association are pouring into that region, their only goal the betterment of its inhabitants. Regardless of what some wayward missionary reports—in singling out a few clashes between natives and Europeans—have unfairly cited as evidence of cruel treatment and a preexisting enmity between native and civilizer, the long view must be taken that it is all for the good of African and European alike.

"Ladies and gentlemen, I have no reservations about this enterprise. Not only will those peoples benefit from our presence and the advancements of what our technology and medical knowledge can give them, but in the course of such advances, the Arab slavers will also be stamped out, and along the way, as I have advocated in the region of Uganda, the light of Christianity will flourish there as well. Yet even as I say this, I can only urge those in positions of power in England to carefully consider our own greater involvement there: Why we have not sought after the riches that are awaiting us by way of abundant natural resources and the promise of trade is beyond my grasp to understand. I may have an affiliation with Leopold's International African Association, but as my heart and loyalties are British, I believe that what is most missing from that scheme is England itself."

Wishing to impress Miss Tennant, he spoke for another twenty minutes along those lines, to the point that she had regretted asking him to speak. But then, abruptly, looking about the room and somewhat annoyed by the fact that, during his remarks, Gladstone had passed the time by moving a soup spoon from side to side, Stanley decided to make a toast.

"However, I am pleased to be here this evening to be saying a few words; indeed, there are some who have not been so lucky. A year ago, when in my dealings with the association, its president, King Leopold, asked me which man I would choose to govern such a region as the Congo, the name that came instantly to mind was that of a very fine chap, a capable and pious gentleman whose absolute opposition to the slavers and whose strong personal faith and bravery I held in the highest regard: I am speaking of the late General Gordon. And so I say"—and he hoisted a glass of wine—"here's to the great General Gordon."

The gathering then followed suit.

As Stanley sat back down, Gladstone's stony gaze was upon him, and whereas Gladstone had been merely condescending with Stanley before, he now glared at Stanley with pure contempt. It was then that Miss Tennant steered the conversation toward literature, which, in her opinion, most people of refinement would find worthwhile to discuss—a neutral zone. In this she was correct, for she had finally engaged Gladstone's interest.

A conservative in his tastes, if not in his politics, and religiously inclined—as religious as Stanley—he spoke tenderly about the books of Saint Augustine, which he had hoped to one day translate himself; then of Horace and Ovid. When it came to English authors, he championed Tennyson and Milton, among others, whose writings, in his opinion, spoke well for the legacy of civilized England. ("I almost liked him for that," Stanley would later write.) Stanley, for his part, held forth on the writers whom he most esteemed. In his opinion, Gibbon and Samuel Butler were remarkable enough, but in the realm of invention, Charles Dickens, so Stanley assessed, still remained the greatest author to come out of England, only bettered perhaps by the Shakespeare of *Hamlet*. Books such as *Nicholas Nickleby* and *David Copperfield* having always deeply moved him.

"Reading Dickens," he said that night, while looking over at the apprehensive Dorothy, "I have often thought David Copperfield was very much like me when I was a boy."

"Dickens was one of Providence's gifts to England, a very prolific and humane writer," Gladstone declared. And he was kind enough to concede that he sensed Dickens's influence on Stanley's prose style: "Your many exclamations and colorful characterizations of people, rather broadly, in fact, do seem reminiscent of Charles's work," he said. "You certainly know how to keep your books moving along at a fast clip."

"I work very hard at what I do, sir," Stanley answered, his tensely drawn face turning red. "And I am decisive in what I do."

With servants pouring liquors, Dorothy Tennant, knowing something of Stanley's background, then asked, "And whom, Mr. Stanley, do you count among the better American authors?"

"A difficult question to answer, Miss Tennant: I have also very much liked the writings of Benjamin Franklin; his autobiography is remarkable. Of current authors, Emerson comes to mind, and William Dean Howells. But I do have a particular favorite—a writer, who, in my opinion, soars over his contemporaries. In truth I am perhaps biased, for he is a longtime acquaintance. An author who is as well known in England as anyone."

"And who is this?"

"Samuel Clemens."

"Mark Twain?"

"Yes, Miss Tennant, Mark Twain."

"And what is it that you like especially about his work?"

"Well, now," said Stanley. "He has a great capacity to recall the minutest details; a knack for capricious language, and, I should say, he is one of the few writers besides Dickens who makes me laugh out loud. Though artful design is not his forte, he's jolly in his choice of language and writes about many remarkable things, with a very sharp journalist's eye. His *Life on the Mississippi* is one of the finest books that I have read about that region in America. As one who has traveled that river in my youth, I know what I am speaking of. It is no easy thing to write as Clemens does." Then: "Even something like his juvenile's novel *The Adventures of Tom Sawyer* has impressed me; his evocation of childhood, in a small town along the Mississippi River, as simply as it is written…it leaves me thinking about the glory and joy of childhoods in general, rare as they may be in some cases. I thought of Wales when I read it: I thought about the farmers I knew.... I can't exactly describe my feelings about it, but for all my experience in this world, I have been touched by that book and others he has written."

Then, as he faltered for words, and as Gladstone looked at his vest-pocket watch, Stanley added, "His books have the warmth of life. A warmth that moves me deeply."

"Would you not say, then, Mr. Stanley," the prime minister asked, "that he is the closest thing the Americans have to a Charles Dickens?"

"I would."

"Ah—so I see that we've finally agreed on something," the prime minister answered. "I have met this Mark Twain on several occasions and have found him a congenial sort. Were it that all writers could be so affably disposed."

With the evening thus salvaged from disaster by literature, Stanley was making his way out from the dining room when Miss Tennant followed him to the door. After thanking him for coming, she said, "Mr. Stanley, if you do not already know, I am a portrait painter."

"I know that."

"And as such, I would be very honored—and delighted—if you would come into my home again to sit for me as a subject. Can you?"

"Well, Miss Tennant, as much as I am touched, my schedule is very full. Can it not be done with some photographs? I can have several delivered to you, if you like."

"No," she said. "I would prefer that you sit for me."

Then, as she smiled in a lovely way: "Oh, please, Mr. Stanley, whatever you are doing, surely you will have a free afternoon. Please say that you will."

This he agreed to eventually do—and that is how things began between them.

❊

THERE CAME THE DAY IN early July when Stanley found himself lingering for some time before the entranceway of the Tennant mansion, a sign beside the door saying: visitors welcomed here. Beforehand, he had walked up and down the streets of Whitehall for half an hour, debating with himself as to whether he should or shouldn't finally keep his assignation with Miss Tennant, and he had nearly changed his mind when Dorothy, seeing him from her front window, opened the door and cheerfully called him in. Over her dress was tied a painter's smock; her hair was up, her fingers smudged with paint, as she was still in the midst of a session with some of her urchin children.

"Do come in—and forgive my appearance, Mr. Stanley. Come now, into my studio." And so it was that she led Stanley down a long hallway, with which he would become well familiar, to a room at the far end of the house on the first floor, which she had nicknamed the birdcage and where her delightful subjects, the little street children of London, fluttered about, lively and as happy as sparrows. With some trepidation—"I do not intend to disturb your labors; I can come back another day," he told her—he followed her into the studio. In it were numerous cabinets, barrels of ragged clothes, a bucket of soot, and all kinds of props: a baby carriage, a cradle, a milk churn, baskets, a large mirror, a wooden rocking horse, and two very small chairs. Two children, a boy and girl, costumed as common urchins in rags, were attempting to play her upright piano, their soot-covered hands banging wildly at its keys; a third child, a boy, pounded at a snare drum; another hit a spoon on a triangle. This little orchestra played to their heart's content, making a cacophonous racket, which, however, did not bother Miss Tennant in the slightest. Leading Stanley to her easel, on which sat one of her "urchin paintings" in progress, she smiled serenely and said, "Come and look, Mr. Stanley. What do you think?"

On a small canvas, was a nicely detailed rendering of a chimney sweep playing with his friends; the studio fireplace before which her subjects posed had turned into a dingy alley and brick wall somewhere in London.

"Most interesting," Stanley said. "Most charming."

Stanley, with his serious manner, brought the children's revelry to an abrupt halt: The leader of this small gang, putting down his drumstick, asked Miss Tennant, "Are we done now, ma'am?"

"Yes, you can go for today," she told him, placing sixpence into his palm. "But I will see you and your friends tomorrow, yes?"

Once the children had gone, escorted by a butler out the door, Miss Tennant, tending to several brushes with turpentine, begged Stanley's forgiveness for her state of dress, adding: "But I did want you to see me as I often am."

Then she proceeded to show him the numerous sketches she had made of her "beloved ragamuffins," mostly charcoal and pencil drawings that she kept in a large portfolio: a little girl watching her baby brother in a cradle; a boy standing outside a café window holding a violin and bow in hand, as if wishing he had enough money for a meal. One drawing after the other, depicting the life of poor London waifs.

"I get my ideas for these scenes from my ramblings around the city. I find some of my children around St. Paul's, or down by the embankments of the Thames. You will notice that poor though they may be, each child is truly happy."

Stanley, who had spent nine years in a workhouse with such poor children and who did not remember them as happy, asked, "And how so?"

"Happy in that they are children, unspoiled by things. You see, I believe that all children, regardless of their circumstances, are more contented than what most people are led to believe— that even an impoverished childhood holds out many delights and joys. The way they are depicted in our newspapers—as thin, pale, and sickly guttersnipes with sunken eyes and hopeless spirits— goes against everything I have observed of them, living, as all children cannot help but do, in the utter bliss and sunshine of those precious years."

"If you ask me, that's a matter of opinion, Miss Tennant." Then: "But have you not wanted children of your own?"

"Oh, sir, I have," she told him. "But I have somehow managed without them." Then: "Is it so that you genuinely like these drawings?"

"Yes."

"Good. Then I hope you will be happy with the portrait I will make of you."

"Are we to begin today?"

"If you would like. But first, let us have some lunch."

⁂

COMING TO HER STUDIO TO pose for her, he got to know her slightly then. Her way of thinking, mostly capricious, seemed intent upon avoiding the obvious; a kind of contrary manner of putting things was her method, or a natural irony. She was very pleasant company, he thought; she let him smoke to his heart's content and seemed such a gentle kind of lady that naturally his innermost thoughts poured forth. The first two times he sat for her, he mainly talked about Africa, but then, by and by, he started to tell her more about his past, a line he rarely crossed with strangers.

"AS I SAID, MISS TENNANT, my father died when I was three, but I know he was a butcher because I have some very early recollection of being laid face-up on a counter of his shop and seeing all these swine heads staring down at me, and I can remember a smell of clotted blood that was most strong, enough to seem thick as mud in my nostrils. At that tender age I was left no better off than an orphan. As my own mother, one Betsy Parry, was otherwise occupied in London, struggling to earn a living, I was given over to the guardianship of my maternal grandfather, Moses

Parry. Now, Miss Tennant, with him you would have a proper subject to paint. He was a farmer, a huge man with enormous hands, capable of easily lifting a heavy stone off the ground, of plowing a field without a mule. He lived in a whitewashed cottage near Denbigh Castle, at the center of town: I can remember that behind the cottage, at the far end of a long garden, stood a shed in which the old man slaughtered calves and split their carcasses in two before taking them to market. This I had often watched him doing; he showed me the slaughter so that I would know where the meat we ate came from. It is a smell, of blood drying on the ground, that remains with me to this day. Now, though he was a gruffly tempered and blunt fellow, he had a caring side to him, and he would sit me down on his lap and teach me how to write the letters of the alphabet on a board of slate. And he'd take me to a Wesleyan church each Sunday so that I might know something about piety, an important thing.

"It was my grandfather who first taught me about the Bible, as he had wanted me to possess some moral sense of things. He taught me discipline with regular beatings, so that I would learn obedience. But he could be tender, too. He always told me that I did not need a mother. 'Even without one, you shall yet become a man,' he'd say. Has it turned out to be the truth? That I cannot say, but it was through him, Miss Tennant, that I felt the first shock of death, for I was watching him tending to some work in a field one morning when, with a gasp, he clutched his chest and, taking three agitated breaths, fell to the ground, dead.

"He had two sons who looked after me for a time, but as they wanted to get married and needed the run of the cottage to themselves, they boarded me out for the price of a half a crown a week to an elderly couple who lived on the other side of the castle. My new guardian's name was Richard Price; his was a pocked and grave face, and his eyes were watery and teeth quite broken; but he made a livelihood tending to the village green. He was also the sexton of Whitchurch and, therefore, like my grandfather, of a very religious proclivity. His wife was a fat old woman who cooked pease pudding each night, which I disliked but was forced to eat because that half a crown did not provide for much more. They had a daughter, Sarah, and it was she who taught me about the devil, who—and I have since learned this to be one of the truths of life—fights with God for dominion over the world... she loved to frighten me with stories about Satan and the ways he had to trick men into sinning... and about witches and evil spirits, too: and she spoke of ghosts, the disembodied spirits of man.

"She so filled my head with such stories that I trembled each night when it got dark. I trembled whenever I was sent out of the house to fetch water from a well; trembled when I had to enter into the castle-wall shadows. Such tales afflicted me with bad dreams. I used to believe that my grandfather's ghost would soon be coming after me, for I was not always so well behaved when he was alive and had wished him dead whenever he beat me. The story of Lazarus, raised by Jesus from the dead, troubled me as well, and I would cry out night after night, waking everyone in that household, thinking that Lazarus had come to visit me.

"Then I take it you believe in ghosts?"

"Of the mental kind, yes. Children, especially, see so many things that we cannot; in fact, I did see a ghost, not in a dream but in actuality, on one of those nights when I went to fetch some water. As I approached the well, I saw a very great shadow moving out from behind some trees: It was no man, just the shadow of a man, stretching high over the castle walls. Well, I instantly ran back into the house, leaving my bucket behind, and from that time on I slept ever more restlessly and cried out from ever more frightening dreams.

"And so, Miss Tennant, as I disturbed their peace at night, and as they found me a difficult sort of child, they demanded more money from my uncles for their troubles. But this extra my uncles refused to pay, nor would they take me back. Shortly came the day when the sexton told me that I would be making a journey; a wagon, driven by his eldest boy, was to take me to the town of Ffynnon Beuno, where I was to be boarded with another of their relatives, a certain Aunt Mary. Being so young and trusting of others, I had no inkling of what awaited me—a very different life from the one I had known."

Then: "But am I boring you, Miss Tennant, with this flight of words? If I do, I apologize, but as you stand behind your canvas making drawings of me—your eyes so kindly—I feel no hesitation in telling you such things."

"Mr. Stanley, what things I can learn of you most interest me: Please do go on."

"Well, then, it was a Saturday in 1847—a Saturday of dreary Welsh weather, the sky gray and air as damp and cold as the sea. With my few possessions stashed in a sack, I rode alongside the sexton's son, who—and here, Miss Tennant, came another instance of hard learning, this time about man's capacity for deception—had allayed my anxieties with stories of how pleasant my life with Aunt Mary would be, saying that hers was a beautiful house with a big garden that bloomed sweet in the spring. With the horse clopping slowly along, traveling the longest five miles of my life, he told me that Mary, like the mother of Jesus herself, loved little boys very much, and that she, having no sons of her own, had always wished for one and had all kinds of delicious cakes and sweets waiting for me to eat. In a lovely voice she'd sing me to sleep with Welsh lullabies at night, and he said no ghosts would enter her house to disturb me. But you see, Miss Tennant, when that carriage came to its destination, there was no pretty house awaiting me, and no Aunt Mary; no, before me, in all its stolid glory, stood an immense stone building, which looked something like a prison, with barred windows all around it. As we waited before its gated entrance, the sexton's son told me that this was only a temporary stop to give our horse some rest, but he had gotten out and clanged a bell by its door. Two clangs of a bell I heard, then footsteps sounding on some paving stones from inside. Shortly a gloomy man stood at the entranceway and had a few words with the sexton's son; with that he lifted me out of the carriage, and as I had started to cry, fearing the worst, because I did not trust the gloomy man's face, he told me, 'Now, wait inside, and Aunt Mary will come to fetch you soon enough.'

"That was the last I saw him; and as there had never been any such person as Aunt Mary, I was taken inside, the gloomy keeper leading me into the inner courtyard of that place, which to my young eyes seemed like bedlam, for I could see, trembling and crying as I was, so many hopeless sorts—elderly paupers who seemed to have no purpose but to walk in circles around the courtyard, talking to themselves; and I saw an idiot speaking to a wall and a bent-over old woman crying in a corner; and when I looked up at the windows of the surrounding buildings, I could see the sad faces of little children, much like your urchins, peering down at me, and I wanted to run away. But this was not to be, Miss Tennant, for on that day I had been delivered into the care of the Victorian state. My new home went by the name of St. Asaph Union Workhouse. I was but seven years of age and very sad indeed."

"You poor, dear man," Dorothy Tennant said.

"Males and females, even married couples, were kept in separate wards. Among the transient population were prostitutes brought in for spiritual reawakening as well as dolts and madmen better suited for asylums but put there by a kindly local vicar. Of the children, there were about seventy: Forty were boys—the girls, kept in a separate ward, were rarely to be seen.

"While the girls were taught by the matron in charge, my schoolmaster was one James Francis, a former collier of some education. He'd lost his left hand in a coal-factory accident as a younger man, and he was of such a bad temperament that at the slightest provocation he often used his good right hand to wield a birch rod. Though this Mr. Francis was a Welshman who could only speak broken English, he taught his lessons, however painstaking and confusing it might have been to his students, in the English language. His words were taken from books verbatim, exactly as they were written, Welsh being strictly forbidden in those classrooms. As I could only speak Welsh, many were the days I spent without knowing a word of what was being taught. But as there were boys willing to teach me some English, I learned to wean myself off the mother tongue—and in a hard way, for whenever I uttered any words of Welsh in the classroom or made an error in my pronunciation of an English word, Mr. Francis would give me a blow on the back of my head or strike a switch against the upheld palm of my hand—I still have two scars to remind me of that, Miss Tennant. But most humiliating was to have my breeches pulled down and be lashed.

"Even though there were many things that pained me greatly about that institution, there was much there by which I profited. We were taught to read and write. Latin and Greek. Geography and history and mathematics. And at the same time, our religious instruction was thorough. It was the practice of the chaplain to post upon the classroom walls and in other public places sheets bearing passages from the Scriptures, such as which might help our moral education. Bible lessons were given twice a day, and among the many books in the library at St. Asaph's were included the writings of the eminent theologians of the day. Services were held twice on Sundays, and each dinner began and ended with a communal prayer, to be recited aloud in unison. So strong were the precepts of faith advocated in that place that the sense of a watchful God, aware of one's every movement and embodied by the stern presences of our guardians, pervaded our thoughts constantly. Of course one had to be humble and pious and never sin, and to this I aspired."

Then, clearing his throat, he said:

"But one day, a very sad thing happened: I am not so certain that I should tell you, but it seems that I will. While sitting in the communal dining hall one evening, I noticed, among the new inmates, a woman whose face seemed familiar to me. She was tall, like you, with a full head of red hair and a somewhat pretty but hardened face. She had a little girl with her, and as she sat down by one of the tables, it came to me that this woman, remote and aloof from the others, was my mother, fallen on hard times. But as I was uncertain of this, I did not approach her until the schoolmaster himself, Mr. Francis, came over to me and said, "John, do you not recognize your own mother?" I went to her, not knowing what to say. Still I managed a few words—"Mother? I am your son."

"In a better world, this lady would have brightened at the sight of me, but in the midst of her own low misfortunes—she had been sent there over some debt—she merely looked at me and said: 'What is that to me?' And then she commenced to finish her meal in silence, her daughter, my half sister Emma, by her side. Though I was deeply wounded by her indifference to me, as I would see her passing in the courtyard or in the dining hall, I maintained the dim hope that she would warm to me, but in the weeks she remained there, as a temporary inmate, her coldness was strongly and hurtfully reinforced in my mind at every turn."

"And did you, Mr. Stanley, see her again?"

"Yes, Miss Tennant, but it was not until some years later."

Then, shifting in his chair and fishing out a match from his vest pocket to light a cigar, Stanley said, "Miss Tennant, you must forgive me, but it is time for me to go—I am due to meet with Mr. Mackinnon over some important matters."

"I understand," she told him. "But please, Mr. Stanley, do come back, and soon."

He was brooding as he left her that day, angry at himself for having let slip the business of his mother's coldness; on the other hand, he remembered the pure kindness in Miss Tennant's eyes, the discerning intelligence and sympathy with which she seemed to regard his sad story. As she led him out, he, feeling duped, did not say much, and while they parted congenially—"Do write me a note and let me know when you can come here again," she reminded him—he remained solemn. As there had been no meeting with Mackinnon—he'd contrived it as a means to escape, the feeling of being locked in by the truth of his emotions having overwhelmed him—he returned to his flat to attend to some correspondence with King Leopold. And yet as he wrote to Leopold, somewhat disinterestedly, about the equatorial territories east of the Congo, which the king was anxious to annex for himself, Africa could not have been further from his mind. Sheepishly, unable to dwell on the matters at hand, he jotted down a note, which he sent off with Hoffman.

> *Dear Miss Tennant,*
>   *I must thank you for the delightful time we spent in your studio. In truth I do not feel myself to be a proper subject for your artistic contemplation, but I still feel greatly honored. I see I have a few hours free the day after the morrow—on Thursday—and if it would please you, I could come by in the afternoon, at about four, and perhaps afterward we might have supper together, if such an idea is congenial to your schedule.*
>
>

Yours,
Henry Stanley

THOUGH HE HARDLY KNEW HER, in early July he accompanied her to several functions; within a few days they appeared together as "friends" at luncheons and diplomatic gatherings, among them one at the American consulate for an Independence Day celebration. Wherever she went she dressed in the highest fashion and most elegantly; at times he couldn't help but imagine what she must look like as she prepared for her outings, but he hadn't a clue and would probably faint at the sight of her in the mornings, so striking must she be, stepping from her bath, her arms crossed over her pendulous breasts, even if her maid had seen her grow from an infant to a woman. (He imagined the scene: *She puts on a pair of bloomers and then a heavily boned corset with its long stays of pink coutil, which her maid tightens, almost to the point that she sometimes gasps, so that her fine figure, with its slim waist and fulsome hips, takes on the shape of an hourglass. Then the stockings are clipped to the corset; and over that she puts on a petticoat, and then a somewhat longer silk skirt over that. Then she puts on a flowered blouse with a high collar; then a fine jacket over it; then her maid gets on her knees to help with her soft leather boots, whose laces she hooks over a series of criss-crossed eyelets; standing before a mirror, she dusts her throat with white powder and finds a hat suitable to the occasion—sometimes a bonnet, sometimes a Parisian concoction of satin and lace and braid, its brim turned upward and smothered in silk flowers—and voilà: She is ready to stun any man.*) He had at this juncture only seen her a few times, but upon occasion, despite his natural disposition against thinking he was part of a couple, he posed with Dorothy for the brigades of photographers, with their apparatus and flashing chemicals.

A week into July he saw her again. Those few days later, he brought along a bouquet of flowers and a box of Belgian chocolates with which to ingratiate himself with her mother, Gertrude. Announced by their butler, he found Gertrude sitting in their parlor, reading by the window light a biography of Voltaire, and though Stanley did his best to present an air of gladness to see her, she was put off by his presence: "I am very thankful for these gifts," she said. "But you shouldn't bring such things to me, for we are merely acquaintances, are we not?"

"I am hopeful that it will not always be so."

She did not respond to that comment, just pointed to a table, saying: "Now, put those things over there." Then he waited for a simple thank you, but that was not her way with him. "Now, go: I suppose my daughter's waiting for you." Taking his leave, and thinking himself foolish for having gone to the trouble to befriend Dorothy's mother, he made his way, somewhat gloomily, toward Miss Tennant's studio, where he found the lady standing behind her easel.

Stanley sat, nervously at first, and passed the first half hour in silence, striking a still pose, his face tilted as if to watch a bird's nest hiding in the recesses of an oak tree just outside her studio window; but after a while, though he was somewhat tempted to speak again of his mother, he, with so many other things that he might relate, and without knowing that it would lead to his mother's door, began with a discussion of his relationship to the disease of malaria, as if, mindful of the distant possibility that they might one day grow closer, he wanted Dorothy to know just what she was getting into.

"THE OTHER DAY, MISS TENNANT," he began, "when I first came in, you happened to comment on how 'well' I looked; and, yes, I would say that on the whole, I am feeling somewhat more fit and better than I have in recent times; just a few months ago, I made a visit to the Swiss Alps to restore my vigor, as, you see, with each of my expeditions a little of my vitality is drawn from me. This is a result not only of the rigors of such expeditions and the want of food and the strange infections that can come over one from a simple cut in the wilds but also from malaria, Miss Tennant, which in Africa is called the mukunguru, or seasoning fever. Even as I sit here, I figure by my own estimation that I have had it at least a hundred times: I never know when it will come upon me. I can be well in the morning and by night laid up in my bed with the fevers and then the chills. The shaking is terrible, and so are the many bad dreams that come to one. In such states, Miss Tennant, one never knows what is real, for many an apparition and demon come visiting the sufferer. In Africa, I heard of an officer attached to one of Cameron's expeditions blowing his brains out because of the fever, and it has sometimes driven men to deeds of violence toward others or to lewd and lascivious and sometimes blasphemous behavior. Of such madness I have been largely spared, though I have had my share of incredible waking dreams, as it were."

"And of what kind?" Miss Tennant asked, her interest piqued.

"Oh, I have seen myself as a child, sitting in my own tent, staring at myself; I have seen my dead grandfather Moses and the very great Livingstone, who died of malaria himself, coming seemingly from the afterlife to offer me some words of comfort. But as you can see for yourself, I am here before you in one, admittedly weary, piece; this I owe to the wonders of modern medicine. Livingstone himself invented a concoction that, in his own case, at least put off the worst effects of the disease for many years—his remedy being called a Zambezi rouser—a concoction of calomel, quinine, jalap, and treacle; but lately, thanks to the efforts of a very fine young American chemist, Henry Wellcome, who has come up with a very useful antimalarial pill.

"Still, if I have survived this disease for so long, I think it is because of my early exposure to malaria as a young man in Arkansas. In other words, Providence intended that I have malaria to later protect me."

"By 'Providence' you mean God?"

"I don't know about that, Miss Tennant: To me, it's a matter of luck, largely, but after a time, when so many incidents of survival mount up, one sees a pattern and wonders if one is protected. When I was a young soldier with the Confederate forces at the Battle of Shiloh, I saw many of my fellow men shot dead or blown to pieces within a moment or two of my having stood by their side: I could have easily been killed on at least one occasion. Not long afterward, when I was captured during that battle and sent off as a Yankee prisoner of war to a disease-ridden camp outside of Chicago, I survived when so many others, more hardy of body than I, did not. I should tell you, Miss Tennant, that surviving such early experiences—and numerous others—made me feel somewhat fearless when it came to matters of physical courage. Through it all, I learned to maintain a coolness of mind under duress. That, Miss Tennant, is one of my greatest talents, and it has served me well over the years, though"—and here he looked at her woefully—"it has apparently left strangers, who do not know me, with the impression that I am a distant sort."

"No, Mr. Stanley," she said. "I would not consider you distant at all; rather, I find that you have much warmth, in your way. From the things you have told me, with your workhouse upbringing and the very difficult path you had to take in this life, it is a wonder to me that you are so remarkably open."

"Dare I say, Miss Tennant, that there is something in your gentle nature that calms me?"

She sketched the contours of his symmetrical Welsh face: He was rather handsome, though if she were to judge his age, on the basis of his careworn wrinkles and the frown lines that crossed his forehead she would judge him to be a man in his late fifties, though a very fit one. She drew his very sad eyes; they must be beautiful when not rheumy, she thought, and she wondered about what he was thinking as he withdrew into himself during those periods of silence.

"You once mentioned your mother to me, Mr. Stanley; and you said that she did not treat you very well at the workhouse. May I ask if you have since made your peace with her, as I imagine you must have?"

"As I have intimated to you, Miss Tennant," he began, "Mother was a very hard case. She never cared too much for me, which I blamed on some very great faults of my own. Of the very few conversations I ever had with her as a boy, I can remember her once telling me that she was not really my mother at all but had found me as a swaddling infant in a refuse bin in London. Why she would invent such a thing I cannot say, but I took it as the truth for a very long time. Harsher still was that she had not spoken to me at the workhouse during her stay there—the small substance of which I earlier related to you—and though it was hard for my young mind to comprehend, I attributed her indifference to her shame about her fallen and lowly state; still, I felt as if I could very much love her, and the truth is that a mother is of very great importance to a child, no matter how callous she may be. And so it was, Miss Tennant, that I continued to love her very much, despite the fact that she never answered any of the letters I wrote to her during my years in America."

☀

"BUT TO NOW EXPLAIN HOW I next saw my mother: As a prisoner of war, though my loyalties had been with my regiment out of Arkansas, and though I saw some logic, even justice, to the

Confederate cause, as a foreign-born recruit I was exempt from normal military laws and therefore seemingly entitled to enlist in the Union army if I so chose, which the only way I could get out of that camp—a slaughterhouse of diseases, by my lights. A commander of the camp thought I would be an asset to the Union army: and, though I was reluctant to do so, after a month in that miserable place, I found myself a Yankee recruit. But I was very sick then, and by the time I had gone south to a camp near Harpers Ferry, such was my state, because of dysentery, that I collapsed into unconsciousness during a common drill. I spent some two weeks in a Union hospital, wherein I was discharged from further service: Sickly though I was, Miss Tennant, I walked into the state of Maryland, and there, taking refuge on a farm, I recuperated—after some two weeks of tender care—and was well enough to participate in the apple harvest. In the meantime, after more than three years in America, and after having endured many a sobering experience, I began to feel a longing for Wales again: The Maryland farm family, knowing of my desires, was kind enough to provide me with train fare to Baltimore, and in Baltimore I went to work on some oyster schooners that fished the waters of Chesapeake Bay until I heard of a ship, the E. Sherman, that was headed for England, and so I signed on as a hand.

"It took me a month to arrive in Liverpool. Forty miles north of Liverpool lay Denbigh, Wales, and as I was determined to get there, I walked most of the way, some carriage drivers taking me for small distances along the route. I came to the district of Denbigh looking like a disheveled and unkempt young beggar. In Glascoed, inquiring after my mother, I was told of the whereabouts of her inn and cottage: And so it was that under the watchful eyes of many suspicious-minded villagers I knocked on her door one afternoon.

"'Do you not recognize me? I am your son, John,' I pleaded, but she closed the door on me quickly and sent me away. Having no place to go, I lingered for a time, until her husband, an earnest-seeming sort of man, came out to tell me that she was in a particularly bad way, since one of their children, a boy, had recently died of meningitis; but it was Mr. Jones who invited me in for the night. I was given a meal and a bed, and while my mother's husband treated me with the greatest of courtesy, I could see that my mother, with her own brood of children to contend with, had neither the time nor the patience to deal with my misfortunes. 'We barely get along as it is,' she told me. 'You are welcome here for the night, but in the morning you must go,' she added. Shortly, with some very great agitation, I forlornly lay down in a bed, a great feeling of dejection having entered my mind."

At this point, Dorothy Tennant, looking up from her canvas, asked, "What did you do?"

Stanley, thinking seriously upon this comment, then said, "I decided to become Stanley, for good, if you must know. If there was any one moment when I decided to put my past completely aside, that was it. If I was already known as Henry Stanley in America, I resolved to become Henry Stanley in Wales.

"Four years would pass before I would see her again. By then I had become a journalist in the American West and had taken up further travels. I was on my way back to America from Turkey when I decided to make a visit to Denbigh by coach from Manchester. By then I had some money in my pocket. Surely an observer who had seen my pathetic self in earlier days would have noticed the marked improvement in my circumstances. I was well groomed and smartly dressed in a naval officer's uniform and brand-new shoes. This time, when I knocked on her door, I am happy to say that I made a much better impression on her. The dear lady was so taken by my distinguished manner and the evidence of my progress in life that she invited me to spend the night with her family—even insisted that I do so—instead of staying in a room in their inn. Ah, but I made her proud then: As she was very pleased by my air of success, she invited some of her neighbors to hear me speak of my adventures in the Civil War and of my recent travels. Afterward she cooked me a good stew, and for that night, at least, I found that I had a little family: my half sister Emma, Mr. Jones, and two of my mother's little children.

Altogether I had a most congenial time with her, and though we were far from close, Miss Tennant, I was deeply pleased by the advances I had made upon her by way of our relations."

What he did not tell Miss Tennant was despair he felt when they were sitting together in a room and his mother, holding his hand and patting it nervously, began to go on and on about his newfound virtues: "Here I am with such a distinguished type of gentleman, my old boy John," she had said. "What, then, can you give me, now? Have you any money for your dear mum?" Her prattle in that regard continued until he fished out from his pocket a pound note, which he gave her, and only then did she seem happy. "Now, then, this is more the way a darling son should be with his mum." Before stuffing it down the front of her dress, she kissed the bill, adding, "And may it always be so, my boy."

"Thereafter, Miss Tennant," Stanley continued, "our relations only improved, I am proud to say, for I have visited Denbigh and her family on a number of occasions since then. But best, Miss Tennant, was the delicious spring—it was 1869—when I had the opportunity to take my mother and my half sister Emma on holiday in Paris. It was in those days, Miss Tennant, that whatever differences there had existed between us—mainly innocent misunderstandings—fell away forever."

Curious, Miss Tennant then asked: "Does she call you John or Henry?"

"Henry, Miss Tennant." Then, more sadly: "I have not seen her in some time. She has not been well. Perhaps one day you would like to meet her. I could bring her here one day so that you might paint her—what do you think?"

"For the time being, I am perfectly content with you as my subject, dear Stanley. Now, hold still for a moment."

≈

WHEN SHE WAS DONE FOR the day, Miss Tennant put down her brush and began to clean it with turpentine, appraising, as she did so, the fine portrait of Stanley that she was making. It was on that afternoon that she detected a speck of something on Stanley's face, and as he got up she said, "You have something here," and, standing before him, as she touched his cheek with her fingers, she suddenly engaged him in a kiss.

"Oh, Mr. Stanley, do trust me," and she kissed him again. Why she, a lady of great beauty and many other male acquaintances to choose from, was doing so remained beyond his comprehension, but just as he began to feel that, however forward her sudden expression of affection was, he should reciprocate—just then, as he allowed his hand to fall upon her hip, to pull her closer, it was his bad luck that Gertrude happened into the room. "My God," she cried. "How dare you!" she called out to Stanley. "Now, please leave this house." She said other things that upset him, and as he went down the steps he heard mother and daughter shouting at one another, the veil of gentility between them lifted.

Out on the sidewalk, a bobby strolled by and saluted Stanley with a tip of his hat, then engaged him in a brief conversation (the usual questions about Africa), and while Stanley attempted to provide quick and satisfying answers, another part of him felt he would be better served to quickly leave the scene of his humiliation. Later that night he was somewhat distracted at a dinner he attended in the company of Mackinnon and Sir Alfred Lyall, and he drank more than his usual "ration"—that was how he categorized such things—of Champagne and brandy.

"You seem a bit low," Mackinnon said to Stanley. "Is there something troubling you?"

"Not at all," he answered. "Just work, nothing but work: I will be better in the morning."

※

AS FOR DOROTHY, HER EVENING was spent in silence with her mother, Miss Tennant not saying a word during their dinner together. By then Gertrude had offered some words she thought would soothe her daughter's angered heart: "Now, now, dear daughter, I am only thinking of your own good. Why you seem taken with that charmless explorer is beyond my comprehension; can you fault me for that?"

"You are just jealous of my youth!" was her daughter's answer.

The irony of it all was that her mother, when in her twenties, had been said to have been a former lover of Gustave Flaubert and, therefore, no stranger to the intricacies of romantic intrigues: Why, then, did she apply another standard to her daughter? In the days that followed her intrusion into the studio, Gertrude tried to convince her daughter that hers had been a natural, motherly response, but Dorothy, whose romantic life to that point had consisted of polite outings with wealthy and rather characterless young men who viewed her as beautiful but eccentric, was determined to never speak to her again. A week passed; several obligations regarding luncheons and dinners bound them together; but throughout Dorothy maintained her silence with her mother. Finally, one night in early August of 1885, when they were turning in to bed, her mother told her:

"My precious love, if it means so much for you to have this Mr. Stanley in your life, than so it will be. Do invite him here again, and I promise that I will be a warmer and more inviting person toward him in the future."

With those words, Dorothy, feeling somewhat triumphant, said: "Thank you, Mother; I will."

☙

THEREAFTER, IN AUGUST, STANLEY AND Miss Tennant were seen in constant company; many were the trips they made to bookstores to browse among the titles; many were the restaurants they dined in. Looking over the restaurant menu at the Hotel Chatham, Miss Tennant ordered a dish called Poularde à la Stanley aux truffes and ate it slowly, with an amused smile on her face, her eyes rarely leaving his gaze. She struck Stanley as being wonderfully happy in that time and always elegant, if not sometimes flighty of nature. In a note to him, she wrote: "To see the Elgin Marbles at the British Museum, we must appear in the exhibition room at exactly 5:45 p.m. tomorrow, when the sun is in its descent and when the light as the ancient Greeks saw it falls precisely on them, illuminating them before our eyes, as they were meant to be seen. Do not be late." Among her closest companions whom he met in those days was one Frederic Myers, her sister Eveleen's husband, a founder of the Society for Psychical Research. Though he struck Stanley as "somewhat touched in the head," the explorer attended the lectures. All the while he was somewhat concerned with her dreams about "other worlds." When she told him one day, "No matter how dreary life may seem to be, there is a more glorious and beautiful world awaiting," he realized that she was still, despite her age, something of a child. And yet he was enchanted by her, and in her absence he thought tenderly of her.

She was of a generally good temperament in Stanley's company, and it was a rare thing for her to show impatience with his timidity; rarer still were the occasions when she felt hurt by him. But during one of their lunches at her home, he had, in an attempt at an even greater sincerity, related to her the story of his former infatuation with Alice Pike: The image of the explorer racked by fever in his tent, or treading through the densest of terrains and thinking about her each day for three years, or riding in the portable boat he had named after her on various lakes and rivers—wherein daily he had not only been consumed by his longing for her but had also, to speak symbolically, entered Alice, in the form of a boat—stunned Dorothy. There he was, looking off into the distance, still speaking about her after a decade had passed and of "a hole in my heart that has yet to be filled," all the while mumbling about the ways she had fooled him and spoiled his trust of women, perhaps forever.

"I cannot begin to express the damage done to my sense of self-esteem over the way she jilted me, Miss Tennant," he confessed.

"A man more sensible and experienced in matters of the heart would have no doubt moved on by now, but you see, Miss Tennant, I am not to easily forget such things: I am afraid it has left me in a bit of a shell these days still." Then: "I hope I have not offended you by mentioning her, Miss Tennant."

"You've only left me feeling a little jealous and regretful that I had not the chance to know you in those days."

It happened that her mother had come in from the parlor: Gertrude had been reading in one of the papers about the life of General Gordon, a pious bachelor, like Stanley, who died at Khartoum without ever having experienced the comforts of love.

"A most interesting thing about Gordon," she cheerfully said. "Seems that in his youth he once had some kind of love affair that ended badly; and as he'd never gotten over it, the rest of his life was spent in a lonely way: What could he have been thinking?"

Stanley had then looked over at Dorothy, their eyes meeting in mutual recognition of the relevance of her mother's comment.

> Dear Father,
>
> How I wish Alice had died while Stanley had gone to Africa, because then he could still remember her with love and would not be so mistrusting of the world. I feel so sorry for him, not only because of Alice but also because of the terrible loneliness that he is too stubborn to let go of... It is a funny thing, then, is it not, Father, to learn so much about someone whom, not so long before, one did not know and to wish to help and care for that person, as if it were the most important thing in the world?
>
> Good night, and sleep well.

❧

ONLY ONCE DID SHE SEEM sad. They were walking in Regent's Park, arm in arm, at dusk, several of Stanley's Scotties on a leash before him.

"What troubles you? You've been very quiet," he commented.

"Do you remember the first time you came to see me at Richmond Terrace? There were three or four children there, one of them a boy named William, the chimney sweep."

"I do."

"A few mornings ago a boy came knocking at our door; it was one of his little friends come to tell me that William had drowned in the Thames."

"That is sad."

"To the boy who brought me that news I gave some coins, for his family: But the fact remains that the innocent child is dead."

They proceeded along in silence, then Stanley, knowing her mind somewhat, said: "Though he is gone, he has surely gone to a better place."

"Thank you, Mr. Stanley; I sincerely hope it is so."

They were heading out of the park when Dolly suddenly swooned and fell into Stanley's arms. The explorer gently sat her down on a bench. "Forgive me, my dear," she said. "I have not eaten for the two days since hearing about poor William."

"Well, then, let us get you something to eat."

And then, regaining her composure, her dizziness having left her, she said: "Would you be sad if I were to suddenly die?"

"That is a strange question, Dolly. But yes, I would be; very much so."

And with that answer she smiled happily. "Ah, then I know that you do care for me; and I promise that I will live a long life, so as to always be by your side."

At Madame Tussaud's: The Story of Kalulu

ON ANOTHER AFTERNOON, WHILE STROLLING in London with Dorothy, Stanley asked her if she had ever visited Madame Tussaud's wax museum, and, as she had never done so, such a touristy attraction having escaped her attention, they made their way to Marylebone Road to see its exhibition rooms. Here and there were displayed the wax effigies of many a famous personage: Henry VIII, Napoleon Bonaparte, George III, among some several dozen others, including Livingstone himself, who was depicted seated at a desk with a Bible open before him. But the exhibit Stanley most wanted her to see, just across from Admiral Nelson, was that of himself with the wax effigy of his young rifle bearer, Kalulu, striding behind him. Stanley's Winchester repeater was balanced on his shoulders.

"Now, Dolly, of all the manifestations of my fame, this display of myself as I once was, and of my dear boy Kalulu, has always struck me as the strangest; while I am very flattered to be included with so many other historical personages, I get a strong feeling of my own mortality, for there is something morbid about being included among the images of so many dead people. When I have visited this place in the past, mainly to look at Kalulu, of whom I was most fond, I get the strangest impression that one day, after I am long dead, visitors will be standing in this very spot, wondering about this version of myself, Henry Morton Stanley; it is akin to the very same sensation I get when sitting down in my parlor to write. The thought comes to mind that sometime, far into the future, when my books will be but dusty remnants of the past on some library shelf, my own life will be observed from afar, perhaps even written about, by some person whom I will have never met. Altogether, it is rather sobering to me."

"And is that why you brought me here?"

"Well, Dolly, not really. I wanted you to get a good look at Kalulu, whom you see here as he once was: a most cheerful and good-spirited lad, of whom I will speak if you want me to."

Shortly they were sitting on a bench, where Stanley began his narrative.

"I was on the march to find Livingstone in the spring of 1871, and heading toward Ujiji, when my expedition stopped at the town of Tabora, an Arab slave-trading center. Such African-Arab towns, stretching west into the interior from Bagamoyo at points along the slave-trading route, were refuges from the surrounding wilds, the Arabs having their mosques, their caravansaries, bustling markets, and their own villas and pleasure gardens with harems. Such outposts of Islamic civilization were marred only by the gross indecency by which these traders earned their livelihoods. There, in a souk, I met with an Arab merchant, and sitting cross-legged on a carpet opposite him, smoking a musky tobacco through the tube of a narghile, I spent several hours in congenial negotiations with him. By giving him several repeating rifles in exchange for some food supplies that would be vital to my expedition, I made such a good impression on the trader that he, in gratitude for my honest dealings, made me the gift of one of his slave boys, Kalulu. And this boy, an orphan with a winning smile, could not have been more affable or obedient in nature. His cheerfulness alone consoled me greatly, and as I much enjoyed his spirit and the boyishness with which he approached our adventure, I made him my rifle bearer. Kalulu, as you see him here, was always by my side or walking a few steps behind me.

"It was Kalulu who accompanied me and Dr. Livingstone on our explorations of Lake Tanganyika, and Kalulu who nursed me when I fell ill from fever. Such a good and cheerful boy was he, Miss Tennant, that when it was time for me to head back to Zanzibar, I could not bear the idea of leaving the little fellow behind. So I brought him back with me to London, where I had taken up residence at the Hotel Chatham. In Africa, we had mainly spoken Arabic, which I had studied and learned in my travels in the Middle East, or Swahili, but by the time we had arrived in London I had taught him to speak rudimentary English.

"I took him everywhere with me, to every banquet and luncheon in my honor, and often into the houses of some very important persons. I took him to the far reaches of England and even to America when I went there on tour. In fact, he made such a lasting impression on Samuel Clemens that years later, he named a character after Kalulu in one of his tales, 'The Esquimau Maiden's Romance.'"

But then there came over Stanley's expression a certain sadness: Though he rarely wept when such feelings of loss came to him, his face grew tense and solemn, and a slight mistiness entered his eyes.

"I was so taken with him, Miss Tennant, that in the months after finishing my memoir of that first expedition—*How I Found Livingstone*—I put my mind to writing a children's novel with which I'd hoped to please Kalulu: It was an African tale set in the wilder climes of Zanzibar, a story that I could not wait for him to read. I called it *My Kalulu, Prince, King, and Slave: A Story of Central Africa.* I held him in such high esteem that when David Livingstone died in 1873 and his body had been brought back to England for his funeral at Westminster, I insisted that Kalulu, of whom Livingstone was fond, be among the pallbearers, a most distinguished group of explorers. Walking directly behind me, as he always had in Africa, Kalulu, in a smart dark suit, comported himself with great dignity and serious bearing. I was very proud of him that day, as I would be until he met his end.

"You see, when I set out once again for Africa in 1874, I had no choice but to bring Kalulu along with me. As I would be away for an indeterminate amount of time, I did not want to board him in some school. He welled up with tears at the mention of being separated from me, his 'white father.' Having no notion of the dangers and difficulties awaiting us, I decided that the only practical solution was that he come along in his faithful role as my rifle bearer. And so we set out. By then the child, who had been a little boy, had grown into a man, springing up, as I would always say, like a palm tree. Taller than I and knowing the run of such expeditions, he was one of my most trusted and beloved companions—and rugged and persevering as well. Kalulu survived many of the calamities we encountered, from near starvation to attacks by the natives. However, there came a day in 1877 when my expedition began a descent down from a plateau along a route of steep gorges and rapids some one hundred and fifty-five miles long—these deafening and impossible cascades I had named Livingstone Falls. Those cataracts were so treacherous that we soon saw our first casualties, among them one of my officers. I almost suffered from the same fate, for I was also thrown into the rapids and would have drowned had I not been rescued by one of my assistants, a strong swimmer, a brave Zanzibari named Uledi. But my dear Kalulu was not so fortunate. As he rode in those same rushing waters, his steersman had allowed the canoe to crash into some rocks, and poor Kalulu was among the six men carried off into the currents. The last I saw of him, from a distance, he was being swallowed up by a whirlpool at the bottom of a falls, which I then named after him—the Kalulu Falls. What he must have been thinking I cannot say, but it is my hope that he went down with good thoughts of me."

Dolly took his hand in her own and lowered her head slightly, as if attempting to look into his heart.

Gertrude

DESPITE HER PROMISES, GERTRUDE CONTINUED to regard Stanley's presence in her and her daughter's lives without enthusiasm. Grudging in the respect she accorded his accomplishments, she found his general demeanor and manner so telling of his lowly roots as to feel embarrassed whenever they ventured out in public. His manner of eating particularly offended her, for he ate quickly, chewed loudly, and so relished his meals that he always finished, as no true patrician would, every last morsel of food. The tics of his digestive system she also found trying.

On country outings, by horse and buggy, to the estates of Dorothy's friends, as they would come to a roadside tavern or inn, Stanley would, on some days, avail himself of the conveniences so often that a two-hour journey stretched to three hours. However much he apologized for his gastric maladies, caused by all manner of lingering African parasites in his digestive tract, Gertrude, with her own fussiness, took his chronic discomforts as if they were something he had contrived to further annoy her. While there was never any telltale sign of personal unseemliness about him—in fact he took considerable pride and care in his grooming—Gertrude thought him filthy inside: More practically, she could not imagine why any woman, let alone her own daughter, who could have her choice of eligible men, would want to bind herself to the burdens that Stanley, in his unsteady health, would no doubt bring to a union. In that regard, he did his cause no good by openly admitting that, from time to time, he would unexpectedly come down with bouts of his recurring malaria, which would lay him up in bed for weeks at a time; furthermore, obviously aged by such maladies, Stanley reminded Gertrude, almost seventy, of her own mortality, and in thinking of her daughter's future happiness, she wondered how many years he, with his worn-down system, would have left to him.

EVEN IF DOROTHY SEEMED VERY much taken by him, for reasons beyond her mother's understanding, by late August, after only two months of putting up with her own unhappiness about their budding courtship, Gertrude Tennant decided that it would not be a bad time for her and her daughter to go on vacation by way of a Continental tour. It was on a late August day, when Stanley had come by the house for lunch, that Gertrude announced that she and Dorothy would be going away until November. Since the tour had been suggested by Dorothy herself earlier in April, before she had met Stanley, her mother's abrupt decision did not come as a surprise; and while it had slipped into the back of her mind by then, Dorothy, in fact, did not mind the prospect of revisiting her favorite museums; nor, by way of collecting her emotions, did she object to the perspective that such a separation might give her—for in midlife, she was somewhat perplexed by her growing attachment to a man whom many others apparently found stern and unlikable.

That day she spoke of her excitement over the prospect of painting from nature, as they would also visit the country estates of friends in Scotland and Wales; besides, though she would greatly miss him, they would never really be apart. As she later told Stanley, "I will write you every day of my thoughts of you, as I know you will write me."

Later that evening, as he lay in bed in his New Bond Street flat, trying to read himself to sleep, he decided, as he occasionally did, to make an attempt at the highest of the arts, the writing of poetry. It was about one in the morning when he, feeling both relieved and disconcerted at the sudden announcement of her departure, wrote out these rudimentary lines:

> Oh, the weary lion am I
> Parched from want of water
> Searching far and wide
> For the respite of dusk and the
> Slumber of the wilds...

Gifts

THAT CHRISTMAS STANLEY VISITED THE shops of Oxford Street in search of a gift for her: He considered sable-lined plumed hats, majestic jewelry boxes, and intricately inlaid mother-of-pearl Swiss clocks with automatic movements (cherubs—how he adored cherubs, poised to ring little golden bells). He looked at elaborate purses woven with gold thread, ornate ivory chess sets, pearl necklaces, silver perfume decanters, gold earrings, an antique leather globe—the possibilities confounded him. But finally he settled on a diamond bracelet (which cost him five hundred pounds) and, apropos of their dinner with Gladstone, a copy of Mark Twain's *Life on the Mississippi*, which he had come across in the J. & E. Bumpus bookshop on Oxford Street. (Her mother called the first gift splendid, the second "somewhat stingy.") Miss Tennant gave Stanley a fine first edition of Dickens's *The Pickwick Papers*, which, in his love for that author, delighted him. (Years later, that same edition would sit among other books in his widow's home.)

Spending Christmas Day by her side at Richmond Terrace,

he, sitting in front of the parlor fireplace, thought it a possibility that he would one day have the kind of Christmas he had never known: with a wife and family beside him.

More than a month later, on January 28, 1886, his birthday, Dorothy presented him with a silver adornment for his watch chain, a coin-like token that bore her monogram and said in Swahili: BULA MATARI, TALA, or "Breaker of rocks, remember me." (While he celebrated his birthday on the aforementioned date, his favorite anniversary of the year was always November 10, the day he found Livingstone.) And she had given him other gifts, for no particular reason—books, mainly. They always came with an inscription such as: REMEMBER THAT LOVE CONQUERS ALL or NEVER FORGET THE ONE WHO CARES MOST FOR YOU. These he cherished and kept in a section of a bookcase that he set aside for her missives.

Seeing her at least twice a week for portrait sittings, or for excursions into town, and always on Saturday for tea, he began to believe that there was some hope for them as a couple. Many of his nights alone were spent not with thoughts of Africa but of Miss Tennant herself. Always chaste in his thoughts about her, he never tried to imagine what she would look like naked, though, as he fought off the temptation to, he would concede to himself that she had a full and womanly body. And for several months, she often confided to her dead father that she had been thinking about marrying Stanley, "if only he would overcome his timidity and broach the subject. Then I would show him that I am passionately loving." When she conceived of their wedding, it would be a grand affair, to be held in Westminster, and she, the blushing bride (so she fantasized) would make her way down the aisle toward Stanley while her father, in the bloom of health, would walk beside her: "Oh, Father, should such a day come, I know that you will surely be there."

FOR SEVERAL MONTHS *LIFE ON the Mississippi*, a gift from Stanley, served as her bedside reading, along with Stanley's own volume on the Congo; of the two, she drew the greater pleasure from Clemens's picaresque and captivating chronicles, though her infatuation with Stanley cast his own book in a continually for-giving light. While his *The Congo and the Founding of Its Free State* contained little humor, such as would make a dreary night pass more pleasantly, she found the personality of the explorer evident in the forced march of its words, its aggregation of details, and its closely observed descriptions of events. Its chronicles of obstacles overcome on his journeys were a testament to his intrepid spirit. What it lacked in tenderness it made up for in thrilling evoca-tions of darkest Africa—and in a sanctimoniousness that Dorothy, despite her dislike of overly pious types, found inspiring. It was a book, much like Stanley himself, that was something to be con-tended with and taken quite seriously.

BY FEBRUARY, HOWEVER, THINGS SLOWLY began to change between them. One evening while attending a dinner at the Ten-nant mansion, he passed much of that meal in silent agony, as his stomach was badly cramped with knots so tight that several times he excused himself from the table and retreated to the study, where, at one point, Dorothy found him writhing about on the floor, doubled over in pain, uttering that with such discomforts as came to him with gastritis, he would rather die than live.

A week or so later, he was still laid up in bed, with his man Hoffman by his side and Baruti, barefoot and in a page's uniform, pacing disconsolately up and down the halls, when Dorothy and her mother arrived at his flat. They found him pale and barely able to move, the room smelling of medicines. Stanley, ashamed of his dismal state, said little and was barely able to do more than hold Dorothy's hand for a few moments, his face, made rigid by his pain, much like a death mask.

February 22, 1886

Dear Dorothy,
    I was very much touched indeed by your visit yesterday.
Though I could barely express myself well, I was sincere when

I told you that it meant so much that you would inconvenience yourself to see me. I am sorry for the atmospheric disharmonies of such a sickroom, but that you remained so long to reassure me gave me a hope and gratitude that, unfortunately, I did not have the strength to express in words at the time, for these pains come and go like the tides of a river.

I hope you noticed that I had by my bedside the silver watch chain token you had given me for my birthday—I will always treasure it, as I will your gracious and attentive friendship.

Your devoted servant,
H. M. Stanley

March 15

Dear Bula Matari,
*   Mother and I remain deeply concerned that your recovery is taking so long; we do miss your company, and though I have remained busy as ever painting my beloved ragamuffins and with the gaieties of my life here in London, I look to the day when you are well again: Please tell me that you will get better.*

Lovingly yours,
Dolly

***

NOT UNTIL LATE MARCH DID he feel well enough to leave his flat, but even then he could barely walk without difficulty and exhaustion. His body having been drained of its strength, Stanley required the assistance of a cane, and he, on a milk diet, had lost so much weight that he was loath to come face-to-face with Dolly. Several times she had written Stanley in those days, asking him to come and visit; or she would visit him, but, as he answered her: "Such is my lamentable condition that I would prefer that we wait, as I would not be very good company: And yet your gracious concern continues to give me strength and hope for better things to come."

In the last week of March, advised by his physician to leave London and partake of the more congenial and healthful climes of Italy, Stanley, packing a portmanteau, slipped out of the city and crossed the Channel to France, his journey taking him to Nice, then to Rome. Thereafter, he headed north to spend a week in a resort on Lake Como. Then he went south: At Capri he visited, astride a donkey, the cliffside Villas of Tiberius; at Ischia he sought the cures of the island's natural mineral springs; a few days later, he was in Naples, from which he visited its archaeological tourist attractions.

BACK IN LONDON THAT SUMMER, while Dorothy and her mother remained on holiday at friends' estates in Scotland, Stanley decided that he had, all along, perhaps been too reticent and guarded in his feelings about Dorothy. Suddenly he felt consumed with "the all-important question"—a marriage proposal; for two weeks it haunted his thoughts, followed him into his sleep, met him at every corner. Finally he sent an uncharacteristically brief letter of proposal to Miss Tennant

Her answer came promptly: a two-page missive along with a pressed rose. Although she made it clear in her reply that she cared deeply for Stanley, to his dismay he quickly realized that he was being rejected—and on the maddening grounds that he was too "great" a man.

꧁꧂

August 15, 1886

Dear Samuel,

Since I have told you somewhat of my ongoing relations with Miss Tennant, and as it the kind of story that deserves some closure, I will tell you, without mincing words, that it has ended badly; in short, she has thrown me off, and it

seems that I have wasted the past sixteen months living in a
fool's paradise. As a writer (and a fine one indeed), you surely
know of the vacancy that occurs when you have let go of a
book—there is a great void of mental activity and emotions
to be filled—and this, alas, is what, upon reflection, made me
particularly susceptible to her cunning and charms. In retro-
spect, it is no coincidence that I fell into her trap just after I
had finished my book on the founding of the Congo Free State;
if I hadn't the time to while away in the first place, I doubt if I
would have spent so many hours in that woman's company or
been swept up in her gush of compliments and fulsome adula-
tions or put up with her obnoxious mother. Without going
into the bloody details, I hope it will suffice to say that I have
decided to stick, henceforth, to those things I do best; as I am
apparently ill-suited for romance, I have resigned myself to my
bachelorhood, for, as solitary as that may be, I can at least
be free of female manipulations. Thankfully I have enough
friendships to make it bearable. Which is to say, Samuel, that
despite this debacle, I feel remarkably well and, truthfully,
somewhat relieved that it is over.

"Not at all true," Stanley confessed in person to his friend several months later, while on a lecture tour of America, arranged by
Twain's agent, Major Pond. "It's not as if I haven't tried to forget
Miss Tennant—indeed I have. But the confounded woman creeps
into my thoughts in the most unexpected ways: I think it is worst
at night, when I am in my bed alone. Have you any idea, Sam, of
the loneliness of such nightly solitude, year after year?"

"I do, fellow traveler. I've had my share of such nights."

"But at least you have the solace of a fine home."

"It is one of my few." Then, impatiently: "What makes you
think I would have an answer to your dilemma, anyway? I wish
there were a potion you could take—or maybe a hypnotist would
be of help to you. Obviously that high dame means a lot to you
still, and I expect that it will take you some time to get over her.

But as you are about the most hard-nerved and steely man I've ever known in my life, I expect you to quickly put her from your mind: Think of her as just another jungle that you have hacked your way through; sure, you're sad and disappointed, but this, too, will pass. Use your noggin on this one, Stanley. It pains me to see you this way. And, at any rate, what makes you think that this life is anything but imperfect? You of all people should know that the best."

Then, more calmly: "In the meantime, dear Stanley, whatever you do, my friend, do not allow your memories of that woman—what was her name, anyway?—to lay you low. Now, with all due respect, buck up."

And that was all that either man said of the Tennant affair.

HUCK FINN IN AFRICA

BACK IN LONDON IN THE New Year, on the eve of setting out to Zanzibar by way of Alexandria and Cairo, in the service of King Leopold, Stanley dashed off several notes to friends; one of them was addressed to Samuel Clemens:

February 17, 1887
160 New Bond Street

Dear Samuel,
This brief ditty is to inform you that I am off on the Emin chase; don't know what awaits me, and the weight of details and preparations boggles the mind, but as I have been making my final preparations and packing away an entire case of geographical and scientific books, I should let you know, for what

it's worth, that among the few books I am bringing along for my leisure (should that exist) is your own Adventures of Huckleberry Finn, *which you were gracious enough to have given me.*

Until we meet again,

Henry M. Stanley

＊

ON MARCH 18, 1887, STANLEY'S hurriedly organized expedition, commencing from Zanzibar by ship, arrived, after a month's sailing, at the port of Matadi, at the mouth of the Congo River, on the west Atlantic coast of Africa. In Stanley's party were some six hundred native Zanzibari carriers, sixty-one Sudanese soldiers, thirteen Somalis, and his own two servants, Hoffman and Baruti. Joining the group was a Zanzibari slave and ivory trader named Tippu Tib, high lord of the Stanleyville region, whose personal retinue included thirty-six wives and concubines and some sixty-one guardsmen and porters. There was Stanley's contingent of European officers: Captain Robert Nelson, a veteran of the Zulu Wars; Lieutenant John Rose Troup, who had seen service at one of Stanley's stations along the Congo and was fluent in Swahili; William Bonny, a former medic in the British army; James Sligo Jameson, an amateur naturalist, who was put in charge of cooking and the distribution of rations for the expedition, and one Arthur J. M. Jephson, who had no qualifications save for the fact that he, like Jameson, donated one thousand pounds to join this glorious enterprise. (Hundreds of others had also applied.) Two more officers, on special leave from active duty in the army, were on hand: Lieutenant William Grant Stairs of the Royal Engineers and one Major Edmund Barttelot of the Seventh Fusiliers, his high-strung second in command. Finally, as chief medical officer, there was Dr. Thomas Heazle Parke, whom Stanley had signed on in Cairo.

At Matadi, the fleet of five steamboats that Leopold had earlier promised to Stanley for the expedition's transport upriver turned out to be useless rotting hulks in total disrepair. Instead of commencing their journey by water, Stanley's column marched uphill for twenty-eight days, along the very road Stanley had built seven years before, toward the Congo plateau.

At first, the column set off in good order: At the lead was a tall Sudanese soldier carrying a banner—not a Union Jack or the flag of Belgium, but the standard of a New York City yacht club to which Stanley's former employer, Gordon Bennett, belonged. Behind him was Stanley himself, dressed in a Norfolk jacket, knickerbockers, and a peaked hat with a sun flap hanging off its back, riding a mule with silver-plated strappings along its side. Following Stanley were Baruti, dressed in white, wearing a turban, and carrying his rifle, and Hoffman, in safari garb; then a contingent of Somali soldiers followed by a hundred porters. Behind them was Tippu Tib, wearing long, flowing white Arab robes and carrying a scimitar, its handle encrusted in jewels, aloft on his shoulders, and his harem, wearing colored robes; their faces were half hidden by veils.

Despite its initial glorious appearance, the expedition was beset with problems of discipline from the beginning. Aside from certain old "faithfuls" from Stanley's last expedition, the hurriedly recruited corps of porters and guards proved to be an unruly lot, prone to desertion, pilfering, and a reluctance to take orders. Within a few weeks of their march, the expedition began to suffer the ravages of malaria and dysentery. By the time the column had reached the first way station of Leopoldville, eleven of his porters had died, twenty-six were too ill to go farther, and twenty had deserted.

When they finally reached Yambuya, on the banks of the Aruwimi River, Stanley left Major Barttelot, his second in command, with a large body of men—his "rear column"—to wait for supplies from Leopoldville, while the remainder of his expedition went on. On June 28, 1887, with several of his officers—Jephson, Stairs, Nelson, and Parke—and his servants Hoffman and Baruti by his side, along with three hundred and eighty of his ablest men, Stanley set out, due east, into the vast Ituri Forest, a dark and dank realm the size of France, so dense with trees that light rarely penetrated to the ground. As they followed the course of the river, the sound of the cataracts was deafening; but to travel within the forest itself was daunting in a different way, often deathly silent and always gloomy, "like being inside a long-abandoned and very dark cathedral," he later wrote. He would ultimately call it the "region of horrors."

꧁

From Stanley's journal:

Camp near the Lenda River, incessant roar of the cataracts maddening: from the soft and viscous topsoil, worms and slugs oozing out of the loamy mud under the worn soles of our boots, the earth smelling of elephant, simian, and antelope dung; from the trunks of rotting trees, swarms of stinging red ants in livid streams in every direction, like lines of fire...black ants, too, crawling up our boots, supping on our spoons, swimming in our thin broths, teeming over our plates and into every open box, every blanket, even crawling onto the pages of my books. Pismires—tiny insects with scissors-like mandibles—cutting into the soft flesh of one's neck; and bees small as gnats and able to pass through the eyes of needles, stinging, biting, attacking with the ferocity of black wasps, so voracious in their appetites that they stripped the hair off my mule's legs. Such little creatures going for the eyes, ears, and nostrils, my skin covered with swelling sores, as if I'd fallen again and again onto a nettle patch; venomous hornets tormenting us as well...and wasps, their baggy nests hanging everywhere off the trees, exploding like darts through the air and attacking man and animal alike at the slightest provocation—a footfall, a voice, the striking of a match...tiger slugs crawling up over my stockings and wriggling onto my skin, a stinging slime left in their

wake; green centipedes with beady eyes falling out of
the trees...and butterflies, too—appearing abruptly in
swarms from the east, dropping down in sheets from the
trees, and so densely gathered they are an obstruction to
one's movement; to pass them is like parting a curtain, a
cloud of them, in a blizzard of fluttering wings, the creatures alighting upon our faces.

Then:

    The Ituri again, clack-clack in the trees; around
me, in the netting of lianas and creeping vines that
crosshatch the woods, and off the branches of the
surrounding trees, femurs and rib cages, spines and
clavicles—human bones of every variety—hanging
everywhere, like clock pendulums or Chinese wind
chimes. Worse is the undergrowth, for with every step,
I feel the ground beneath my feet oozing with blood, the
syrupy mud rising up onto my boots with every step.
The leather of my shoes coming apart like soaked, mealy
bread...such disagreeable things I ascribe to bad digestion
and a very severe headache before turning into bed....

Or:

    On the trail came across a dying native, his head
cracked open by a rifle butt, the side of an eyeball visible
through a split in the forehead of the skull, his smooth
belly expanding ever so slightly with his last breaths—
the oddity of it all, not a drop of blood issuing from the
gaping wound, as if the blood had been stopped like mud
in his veins...had no choice but to discharge my pistol
into his head, to put the poor fellow out of his misery, the crack of the gun, the body writhing for a final
moment...a nightmare, to be sure.

And his journals go on and on: with opinions about his officers, reports of the dead and wounded, and counts of deserters in his caravan.

WITHIN THE HUNDREDS OF PAGES of his journals, there exist these scant references to *Huckleberry Finn*:

September 20, 1887

> My eyes are slowly going bad...have been reading Clemens's novel again, in my tent, before sleep; some parts I have found less than what he is capable of, some of it strictly picaresque, but some parts profoundly moving. I particularly find Jim to my liking and not unlike my good-natured man Uledi...The river of freedom is an idea I enjoy, but an illusion, no doubt, especially given the reality of the river that exists in this place. A river of death...But I find that just thinking about the Mississippi and my old life does wonders for my spirit, even when I know it is just a made-up story.

October 8, 1887

> On a reconnoitering excursion across the black lake of———when, because of a heavy and sudden fog, we could not see far into the darkness or take our bearings by the stars, I had no choice but to light a torch, even though that light might well have brought a hail of poison arrows from the shore toward our canoe. But I had no torch, so I asked Hoffman to hand me my knapsack, wherein were contained several books, including the Bible and *The Adventures of Huckleberry Finn*, as I had thought to burn one of them for light—but which one? Though it troubled me to use the Bible, I could not bear the thought of tearing to pieces and making ashes out

of Clemens's gift to me, so putting it aside and begging Providence's forgiveness, and bearing in mind that I had another Bible back in camp, I ripped from my Bible's binding clumps of its pages, which I put to a lucifer match, its sudden glare giving us a sense of where we were in relation to the shore, which we shortly could make out was to our right. We were fortunate to find some of our party (Lieutenant Stairs and well-armed Somalis) awaiting us there, for seeing our light, they set afire some of their own torches, and we were saved.

IN A PHOTOGRAPH TAKEN IN a Cairo studio, circa January of 1890, Stanley is posed with the surviving four officers of his expedition (Jephson, Stairs, Nelson, and Parke) against the painted backdrop of an African plain, potted palms surrounding them. These gentlemen—in their dapper, high-collared white Victorian shirts and walrus mustaches—are either seated, canes and bowler hats set on their laps, or standing, at ease, looking bemusedly into the camera, as if they had still not gotten reaccustomed to the trappings of normal modernity. Stanley, his face gaunt and his expression weary, seems by far the eldest; with his hair turned completely white, he could have been an uncle posing with his nephews or a schoolmaster with his teachers instead of an intrepid explorer who'd just turned forty-nine.

☙

Dearest Samuel,

How are you, my old friend? As for me, I fear the best years of my life are gone, and now, at fifty, whatever glories might await me, my personal circumstances remain as solitary as before, but with the difference that I am now feeling my age—Africa will do that to a man.

I mention this because it is you who tried to dissuade me from undertaking the whole business during my last visit with you in Connecticut, in the winter of '86. As we talked about Africa one night, you doubted the value of the mission, calling it an excuse for "wholesale colonization" of the region, and as you, dear Samuel, by the example of your happy home life, made me think heavily about the prospect of spending endless months in the wilderness without the ordinary comforts of domesticity, I nearly changed my mind. But the eyes of my peers were upon me, and besides, I did not think the mission would be as difficult as it turned out to be.

As you may recall, certain extenuating emotional circumstances were at work on my spirit at the time—I am speaking of my misbegotten attachment to Dorothy Tennant, the London society dame whose initial romantic attentions had been a great surprise to me. To have been lulled into a dream of love, only to be rejected, perhaps clouded my judgment at a crucial moment: In the end, I welcomed the distraction and am still convinced that I was the best man for the job. I expect that all the parties who had diligently persuaded me to do so—King Leopold of Belgium and Mr. Mackinnon—have been quite satisfied with the results, for central equatorial Africa is now better known and will be portioned off, to mutual satisfactions, among the Europeans, and the strange and mercurial pasha was brought to safety.

And remember how much of Europe was in an uproar over the fate of one Eduard Schnitzer, or the Emin Pasha, as was his title after the khedive of Egypt elevated him? A bookish and quite brilliant man, a linguist and naturalist assigned to the governorship of Equatoria, he had been stranded with a contingent of Sudanese forces in a garrison near the Albert Nyanza—Lake Albert—and apparently surrounded by the forces of the Mahdi, bent on his extinction. As you know, nothing had been heard from him in several years, and in Europe there was the fear that he would surely suffer the same fate as did my old friend Gordon of Khartoum—which was to be hacked to pieces by Islamic swords. As you know, I was

"retired" from explorations and missions, etc., having grown
weary of such challenges. Nevertheless, it was during the second week of my American tour—as it happened, I was visiting
with you in Hartford on that leg (and a most pleasant one it
was) of the tour arranged by Major Pond—when I received the
summons to lead the expedition. Both King Leopold of Belgium
and shipping magnate William Mackinnon, of the British
India Steam Navigation Company, had been after me for some
time to undertake that journey, and though I had my reservations, my sense of civility and duty prevailed. Once the funds,
some twenty thousand pounds or so, were raised by subscrip-
tion and I received the summons, it was a matter of honor and
integrity that compelled me to accept the assignment.

No doubt there will be much talk about the loss of life and
the necessary measures we had to take in subduing hostile villages to ensure our survival, but in the end, given the sheer
magnitude of my accomplishment—tracking through a previously unknown region the size of France to rescue the pasha
and recording the geographical discoveries that resulted—I can
take some pride. Rarely can any man (or men) lay claim to
have actually entered into Dante's dark wood, as I can now:
For one hundred and sixty days, we marched through the
immense Ituri Forest without ever seeing a bit of greensward
the size of a cottage chamber floor. Nothing but endless miles
and miles of forest, and never as much as a patch of sunlight,
the gloom of being in such a godless place so great that, indeed,
the small emotional troubles that come to a man in the discharge of ordinary life seemed hardly of consequence; even one's
own name in such conditions hardly matters, only survival.
My dear friend, to say that it was like a dream, and often like
a bad one, is no understatement.

However malevolent were the conditions throughout (of
which I will not further elaborate), I had the consolation of my
books: my Bible, my atlases, and your own The Adventures
of Huckleberry Finn, which you had given me back in '86,

during our most agreeable visit in Hartford. I began to read it aboard ship en route from America to England that winter, when I had been called for this mission. Then I read it again in the New Year, on my way from England to Alexandria en route to Cairo—so much of my time otherwise was preoccupied by preparations for the expedition. Thereafter, once the expedition had set out by ship from Zanzibar—easterly around Cape Horn to the mouth of the Congo and onward up by steamboats along the Aruwimi River to the edge of known lands—I began it again as a matter of comfort to me. Through the many months afterward, on many a night, I would remove that book from its protective oilcloth wrappings, for soft paper rots quickly in the dampness of the climate, and light a kerosene lamp by which to read under the mosquito netting (it was impossible to read anything during the day; aside from the heat, there were so many insects about that to open a book, smelling to them of delicious ink and nutritious pulp, would be to attract these famished creatures in great numbers, for they loved the taste of the pages of books). As I reread portions of that novel, your evocation of the Mississippi and thereabouts provoked in me a flood of pleasant reminiscences about our own youthful days in the American South: Or, I should say, it reminded me of the times, so long ago, when we first recognized each other as friends—and lifelong friends at that.

Well, as I am one of the few living Europeans who have been to such a place, I am hoping that you will be amused to know that Huckleberry Finn and his good friend Jim traveled to the land of the Negroes with me. I liked your portrait of Jim, I should add: The scene where he cries (chapter 23) while describing how he had once beaten his little daughter for not speaking to him, then realized she was a deaf mute, remains among my favorites—why I cannot say. As for Huck Finn—that he, like me, was practically an orphan made him a most sympathetic character, and I found his desire to escape from the "civilizing influence" into the freedoms of the river a quite intriguing *and amusing idea. As you know, to bring the "civilizing influence" into Africa has been one of my goals, though my own experience, based on what I have seen and on the moral unfitness of the many men now operating in the region, finds me, like Huckleberry, longing for the purer world of the wilds.*

As a parting thought, a line from Browning in which I took much comfort during the expedition:

I count life just a stuff
To try the soul's strength on.

Yours,
H. M. Stanley

HIS RETURN

HAVING COME BACK FROM AFRICA by way of Alexandria, in April of 1890, Stanley set out from the port city of Brindisi by rail along the Italian countryside to Rome. His progress was met in every little town along the way by ecstatic crowds who, thronging around him, greeted him as though he were a new Caesar. At each stop, the train would pause for about twenty minutes, Stanley, somewhat bronzed from the sun, appeared at the aft and waved at the crowds. In the piazzas of many towns, festivals were held in his honor, and he found himself, however briefly, stepping down into the midst of elaborate celebrations to shake hands and pose for photographs and receive laurels and medals. Along the way he had heard that mothers were naming their newly born babies "Enrico" after him.

In one town, fragrant with wisteria and potted flowers, as

Stanley stepped off the train for a few minutes, he found a rotund and affable majordomo pointing out his young daughter in the crowd, all sincerity and good will, asking: "Vuole sposare a mia figlia?"—"Would you like my daughter as your bride?" He turned a livid red, bowed, and, in a state of agitation, walked away.

For all his glory, sleep did not come easily to him; having no use for such pithy emotions as guilt, and not feeling any blame for having performed the necessary task of burning down two hundred and twenty-six African villages on his marches ("reduced" is the term he used to refer to such events), and in general equating any inkling of shame with weakness, he, in full control of his emotions—save for rage, impatience, and envy (among others)—found himself vexed over the capricious and troubling thoughts that would come to him in those moments preceding his sleep, and during sleep itself, when he felt very much alone in the world, only Stanley and God existed in the room.

⁂

BY THE TIME HE RETURNED to England, in June of 1889, after triumphant processions in Rome, Paris, and Brussels—where Leopold bestowed upon him the Grand Cross of the Order of Leopold and the Grand Cross of the Order of the Crown—he found that his recent exploits, above all others, had not only made him more famous than ever before but had also enhanced his standing with the aging Queen Victoria, who invited Stanley to dinner at Windsor Castle so that she could hear his stories.

The great dame was far more receptive to me than she was on my previous visits. Something in the outpouring of congratulations from all over Europe and the universal publicity—which reflected well on the "English goodwill" accrued by my adventure—seemed to dispose Her Royalness well toward me. I was received in her private quarters, where she showed me some of

her drawings of persons and landscapes (not a bad artist, for an amateur) and asked me if I would be disposed
to a knighthood; but for many a reason, I had to defer
the honor until some other time, mainly (and I could
not tell her so without offense) because of my status as
an American citizen, which was conferred on me during my trip to the United States in 1885. As she would
not have understood the practical reasons for it, involving copyright protection in the United States, I informed
the queen that I was not yet worthy of such an honor.
Though it did not sit well with her, I am told that, after
I held forth on the difficulties of the Emin Pasha expedition before a gathered assembly at Windsor Castle, she
was greatly pleased and considered me a "wonderful
traveler and explorer." It had been a help, I think, that I
named several geographical sites after her.

A grand reception was given in his honor by the Royal Geographical Society in London. Royal Albert Hall was packed
with some ten thousand important spectators, Dorothy Tennant
among them. For reasons that were of an intestinal origin, Stanley, hearing one wave after another of applause in anticipation of
his appearance, fainted three times. ("What brought that about I
do not know," he wrote.) Finally coming out onto the stage, he
stood before Sir Mountstuart Grant Duff, president of the society,
and, hearing his praises sung as a great and intrepid explorer, and
as Sir Mountstuart placed around his neck the red ribbon and gold
medal of the RGS, bearing an image of Stanley's profile imposed
upon an image of Africa, he was dearly tempted, in the name of
truth, to expose the whole enterprise as a "bold, certainly brave
procession of madness, come to a good conclusion." But when
he accepted the medal, he spoke instead of the many great things
he accomplished—of the advantages that were to be gained by the
European presence in Africa and about the "high moral road to
be taken by all." Methodically, and with the assistance of several

maps, he described, in the simplest of terms, the results of his expedition, the high point of his exegesis being a description of his definitive establishment of the exact location of the legendary Mountains of the Moon on his return route, which brought about yet another great ovation. Humbly thanking the gathering, he left the stage to sustained applause—archbishops, scientists, noblemen, and even cynical journalists were on their feet. Shaking many hands backstage, Stanley then inquired as to the whereabouts of a water closet; led to one, he closed the door behind him and vomited. Though he would publicly say that the RGS reception was by far the grandest he had ever known, in the privacy of the loo, he repeated to himself: "This is s—t, all of it the d—est s—t."

≈

IN HIS CORRESPONDENCE ONE DAY, after he had settled back into his New Bond Street flat, was a letter from Dorothy Tennant. It had been written one morning when she had awakened from yet another of her dreams about him.

June 7, 1890

Dearest Stanley—

I know that you may have thought of never hearing from me again, but I should let you know that although I behaved foolishly in regard to you, for the many months of your absence—four years now—I have often reflected tenderly on the matter of our mutual affections; these thoughts came to me when I realized my own despair over the possibility that you might have come to harm in Africa. I prayed for your safe return nightly—I consulted often with Lord Mackinnon as to word of your well-being... In short, dear Henry, I realized how dearly I held you and regretted my grievous and selfish actions. Though you must surely think me bold to write you now, after so long a time, it is because I have been struggling to change...

to turn away from the selfishness that blinded me to your
worth as a man. If I have been neglectful in this regard, then
understand that I am more than what I was then and would be
honored and deeply glad to see you again, not because you have
done great things but because I fear I might never see you again.

Your sincere friend,
Dorothy Tennant

STANLEY DID NOT ANSWER THIS letter and did his best to avoid her. Each time he went to a reception or banquet in his honor, his face would heat up at the prospect of meeting Miss Tennant. But in the small circles of London, it was inevitable that they would meet again. It happened one evening at a reception held by Mackinnon in Stanley's honor at the Langham hotel. With Mackinnon by his side, Stanley—dressed in the same white corded Egyptian officer's uniform that Dorothy would immortalize in her painting of him—stood about, gloomily sipping Champagne. Then he saw her, in the bloom of her beauty—even more beautiful than he recalled—standing in the corner of the room demurely with her mother, the old bat nodding at him when she caught his eye. Why was it, he wondered, that Dorothy then beamed a smile at him, despite all the public humiliation she had put him through? (Everyone in London knew about her rejection of his proposal.) And why did the very air around him seem to take on such a heavy weight, as if its molecules had grown dense? Why did his pulse race—either anger or nascent love teeming through him? He could not say. Hoisting her own Champagne glass up to him, Dorothy nodded, and he turned away, his face flush. Mackinnon, who had taken the liberty of inviting the Tennants to his fete on the chance that Stanley might reconcile with her (for she had seemed genuinely affectionate in speaking of Stanley in his absence), turned to his explorer friend, asking: "But Stanley, what harm would there be in your speaking to her?"

"I would sooner be back in the swamps and up to my neck with leeches," he snapped.

As he occupied himself in petty conversation with his admirers, she noticed him turning to look toward her despite his efforts not to do so—an effort he would never admit to undertaking. Inevitably, she worked her way across the room, her progress slow, for in her way she was famous, too, and she often stopped to speak with her own admirers. Finally, when she found herself standing a few paces from him, she was startled to see how the great man had been aged by his travels. It was not so much that his hair had turned completely white but that his whole being, which had seemed, in his moments of good health, tireless, now seemed subdued, even frail. She was suddenly aware that he had seemed to have shrunk somewhat, not in matters of height—she was some three inches taller than he was—but by way of a diminished vitality. His air of immortality had faded. All at once, though he refused to look her squarely in the eye, she found this softer, more world-weary Stanley somehow more appealing than the previous Stanley, and without even considering how it would look to others, Dorothy took hold of his hands and held them close to her heart: "Oh, Mr. Stanley, if you only knew how long I've waited to see you again." Then: "But will you not speak to me?"

"Miss Tennant," he said somewhat coldly, "I appreciate your sentiments, but please, do me a service: Go off into your fine life and leave me alone."

"I don't believe you mean it," she said—and the truth was that he trembled when speaking it. "You will hear from me—again and again until we can be as we once were."

And that was how they left it.

❧

MORE NOTES FROM MISS TENNANT continued to arrive at his flat: He chose to ignore them. Still he received more letters—first of farewell ("When shall we say our proper good-byes?") then others of devotion ("Having been so foolish a girl, unacquainted with love, I rejected you; but now I feel as if by doing so I have exiled myself to a lightless land of complete unhappiness"; "I am yours whether you will or will not be my husband"; "I am ready to be yours"; "I will obey as well as love").

These were letters so humble that Stanley, in a maudlin and solitary mood himself for some weeks—finally chose to respond to her:

> That you have put me, a man of importance and high self-esteem, in such a bad way; that you, whom I have told so much to, especially about the misery I had known in terms of family relations...that you, who had seemed so maternally kind to me, had in a callous mood refused my sincerest emotions, denying such emotions and whatever feelings you had, if you had them at all—all these, taken together, have made any future arrangements between us impossible: For your refusal has entered me like an arrow deep into my heart. There is nothing I can further say on this subject: You must leave me alone.

Then came this missive from her:

> Of course I understand. And if I am never to see you again, never to hear the timbre of your powerful voice, and if I must expect to go on regretting such things as I have done for the rest of my life, then so it must be. But if you can believe that there can be a different outcome to a story that began brightly, then darkened because of my own faults and inexperience, then I know that we can make a life of happiness: For I know that deep down you want the same wonderful things as I do. So humbly, I ask you to marry me, Mr. Stanley. Should you refuse, then this will be the last you will hear from me. But oh, Bula Matari, say yes, and a new and glorious life will begin.

RECEIVING THIS LETTER ONE JUNE morning at his New Bond Street flat, he sat down, without moving, for several hours. He half crumpled the thing in his hands. He got up to shave. Looking into a mirror, he thought that he had lost the innocence and openness of his expression, each line equal to a year of passing loneliness and struggle in his life. Well into his twenties he had been boyish in appearance, but slowly his visage began to change, not just because of the ordinary passing of time but also from having witnessed so much death. It had been a companion since his boyhood days in Wales; it had followed him to New Orleans, then to Cuba, and then, during the Civil War, at the Battle of Shiloh, as a Confederate. Thereafter he watched death multiply before him in Africa time and time again. From native attacks. Fevers. Dysentery. And he had witnessed all of it from the vantage point of his solitude—would it ever pass, that loneliness?

Once, in an African forest, he had come upon a clearing where the trees were shimmering blue, their leaves vibrating rapidly. He stepped closer. Thousands of butterflies of many colorations had been resting there, wings flickering like candle flames—but all he could identify with was the lowly beetle that had scurried by his mud-encrusted boots.

"I'll take the hardy over the beautiful," he had thought.

He could have died a hundred times save for his fortitude. There was a big difference between stepping down on a thistle and thereby cutting the sole of your foot while hiking in Wales and doing the same in Africa. He remembered a minor "cut" he'd gotten in the jungle, the sharp tip of a reed having gone through the sole of his boot. Within a few hours the skin around the wound had swollen and turned a livid pink; within a day it became black and blue. The following morning it had begun to seep pus, and he fell into a fever for days—but even that had been easier to bear than Miss Tennant's rejection of him. No wonder he was sometimes so foul of mood and enraged during his last expedition; no wonder some of his porters had come to fear him.

"What is love, anyway?" he asked himself over and over again.

STANLEY BEGAN A HALF DOZEN different letters to her before sending her this:

Dear Miss Tennant,

In all truth I have wondered if the sea change of your feelings toward me has to do with my fame, and I have not found it easy to forget your past rejection of me. I have treated even the lowest pygmy better than you treated me, but I will admit that your claims to have prayed for my forgiveness—and love, if that is so—have moved me from a settled indifference to what might happen between us to a greater and more profound sympathy for the enterprise; and while I have yet to become completely convinced of your good intentions, I will make an attempt to reach that faith. But be warned: I do not find it a paltry matter.

And he went on for page after page, as if on a forced march of his emotions, until he had filled eighteen such pages: "If this is some piracy of your emotions to trick me again, than do not answer this; if you are sincere, I will be willing."

He was, after all, feeling that he would not live forever.

〰️

FROM SAMUEL CLEMENS TO WILLIAM Dean Howells:

June 25, 1890
Hartford, Connecticut

Dear Howells,

A curious thing: You remember meeting Henry Morton Stanley a few years back? The poor fellow had been going through a rather sticky and disappointing romance with a London society dame who had put him through the wringer. It put him in such a bad way that he had forsworn contact with the feminine universe until further notice; but lo and behold, I have just received an invitation to attend their wedding ceremony, to be held in the hallowed halls of Westminster in a

few weeks' time; apparently Stanley, back from his Africa trav-
els, experienced a change of heart—just one of those things, I
suppose, that will happen to a man when he's cooped up in the
wilds and malarial. Bemused as I am by the whole business, I
wish that brave Hercules all the good luck in the world. Much
as Livy and I would like to attend, and as curious as I am
about attending a wedding at Westminster, we won't be going.
(Among other things, Livy is under the weather and has been
told that she needs a few months to recover from a recent heart
ailment.) But I do wish the boy the best, and I am sure to meet
the lady who snared him sooner or later.

THEIR WEDDING

From Lady Stanley's Unpublished Memoir, circa 1907

ON THE AFTERNOON OF JULY 12, 1890, when I wed Henry Morton Stanley in Westminster Abbey, most everyone of importance in
London—including the Prince of Wales and Gladstone himself—
turned up for our ceremony. (Of the five thousand requests for
seats, only one-third of them could be honored.) Along the rainy
streets outside the abbey a great crowd of well-wishers gathered
to view the procession of dignitaries entering the sacristy, a flank
of bobbies and mounted Life Guards keeping clear a path into the
square as carriage after carriage veered into sight of the abbey
doors. I'm told that within that gathering were pennywhistle
musicians and jugglers; vendors hawked apples and taffy candies,

as well as souvenir pamphlets and pins and postcards featuring pictures of Stanley and me and commemorating our union.

At about one thirty, when I disembarked from my carriage in the company of my mother and brother, Gertrude and Charles Coombe Tennant, I alighted into a crowd of well-wishers, the ladies and young girls among them oohing and aahing over the nature of my wedding gown and train. It was a costume whose specifics I had dreamed about and made sketches of in my studio. My petticoat, bodice, and skirt were of white satin and trimmed with lace and silk cording, their edges decorated with garlands of orange blossoms and pearls; my bodice's high collar, in the Medici style, was similarly embroidered with pearls. I wore a tulle veil fastened to my hair with diamond stars, above which sat a crown of orange blossoms held in place by an aigrette, also of diamonds (a gift from Stanley). My shoes were of silver leather with diamond buckles. These were complemented by a long diamond necklace, a gift from Sir William Mackinnon, shipping magnate and head of the Imperial British East Africa Company, who helped to finance Stanley's last expedition. From it hung a brooch consisting of thirty-eight diamonds that had been arranged around a cameo of our good Queen Victoria (a gift, appropriately so, from Her Majesty).

During the days preceding our wedding, Henry had been laid low in his New Bond Street flat, unable to stir from his bed. He had fallen fiercely ill from a bout of chronic gastritis. Though he had continued on in great pain and was pale and feverish on the morning of our wedding, Stanley, fretful of missing out on what he had described to me in one of his daily letters as "the occasion of his greatest hope and promise in life," roused himself from his bed and, hobbling, managed to bathe, shave, sit for a proper haircut, and dress. His valet, Hoffman, and Dr. Parke assisted him into a fine ensemble that included a silk top hat and dark frock coat, to whose lapel he affixed a white carnation.

By the time he came by carriage into the square, buoyed by the jubilation of the crowd, who greeted him with whistles and applause and shouts of joy—"Long live Stanley!"—he was barely able to walk without a cane, but with his usual fortitude and resilience he summoned enough strength to get out of the carriage unassisted.

With a pipe organ playing and a choir singing, I made my entrance into the abbey shortly after my husband's arrival, a relief coming over me at the sight of him fidgeting with a pair of white kidskin gloves, for until a few moments before, we had wondered if Stanley would make it at all.

With my brother by my side, and with my two bridesmaids, bouquets of white roses in hand and jasmine wreaths upon their heads, leading the way, and with my two plumed squires carrying my lustrous train following at a distance of some twenty paces, I proceeded toward the altar into a realm that felt sanctified, supernatural, and protective. In the towering nave of Westminster, its stained-glass windows glorious with light, candles and lanterns aglow, in my trembling hands I carried a bouquet of white jasmine, gardenias, roses, and *pancratium* lilies.

When I joined Stanley by the altar, he was pale, his rheumy eyes betraying to me the gravity of his illness, his face drawn and his hair turned completely white. But he still managed to greet me with a slight smile and a nod of his head, and there was strength in his hand when he took hold of my mine. I can remember looking at Stanley and asking him, in a whisper, "Are you certain in your heart about this?" At that point he took a deep breath and stood straight, saying firmly, "Yes."

When we left Westminster, rose petals tossed from the balconies of surrounding houses were falling upon the pavement and street like snow in our wake. And as the tower's bells were ringing and the bystanders lining the street were waving miniature Union Jacks—as well as a few American flags, in honor of Stanley's American association—I realized that my new husband had quickly fallen ill again. As we made our brief but jubilant procession by carriage to my family's town house in Richmond Terrace, he let out a shallow breath and slumped back into his seat.

Eventually, the carriage compartment, jostling along the cobble-stones, brought him enough discomfort that he doubled over. But then he would open his eyes and ask, "Are we there yet?"

We held our reception in our back garden on Richmond Terrace. Tents had been erected in the event of bad weather, which was a good thing, as it had rained most of the day. Stanley, I should regretfully say, was not up to the occasion. When he had first come onto the green, assisted by Dr. Parke, he had simply said hello to a few folks, then retired inside to rest. After a while, Mother, being a determined soul and very aware of formality, went in to give my husband a rousing talk about his responsibilities. And so my husband, summoning his strength, chose to address the gathering from a lawn chair. For about five minutes, he named, from memory, nearly everyone in attendance and thanked them, ending his oration with these words:

"This is the very finest day of my life. Who would think that this old soldier would be so lucky as to have, at this stage of his life, a woman as good and lovely as Dorothy? How strange it all seems that I now, so unexpectedly, possess a wife."

꙳

HERE THE NARRATIVE BREAKS OFF; at the time of writing, her mother entered her study to remind her of an impending luncheon appointment, and so she put down her pen, withdrawing into her dressing room.

Part Two

MEETING MR. CLEMENS

DOROTHY SITS TO WRITE ON an early spring day in 1908. Near her writing desk is a cabinet photograph that Samuel Clemens had given her in 1891, signed "With kindest regards to Mrs. Stanley, Mark Twain, Hartford, Connecticut, Jan. 29"; in the picture, Clemens was posed on his porch, his arm wrapped around a pillar, his legs crossed—a most intense expression on his face. The occasion of this gift, coming during Stanley's last tour of America in late 1890–91, when he and Dorothy, or Dolly, as he had come to call her, and her mother, the pestiferous Gertrude Tennant, had met up with Clemens in New York City.

From Lady Stanley's Unpublished Memoir

DURING THE FIRST MONTHS OF our marriage, when Stanley began to move his most valued effects and books into my house on Richmond Terrace, we turned one of the large guest chambers into his study; as crates arrived by wagon from his New Bond Street flat, he would spend part of his days carefully unpacking them, and shortly that room, filled with those objects and books, became the one he found most inspirational to his thinking. Elsewhere in the house, we found space for numerous other photographs of Stanley in Africa and allocated one of the empty servant's quarters for the storage of his travel podium, portable writing desk, medicine trunks, and the piles of tribute plaques and coffins and other commemoratives that came nearly daily.

Once he'd put his large and formidable writing desk, which resembled a preacher's pulpit, near the fireplace, and once he had installed a correspondence cabinet, he attended to his books—one such crate, marked THE ONE HUNDRED WORTHIES, bore those volumes necessary to a gentleman's essential education. There were also geographical books, books in Latin and Greek, books on ornithology, many books on religion and theological thought, and numerous biographies. ("It is my intention," he told me in those days, "to write my autobiography so as to get the record of my life straight.") For his pleasure, there were novels. In fact it was my observation that, when he was not writing, he considered the companionship of a book—nearly any book at all—indispensable to his well-being. He read everything, from the cheapest shilling novels—the kinds of shockingly bad yellow-backed romances one would find in the kiosks of railway stations—to books written by the great past masters, such as Cervantes, as well as authors of current interest—Kipling, Tolstoy, and Dostoyevsky among them. (It was a habit, I would learn, that he did not share with Mr. Clemens, who was not quite as well read as my husband, particularly in the realm of novels.) But among the books that he most cherished he included the works of Mark Twain, to which, I noticed, he returned again and again.

Despite the great acclaim that had met his initial return from the Emin Pasha expedition, it was not long afterward that his actions were being daily condemned by missionaries and humanitarian groups in the newspapers. One of the officers in his party, a certain Lieutenant Troup, with whom Stanley had a falling-out, had written to the newspapers describing the expedition as a "mad mission, supposedly dedicated to the spread of civilization but really about exterminating the natives in the way the Americans had exterminated the red man."

"My dear," he once told me, "it is one thing to command the physical body of a man to do such and such a thing: But to command the mind and the soul is not so easy at all. The conditions of such an unearthly world produce in normally civilized and reasonable men many a strange response, which no one man can predict or control once soul-altering madness has descended. In a place like Africa, where the 'wilds' quickly find a man out, there is no substitute for fortitude and character."

Some accused him of being power-driven and merciless in his treatment of the Africans. This, I knew, was far from the truth. Nor was he pleased to find himself the butt of jokes. One evening, out of curiosity, we had occasioned to attend a theatrical venue in the East End and saw a play called *Stanley in Africa*. To my husband's dismay, he was portrayed by a baboonish actor who played Stanley as a daft British officer, oblivious to the sufferings of the column in his charge. The guffaws of the audience when his character would bellow out, "March on through the dismal swamps to find the snippety pasha—and ivory, too!" so upset him that we left quickly.

"What I did was for the good of the future of Africa," he told me again and again from his sickbed one day. "Those who do not believe me can go to H—s and stay there forever."

☼

THANKFULLY, IN NOVEMBER OF 1890, just as he had begun to grow overly testy and weary of the public atmosphere in England, we traveled to a far more evenhanded place where such controversies did not exist: America. The reason for our sojourn was a lecture tour of that country arranged by one Major James Burton Pond (who, I should add, happened to be Samuel Clemens's agent). With my mother, Gertrude, two of our Swahili servants, and in the company of Lieutenant Jephson and my cousin, we set sail from Liverpool to New York, aboard the SS *Cuba*.

Upon our arrival, Stanley's mood, dour in recent weeks, greatly improved: A military band had gathered on the chilly, windblown dock, performing both "God Save the Queen" and "The Star-Spangled Banner." As we passed into the customhouse, there was a contingent of press on hand to ask friendly questions, most of them having nothing to do with Africa. But then, for whatever reason, it seemed a funny thing to the local press that Stanley had escorted my mother down the gangplank and across the pier to the customhouse, his elbow locked on her arm while she, with her other hand gesticulating toward his person, seemed to be expressing some strong opinions. Then an argument between them erupted over a trivial matter: I can remember that the steve-dores and dock workers found this incident quite funny and began calling out many foolish things. Just then, I had counseled my husband to remember the glory awaiting him, and he resumed escorting my mother with courtesy. But a seed was planted: By the time we had finished our progression to the customhouse, the press had formed the unfair opinion that Stanley was under the sway of a nagging mother-in-law, a motif that would follow us, to his annoyance, in humorous newspaper accounts throughout the land.

☆

WE STAYED AT THE PLAZA Hotel, just off Central Park, a large suite of rooms at our disposal. Telegrams and notes lay in piles upon the desk of Stanley's temporary study, including an invi-tation from Thomas Edison to visit with him at his laboratory in Menlo Park, New Jersey, one of the few outings that Stanley seemed to genuinely look forward to. Stanley on that occasion also received a great number of telephone calls—among them one from Gordon Bennett, publisher of the *New York Herald*, and one from Mrs. Astor, who had arranged a dinner in her Fifth Avenue mansion in his honor. Thoroughly prepared for the lectures that he would be giving in New York—at the Century Association, the Cooper Union, and in Steinway Hall, among other places, he would address both geographical societies and ordinary audiences on "The Founding of the Congo Free State"—he still felt hard-pressed to make a good impression about his activities there.

With so many engagements, dinners, lectures, and luncheons and such, we were always making our way through the streets of the city by carriage. Stanley found the city barbarically noisy and in a state of disorder: The elevated trains he despised; the many posters and advertisements that were thrown up everywhere, without regard to any aesthetic concern, troubled him as well. He on one occasion took the time to count the telegraph and telephone wires that crisscrossed above the street outside one of our windows—some one hundred and seventy four, he counted: a web of wiring; an ugly scene.

Late one Sunday afternoon, Stanley mentioned, with some delight, that he wanted me to meet someone who was waiting below in a lobby sitting room with Stanley's American agent, Major Pond. "And who is this?" I asked.

"Come; you will see."

Descending to the Plaza lobby, Stanley and I found the supremely tall and bearded Major Pond sitting in a banquette in a dark corner of a salon. Beside him was a quite pleasant and genteel, rather angelic-faced woman who immediately smiled upon our approach. Just as Major Pond stood up to greet us, the gentleman by her side struck a match for his cigar, his distinguished face, with its high, curling brows and handlebar mustache, glaring like sculpted stone in that sudden flaring light—like a jack-o'-lantern, perhaps; the very sharp features of his face, with its aquiline nose and deep-set, hawkish eyes flashed brilliantly white and yellow, then faded low into a sudden bluish shadow as the match went out. In that moment I knew that he was none other than Samuel Clemens, or Mark Twain, the lady at his side being his wife, Livy.

"Hello, Stanley," he said. And, looking at me, he added, "And so this is the one and only gracious lady?"

We spent that evening together; throughout I saw in Stanley certain qualities of behavior that I had not seen before. He seemed much relaxed in the company of his friend and quite willing to allow the great man the floor when it came to conversation. In truth, after a week of engagements Stanley was feeling somewhat fatigued, but he also seemed relieved to be hearing about subjects

254 | OSCAR HIJUELOS

other than Africa, about which he was continually expected to hold forth.

Of that felicitous occasion I can remember asking Mr. Clemens by which name he liked to be addressed.

"Our dear friend Major Pond here treats Mark Twain like a nom de plume, which it is, of course: In his letters, he puts Mark in quotes, even in his salutations to me—which is a professional idiosyncrasy that I have not yet figured out. I don't mind Mark—I've done well by it—yet sometimes it sounds too short by itself, while 'Mark Twain' doesn't: Now, Livy calls me Precious and Youth so often that I have been known to accidentally sign my letters to complete strangers in such a way; whereas Henry here refers to me as both Samuel and Mark, depending upon how biblical his mood is. Personally, if I am feeling lazy, I will use the short form, Mark, to sign my notes; because it has two fewer letters than Samuel it conserves great amounts of minute energies when added up over the years. Now, with you, dear Madame Stanley, I would consider it an honor to be addressed by whatever name you choose to call me, just as long as it's one of them, so as to avoid future confusion."

☼

TO HAVE WALKED ARM IN arm with Mr. Clemens along Fifty-Ninth Street that evening would remain for me a greater honor than would meeting the American president, Benjamin Harrison, and many an illustrious senator at the White House the following week. With a woolen cape slung over his shoulders and a Russian trapper's bearskin cap upon his head, Mr. Clemens (to this day I cannot think of him as Mark or Samuel), though of medium height (he was by his own account five feet, eight and a half inches tall), he seemed taller in his cowboy boots. Passersby recognized him, and even carriage drivers doffed their hats or whistled to greet to him, calling out: "Hello, Mr. Twain!" We made our way

along toward the cobblestones by Central Park, a light snow falling. As my husband, escorting Livy, in the company of Major
Pond, followed behind us, I inquired of Mr. Clemens just how he
and Stanley had met.

"My husband told me that you became acquainted long before
you became known as writers. Stanley has never described the
exact circumstances, other than that it happened long ago. I don't
understand his reluctance to discuss it."

"Madame Stanley, among us writers there is a sacred code
that prohibits us from revealing too much about certain things.
For reasons that I cannot convey to you—and perhaps I one day
will—Stanley and I have agreed to keep it a private thing."

Parting congenially after a nightcap at our hotel, I presented
Mr. Clemens and his wife a gift of my book *London Street Arabs*,
and we expressed the mutual wish of seeing each other again. I
told him that it was my hope that he would have the opportunity
to one day meet my mother, who was an admirer of his writings;
and perhaps, I had asked him, he would sit for me as a portrait
subject, as Stanley had—he said he would.

Later, I mentioned to Stanley my complete enchantment at
meeting Mr. and Mrs. Clemens, but when I voiced my curiosity
as to why he remained so secretive about his early friendship with
Clemens, he was curt in his answer: "Do I have to tell you everything? Cannot a man have his own private thoughts?"

Even when we eventually made our way to the cities of St.
Louis and New Orleans, where he had once worked and lived as
a young man, he never went into detail about Clemens.

Another Journal Recollection, from January 27, 1891, a Tuesday

ON A DATE WHEN STANLEY was scheduled to give a lecture
in Trenton, New Jersey, Mother and I had an invitation, received

some days before, to visit Samuel Clemens's home in Hartford, Connecticut.

We arrived in Hartford at about 9:30, and Mr. Clemens was awaiting us in a carriage, his youngest daughter, Jean, by his side. Along the way we stopped at a country store to pick up various vegetables to be cooked for supper. He called me My Lady, and he could not have been more courteous. He seemed quite delighted to play the host, though he missed Stanley's presence.

"Well, I'm happy that you've come," he told us.

As I had imagined, and as described by Stanley, his house was majestic, a fairy-tale-like place with turrets that suggested witches' hats, great hallways, and winding stairs. Its shape reminded me of a riverboat. In his parlor was a large Gothic fireplace transplanted from a Scottish castle, and one of the ceilings had been inlaid with mariners' stars, I believe. And though there was a sense of gaiety about the place, Mr. Clemens seemed more solemn than he had been when we saw him in New York. Nevertheless we had a pleasant discussion that day about the novelist Anatole France—Mr. Clemens was reading *The Crime of Sylvestre Bonnard*, a book that greatly impressed him. He seemed to dote on Mother, who took an immediate liking to him. His daughter Clara performed songs for us on the piano; and Jean, having experimented with some poetry, declaimed several new verses for us. Mrs. Clemens was still in mourning over her mother's recent passing and was laid low with what Clemens hoped was a "mind problem." She did manage to muster herself from her bed for most of the day, and it was obvious to both of Mother and I that our company was a burden on her: Yet she was cheerful and grateful, filling us in on the latest caprices of one of their famous neighbors, Harriet Beecher Stowe, author of *Uncle Tom's Cabin*, who lived just next door and would, even while we were there, arrive unannounced and wander through the rooms of the house in her bedroom slippers, whooping and howling at times. She would sit down at the piano and even as we were in the midst of a conversation begin to play and sing, and then just as suddenly, she would get up and leave the room. She returned with some flowers cut from the Clemens's own greenhouse, which she presented as a gift to Livy; then she began to question Mother and me as to whether we had read her most famous novel. When we told her that we had, she asked if we had a copy of it to reread on our journey. When we told her that we did not, she insisted on bringing over a copy. We went along with it, taking into account that she was obviously plunging into senility—Mr. Clemens made several discreet comic gestures with his eyes at her eccentricity, and Mrs. Clemens told us that as a general practice the neighbors in Nook Farm had grown accustomed to her waywardness. Clearly she had descended into a second childhood of sorts. I could not help but wonder if the solitude that writers experience day in and day out, with work that does not bring them into close intercourse with "society" might hasten such mental decline.

In this regard I would say that Clemens was about as well balanced as Stanley, who looked upon his writing duties as plain work, disturbed as he might be by its tedium. Like Stanley, Clemens, on the whole, seemed remarkably grounded: a famous family man, pestered by responsibilities, moody—I had seen him shouting at one of the cats in a sudden spurt of anger—but generally even-tempered.

As I wanted to make a painting of him eventually, I took the liberty of making some pencil sketches of Clemens as we sat by the fine fireplace. Sitting before the hearth, he had dozed for some minutes, but then a snort, when one of his cats jumped up on his lap, awakened him. He apologized: We laughed. I showed him my rudimentary sketch. Pleased, he said: "I don't hate it, which is a good thing for me."

After dinner, a sleep of quietude—a welcome change from the incessant clamor of New York. In the morning, after breakfast, he drove us to the station; shortly we arrived back in New York, where I rejoined my husband and his colleague Dr. Parke. A few days later, we embarked on our tour.

∾∕∽

THEY WENT FROM NEW YORK to many cities on the East Coast, then they came back for a banquet at the New York Press Club; then they went to Chicago (on February 14), then on to California (Los Angeles) on March 21. On Sunday, March 29, Stanley reached New Orleans after a thirty-two-year absence.

From Stanley's Journal, circa 1893, Relating How
He Later Came to Write about His Early Days with
Samuel Clemens

HAVING JOURNEYED TO NEW ORLEANS by private train in early 1891 as part of an itinerary of some one hundred engagements across the United States, with several stops in Canada, I had not expected how touched I would be by those distant yet familiar surroundings. The tour itself had, to that point, been a matter of fulfilling an obligation. Though I was still exhausted from my recent Africa travels and would have been content to stay home with my new bride in England, I had undertaken this tour to make amends to my American agent, Major Pond. Four years earlier, in the autumn of 1886, while lecturing in the northeast—after having attracted some very good press notices, a result of successful engagements in Hartford and Boston, where I had been introduced to my audiences by old friend Samuel Clemens—I was soon flooded with offers from all parts of the country; so many, in fact, that Major Pond was kept quite busy in his New York office making adjustments to my schedule day by day. By that mid-December of 1886, just as the offers continued to pour in and I had completed my eleventh lecture, in Amherst, with some eighty-nine more to come—as per my original contract with Major Pond—a telegram from William Mackinnon arrived at my hotel. It was an urgent summons to England, advising me to drop everything and move forward with the final preparations for an armed expedition to relieve the Emin Pasha, governor of the southernmost province of Equatoria, then under siege by the forces of the Mahdi in a stronghold near Lake Albert, his life being in imminent danger.

As it had been a condition of my original agreement with Mr. Pond that I could cancel my tour at any time given such an emergency, I quickly booked passage back to Southampton—to Mr. Pond's heartbreak, but not without having first given him my word that I would later return to complete my contractual obligations should I survive the ordeal that awaited me.

So it was that after four years of rigorous travel I found myself in the limelight again. It was no easy thing for me to face the public at that time (or any time), for though my return from Africa had been at first received with great jubilation, some rather severe and startling attacks on the nature of my command had begun to appear in the press within a few months. One particular aspect of my account in *In Darkest Africa*—in regard to the cruel and irrational behavior of the officer commanding my rear column, the late Major Barttelot, who was responsible for many unnecessary native deaths—had come under question. His family, rushing to the dead man's defense, and naturally wishing to restore his good name, had launched a campaign to discredit my reputation and abilities. Joining them were others, principally Lieutenant Troup, who not only made claims against my moral character but also reported, without a hint of shame, on the unsavory activities of certain of my other officers. Altogether, though I ultimately made a successful case in my defense, it remained an ordeal, for I had to spend countless hours, in England and in America, submitting myself to long and tedious interviews with journalists, answering every kind of inquiry, and living under magnified scrutiny, as if I were in court and under indictment for a crime.

Thankfully, on this journey I was accompanied by my new wife, Dorothy, the pearl of my days, whose sunny temperament and joy for life remained a solace to me. My mother-in-law,

Gertrude Tennant, and her nephew, Hamilton Aide, and one of my old (and most loyal) Africa hands, Lieutenant Arthur J. M. Jephson, comprised the rest of my party. Our private train cars featured all the amenities of a fine hotel, and as we crossed the country, I had the use of a small office and writing desk on which to make improvements to my lectures as needed. Because I had always experienced some unease before audiences and remained wary about going over certain distasteful details in regard to my recent expedition, I was plagued all along by a great reticence. (I worried, mostly, about being boring.) Here my clever wife's input was invaluable to me. It was her idea that I somewhat broaden the scope of my talks so as to include the story of my encounters with the pygmies of the forest and other remarkable, somewhat pleasant discoveries. My lecture, which had at first been advertised in New York as "The Relief of Emin Pasha," became "The March through the Magical Forest," a change, that, according to Major Pond, much invigorated box-office receipts. (We did many thousands of dollars' worth of business at each venue.) No amount of what I said could begin to capture my experiences, but I tried to put my listeners into my shoes: It was exhausting, to say the least, but I was applauded everywhere I went.

Since I had given over most of my spare time to the refining of my talks, I mainly left sightseeing to my wife and her mother. Dolly could at least use that opportunity to take in something of my adoptive country and meet some of our many friends. In New York, that chaotic metropolis (a city planner's nightmare was my impression), I had the pleasure of introducing her to Samuel Clemens for the first time—he liked her immediately, I am happy to say, and one evening they attended a Buffalo Bill rodeo show together. And Clemens—that is, Mark Twain—was also on hand during some of the lectures I gave in Hartford, his hometown, and in Boston. It was joyous to me that they got on so well.

On one of those afternoons in Boston, after a fine snowfall, Dolly and Clemens, along with his youngest daughter, Jean, went out for several hours of sleigh riding. Upon their return, my wife was rosy-cheeked and ecstatically happy. "Oh, Bula Matari, come and have a ride and breathe the most delicious air under heaven!" she said to me in her endearing way. Clemens, smiling, his hat of Russian fur and his long coat still dripping with particles of snow, joined in: "Yes, Bula," he told me. "Your winter chariot awaits." But having my duties, I excused myself and returned to work; besides, I liked the idea of Clemens befriending my wife. She was, after all, quickly becoming my "better half" and an asset to me socially, and I knew that Clemens would have a more congenial time with her than he would with me, so preoccupied was I about saving my energies for my nightly performances.

�☀️

NOW, BY THE TIME WE arrived in New Orleans, in March, I was somewhat ready for a diversion beyond the endless dinners and fetes in my honor, which I, being cautious around strangers, would have been happy to avoid. Nevertheless I gave lectures in the elegant salons and society halls of the city. Playing up my "southern roots" for the crowds, I spiced my stew of African tales with frequent mentions of having worn the Confederate uniform and participated in the Battle of Shiloh, though I had since become better known for "other things." I spoke of southern bravery and resolve during that war and ventured the notion that if I had remained cool in some very dangerous situations in Africa and other locales, I owed it to those earlier formative experiences. But while speaking of these things, my life before the Civil War began to come back to me, having lain dormant under a multitude of other memories; and so, breaking from my normal routine, I decided to spend a morning with my wife and her mother, sight-seeing around the city.

On that occasion, I showed them the places where I had once wandered, the harborside and levee, the labyrinthine center of the French Quarter, even the old coffee stands where I used to dally as a young man. And I took them up the main commercial strip, where I had once worked for the better part of a year as a clerk in a store. When we came to that location, at number 3 Tchoupitoulas Street, we found that a store still existed there, selling, as far as I could tell, much of the same kinds of goods, though with a many modern addition to its inventory. I could not resist going inside to take in the old ambience.

Then we strolled over to my first boardinghouse, an old clapboard affair on St. Thomas Street. I was very touched to see that with the exception of some physical improvements to the premises and the addition of some rosebushes clustered by and adorning the front yard's white picket fence, it was much as I remembered it. And because it had been such a happy place for me, a home where I had received much kindness, I felt a great curiosity to see if my former landlady Mrs. Williams still lived there. And so with my wife and mother-in-law in tow, I knocked on the front screen door. Shortly, as we waited in the heat of the day, we heard a voice calling from inside—"Hold on!" Though I had not heard that voice in years, it sounded like Mrs. Williams, and within those moments, I experienced a drawing back in time to my youth, when I knew little about the world. With those years falling away from my travel-worn self, I felt a strangely invigorating grace come through me. To my delight, when the door opened, there stood before us a pretty black woman, her hair all white and tied up in a bun; she was wearing a floral-patterned dress and an apron and smelled sweetly of lilac perfume. She was perhaps seventy or so, though her bearing and manner were youthful.

"What can I do for you folks?"

At first, she displayed no awareness that the well-dressed gentleman with his hat in hand and in the company of two ladies had been one of her boarders many years before. I had, indeed, changed: The lad of eighteen, with his youthful countenance and ruddy cheeks, who until he was twenty-five had never seemed to most people older than fifteen, now stood before her with his hair turned white, a weathered face, and a great walrus mustache.

"Good afternoon, madame. Are you the same Mrs. Jessica Williams who ran this boardinghouse in the years before the war?"

"I surely am and still do. And who might you be?"

"You may not remember me. My name is Henry Morton Stanley, but I once stayed here for the better part of a year in the late 1850s, under another name, Mr. John Rowlands."

Looking me over, she finally declared: "Why, the little Welsh boy, Mr. Johnny! Come in, come in!" And she beamed so delightfully, shaking all our hands and smiling so gratefully, in a way not often seen in our lofty London circles, that even my most aristocratic mother-in-law was charmed. "Oh, my," Mrs. Williams said with excitement. "Ain't you the very one I have been reading 'bout in the papers!"

Indeed, my arrival in New Orleans had been much publicized in advance, thanks to my agent, Major Pond—my every lecture advertised and every luncheon and dinner engagement duly noted. Extensive, too, had been reports of my African exploits and the celebration of my return as an "adopted son of the city." Yet I felt somewhat humbled to be in Mrs. Williams's presence, for she had known me before I had become the "great Henry Stanley."

We sat in her parlor and reminisced, but as I had some pressing engagement awaiting us later that afternoon, we could not stay as long as I would have liked. As we took our leave, Mrs. Williams told my wife—"Your husband, ma'am, was one of the most polite and studious of my boarders, and neat as a pin and grateful for the littlest things. Always thought he would land on his feet one way or the other. But never in all my days did I think to see him go so far in this world; you've made an old woman happy, coming here, you certainly have."

When we parted, though I wished to embrace her, for the thought occurred to me that I would probably never see Mrs. Williams again, my affectionate side, seen by so few in this life, remained within, buried under the shell of my long-practiced formality. So in farewell, I simply took her hand in mine and held it for a few moments. She smiled, and I could see a few tears in her kindly eyes. I came away from that visit in a solemn rather than joyous mood, as in those moments, I had repeated one of the great failings of my life—an inability to express, regardless of my desire to do so, just how deeply moved I could feel by a person.

IN THE COURSE OF THAT lecture tour, I had been presented with honorary university degrees and keys to one city and another and with medals and plaques and certificates singing my praises, but as my visit with Mrs. Williams had come on the heels of so many formal occasions, that brief meeting, standing out in my mind, seemed to have a subtle effect on my emotions. For I continued to think about our visit together, my mind vexed by how so simple a soul, whose importance to the greater world was negligible, had certainly found contentment, while I seemed to be in the midst of a perpetual mad scramble to preserve my fame and reputation.

WITH MR. TWAIN

From Lady Stanley's Unpublished Memoir

THE YEARS 1891–92 WERE OCCUPIED with much travel. When we returned from America in April, after a short rest in London, Stanley was pressed to fulfill a commitment to tour the British

Isles, our journeys taking us, by private train, out from London to the far reaches of Scotland and Wales. Wherever he appeared—to champion the cause of England's further involvement in Africa—the public gathered. (There was another category of lecture as well: Stanley would receive a heartfelt summons from an earnest vicar speaking on behalf of his parish. Because he was known, in some devout circles, for his pious work of bringing the Word to the savages of Africa, as per the example of his "second father," David Livingstone, he was often sought out by the common religious folk, those lordly people of the earth who always asked Stanley to come to their churches to speak.) Aside from advocating that England build a great Congo railway, so as to link the isolated interior with the rest of the continent, he wanted the British people to rise to the challenge of fostering English civilization in East Africa—in the regions of Uganda and Kenya. He spoke before antislavery societies about the repression of the Arab slave trade, to medical societies about the training of medical officers, and to medical missionaries about the treatment of tropical diseases, for from his own experience with malaria, he saw that such diseases, unchecked, would eventually evolve into new plagues, impeding European progress in those countries. But many a deaf ear was turned to him.

Such tours were exhausting for my husband. While Mother and I sometimes accompanied him and could enjoy the amenities of luxury travel, we did not have to mount the stage and speak for several hours at a time. (Hard as he tried, he had only been able to get his Emin Pasha speech down to one hour and forty minutes.) Nor did we have to answer the unending questions of journalists or put up with the demands of holding forth with strangers at those meals. We were something of a buffer for Henry, and he had become grateful even for my mother's company, for people are not so forward if you are not alone. What private moments he had, on such tours, when he was traveling without us, he cherished: His free time was spent reading or writing. Still, when ensconced in a room in a small-town inn, my husband, craving the fresh air, got into the habit of slipping out at every opportune moment.

Thankfully, when the English tour ended, by the end of July, we went to Switzerland, where Stanley began a well-deserved rest. By then he seemed so fatigued and weary that I questioned the soundness of his reasoning in having accepted yet another tour that coming October, to Australia. He was not looking forward to it, but as he was a man who believed in keeping his promises, he could no more change his mind than, as he put it, "a bee could turn into a butterfly." But in Switzerland, he took advantage of the fresh air, and our days were spent in long hikes in the meadows of Mürren. On one hike, however, along a field of damp grass, it was his misfortune to lose his footing—the man who had traveled for years throughout equatorial Africa without once breaking any bones shattered his ankle from a fall. The painful injury precipitated yet another bout of malaria.

For some months he could only walk with the assistance of a crutch. He hated the thing, but on at least one occasion, my husband found that it worked to his advantage. It was in October of that year, 1891, just before we were to leave for Australia, that King Leopold summoned Stanley to his palace in Ostend to discuss the possibility of Stanley's returning to the Congo. When the king broached the subject, Stanley pointed out the lameness of his leg, from which he had yet to recover. "Well, it will be healed by the time you return from Australia, will it not?" the king said. "Then I will have a big task on hand for you, when you are ready."

Throughout our long tour of Australia and New Zealand, Stanley underwent numerous relapses of gastritis and malaria; the latter would usually come over him after he had been weakened by the former, which is to say that the conditions of touring and travel in general, particularly given the very long periods at sea, were proving too much for my husband's flagging constitution. Loving him so, I, for one, did not want him risking his life in Africa again. For all the praises heaped upon him by the likes of Leopold, I began to remind my husband that however immortal he might sometimes feel, he was very much a man of flesh, of a finite duration, one who, in his matrimony, should prepare himself—give himself over to—a more domestic and safe life, an idea that he only reluctantly came around to.

Strange dreams plagued him. He would report these dreams in a most factual, almost casual manner over breakfast, and we, alarmed that most of his dreams were about death, began to wonder if Stanley were having premonitions about his own.

"Please, Henry," I would say to him. "Allow me to take care of you."

But his illnesses—his malaria, in particular—were more persuasive than my words. Physical pain, such as what he suffered when he broke his ankle on an ordinary hike in Switzerland, he was indifferent to. But, as I would learn, what he most feared was a diminishment of his faculties—his memories, his ability to organize his thoughts and write through the long hours, and the very physical aspect of his written script, in which he had always taken great pride. These became the things he wished to preserve, the loss of which he feared the most.

Thankfully, when we did come back to England some eight months later, in June of 1892, Stanley had begun to take my own many reservations about such rigorous journeys to heart. "My love," I said to him. "Having worked so hard, should you not now begin to enjoy your life?"

"It is the better idea," he admitted. "I will not return to Africa," he told me.

☀

WHEN HE WAS NOT ILL, he remained as energetic as any man. The lack of a great challenge had left him restless. As he easily tired of London society, Mother and I, thinking it an honorable profession that Father would have approved of, persuaded Stanley to give up his American citizenship and stand for a seat in the House of Commons as a Liberal Unionist candidate for the

North Lambeth district in London. Ours was a rushed decision, and Stanley entered the contest just ten days before the polling would take place, in late June. Refusing to go door to door, to call personally on voters, or to loll about in pubs and meetinghouses, he preferred to rely upon the carefully prepared speeches that he, as a son of the working class, would give at labor clubs and assemblies. Such experiences, however, did not go well at first. During a speech at Hawkstone Hall, Lambeth, it seemed not to matter what he said, for he was heckled by an organized rabble from the opposition, his every word shouted down.

"Whatever I have achieved in life has been achieved by my own hard work, with no help from privilege or favor of any kind. My strongest sympathies are with the working classes...and as such I see myself endeavoring to better the conditions of the masses..." He had just finished saying these words when the stage upon which we were seated was stormed and we were forced to flee to our carriage.

Despite our late entry into the fray, Stanley, on the strength of his reputation and great patriotism, lost by only one hundred and thirty votes. And while he had no great love for electioneering, he promised to continue on as a candidate for the next election, Along the way came other interludes of travel, mainly for reasons of his unsteady health, which by then had begun to trouble me, as these affected his mood. We rarely argued, but what arguments did take place seemed to come about from his continuing discomforts, which enfeebled him, and being put in the care of others seemed to shame Stanley. In that state, he preferred to be left alone; he would enter into weeklong periods of isolation, when he would rarely venture from our house. Otherwise, even when good health found him, it was only an exceptional person who could rouse him from his seclusion, as happened one June afternoon in 1892, when we learned that Samuel Clemens had arrived in London from Berlin, on his way back to America.

On Mr. Twain

WHAT I UNDERSTOOD FROM STANLEY of Mr. Clemens's situation in those days was that the great American writer had been undergoing some rather difficult times in regard to his finances and health. An entrepreneur, Clemens had started his own publishing house in the 1880s, Charles L. Webster and Company, through which he put out his own books, *The Adventures of Huckleberry Finn* being the first. His greatest success came with the publication of the autobiography of Ulysses S. Grant, in 1885, which sold many hundreds of copies. Despite profits from it, Clemens had taken a ruinous loss through a gamble on another book, *Life of Pope Leo XIII,* as neither Catholics nor Protestants bought that pious volume, and several other of his publishing ventures had also failed or not come to fruition. But what money he had made over the years from his own popular writings and from the Webster publishing company turned to air, for he had poured huge amounts into the development of a typesetting machine. Its inventor—a certain Mr. Paige—much delayed its completion, at great expense to Clemens.

Clemens had written Stanley a few letters that mentioned these reversals, but never had he prevailed upon my husband for any funds and referred to his decision to move with his family to Europe as one made out of a concern for his wife's health. Since we had last seen them, two years before, Livy had begun to suffer from a crippling rheumatism and heart palpitations that left her faint, short of breath, and listless. And one of their daughters, the youngest, Jean, at the age of twelve, had come down with some unusual symptoms of her own, her sweet personality suddenly changing. Clemens himself, in the urgency of his financial need, was driven to write many hours each and every day to raise money, to the point where his right arm became practically paralyzed. One of the letters that awaited Stanley on our return from Australia, in mid-1892, had arrived from Berlin, where Clemens and his family had been staying for some months. Clemens's script was unrecognizable, as he had taken to writing with his left hand.

"What's hardest," he had written to Stanley, "is that we have decided to leave our beloved house in Connecticut. When we will return I do not know—I hope it will be soon; but I have found positions for my coachman of twenty-one years and my butler, George, and have left behind my two most trusted servants to look after the place. You may ask if I am happy to be traveling again: The answer is no! But I do find it necessary. The 'cures' of Europe will be good for us all; and it's a cheaper way of living, to be sure."

It is a curious thing that while we were vacationing in Switzerland, Clemens and his family were at Marienbad, taking the bath cures. Knowing Clemens, he had become convinced that his old friend, with so many pressures in his life, had entered into a melancholic state.

"Were I in a better condition," he told me, "I would go to him tomorrow."

☀

THEY FINALLY ARRANGED TO MEET at Claridge's for four o'clock tea, with my mother and I coming along. Stanley took a place beside us at a banquette, his hands cupped over the head of a cane, which he still needed, looking about each time someone entered the room. When Clemens walked in, some few minutes after the hour, he was instantly recognized by the patrons, who applauded his entrance. Clemens, majestic in a white linen suit, his hair streaming madly from his head, nodded and smiled at them as he made his way toward us. Stanley got up immediately and seemed genuinely moved to see him again. Not one to smile, Stanley easily did so then.

"Samuel Clemens, how the deuces are you?" Stanley happily said.

Clemens was affable that afternoon, quite complimentary of me, and actually doting on my mother. He seemed to find it amusing that Stanley was running for Parliament—"A dark rumor I heard at the Blackfriars Club; is it so?"—but he also seemed rather weary, even apprehensive. I do not recall if he made a joke about being in reduced circumstances, but as he sat with us he mentioned that his trip to America was necessary because of "urgent business matters." His right arm seemed somewhat better than what we had expected: The cures he had taken had improved his condition to the point where he could lift his elbow above his shoulder, something he said he could not do for the longest time: "Made me feel like an injured bird," he told us. The baths in mud are messy but remarkable, he allowed. Another help to the bodily maladies, he mentioned, was something he called the mind cure.

"Do you folks know of it? Learned it years ago from a governess we once had. It works by sheer willpower. But you have to really concentrate on putting the malady out of your thoughts. Anyway, this method seems to work nicely with stomachaches and such, if you can stop thinking about your troubled innards."

"I doubt it would work with malaria," my husband said. "Many is the time I have been stricken and wished it would go away. It just doesn't happen."

"Everything is harder in our years, Henry. We are no longer at an age when such things come easily. Even my memory is lagging lately: Don't know if it's business that does it, or just plain worries, but names leave me more easily these days. It's getting old, isn't it?"

"I think not," my husband said. "The longer you live, the more things you have to remember, and I would imagine there's only so much room in the human mind."

"I'll allow that might be so, Henry, but why is it—and I address this to Mrs. Tennant as well—that it is easier to remember some things from childhood than the name of a gentleman you just met in a crowded room?"

"You will always remember persons of interest," my mother said. "Most individuals are not worth remembering."

"I can see that—and yet even the best-remembered and fondest things get all scrambled up when you remember them, don't they? How I wish in these days to recall only the things that make me happy. It would be a kind of paradise, wouldn't it?"

⁂

HE TOLD US THAT HE would be giving a lecture at the Garrick Club in London, and he asked if Stanley would be kind enough to introduce him. (Stanley said he would.) He said that he was writing travel letters for a New York paper, the *Sun*, as I recall, and working on a book, a historical novel, the subject of which he would not mention, having some superstitious sense of secrecy about it. (This I would read years later; the book was about Joan of Arc.) And, as a gift, he had brought along "another ditty that has somehow tumbled out from my pen," a copy of his latest novel, *The American Claimant*, which had just been published in May. "A humble effort for your library," he told us.

Stanley was delighted to receive it, searching, as he always did when receiving anything from Clemens, for an inscription on its title page: Reading it over to himself, he showed it to me. It said: TO THE HAPPY NEWLYWEDS. MAY IT ALWAYS BE SO FOR YOU. SAM CLEMENS.

"This is fine indeed: I will read it tomorrow," Stanley told him. Then: "I do not know if you have received my latest on the Emin Pasha expedition, *In Darkest Africa*," he said. "I know that I asked Major Pond to make sure that you had a set."

"I do."

"And your opinion of it?"

"You know I like your writing, Henry; you must work harder than anyone—I was in on the birth of it. I remember your letter from Cairo about the book and how quickly it was written. How many words are in it?"

"About six hundred thousand, more or less."

"In how many days?"

"Eighty-six."

"My God! And all the things you put in it—maps, drawings, letters, lists—how on earth you did it I cannot imagine, but you did! It reads like a novel, almost—but some new kind of novel, I should say. Closest I ever got to something like that... well, it was *Life on the Mississippi*. Of course I admire it for the sheer audacity of the thing. Well done, Henry: And I am saying that despite my own feelings about the situation there. But as a work, well, I've got to hand it to you. I am admiring of it."

"Thank you, Samuel. Coming from you, that means a lot to me."

Stanley's face had flushed, and he looked into Clemens's eyes, which had briefly but intensely focused on his own.

"I do mean it. You've turned into one of the most muscular writers in the world. But I couldn't help noticing that you dedicated that book to King Leopold: I don't like him, Henry."

"That is a pity. He is a well-intentioned man in a difficult situation: The Congo does things to men's souls. Unkind things sometime happen."

(HERE STANLEY DAYDREAMED FOR A moment. He remembered the first time he spoke with Leopold. One evening in 1878, in the wake of his second expedition, after the most lavish of dinners, they had gone strolling in the gardens of his palace at Ostend, and the king, humbled by Stanley's explorations and lavishly praising him, a "common churl," as the greatest of explorers, had broached the subject of retaining his services in the Congo. The king had an immediate advantage. At some six feet four, he towered over Stanley, but despite this, he continually dropped his head low and slouched his shoulders; at every other moment he seemed to pause, bending low to pick at some blossom, his sentences coming when he, at a lower altitude, met Stanley eye to eye. That night he confessed his personal failings.

The sky was a dark blue, and the silhouettes of cypress trees, punctuating the horizon, dozed under the stars.

"What am I but a king who looks around and sees the world in a state of sorrow? I see the suffering all around me, and I become ashamed of my easy life. What is the purpose of mankind other than to better the condition of the lower orders?" Then: "What have I, a master of a great but modest land, to gain from risking my wealth to help some heathens, unless it would come to some good? No, Monsieur Stanley," he said as he slipped into French. "Je suis sincère." That very night, as the king paused to sniff some blossom's fragrance, Stanley told him that, upon returning to England, he would give the matter about Africa some thought. It involved Stanley returning to the Congo, with the aim of acquiring, by lease, native territories that the king would over-see. England—and, for that matter, the United States—with other territorial ambitions, had no interest in such enlightened expansions. When Stanley looked at him somewhat apprehensively, the king, a merry fellow who loved the fellatios of Paris brothels, laughed. "Besides, I will pay you well." Then: "Come, now: You are already greater than any other explorer—why not become the Alexander of Africa?")

CLEMENS, NO DOUBT, HAD BEEN exposed to certain exaggerated reports of violence done to the Africans in that region, a subject that always soured Stanley's relish of his own accomplishments. Even I sometimes imagined that my husband despaired that he could not do more to control the cruel actions of men, which were far out of his control. It was the one thing that made him regret his decision to disengage himself from the activities there—for even if a small percentage of such reports were true, it would reflect badly upon his legacy as a man who had sought to bring good to the region.

"At any rate, Henry: As you know, I have a publishing venture back home; it's often occurred to me that we should do something for it. Perhaps a book about the 'old days' of our youth. Does this hold an interest for you?"

"It is something that we can surely discuss."

This was followed by a silence.

"And how do you find Germany?" I asked Mr. Clemens.

"Oh, it's a fair enough place. The food is so-so. Not as good as the French make. But the culture is high, though wasted on lowbrows like me. Wagner operas are pretty but too long. A few months ago we went to a ten-day opera festival in Bayreuth. I slept through most of them—they work like a knockout potion on me. But note for note, you get your money's worth. Still, I have to say the Germans are a civilized people. And they are into pomp: I've taken my older daughters to the kaiser's fetes—grand balls held in his palace. I've signed books for him—'to William II': Imagine a boy from Hannibal doing that. We meet everyone of importance but live humbly there. At our hotel in Berlin, we can see the kaiser's carriage passing by on the street in the mornings—we're on the first floor, as Livy's not much on climbing stairs these days." Then: "She hasn't been well of late."

The thought subdued him.

"Is she all right?" my husband asked.

"I would like to say that she is, and she works hard to seem like she is. She never wants to bother me with her condition—and she has some days better than others. But it makes one start to feel old."

Then: "Anyway, Livy has gone from one thing to the other. She has something called erysipelas, a skin infection; and worse, she suffers from Graves' disease, which has a bad effect in weakening her heart. I have only left her out of the most urgent necessity. It's not been an easy time." Then: "And you, Stanley? How goes your health?"

"It goes as always, Sam. I never know from month to month if something will trigger my malaria."

"If that's the worst of your troubles, it deserves a toast. Let's find the bar."

And with that, Clemens asked our leave. He and Stanley went off to the men's billiard room of the hotel. As I left I heard Clemens toasting, "To malaria and all the goddamned things in this world!"

∿

WHEN STANLEY LATER RETURNED HOME, sometime past seven, with Clemens in tow, I should say they were in rather high spirits. Clemens was singing some old spiritual, cheerfully; at first Stanley brought him into our parlor to show him the Edison cylinder machine we had received as a wedding gift from the inventor. Then he took him into his study to show off the many African artifacts he had mounted on the walls—spears and war axes, necklaces and pieces of primitive art (among many other things), as well as the great many volumes of books in his library. Clemens sat smoking, with a whiskey in hand, looking over one book and the next while Stanley, excited as a child, pulled some special and very old volumes off the shelf.

"That is an original edition of Suetonius's *Twelve Caesars*, as published by Bettesworth and Hitch in 1732." Then: "Here is De Quincey." And: "Gladstone's *Gleanings*, signed for us. Not a bad book at all; quite Christian in its outlook." Then: "These are my Dickenses: *David Copperfield. Great Expectations. A Christmas Carol*, each bearing the great writer's signature!"

I was standing by the door to my husband's study to call them in for dinner—for Clemens had agreed to stay—when I heard Stanley saying: "Old friend, do you mind that I show you these things?"

"Mind? I'd rather sit here comfortably with these books than anywhere else in England," he answered. I felt slightly intrusive as I reminded them that dinner was waiting: I had not seen Stanley quite so enthused about anything in quite a while. "If there are any of my books that you would like for your own," he declared as we made our way to the dining room, "feel that they are yours to take with you." I'd never heard Stanley say such a thing before, not with any other visitor. "You are my friend, after all. A brother in letters, if not more." Then, tenderly, Stanley said: "You know, Samuel, I will never forget some of the things you have done for me."

THE DINNER—WHAT COULD BE SAID of it? Roasted quail and potatoes with a pottage of vegetables—our usual kind of fare. My husband, enlivened by having shown Clemens his new study, could not restrain himself from describing more of it. It was as if he were a boy rather than an explorer that evening, so happily disposed was he to Clemens's presence. He'd even gotten up to bring a large framed montage of explorers' photographs he'd made from the likenesses of Baker, Speke, Burton, and Livingstone. And if Mr. Clemens's wineglass went empty, Stanley filled it himself; and he loosened his collar and spoke exceedingly highly of his friend: "Yes, you are the best that America has to offer in letters—there's no finer writer than you."

Such kind words, however, seemed to make Clemens uncomfortable, as he kept shifting about in his seat and looking around the room, as if glancing over at our curio cabinet would change the subject. But once Stanley had decided upon a friendship, there was no limit to his capacity for adulation. In any event, cutting Stanley off just as he began to list the many admirable qualities of Clemens's work, I had thought to broach the subject that Clemens had brought up earlier at Claridge's: "And may I ask, Mr. Clemens—you mentioned a collaboration between you and my husband. What have you in mind, sir?"

"Well, it certainly wouldn't be about Africa. I would say it might be something along the lines of a dialogue between two grizzled codgers, talking about the old days on the Mississippi, just before the Civil War: your husband, in a previous incarnation, madame, plied those waters for several years, as often as I did: in fact, it was on the boiler deck of a riverboat that we met as young men, isn't that so, Henry?"

"Yes," Stanley said. "But Sam, surely you have written of it in *Life on the Mississippi.*"

"I have indeed, but you and I—well, did we not make a

journey together that might be somewhat interesting to our read-ers?" Then, for my sake, he added: "That was before I became Mark Twain and just when Henry became Henry." But then as my husband's face began to turn red, as sometimes happened with him in moments of discomfort, Clemens, seeing him so, dropped it. "What I mean, Dorothy, is that Stanley and I could make some kind of book together. My own company would give it a first-class treatment, of course. It's just something to consider. I under-stand if you would not want to tie your fortunes to me, as lately I seemed to attract disasters, businesswise. But with our names on such a book, whatever it might be about, I am certain that we could sell at least one hundred thousand copies of it by subscrip-tion." Then, gloomily: "On the other hand, I could be wrong."

"Should I end up winning this election in Lambeth, I doubt I would have the time to give this book you propose the proper care; but then if not—we will see." Getting up, he said: "Come, Sam, to the billiard room."

"Just one thing before you gentlemen resume your evening of revels," I said as they were about to leave. "May I ask you, Mr. Clemens, how long you will be staying here in London?"

"Just a week," he said. "I've got a few talks to give at several clubs and a meeting scheduled with my publisher here. I've heard some rattling about a reception with the queen, but I'd rather wriggle out of that one."

"Would you," I asked, "have any time to sit for me as a sub-ject? I've already got several portraits in the National Gallery and a show coming up at the Royal Academy next year: It would be an honor that would please me greatly."

"Well, I know how long such portraits take. I haven't much free time," he said warily. "I suppose I could give you a few hours. But if you begin it now, I can't say when I'll be able to sit for you again."

"Two hours would be fine for now. Would tomorrow at two be possible?"

He thought on it briefly.

"I can't tomorrow. But Wednesday, maybe."

"At two p.m., then," I said to him. "You've made me happy—and you will be pleased with what I do."

※

IT WAS ABOUT TEN THIRTY at night when Lady Stanley finished writing: Her three hounds had started barking at some disturbance in the yard; she put down her pen to attend to it one evening in 1907.

A Note by Samuel Clemens on Meeting with the Stanleys in London, 1892

ABOUT FOUR, MET WITH HMS (His Majesty Stanley) over at Claridge's for tea and found the chap cantankerously happy, as he had his new bride along with him, the beautiful and gifted Miss Dorothy Tennant, as she's known in London; real society dame, a little haughty but not quite the snob, like a lot of the ladies who hang around the queen's stiff upper-crust circles, the title-crazy dames who never really get around to looking you straight in the eye. But Mrs. Stanley was different. For lack of a better word, I would say that her eyes "sparkled" with friendliness and interest, as brightly as the pearl-studded choker she was wearing around her neck. As a matter of fact, I would say that she was a pretty attractive lady altogether—swan-necked, full-bosomed, with an ingratiatingly full head of lovely hair, which she wore in the coiffure of Empress Eugenie of France. Her first reaction at my approach was to surprise me by kissing my cheek, even when I had a cold. She said: "Oh, Mr. Clemens! A delight! It's so wonderful to see you again!"

I sat down with Stanley and this gracious lady. With them was Mrs. Stanley's famous and cranky mother, a grande dame of a bohemian, who still wears the widow's black—but velvet—and all kinds of outlandish jewelry, including rings that would choke a horse and a cameo of her late husband prominently displayed beneath her goosey neck.

As for Stanley, he was looking well, considering his ailing health and a fall he had taken. He was fairly bronze-skinned; and while he seemed more tranquil, even content, in his matrimonial state, his eyes were unmistakably his own—the eyes of a caged lion, I would say. His mother-in-law seemed to put him on his best behavior, but in certain moments he was his old grim self. How I have often wondered what he was really thinking around me, but like a shrewd card player—even if he didn't play cards—he remained a good actor, never revealing much about himself, at least in public. But his hair had turned so white, like dove feathers, that I wondered if it had come about from Africa, as he always said, or if it had come about from putting up with his mother-in-law. Though we had a butler standing by our banquette, she kept asking him to pass this and that over to her, as in, "Henry, would you ever so kindly please pass me the cream?" And: "Henry, my son, a few sugar cubes, please." He seemed to be suppressing a lot of sighs—seemed fidgety, too, around her, as if he would rather be out in the wilds of Africa with the cannibals than having tea and crumpets on a rainy London afternoon. In any case, I had the impression that he was intensely bored by the whole business of dealing with Dame Gertrude, but upon his wife he truly doted. Seems that the domestic life was softening him up a bit: Now and then I caught him just staring at her in admiration, even affection. His transformation left me touched.

We made some small talk—I filled them in on my situation, more or less; these teas can be awkward, sort of like being trapped in a corner at a party. One has no choice but to yap and yap. But I must say I was happy to see Stanley doing so well. Of course, neither of us felt like bringing up the goings-on in Africa.

I haven't felt too happy about the news out of Africa: It is true that Stanley had inadvertently set up for King Leopold a quite unpleasant and cruel colonial regime down there, brutal to the natives. I can't imagine that Stanley would have done so on purpose. That's one thing, and I can't fault the man, though I have to often hold my tongue around him on the subject—that is, until we've had a few drinks, and then we come down to the brass tacks of it all. Still, I want to believe him when he tells me, as he has done on occasion, that to bring "civilization" to the wilds is going to be a long process, at some cost to native lives; that even if things might be bad right now, the longer view of history will have proved him and folks like Leopold correct. (Yet I dislike that king!) In any case, it's not a subject that we care to discuss in public.

After a while Stanley and I left the ladies to have a few drinks in the gentlemen's bar and billiard room. We were in the middle of a game when a gent, a stringy fellow in a dark, rumpled suit, a porter of some kind who had been sweeping the floor, came over to us—or, more precisely, to Stanley.

"Have I the honor of addressing Mr. Stanley, the great explorer?"

"Yes?"

"Eh, then I should say, it's a great day for me, and one that I will share with my family for all time to come." Then: "Is it true, eh, I dunno, without meaning to question your 'complishments, sir—but me cousin, a confectioner on Waterloo Road, seems to think you've been quite wrong in the handling of the African savages; I, of course, don't believe so, but some do. Can you tell me wot I can say to 'im in that regard?"

Stanley bristled: "Cannot you not see that my friend and I are simply shooting billiards?" But as Stanley continued to play, the same fellow stood about, somewhat forlornly, grieved to have offended him.

"I'm so sorry, sir. Myself, I am your admirer. Can you forgive my intrusion?"

"Yes. Now go away!"

"But begging you pardon, again, sir, I was just asking you a civil sort of question. I meant no disturbance."

"My dear fellow," Stanley said. "I do not know you; I do not want to know you. And I do not care to begin any form of conversation with you. Is that clear?"

"Ah, then," he said. "I guess I have been mistaken about you. It wasn't much that I asked of you, was it?"

Bowing, he left to take his broom again, muttering to himself.

※

"IT HAPPENS ALL THE TIME," he said to me. "Once I am asked such a thing, I am robbed of time, as surely as flour passes through a sieve." But then he began to sulk about it. "Samuel, do you think I was unfair to the fellow?"

"A few words to soothe him might have been all right."

He made no further mention of the incident until later. He had perhaps realized his rudeness or, thinking of his electioneering, had thought about how such a trivial incident could hurt him, but when he saw the same man solemnly polishing some glasses behind the bar, Stanley did the right thing, which was to approach him with a kind word.

"Dear sir, now that I am done with my billiards, to address your earlier query...the situation in Africa, and this information you should share with your relations, is of such a complicated nature that there is no way for me to provide any easy answer, except to say I am absolutely certain that, as surely as you and I are standing here, Providence is seeing to the evolution of better conditions in that place. Whatever falsehoods are bandied about, it is civilization—and by that I mean railroads and hospitals and civil order—that is being established in the Congo. It is for the greater good of all the people there, Europeans and Africans alike, that my efforts have been made." Then: "Now, how can I be of further service to you?"

The porter stammered some words of thanks, then asked Stanley to sign a piece of paper as an autograph; as Stanley did so he heard a litany of praises, his few phrases having made the right impression.

That afternoon we'd probably had a few more drinks than was necessary, but I had hoped to persuade a relaxed Stanley to publish a book with me. The subject I had seized upon was a journey we had made together to the Antilles as young men, the story of which Stanley, for stubborn reasons of his own, had never wanted to convey. But as so many years had since passed—more than thirty—I found it surprising to see that he had kept the same strong feelings against such a book.

"Why not, Henry?" I said.

"If I should decide to write of this, it will be in my autobiography. Besides, Samuel, it is something that still pains me all these years later. I have not even told Dolly about it."

I understood, to a certain extent, his desire for privacy, but I could not understand his apparent shame about what had happened in Cuba—and so, for the time being, I dropped the subject but considered it an out-and-out pity.

BACK IN HIS HOTEL ROOM, in an establishment not quite up to the standards of what he was used to, Samuel Clemens drank a warmed whiskey and, putting aside his notebook, went to bed.

PORTRAITS WITH TWAIN

Third Fragment from Lady Stanley's Unpublished
Memoir

On Wednesday afternoon, while Stanley was out at a meeting, Clemens made his way to our home. He brought roses for my mother, and after he had refreshed himself with chilled water—he had been tramping around from office to office, and it was unusually warm in London that day—I brought him to the place where I had set up a row of easels on which I displayed my paintings of street children; the most well known of them he had seen before, and another, *Sprites at Sea*, had been reproduced widely as a print. The others were reworkings of drawings I had done for the magazines *Little Folks* and *The Quiver*. I also had some of my drawings and paintings of Stanley to show Mr. Clemens. It is a funny thing: No matter how often one has looked at and attempted to draw a subject, something always seems to be missing; and yet with Stanley, I felt that I had captured everything about him, even the particular way his brow furrowed when he was having a special thought. But he never smiled.

Clemens was very courteous and generous in his praise of the Stanley portraits. I had made three: one of Stanley standing, one of Stanley sitting with a book open before him, and a more conventional portrait of Stanley contemplating a map of Africa, which the National Gallery liked very much.

"Goodness," Clemens said pleasantly. "These are all fine. Well done. You've even captured the opaqueness of Stanley's eyes."

"Opaque? But they are blue and green, like yours."

"I meant opaque in that they are hard to read: He's like a sphinx, that husband of yours. He never shows what he has seen or sees, does he?"

"He doesn't, but he expresses himself in other ways."

"Oh, but I know that." Looking about, he asked, "Where do you want me to sit?"

"Just there, in front of the hearth."

"You mind if I smoke?"

"Not at all."

I was used to Stanley smoking whenever he sat for me: Thusly anticipating my new subject's similar habit, I had my butler put out an ash urn beside the chair for Clemens to use. Wearing my smock, and with a fresh sheet of paper on which to draw my preliminary study of him, I tried to determine the position in which Mr. Clemens would be most comfortable and which pose would be advantageous to him.

"Just relax, as if you were talking to me, but sit generally still."

"That's something I generally aspire to, madame," he said.

I began to draw him in pencil, and, as I did so, I noticed that he had started to hum to himself; looking out through my studio window to a great chestnut tree, he took on a tranquil expression.

"And what is that you've been humming?"

"Oh, an old Negro spiritual taught to me by slaves on my uncle John's farm, back when I was a boy. He lived about four miles out from Florida, Missouri, he did. A finer man there never was." Then: "Do you know, Mrs. Stanley, that whenever I am troubled I think of my days there and in Hannibal?"

"Are you troubled now?"

"Madame, I am like a cucumber soaking in a vat of vinegar, but I am still optimistic enough, I suppose." Then: "It is a funny thing, Mrs. Stanley: The older I get—and I will be fifty-seven come November—the more aware of the minutiae of my past I become. As your wise husband told me the other day, there's so much to remember that, as the years go by, there's hardly any room left in the brain for something new. Each day I ask myself, 'How are things remembered, Sam?' Then I say that I remember things as if my brain were some kind of camera—a camera that has taken a million photographs. Why some of those pictures stick in the mind more clearly than others, after so many years, is a mystery to me. Take my mother, Jane Lampton. She passed on two Octobers ago, in 1890, at a mighty age, her eighty-eighth year. That she lived so long was miraculous in a way, for she was as frail and delicate in her youth as my own wife, Livy, is now; and yet if there is such a thing as the spirit keeping the body sound, despite its maladies, she did so, year after year."

Then he fished out from his vest pocket a watch: Within its top encasement was an image of his mother.

"Here she is, Mrs. Stanley—my little reminder of the great

lady that was my mother, Jane Lampton. It's just a photograph, but each time I see her I am both warmed and grieved. How can it be that one simple thing can bring so much to mind? She's about fifty in this picture, slender and petite, but she was so sturdy of heart that she always stood as a great example to me. If I have a kind bone in my body, it's because of her. You see, she was one of those rare Presbyterian souls who actually cared about the condition of her fellow humans: She loved people and animals—took in every poor bewildered cat in our neighborhood when I was a boy—and was always a lively sort, despite her infirmities. Far from being an invalid who allowed herself to wither away, she relished every opportunity, whatever her misfortunes, to enjoy life. She danced and loved music, loved the circus and minstrel shows that came to town; she was kind to our slaves, and she taught me something about books.

"Once, we had a little slave, brought to Hannibal from Maryland, a gentle and cheerful boy named Sandy. He was always singing and whooping, whistling and yelling—so noisily that he drove me to distraction. One day when he had been singing for an entire hour without stopping, I lost my temper and went to my mother in a rage asking her to please shut him up; but instead of becoming angry with the boy, tears came to her eyes and she said, with much kindness: 'Sam, when the poor thing sings, it's because he doesn't want to remember he'll never see his family or mother ever again; if he's quiet, then he will surely think of them and become very sad. So just remember this when you hear that friendless child's voice again.' After that, I kind of took comfort in hearing him, and his carrying on never bothered me again, for in my selfish boyishness, I had forgotten his sad situation; that he was so terribly alone in the world and trying to cheer himself up with songs and all kinds of wild whistling suddenly made sense to me. Thereafter I went out of my way to befriend him—later I put him in my book *The Adventures of Tom Sawyer*. But that was the kind of thing in which my mother instructed me.

"All in all she was one of those proper churchgoing ladies for whom every occasion, whether it was a Fourth of July celebration or a revival meeting, a lecture or even a funeral, was an opportunity to turn out and show her sunny side. To the day of her death, she remained fair-minded and compassionate—that's the word, 'compassionate.' What I am, what good qualities I have, I believe I owe largely to her. Her strength of spirit is what sustained her for so many years, and it is something I have tried to summon up for myself in times of darkness: For despite the downturns and tragedies of her life, she never allowed herself to get beaten down. It was faith, I suppose, that made the very great difference in her attitude. A faith in a God I have never seen any evidence of but whose imaginary presence in so many lives, like her own, has been a solace. Needless to say, Mrs. Stanley, I miss her.

"But memory is a funny thing. Lately certain things still come back to me about her as clearly as if they had happened this morning. Some come as clear as a photograph. One picture I most vividly remember is fifty years old: I was six, my mother forty. We were in a bedroom of our house in Hannibal, Missouri, where my older brother Benjamin——he was ten—lay dead, the poor boy having succumbed to a fever; my mother had brought me in to say good-bye, I guess. We knelt down by the bed, my mother holding my hand, when all at once she began to weep and moan in a way I had never seen before. I can remember feeling ashamed of myself for not crying along with her and ashamed that I was powerless to stop her tears. And as for my poor brother, well, being so little I wasn't completely convinced that he was gone. And that's perhaps why my mother, in her wisdom, had me lay my hand against his brow. It was cold and still and so sad a thing that I could not understand why it was so. He hardly seemed a person at all anymore: I can remember feeling a terrible guilt about it—you see, Mrs. Stanley, I had been the sickly child of the family. I had been born two months premature, and so frail, slight, small-boned, and prone to diseases that until I was about six or so, little hope had been held that I would survive childhood. But there I was beside her, with my hand held against my brother's face, somehow thinking—for I was so young, just six, when everything in life seems a paradise—that it should have been me and not Benjamin in that bed. Somehow I believed that I had been spared and he had taken my place. It's the kind of reverse thinking that comes to children, I suppose. But just the same, all the occasions when I had acted the brat out in the yard and wished him dead over some stupid thing landed on my conscience so badly that for the longest time I suffered terrifying nightmares from it. That kind of thing never leaves you. Even now, when I see a late morning sunbeam drifting in through a window, I can close my eyes and, ever so fleetingly, find myself in that room again, my brother lost to the world, my dear mother by my side."

In that moment Mr. Clemens's expression, as I recall it these years later, was nearly beatific. He seemed caught up in a distant moment, his face taking on an air of concentration, as if he were composing something inside his head. But then the spell left him; he shifted in his chair and drew from his jacket pocket a cigar—"My own brand, Mark Twain," he said. Lighting it, he went on:

"Even when I know that I was not at fault, there's a part of me that still thinks it is so. And it's not a feeling that I've since become immune to: Folks say that we should count our blessings—and I have had many, Mrs. Stanley. I've been blessed to have been raised in Hannibal. Blessed to have a good wife and three precious daughters. I've had my share of fame and fortune, along with all the nonsense that goes with it, and I have seen a lot of this world along the way. But for all that, as many blessings as I can count, I am always aware of how weakly tethered they are to this life. As I said, I'm lucky to have three precious daughters, but my first child, Langdon, born premature, like myself, in 1870, was a different story.

"As newlyweds, Livy and I had moved from Buffalo, New York, to Hartford, Connecticut, and were living in our first house in that pretty town—a wonderful cottage set down in the midst of a quite literary neighborhood called Nook Farm. Livy was then in mourning over her father's death the year before, but my spirits were high, as I was just managing to make something of a living as a writer by then, but my main livelihood depended on the lecture tour, as I was in some demand, having become the next best thing after Bret Harte. But a cloud followed me around just the same.

"For the first year of his life Langdon was so sick that he cried and cried to the point where I thought I would go mad. Livy was sick constantly, too, with colds and the flu, and she came down with typhoid fever, which almost killed her—of course she recovered—but for the longest time I was both a writer and a nurse in a gloriously comfortable sick house. A beautiful sick house that had to be paid for. And so when Livy finally recovered from her various maladies, that second year of our marriage mainly found me out on the road traveling by rail from town to town in the northeast, lecturing. I hated that life—the late trains, the bad weather, the cold and graceless hotel rooms. I worked so much that I missed my second Christmas with Livy because of it. All in the name of making money, and not much, at that. But in the midst of that drudgery, something wonderful happened: Our little Susy, a healthy baby and fat as butter at birth, came to us in March of 1872, a very great blessing and joy indeed, but a joy that—and forgive my entangled way of speaking, Mrs. Stanley—was short-lived. A few months later, on a raw and chilly morning, I took little Langdon out with me in an open barouche for a ride through the countryside. Wrapping him up in furs, I believed that I had attended to him with the best of care, and as our coachman drove us, I fell into a reverie of thoughts about some story or other, which I went to jotting down in my notebook, and while I was thusly occupied, for such thoughts envelop all my attentions, I had failed to notice that the fur wrappings had fallen away and exposed his little legs to the cold air. By and by the coachman noticed this, and I covered him up again, but by then it was too late, as he had caught a chill. And shortly this turned into a cold and the cold turned into diphtheria and he died at nine one June morning in his mother's arms. He was only nineteen months of age."

Clemens's face flushed, and he sneezed, still suffering from a cold. Why he was being so candid with me I cannot say, but in my experience I have found that when persons sit for you and are allowed to speak freely, the small talk that passes for conversation under ordinary circumstances does not do: There is something about being looked at carefully that induces in a subject a profound starkness of feeling. Clemens, in fact, seemed quite willing to share his thoughts with me on this occasion: I can note here as well that he spoke very much as he wrote—a searching and sometimes meandering course was traveled before he came to a stop. These sentences I have been trying to capture.

"And I can go on in this vein," he continued. "If you've read *Life on the Mississippi* you will already know that my brother Henry's death came about because of a riverboat accident. A boat he would not have been on except for me. There had been an explosion of steam and fire...He was too heroic for his own good...tried to save others instead of himself and paid dearly for it. All these years later my recollection of him, as he lay scalded and in pain upon a hospital bed in Memphis, remains with me as another picture I'd rather forget. Somehow I blame myself for these things. Somehow I feel ashamed of myself when I allow myself to have such thoughts: But when they come I do not relish them."

"Surely you know, Mr. Clemens," I said to him, "that these incidents were not your fault. Some things simply come about because, as Stanley himself has told me, they are a matter of Providence. Fate. But I understand such feelings of loss; my own father left us twenty years past; and yet not a day goes by when I do not think of him. I know it may seem a silly thing, but I have kept him so close to my heart that I have made it my habit to think of him when I am addressing my diary at night: Whether he is really there or not—for we can never know, really—I like to believe it is so, for the lack of his companionship, in spirit, is unimaginable to me."

"So you believe in an afterlife?"

"Of a kind. Yes, I do."

"And what is that? I suppose you see Elysian fields, do you?"

"Not quite, Mr. Clemens: I imagine that the very many memories we have of our lives—what you called the million photographs of the mind—come with us when our souls are released from our bodies. The body passes, and the soul does not."

"And what proof do you base this on?"

"Faith, Mr. Clemens. Simple faith."

"Well, the idea of lurking about for all eternity doesn't particularly enthrall me, though a bit more time with our beloveds, or at least some evidence that all is well with them and the world, does appeal to me. Probably something like that happens anyway when the brain shuts down at the end—it's supposed to be something like a fine and whimsical drunkenness, filled with numerous dreams—and possibly nightmares. What does Stanley think about that, anyway?"

"I don't really know. He's religious but not superstitious; he's a bit too much of a realist in his thinking and not very imaginative in that way. When I have asked him about this, he has tended to wonder what difference it would make. As he told me, 'We'll find out anyway, won't we?'"

"Sounds like him," Clemens said. Then, after sitting for a time, he began to grow restless and asked how much time remained: He had only been with me for an hour, but it had been sufficient for my preliminary sketch. Releasing him from his servitude—I knew that he was a busy man—I showed him the drawing so far. "Egad, but I'm getting old!" he declared. And then, as I led him out, I asked if he could return again on another day.

"Day after tomorrow, around the same time," he said. "But only for an hour, you understand?"

☀

Dear Father,

This afternoon I had sit for me the great American writer Samuel Clemens, or Mark Twain. He is a congenial but very sad man with many burdens upon his shoulders. Though he does not speak of such things openly, both Stanley and I are aware of his troubles, but we say nothing to him, as he is so proud as to never seem in want, which he would consider a great shame. As a subject he is fine to draw: Unlike a child, he has much history written on his face—his life experiences and his many hours of labor show in its furrows and wrinkles. He is an interesting and pleasant-looking man: His hair, white, shoots out in a shock that he seems proud of; his nose is aquiline, and his eyes, very intelligent, are narrow, like an eagle's. I am somehow reminded by them of an American Indian. His brows are hairy and shoot upward, as if he had been charged with electricity, and he wears a thick mustache that does little to conceal the delicacy of his lips, which are as finely shaped as a woman's. He spoke to me of touching and personal things, I suppose in an effort to befriend me. I would further say that, like Stanley, he is at heart a shy man, perhaps even melancholic, quite different from his famous persona. With Stanley and Kipling, he is one of the best-known writers in the world. My sense of him is that he is a man of boundless and dogged energy, like Stanley, who would prefer to enjoy his life but is pressed by financial circumstances to take on many labors. He is in London for only a few days more, as he must return to America on business: Stanley considers him a good friend.

⁂

Our Second Sitting

My husband greeted Clemens at the door, and they spoke of meeting up later to visit some bookstalls or head out to a club for a drink. As Stanley excused himself, Clemens, finding me lingering in the hallway with a paintbrush, said he would shortly come into my studio. As I stood moving from side to side to perceive the angles of his head, he sat down on a high stool and, lighting a cigar with a vesta that he struck on the heel of his boot, began to speak again.

"Seems that I got carried away the other day, Mrs. Stanley," Mr. Clemens said to me after he had settled down. "Being away from my family gives me too much time to think about things that I should not be thinking about. As much as I carry on to myself about the distractions of family life, my wife and daughters are my greatest solace. Without them I can't imagine how I would get along. It's unimaginable to me. For what is any man without his family, his little kingdom? Not even the amenities of fame—meeting the queen herself or having lunch with the kaiser—can fill the heart the way a simple conversation with your daughter can. But it goes too quickly, Mrs. Stanley; the years slip by as quickly as the summers once used to.

"At my age, time itself becomes the greatest trickster in one's life: I, for one, cannot understand what has happened to that unit of measure we call an hour. Once a single hour seemed an endless thing, passing as slowly as a shadow shifting in the sunlight in mid-July. But now it zips by—tumbles into the next hour and then the next—until before you know it five or six hours have passed, and yet those hours don't seem to possess the same richness as a single hour from childhood. Lately I have been puzzling over this. As an experiment I have mentally listed the things I can remember from a single hour during an afternoon on my uncle John Quarles's farm while I lolled about under a shady tree, lazily reading Walter Scott's *Ivanhoe*. Do you want to hear about this?"

"Of course."

"It goes like this: Let's say I'm hearing the mantel clock chiming the hour of three. It goes *ping, ping, ping,* and I'm looking across the yard and watching a female slave beating the dust out of a rug slung over a rope, each *whap* of her stick like the ticking of a clock, but one that ticks ever so slowly. I can remember watching as some hands put bridles on a team of horses and hitch them up to a wagon. Then my uncle John, as fine a man as any I have ever known, comes out onto the porch, lights his corncob pipe, looks around, then slips back into the house. And my mother's sister, Aunt Patsy, comes out to that same porch and calls to me to ask if I am thirsty, then reminds me that she would be grateful if I didn't bring any more garter snakes home—these I liked to slip into her work baskets. Then Aunt Patsy tells me that if I am a good boy I might be rewarded later with some fresh-baked apple pie, the kind of bribery I generally ignored. Then I see my little brother, Henry, out by the fence near the road, flicking stones into some cans. He has a little bowl of sugar by his feet and is surprised to find it overrun with ants. This he brings over to show me, then runs away to play some more: I can remember thinking that I loved my brother but had to be on my best behavior around him, as he was as righteous as my mother and tended to report my wanderings and mischief to her. I've since immortalized him, I suppose—if being in a book is that—as the do-gooder Sid in *Tom Sawyer*.

With that he paused for a moment, looking out through my window at a patch of sky. Then he continued:

"Some slaves come along—my uncle had some fifteen or twenty of them—taking a cart to the barn; they are followed by a pack of little children, one of whom stops to greet me and says that they will be playing hide-and-seek in the woods and asks if I want to come along. But I'm into my book and much enjoying its tales of the knights of olden days when I notice the green and curious-looking head of a centipede peeking at me; he's crawled up the spine of the book and seems intent on exploring the valley between the pages. He's a cute fellow, and I jiggle him onto the palm of my hand and set him down, gently as possible, among the blades of grass and watch him go off to wherever such creatures wander. My good deed—for some boys would have killed it for fun—makes me feel virtuous and at one with nature. Then I'm back into my idyll and am reading some more when I hear a purring: One of the yard cats, a calico, has for some reason decided to accompany me and lies down by my side, happily licking his paws, his ears moving like antennae whenever he hears a bird chirping in trees. I pet him a few times, scratch the fat part of fur under his neck, and he's purring even more loudly, then I make the mistake of scratching at his belly, which he doesn't like, and suddenly he bounds away. I eat a piece of licorice and am chewing it happily when Henry comes back and decides he wants to play the Indian with me. Whooping, he puts his arms around my neck and starts slapping the top of my head as though it were a tom-tom, and we wrestle around for a bit, both of us giggling. Then I read to him for a spell, and a drowsy feeling comes over him, and the next thing I know he's asleep, his head settled against my shoulder, his breathing ever so quiet and gentle-like. It's just then that I hear the mantel clock chime, ringing in the hour of four."

He then pulled a cigar from his jacket, lit it, and said: "And that's just from a single hour, and even if I'm mixing up a bit of the details, for they come back to me in a scramble, I am certain my recollection is true."

⁂

THAT NEXT FRIDAY EVENING STANLEY and Mr. Clemens appeared together at the Garrick Club in Covent Garden, where a great many persons had arrived for the occasion. In the afternoon Stanley had prepared a little introductory speech for his dear American friend. He had jotted down notes and paced about his study in a state of apprehension, as he hated the idea of his words seeming like something sloughed off. And he seemed anxious about his stage bearing. Though I had reminded him that he would be at the podium for only a few minutes, he seemed very aware of Clemens's power and wished to do him justice.

Indeed they were a study in contrasting styles—my husband preferring to make quite deliberate, long, rehearsed statements and Clemens relying upon an improvised and colloquial manner of speaking. It was in that realm that Henry envied Mr. Clemens, for in his persona as Mark Twain, he always displayed a lively sense of humor, a quality that my husband perhaps wished he had himself. For all his virtues of character, and despite his prolific writings and the grandeur of his accomplishments, he was ill at ease in public settings. Giving speeches had never come easily to him: He suffered from a kind of stage fright, and though he was very much a man of action, afraid of few things, he was an awkward and self-conscious speaker—stiff and overly formal, some would say. But Clemens knew how to work a crowd: While he spoke privately of his weariness with tours and public events, he approached his presentations with the aplomb and confidence of a seasoned stage actor. His charismatic qualities and funny way with words, which he translated successfully into the warmth of his prose and language onstage, constituted the greatest advantage that Clemens had over my husband in the public arena.

(A note: In this aplomb, Clemens was distinctly linked to his predecessor in letters, Charles Dickens, whose own stage presence was remarkable. I knew this firsthand, having seen him perform in London when I was a little girl, a fact that I think Stanley somewhat envied. Clemens himself had attended a Dickens lecture years before in New York with his future wife, Livy, or so he had told me at some point: The irony of it is that Clemens, a great performer in his own right and the "American Dickens," as Stanley has called him, found the performance flat and uninteresting. Dickens "muttered though the whole thing," Clemens told me.)

But while Stanley believed he had many a devoted admirer, from the highest lord to the most common man, he always felt that Clemens enjoyed the greater measure of the public's affection and esteem. Still, he never conveyed any sign of being envious around Clemens.

⚜

"MY DEAR FRIENDS," STANLEY SAID before the crowd, which included Sir Lawrence Alma-Tadema and Sir Arthur Conan Doyle. "I begin by asking, 'What is literature?' Our world is founded on deeds, but it is by words that we remember them. But deeds cannot be relived except through words: Written history is but a reminder of things that happened. Even the myths as recounted by Homer and Ovid reflect what we must know." Here he cleared his throat. "All that has been lost to us is certainly a pity, but what we do have of living vital records we can cherish because someone cared to write them down. What is literature but the record of men's lives? No less can we cherish the infinite numbers of authors whom we will never know; and yet the effort is vital, worthy of us as civilized persons, for without them the past would be vacant, meaningless, except as a shade we would be vaguely aware of. Imagine now, as we are gathered here, that some many years later—even a hundred or two hundred years later—you and I, each one of us, will be in some way seen again. Even as I stand before you, I am fairly certain that our age and its deeds are being known in the future. We are being read about in the same way that we as children once read of the ancient Greeks and Romans. It is a fact: Years from now someone will be reading about us, of that I have no doubt. But this"—here he coughed—"is no mere matter of tautology; for our lives, once written down, are simultaneous with another time. Our literature is our legacy, and if there is such a thing as ghosts, literature will be the only verifiable version of them.

"There are many dead authors from whom we will never hear. But fortunately there are living authors among us as well. Tonight we have the special privilege of having a very great friend speak before us—a man of letters, of goodwill, of mirth and charm; a man from America, now residing in Berlin: Samuel Clemens, or

Mark Twain, as he is also known. One of the finest—if not the finest—exemplar of a writer. Surely he will be remembered as most of us will not be. He is a library of wisdom, a pantheon of insight: He is, I am grateful to say, a dear friend of mine, but he is a friend to us all just the same. All of us, fortunate to have been there at the time, can remember his splendid debut in London, in 1872, and I know he will equal if not surpass that early impression tonight. I know not what he will be speaking about, but I know that surely they will be words for the ages. Ladies and gentlemen, the inimitable Mark Twain."

Clemens looked at Stanley; smiling, they shook hands, and applause followed.

Clemens shifted from foot to foot at the podium.

"To begin with, a writer makes books. In that we are like undertakers; as we put things into places where they will never be touched or changed—a kind of timeless limbo, or heaven, to be a bit more cheerful about it—we are like those Swiss tinkers who fidget around with little gears and make clocks. For each book, whether novel or travelogue, history or memoir, ticks according to its own time: Its gears run perpetually as long as there is some-one to wind it up and scan his eyes over its creamy papers. The beauty of it all, as Stanley has pointed out, is that books will last as long as there are men to read them—far longer than any one individual. Shakespeare's gone, and so is Cervantes, their bones have long since turned to dust, and yet their books bring them back: Even now, as I speak, the youthful Cervantes, a prisoner of the Ottoman Empire after the Battle of Lepanto, sits in a cell in some dank Muslim dungeon in Constantinople, dreaming up *Don Quixote*. Shakespeare, drinking ale in a tavern in Stratford-upon-Avon, looks up and sees the face of Ophelia in the tavern keeper's buxom daughter; one idea leads to another; a single expression, a moment, a patch of thoughts, amounting to one splendiferous idea or person. Added up and written down, they become a book.

"What books I make—any of us makes—are expendable in

the face of the actual rumblings of history, yet without them, imagine how dull and listless life would be. Think about it—a world without books, with nothing to remind us of how other men thought and lived. I've once dreamed of such a world, and the very thought left me so gloomy that I could not speak to anyone for days and was only resuscitated by reading Carlyle's history of the French Revolution. Books, I then concluded, are my water, my evening and morning meal, my sunlight and garden, and what words spill from my pencil are my gestures of thanks for that fact.

"I could speak of the greatest literature, but because you all know me as a man of simple tastes, and because many of you are gainfully employed artisans of the word, as I am, I thought I would confine myself to my own life, with which I should be familiar by now."

He shuffled past a few pages.

"Now, I only meant the aforementioned thoughts as a kind of preface, not to put you all to sleep. But about one of my books I will briefly speak—*The Adventures of Huckleberry Finn*. It took me seven years or so to write, maybe more. I had at the moment of its conception been sitting in my study in Connecticut and daydreaming about Hannibal when in a moment's flash I saw the story about the adventures of a crafty boy, Huck Finn, and a runaway slave who set off on the Mississippi together, heading north to freedom. Just as a context, the story was set in the late 1840s; at the time I wrote it, though, the Underground Railroad and the Civil War were receding into memory, and slaves, ostensibly freed—I will not discuss the failures of the Reconstruction in the South—were of the past; but I still could not keep myself from telling their story.

"In that book I confined myself to the boys' life on the Mississippi because that had a peculiar charm for me and because I knew the slave's world a little from my youth. Out on my uncle John's farm near Florida, Missouri, where I spent many a glorious summer, the slaves were my friends. I played with their children, went tramping through the woods with them, heard their songs, and felt bad when one of them cried over some little misfortune. I knew them as part of my uncle's extended family and was not aware of the low regard in which they were held by the outside world. I knew nothing of their standing in society. But they were slaves. I had no aversion to slavery; I didn't know there was anything wrong with it. But years later, once I knew that it was wrong, and after a whole unholy war had been fought over the issue, I thought to put my feelings about that mighty subject into a book. Jim—he was based on one of my uncle's slaves, a fellow I loved and respected. Huck was based on an old friend from Hannibal, Tom Blankenship, a knockabout and young heathen whom I knew well. His pappy was a drunk, and his life was low, which, in my eyes, made him an especially sympathetic fellow." There was laughter, which Mr. Clemens, scratching his head, did not quite understand.

"Liking Jim, I rooted for him in every part of the tale. They were friends and mutually respectful, as imperfect a pair as they might have been.

"Setting them adrift on a raft, I peopled the river with the confidence men I knew from my days as a pilot on the Mississippi and made a book that I hoped would be seen as an homage to the idea of freedom—and friendship. It sold well in America, but the critics did not like it. Since I used a vernacular kind of language, it confused folks. Some critics found it wanting in 'literary quality'; some said I was trying to elevate the lowliest subject to some high pinnacle of honor. In several places it was banned, for the coupling of a sassy white boy and a befuddled, freedom-craving Negro did not sit well with some. Having poured so many years and my deepest understanding and affection for my subject into the book, I was perplexed. Is it literature? I hope it is.

"You here in England were very kind toward it, which says much about your civility and understanding of words and the idea of the novel as something that should be new. I suffered somewhat at its American reception, but when I ask myself if I would write that very same book now, knowing what I do of its reception,

I say yes. But could I? I doubt it. Let me put it this way: Books represent a confluence—of memories, impressions, emotions, and will. They come out of a certain moment, and I am beyond that moment now.

"I did write it, and am proud to say that *Huckleberry Finn* has traveled far and wide—I've been told that the both the czarina of Russia and the kaiser have it in their libraries, and I understand that my dear friend Henry Stanley took it with him on his last expedition into the Congo. What an honor (not a blasphemy) that is.

"When I am writing I am not Samuel Clemens but Mark Twain, and through that portal flows everything. I am my books, and I am not. I admire them, and I do not. It was me, and it wasn't, but I hope the effect on the reader remains the same."

⚜

AFTERWARD WE WENT BACK TO Richmond Terrace for dinner. Mother was waiting. She liked Clemens; I do not know if he liked her, though my impression is that he did. But upon our arrival, she was pacing about the foyer outside our dining room, inside of which many guests were gathered. As we walked in, Mother instructed Stanley to put his walking cane aside, then she greeted Mr. Clemens, catching him by the inner foyer as our butler removed his coat. She said, winningly: "Before you go in, you must sign some books of yours that I have purchased as gifts." She led him into her study: She had some twenty of his books set aside in a pile, and she stood by him, thin and opinioned and adamant as she could be, instructing him over every signature. They fell to talking. Clemens, in speaking of his stopover in London, seemed sincerely enchanted by her company, holding her hand and nodding agreeably as she praised him. Meanwhile, Stanley was pacing irritably about. "Dear lady," I heard Clemens say, "My mother is gone, but you seem very much the lady she was." And he made the graceful gesture of kissing the upraised knuckles of her hand. "You seem delightful for your age, my lady," he added. "Consider me a friend." Then my mother, who I cannot say was the most emotional of women, stood up and shocked me, kissing Clemens on the face. "Well, then," she said. "As you are mine, I am yours—a dear, dear friend." Nearly weightless, buoyant over their exchange, and with a fan in hand, she left Clemens and made her way into our dining room, where were gathered many eminent persons.

☙

The Man Inside His Head

It was my good fortune that Samuel came to sit for me again that next afternoon. He only had an hour, being kept busy with appointments, mainly with his London publishers. He did, however, seem most happy to spend time with me and made the flattering gesture of bringing two bouquets of roses, one for Mother and one for me.

I had made a few rudimentary oil studies of his most interesting face; while his heavy, ridged brow cast his eyes in perpetual darkness, they were lit with wisdom and intelligence—like Stanley's. His longish nose and prim mouth, hidden under a reddish, gray-streaked walrus mustache, along with his great head of hair, seemed easy enough to capture; yet the subtle quality I most wanted to convey in my portrait of him was elusive. Clemens, at every moment, seemed to be of two minds, which is to say that while he, with a cigar held in his delicate hand, would speak of one thing, I always had the impression that at the same time he was secretly thinking of another. At first, he was quiet that day, but then, while speaking sincerely about how much he missed his family—so many Atlantic crossings, precipitated by financial concerns, taking him back to the States in those days—I asked him how he, with so many demands on his time, could manage so many things at once: his publishing house, his writings, his financial affairs. In a mood to amuse me, he told me a story about "the little man" in his head.

"Indeed, how I manage so much is a mystery to me, particularly since I aspire to laziness and lolling about, which has not been my destiny of late; I really have no choice, but when I am out and about and faced with numerous decisions, I rely upon a friend of mine, a fellow who is always sitting around on a bench in a railway station, waiting for a train. I call him the little commuter. He is an admirable fellow, brighter than I by far and more sensible, especially when it comes to business matters—and he's far more tolerant of people: Altogether he is my better and smarter self, though I never imagine that he looks anything like me. He is Everyman, a pleasant, no-nonsense fellow, and he must have an intelligent face, but as he often wears a bowler and as I only see him from a distance, as if I were standing on the far end of a train platform, I have never known what he looks like up close. But he always carries, regardless of the time of the year, an overcoat and a valise: I imagine that he is the editor of a publishing house—a successful one—or perhaps he is an attorney. Occasionally I have seen him open his valise and look over some papers, but what they contain I never know. He often sits, the valise by his side, and always removes his overcoat, setting it down beside him, as he, looking off down the tracks, awaits the train. What this train represents I don't know—it is possibly just a train—but I sometimes think it has to do with a coming opportunity. Often, when I am in the midst of a conversation, it seems to represent an opportunity for escape. That is to say, Mrs. Stanley, that when I happen to find myself in the midst of a boring conversation, I check in on the little commuter; and as things get duller and duller, and just when I am thinking I would be rather somewhere else, the train comes chugging into the station, sending up trails of smoke and clanging its bells. With that he always stands up, puts on his hat and overcoat, stashes his papers into the valise, and, much relieved, gratefully boards.

"My thoughts go with him. Though I may nod thoughtfully

and grin at the person I am entrapped with, I have the solace of thinking about the little commuter—even if he and I are not one and the same, I somehow feel that I can see what he sees—and I drift off, thinking that I am looking out at the passing countryside through the window. But then, once my interest has been newly engaged, my little commuter is back on his bench just like that, awaiting the train again, his valise and overcoat and bowler by his side, as before.

"This little man has seen me through many a drudgery— business meetings, visits to lawyers' offices, court hearings, and many a tedious reception. As to where the train sometimes goes once it leaves the station, it travels the world. I have, while accompanying this chap, revisited the Sandwich Islands: I have gone to San Francisco, to Venice, and sometimes back to Hannibal. And while I have often enjoyed these travels, I have unfortunately boarded that train many a time, especially during matters of business, when I shouldn't have."

"And where is this little man now?" I asked.

"Oh, he is still sitting in the station. He rarely gets on when I'm in your company."

TWAIN'S SADNESS AND OTHER EVENTS

AS HE HAD PROMISED DOLLY that his days of exploration were over, Stanley became an election campaigner again. Giving speeches in social clubs, pubs, and meeting rooms throughout the North Lambeth district—just across the river, over Westminster

Bridge—he never deigned to canvass his constituents door-to-door or to shake a single hand if he could avoid it. However he stood on the issues—regarding Africa or regarding the ongoing debate about whether Ireland should be given home rule (he was against it)—and despite the lackluster nature of his speeches, because of his fame, and because he was running as an "illustrious son of the working class," he won. The very night his victory was proclaimed—at midnight, by way of a red flare fired over the rooftops of North Lambeth, the sky flushing pink—his wife, Dorothy, dozing on a lounge in the attic of the Liberal Unionist Club, awakened to the cheers of Stanley's constituents, who, gathered as a great and frenzied crowd below, had carried Stanley into the hall on their shoulders. Rushing down the stairs, she was on hand to see Stanley, ashen-faced and listless, as his supporters set him down atop a table. In contrast to the jubilance of his constituency, he was neither excited nor happy in his bearing, as he regarded the whole business as a mistake, another burden to contend with. His expression was solemn, and though just a few scant years before he might have attempted to make a stirring speech—as if such fleeting moments of glory were of importance—he simply looked around and, thanking the boozy crowd, bid his constituents good night. No speech, no flowing rivers of appreciation—he just wanted to go home and smoke. His hands were cold, his manner sullen, and when he and Dorothy rode a hansom cab to Richmond Terrace, the subject of his election had already settled in his gut as a most disagreeable thing. En route home, he told Dolly that he did not wish to discuss it. Settled into a chair in his library, he sat alone until the early hours of the morning, smoking Havana cigars—his only movement to dash out a cigar and light a new one. Occasionally he would reach out for some book or other to leaf through it—but he did not speak to anyone for days.

STANLEY TOOK HIS SEAT IN the House of Commons in August of 1895. The atmosphere at Parliament he found asphyxiating. To be herded in, like sheep, in the mornings—to sit in an airless, overcrowded room among some three hundred and fifty members, listening to addresses, mainly about the "Irish question," in which he had no particular interest—was beyond him. Even when issues pertinent to his knowledge about Africa were being debated, he rarely caught the Speaker's eye: his raised hand, his thumps on the table, and his cane clacking the floor went unnoticed. Worse was the absence of light, which he found depressing, and for a man who had spent endless hours walking in the open air of the wilds, the atmosphere of those chambers, with their closed windows—the Thames stank—was stifling. The river's bilious and unsanitary miasmas were kept at bay by panes of glass, but the air inside, defined by body smells, colognes, tobacco smoke, and hair tonic, was nearly nauseating. He'd come home at a late hour feeling more exhausted, he'd say, than he had been on his marches.

He might have had a future as a statesman had he the patience for the consuming intricacies of parliamentary procedures, but it all bored him: Further, he felt himself a loner, and he found the clubbishness of the house's members, who separated themselves along class lines, irritating. Prone to the nostalgia of a man who thought his best years were behind him, and missing his adventures, he often felt that his life was over.

YET DOLLY SEEMED CONTENT, AND, all in all, during those rare moments when Stanley had a few hours to do as he pleased, which was to sit in his study and read, the enterprise of matrimony seemed to him reasonable enough. Dolly, however spoiled she had been in life, seemed to truly care for him; on many an afternoon, that thought alone was enough to assuage his occasionally bitter feelings of containment and the sense that the domestic life he'd always longed for was nothing more than a prison.

He rarely wrote anything that he considered important—countless notes relating to social engagements; a few letters to the newspapers (but mainly his old fire and indignation had left him); lectures he would give here and there about Africa—but in those years, with his original glory faded and with his reputation somewhat eroded by increasing reports about native abuse in the Congo, he did so as a relic of the past, the specter of greatness having faded from the public's perception of him. Even his attempts at writing his autobiography stalled: Relegating the pages he had once written during his tour of the States and Australia to the bottom of a trunk, Stanley managed, during several bouts of concentrated writing at quiet seaside resorts, to produce the portion of manuscript relating to his youthful years through the Civil War that would serve as the official version of those years. But once he had reached that point, wherein he much enjoyed the process of describing just how Henry Morton Stanley came to be, it was if he could write no more on the subject, his will to do so sapped by emotions he found unbearable.

At fifty-five, as much as he tried to, he could never forget that, once upon a time, he had been an unwanted child, a lowly sort loved by no one. With each new line he wrote that awareness came back to him: That he still felt himself an "orphan" rankled him. It was an illusion, of course—all men end up being orphaned by death—but as he ruminated over the fact that his life had been spent in the servitude of others and in the pursuit of "empty glory," he searched his mind for the single thing that might make him happy—to give someone what he had wanted himself: a father.

HERE FOLLOWS A LETTER STANLEY wrote to Samuel Clemens at that time of his ruminations: Clemens, then staying at Quarry Farm in Elmira, New York, was about to embark on a worldwide tour to pay off his debts; Stanley had helped Clemens with arrangements for the Australian leg of his journey by introducing him, by mail, to his own promoter in that country, Carlyle Greenwood Smythe.

June 12, 1895

Dear Samuel,

It seems our correspondences as of late have had much
to do with business and the details of tours and lectures: I do
not mind sharing my practical knowledge of such, in answer
to your inquiries, and I have been happy that you have made
good connections through me—Smythe, my agent in Australia,
is a good hand, and should you make that antipodean journey
he will serve you well. I do not mind at all the sharing of other
practical information: What I can do for you, in a professional
capacity, is always the easy thing; when I come across your
notes in the morning mail—from Paris, or Italy, or wherever
you, in your wanderings, happen to be—I answer them immediately, regardless of the glut of other correspondences and invitations that cross my desk daily.

I am, as you may deduce, a little weary from my post-
Africa life. I am now declining, without a doubt, in vitality: My marriage has been the best of it, but in other ways,
Samuel, I have been feeling restless. Spiritually, I have come to
regret my foray into the House of Commons—for Dolly's sake,
mainly. You have often used the term "hot air" in reference to
the pedantic people in life, and I do not look forward to the
prospect of being surrounded by them: I am told by my wife
that I have lately acquired the most solemn and withdrawn
air during our social outings. It's not that I do not enjoy the
company of people, but there is so much small talk and so
little time for the important things that I have been feeling
robbed: If I were an hourglass, I would be one for whom most
of the sands have run out. Time—what is it but a measure
of mutually agreed-upon units marking our passage through
the world? I have little doubt that the endlessness of it all, or
our illusion of its endlessness, is just a psychological device
that we humans employ to keep ourselves sane. How else can
one bear the quickening of the gap between the dawn of one's

*consciousness in infancy with the indifferent and rushing
present?*

*Lately the very words I once mentioned to you long
ago—the Reverend Hughes saying, "All men think other men
mortal but themselves," a maxim that drove my ambition as
a youth—now seem so much truer, and ironically so. Imagine
my current state of mind when I am feeling my time is being
wasted: What was once as abundant as an ocean has now
trickled down to a stream, and where I once imagined countless journeys for myself, I only see a few more awaiting me,
if any.*

*Part of this has to do with a sense of mortality. In the
past few years I've lost some good friends: Two of my officers
from the Pasha expedition, Captain Nelson and Lieutenant
Stairs, died in Africa in 1892; my medical assistant, Dr. Parke,
the picture of health, died suddenly of a heart attack in 1893;
and William Mackinnon, whom I valued greatly, has also
recently gone on. The Emin Pasha himself was murdered along
a trail in the Ituri Forest. I could go on but won't (forgive my
moroseness).*

*At least in the days when we met, back before the pleas-
ant illusion that was the South crumbled and became what
it is today, before the romantic caprice that said slavery was
a noble thing as long as it was conducted equitably and with
concern for the slaves' "human comforts"—as long as "civilization" flourished splendidly—you and I could enjoy our youth.
Remember then, Samuel, how lovely the Mississippi once
looked to us? It was not so much the actual physical nature
of the river itself, lovely as it was—with its luminous moons
at night, the shredded violet skies at dusk, the scent of marsh
flowers and burning campfires wafting over the waters—as the
aspect of the river unfolding endlessly before us, a symbol of
our own endless-seeming youth.*

*How could we have known, as young men, what life held
for us? Two famous budding writers were we: on the one hand*

there was you, the steamboat pilot Samuel Clemens, whose occasional ditties and observations about river life found their way into the region's newspapers, and on the other hand there was me, a common sales clerk from New Orleans by way of England whose only jottings were of numerical things, such as would concern the commerce of a riverboat trader like my adoptive father, Henry Stanley. Neither you nor I knew anything about what awaited us in the world of letters, and yet from the beginning, our mutual respect and liking for books brought us together. I can still remember your general amusement at the fact that you found me reading a Bible by the riverboat railing. That you deigned to speak to me, out of a hunger to converse with someone besides bored widows, was the beginning of a friendship.

Of the Bible you have always had your opinions: You have always regarded that "Good Book" as a great mythic fantasy—heartening to human resolve, moralistic, etc., but a tall tale—whereas I, in my innocence, believed in those words deeply. Since then—in the years, nearly forty, that have passed—I have generally come to agree with you: The Bible, in its sweetest and highest-aspiring parts, is wholly inapplicable to actual humanity. By Providence, we human beings simply fall short of the idealized way of living laid out before us. And what is God? You have told me that, at best, you have a general idea that God exists in the world only when "luck" or "destiny" falls in stride with a person's good fortune and that His absence from most events speaks to His general indifference if not nonexistence. I agree with you insofar as "God" is an impassive veil over our lives. I think He watches us from afar and does not intercede, as most people want Him to: The violent and needless deaths I have witnessed over the years, in regions where life is cheap and as exchangeable as an English pound, have been the proof.

I can tell you these things because, in a way, though we are separated by only a few years—six, as I remember—we have been treading the same ground: That you, Samuel, have managed to draw upon your own resources at this stage in your life to undertake a great tour to ease your debts has left me with an even greater admiration for you. Though you have never been a true soldier of the field, you have a strength of will that would have served you well in war, in spite of all the jokes you make about it. I have often thought, in this regard, that the greatest source of your strength must be and always has been your family—your lovely daughters, Jean, Clara, and Susy, of whom I have cherished memories, and of course your charming wife, Livy (I hope she is not ailing of late). What empowerment and confidence they must give to you, knowing that whatever your travails, at the end of the day you can be joined with them in the blissful and soothing atmosphere of domesticity.

If I have asked, "What is time?" then I must also ask, "What is fame?" To be recognized, applauded, introduced to persons of note, for a few moments; to travel a great distance to spend a mere half an hour at lunch with the queen—what does it add up to?

I have been thinking lately of my great enjoyment of children: Perhaps it is because I did not have much of a happy childhood myself—nothing nearly as sublime or comforting as the things I have read of your own past and the things you have told me about it. I had no paradise such as you did in Hannibal and at your uncle John's farm. The closest I have come to that kind of happiness has been in the wild and in friendship. Call it an honor to dine with the queen, but one is so blocked up inside from the formality, the protocol. There is honor but little joy in such things: For me, aside from the enjoyment of a few select companions and the company of my own very sweet wife, there is little else until I find myself with one of the cherubs I encounter. Around them, the great explorer becomes a child himself. Lately I count my happiest hours as the ones I have spent acting out the way the creatures of the

*African jungle move and roar: I was out at Cadogan Gardens
not so long ago, entertaining a group of children. I was, for
their amusement, pretending to be an African elephant, a lion,
and an antelope to teach them about the wonders of nature.
The essential integrity and uniqueness of the African "beas-
ties" brought no end of joy—through the children's laughter
and delight in seeing an old, white-haired explorer prancing
in a yard, I am drawn back, then, as I get older, as the body
fades, to a second childhood, I suppose, for to see the world
as children do is to reenter that paradise, a place or state
of mind far removed from the sorrows of this world. In that
exposure to such unsullied innocence I have found much that
is wonderful.*

*Which is to say, dear Samuel, that Dolly and I have been
considering the adoption of a child: As we have come to an age
when having children is no longer possible, I have been giving thought to the benefits of looking for a little one—a Welsh
child, of course—to call our own.*

*It is our plan to head up to Denbigh for such a purpose. It
would be a lovely thing to make happen.*

*As I know from Major Pond and Mr. Smythe that you are
to shortly to embark on a long world tour, I can only offer you
a word of encouragement; but should you need anything I am
always here for you.*

> *My best wishes to you and your family—*
> *Stanley*

STANLEY AND DOLLY SPENT SEVERAL months visiting many
an orphanage without finding a child appropriate for them—one,
as Stanley demanded, who had the "vital spark of intelligence and
alertness." But one day in the spring of 1896, a letter arrived from
Denbigh, written by a woman named Mary White, mentioning
that she was in guardianship of a thirteen-month-old boy who
had been born out of wedlock to a distant cousin on his mother's

side, a disgraced servant in the house of a wealthy man. With no one to assume paternity, and with the mother too poor to support him, the child had been passed along among uninterested relatives until he had come into her care. And so, in Denbigh one afternoon, after making a brief visit to St. Asaph's, where he donated a trunk's worth of books to their library, and after wandering through the local cemetery in a daydream about the passage of time, Stanley and Dolly alighted in the rustic hamlet of Corwen, in Denbighshire, where they made their way by carriage to a stone cottage by whose door stood a stout and grandmotherly old woman. Exhausted beyond her years, she wore a frayed cap and a sorry dress and was bent over a washbasin. Behind her, a wicker cradle held a child who was crying. The child was a pink-complexioned, brown-eyed Celtic infant, helpless and more or less destined, without the intercession of Mr. Stanley, to a foundling home or orphanage.

Stanley, for the occasion, had put on a blue frock coat, and as a matter of authority, and to impress the locals—for he had never wanted any of them to forget his accomplishments and rise in the world—he had attached a number of medals to his lapel. Dorothy Tennant wore a fine French dress. The driver opened the carriage doors for them, bowing.

"So," said Stanley. "Is this the residence of Mary White?"

"It is."

"I am Henry Stanley. Is this the child of whom you have written?"

"It is."

"Has he a name?"

"None yet." Then: "Go ahead—take a look. I believe he is a distant relation of yours."

With his wife by his side, Stanley stood over the infant, and, as he had done with other infants they had seen, he performed a test. Removing from his pocket a watch and chain, he dangled it before the baby and was pleased to see that the child's bright eyes followed its motion as it swung from left to right. Stanley then snapped his fingers and saw that the infant reacted quickly to that. He touched the child's head, with its traces of florid blond hair; then, leaning down to take a closer look, he was pleased to see that the infant seemed to be smiling and was reaching out to him with its little hands. He was thinking that this was a delightful child when Dolly, unable to contain her excitement and pleasure, and who, having always loved children, found the creature, in its innocence and perfection, irresistible, declared: "Oh what a joy: He even looks like you!"

It was not long, then, after conferring privately with his wife that Stanley told Mrs. White that they would be most interested in assuming possession and care of the child.

"Are you saying then, sir, that you want him?"

"Yes, we do."

"Then if you do, would you be willing to pay me something for having looked after him so well?"

"How much?" Stanley asked.

"I think ten pounds would cover it. I've had him for four months, after all."

This Stanley paid her on the spot: Other considerations, involving legal matters and fees, were resolved with alacrity because of Stanley's great standing in Wales. Within a few days, after a visit to Carnarvon, they came away with the papers of adoption and the infant himself.

DURING THE TRAIN RIDE SOUTH from Wales, Dolly held the baby closely: All her affection for children, which she had previously expressed in her paintings of London street urchins, multiplied, and her maternal side blossomed. Her journey was spent kissing the baby's face: Stanley, for his part, could not have been more attentive. He often sat back, beside his wife, thinking about the fact that he, as an abandoned waif, never knew where he really came from and never felt that anyone really cared: But this child would have a different fate. All around them, the countryside was rushing by—the incredible sun glaring through the treetops cast a shadow in the shape of a lunar crescent upon the compartment's wooden walls. The baby looked at it, enthralled, and Stanley remarked, "How alert! He'll be a good soldier one day!" Later, as the train jostled along, and as his wife swaddled the baby in her arms, Henry Stanley made it a point to dangle before the child's large brown eyes a key. And as he did so, he said: "You are now my son."

⚜

FROM HIS LAST MISSION IN Africa, Stanley had carried back a vial of water taken from Lake Albert, and with this water he had the child baptized. The name he chose for the child, Denzil, a variation of Dennis, was traced back to some distant ancestor of Dolly's who had been one of Cromwell's captains. Stanley gave the boy his own invented middle name, Morton, and a nursery was set up in the house on Richmond Terrace. A nanny was brought in, and the explorer himself, moved to excitement, set out to add his touches to that cheerful, sunlit room: Besides some scenes of fairy tales—colored lithographs by the elf artist Richard Doyle (uncle of Arthur Conan Doyle, inventor of the famed Sherlock Holmes and a family friend)—and several drawings by Dorothy, Stanley put up over the crib a framed map of Africa, so that in infancy the boy would grow up familiar with his adoptive father's accomplishments.

Then Stanley wrote to his friend: "Dear Samuel—When you are done with your touring you and the Mrs. must come to see the enchantment that has entered into this old soldier's life."

From Lady Stanley's Journal, 1896

IT WAS LATE JULY WHEN Samuel Clemens arrived in England from South Africa with his wife, Livy, and daughter Clara. He had finished the last leg of his yearlong world tour, undertaken to pay off his considerable debts. We had been kept informed of his itinerary by Mr. Smythe, Stanley's own Australia agent, who had booked Clemens's antipodean lectures, but in addition, every so often there arrived in the mail letters from the weary traveler and *cartes de visite* from various exotic locales. Clemens had set out the year before from Vancouver, bound for Australia and New Zealand, then he had traveled onward to India and Ceylon and other points of interest. His plans were to settle in England for a few months before proceeding home, and, to that end, he had come to London to find an appropriate house to rent. Shortly he would be joined by his two other daughters, Susy and Jean, from America—and a much-belated reunion would ensue.

"What is hardest," he had written my husband from Agra, India, "are not the bugs and snakes and the incessant heat of this dusty land, nor is it my own persistent colds and carbuncles, and it is not even the misery of the poverty that exists everywhere and spills onto the steps of the most opulent maharaja's palace; rather, my dear Stanley, it is the powerful loneliness that I feel when thinking about my daughters and how this separation must weigh upon them—particularly Susy, my eldest and most sensitive one, who, I know, was none too happy that we were going away for so long. It's my dream to put my debts to bed for good and abandon this nomad's life, and I look forward to a normal and civilized family existence back home in Hartford. I, for one, cannot wait for my burden to be lifted again; I hope that will be the case when I come back through England, in the spring or summer—the sooner the better."

The first week of August, we were therefore pleased to hear from Clemens by way of a telegram conveying the news that he was in London for a few days; straightaway Stanley, despite some recent maladies, went to the Langham hotel to find Clemens somewhat indisposed in bed. They spent several hours speaking—mainly about South Africa, which Clemens had recently visited.

"He was worse for wear, physically speaking, and looking somewhat more gaunt than I remember, and Livy seemed to be having some problems walking because of a fall," Stanley told me. "They were in very good spirits, though, much relieved that the whole business of the tour was behind them." On this occasion, Stanley invited them into our home for dinner, and to this Clemens agreed, as long as it was not a big affair at which he would feel compelled to entertain an audience. "I am too tired of being Mark Twain lately," he told my husband. "But I will be happy to turn up as Sam and see your sparkling new baby."

We kept to our word, though Mother was beside herself that she could not make it a society event, my husband having demanded that it be kept an intimate thing. "Mr. Clemens may be a famous man, perhaps the most famous American in the world," he told her, "but his privacy is to be protected, at least in this household!" Thereafter Mother and Stanley did not speak for several days, but when that evening came, for the sake of our guests' comfort, they made their peace, and in any case, such momentary differences between them always passed with time. Besides, the truest guest of honor was our Denzil, whom we brought into our parlor and kept in a fine crib. Stanley sat beside him, often just staring at the young, untarnished face, ever so proud of his "darling and pure cherub." It pleased him that he was always able to calm Denzil down when he cried: Holding the child in his arms, he'd delight in sniffing at his head, which he claimed smelled like freshly baked bread. He was so attached to our infant that it was as if nothing in his life before that, not even Africa, had counted for much. He called the baby "my truest treasure" and came to often say: "Every moment I am away from him seems a wasted moment: If all I can do for the rest of my life is to see that he is brought up well and cared for—well, then, that will be a most worthy occupation."

Such was his pride that when Clemens finally arrived with his wife and daughter Clara to our home, Stanley led him immediately to the crib and surprised us all by introducing Mr. Clemens in this way: "Now, dear Denzil, here is your uncle Mark!" a distinction that led our honored guest to blush. "What can I say," remarked Clemens, "but that I am honored?" Then: "Ah, a new and fresh life!"

A congenial evening passed. Whatever fatigues and concerns had descended upon Clemens from the strain of his worries and travels were forgotten for a few hours. The high point of the evening, I should say, were Clemens's most colorful descriptions of India, which intrigued me, especially where they concerned the country's religious aspects. He called India "a land of ten thousand gods, one for every single thing you could ever think about; religion, pungent as burning incense, is thick in the air. And mosquitoes, too." (But did he believe in all that? I think not, because he called the Hindu beliefs "a system by which the poor masses are kept in their lowly state.") Later, as it would be an early evening for them, I prevailed upon Clemens to come and look at one of the paintings I had worked up of him, my memories of those sessions still fresh in my mind. After I took him into my studio, he was charmed by several of my new ragamuffin drawings and expressed a great interest in my methods.

"Will you come back another day?" I asked him, but he confessed that because of Livy's frail health, they would be leaving London shortly. They had rented a house in Surrey, in the town of Guildford, where Livy might rest and he could quietly pursue his writing—a new book about his recent travels—away from the clamor of London.

"Well, then, we will visit you," I told him.

"When my daughters arrive from America we will have you over; and bring the little one, too, if it's not an inconvenience."

"But you will sit for me again, won't you?"

I could not help but press that point, and he was agreeable enough to say he would once he and the family were settled.

Unfortunately it would be a long time before that day would come to pass.

☀

SEVERAL DAYS HAD GONE BY when there arrived a letter posted from Guildford.

August 16, 1886

My dear friends,

If you have not heard from me in recent days it is because a crisis has arisen regarding the health of my daughter Susy. In the heat of a horrendous Hartford summer she has fallen ill from a fever. The brave girl has apparently been ill for some weeks and had the misfortune of depending too greatly on a spiritualist healer who advised her badly; she is now staying with some family friends, and I am glad to say that under a doctor's care she is apparently coming along, though she at this point will not be well enough to come here for quite some time. All this has, of course, left my dear wife and daughter Clara in a state of concern, and yesterday I saw them off at the station, for they have booked passage back to America from Portsmouth to attend to her convalescence. Even now they are at sea; in the meantime I have been sitting on pins and needles, racked with anxiety. Last night what sleep I managed was filled with sad dreams. Though her doctor—Dr. Porter—has assured me by cable that her cure is a matter of rest.

Which is to say that once I hear better news nothing would more please me than for you to join me here for a day; it is a pleasant enough little town, without much to do but go walking. The surrounding countryside is idyllic, in a Surrey way.

Yours,
Samuel

Naturally Stanley wanted to head out to Guildford to reassure his old friend that all would turn out well, but he had come down with some very bad symptoms of his own—gastritis again—and could barely work up the will to leave his bed save to look in on the baby—in such moments, despite his awareness of the flagging resources of his body, he always managed to get up and drag himself, ever so slowly, to the nursery. Always a stoic about pain and somewhat indifferent to any fear of his own death, Stanley had been changed by Denzil's presence in our lives. If anything pained him it was the thought that his wish to live for another twenty years, or at least as long as it would take for Denzil to grow into a man, was unlikely given his own ever-declining health.

∿

SOME MONTHS BEFORE, IN THE early spring of 1896, while traveling in Spain, where he, in his fluent Spanish, had held forth before a geographical society in Toledo, Stanley was on a train to Madrid with Dorothy when he came down with an attack of gastritis so severe that he doubled over in his compartment and was soon nearly rendered unconscious. The pain was so great that he could barely open his eyes. From a carry bag, in which he kept charts of Africa that he used in his lectures, his wife took out a bottle of medicine, an elixir that provoked a great drowsiness in Stanley. For all his fame in the British Isles, when they arrived in Madrid's main station, teeming with activity and with crowds, Dolly, who spoke no Spanish, had difficulty finding assistance. She barely managed to get Stanley off the train by recruiting the aid of a porter with her repeated cries for help, but in the terminal itself, a beehive of activity, there was no first aid station, and the heat was so intense that Stanley, barely able to walk, passed out again. When she finally got him to their hotel—the Velázquez—the frustrating processes repeated itself. A doctor finally arrived on the scene and offered some bromides by way of remedy, but Stanley steadily worsened and grew weaker. Within a week, Dorothy, fearing for his life, resolved to get him back to England, an episode that disheartened and exhausted her: He survived, but for three months he suffered greatly, his cries of agony punctuating the nights, his spasms steadily recurring, and his hours passing in a veil of stoicism and silence.

At least he had Denzil: All at once, it seemed that the horrors of life, the petty nuisances and myriad responsibilities that had made his days an unending progression of work and fretful concerns, fell away. It was if the child's presence had created for Stanley a new world; as if emanating from that innocence came a sanctuary of sweet and reassuring emotions: "To think that I, for so many years, had lived solely for the approval of others and had wasted so many of my energies on 'progress' instead of ensuring what should be most important to a man, the pursuit of simple affections—life's main reward."

☙

THEN CAME A DAY OF sad news. Stanley had been sitting at the dining room table reading the morning newspapers when he came across an item on the front page of the London *Times* that much grieved him.

Mother, sitting across from him, noticed the explorer's face draining of color. "What is it?" she asked. "Read it," he told her. What met her eye was a headline: MARK TWAIN'S ELDEST DAUGHTER DIES OF SPINAL MENINGITIS.

A few nights before, on the evening of the eighteenth, Susy Clemens, after several weeks of suffering, passed away at her father's Hartford home; in her company were several family friends, among them the Reverend Joseph Twichell, their housekeeper, Katy Leary, and her aunt and uncle Charles and Susan Crane. "The famous author's firstborn daughter was called to peace at approximately 8:30 that night," the article said. No sooner had Stanley deliberated on this tragic development—"Oh, why, dear God, should this happen to such a dear and decent man?"

he thought—than he called out to his wife, Dolly, in her studio. Though he was having some difficulty walking, relying upon a cane, and although he had several appointments that he would have to cancel for the day, he had no doubt what they would have to do: "Come on," he told her, showing Dolly the newspaper. "We've got to go to Guildford and find Clemens." Her own distress was great—that this should happen to their friend in the midst of their own happiness seemed most unfair. "Yes, of course. We'll go," she told her husband.

THE DAY BEFORE, CLEMENS HAD been in the dining room of his rented cottage in Guildford, trying to distract himself from thoughts about Susy. The messages he and Livy had received before Livy's departure for America had been mixed; the first few said that their daughter had fallen mysteriously ill, perhaps from her tendency to practice her singing for too many hours a day in the heat of an uncommonly warm Hartford summer. Indisposed with a fever that was "nothing serious," she would have to recover before coming to England with her sister Jean and Katy Leary, their housekeeper, a journey that was to have begun on August 5. But later telegrams, while predicting an eventual recovery, were riddled with alarming phrases: "She is still weak and faint but in good spirits" and "In some pain, she is getting better" among them. Still, those telegrams raised such apprehension that Clemens spent nearly every evening at the town telegraph office, awaiting the latest word. On such nights, neither he nor Livy could sleep. The very possibility that her condition could take a turn for the worse precipitated his wife and daughter's journey back to America. Even as they set sail from Portsmouth, and even as Clemens received yet another telegram saying that her recovery was all but certain, her spinal meningitis was diagnosed in Hartford. Yet for the life of him, as he would sit to work on his travel book, he couldn't figure out why his thoughts—of meteorites flashing across the night skies beyond Hawaii and the luminous lunar eclipse they had seen on their way to Fiji, memories of a beautiful universe in motion—would turn into visions of Susy helpless in bed, a look of despair and loneliness upon her face. No, he couldn't write much, hard as he tried to: A tightening of his legs, a flaring up of his rheumatism, a twisting of his gut accompanied the inescapable sensation that his daughter was, in fact, dying. All of them had experienced that sense without saying so, but Clemens, who refused to believe that it could possibly be true, still awaited the knock on his door, the arrival of the friendly telegraph man, with good news from Katy Leary or Joseph Twichell: "Your daughter Susy has recovered and is now well" was the nine-word sentence he wanted to read; but that morning, August 19, when he had been thinking about whether he should take a walk to the local bakery to buy some bread, then make his way to the newsagent's shop to collect the daily papers, then later drop a note to his friend Stanley, there indeed came, as he had hoped—and dreaded—a knock at his door.

Twain looked out: A ruddy-cheeked telegraph man with kind eyes, who had no doubt taken down the message after it had been conveyed across the Atlantic to London and then to Guildford, didn't seem to know quite what to say. "Mr. Clemens, this is for you, sir." And there it was, contained within the telegram, a simple phrase, sent by the Reverend Twichell, informing him of his daughter's passing the night before.

"I am sad to report that Susy was peacefully released from her sufferings today."

Clemens gave the telegraph man a shilling for his trouble. Heard the words "I'm sorry for you, sir." He seemed to sit down, the actual contents of the telegram not quite registering upon him. He thought, for some reason, about molecules. How much does a molecule weigh? he asked himself. Why is it that when one is happy—say, at a time of love or when first beholding a newborn child—one experiences a nearly weightless density, as if one can nearly fly? And conversely, he wondered, what does a molecule weigh when one is feeling grief? And while he could not exactly determine what had just made him think of such things— the immediate fact of Susy's passing having been occluded behind a wall of disorientation and denial—he fancied that the molecules around him were rapidly growing denser with alarming emotions, until each, as he would later put it, weighed "a ton of sadness, five tons of guilt, then twenty tons of gloom." On that morning, as he sat with the telegram in hand, he found it a physical impossibility to even move, so great was his pain at being unbearably alone and beset by the sadness of this existence, which like the wind, could suddenly come upon him from any direction.

From Lady Stanley's Journal, Friday, August 20, 1886

WHEN WE SET OUT FOR Guildford on the afternoon train out of Waterloo station, Mother insisted on coming along, as she, too, had been sorely concerned for our friend Clemens, with whom she had been having a regular correspondence. What she wrote to him I cannot say, but clearly she had taken to Clemens with a natural liking that I wished she had for Stanley. Not that they were not getting along; Stanley, for the most part, had gotten used to her demanding and exacting ways.

As we prepared to leave, Stanley and I were at first at a loss at what to bring along with us, but it was Mother who, in the practical wisdom of her years, suggested that we gather together a lunch basket for Mr. Clemens should he be hungry. Stocked from our abundant pantry, it contained a basket of cheeses, good bread, and some cured French sausages along with some chocolates, which Stanley remembered Clemens liked. Stanley himself had pulled out a bottle of good port and several bottles of French wine from our cellar; from his library he found a volume by the eminent Anglican theologian Reverend Everett Thomas, *Meditations on the Passings of Man*, and brought that along. My own contributions consisted of several pamphlets from the Society for Psychical Research about the everlasting nature of the human soul: Whether Clemens would be receptive to this I did not know.

Arriving in Guildford, we learned that the town's residents were very aware of Clemens's existence in their midst: At the train station, when we told the carriage driver to take us to the residence of Samuel Clemens on Portsmouth Road, he looked at us from beneath a stovepipe hat and said, "Of course—you are the third party from London I'll have driven there today." As our carriage came to a halt, the street on which he currently resided— a quiet stretch of ordinary houses off the main thoroughfare of shops and taverns and inns—was filled with curious townspeople gathered on the curb opposite his house. Among them were several journalists waiting, I assumed, for an interview with Clemens. One of them, seeing that I had looked his way, and perhaps recognizing us, tipped his bowler at me.

Before the doorway of Clemens's house stood a giant of man, recruited, no doubt, from a local pub to prevent any incursions against Clemens's privacy. He glared at us when we alighted from our carriage and approached the door. "Who are you, and what do you want?"

My husband, in a commanding military tone, addressed him: "Please tell Mr. Clemens that Henry Morton Stanley has come to see him."

This person, ignorant of my husband's standing, told us, in his gruff manner, "Wait a moment, will you? But don't expect anything." As he went inside, I noticed that several bouquets of spring flowers had been set along the pavement beside the house, likely from sympathetic locals; and even as we waited, however briefly, two journalists crossed over, calling out: "Mr. Stanley, can we have a moment of your time, sir?" But my husband would have nothing of it: "Can you not see that this is a private moment?

Now go away." Stanley himself, not at his physical best, had put his hand up on the wall beside the doorway to support himself: His hair was as white as I had ever seen it.

"What is taking so long?" he asked while we were waiting.

Finally the door was opened by the burly fellow.

"You can go inside now."

We entered. To our left was a fully furnished parlor containing an upright piano and a billiard table, and to the right was a dining room, which Samuel had made into his study. Spread all across a long oak table were piles of scribbled-over manuscript pages and several plates holding uneaten portions of meals; an ashtray filled with black cigar butts; many crumpled pieces of paper; two candles that had completely melted down, their wax overflowing their holders onto the wood; a few glasses next to a half-empty bottle of whiskey; and a small clock. A musty and smoky odor prevailed, and the room itself was dark—none of the window shutters had been opened for some days, it seemed. And in that darkness sat Mr. Clemens, wearing a bathrobe, his face unshaved, his eyes red-rimmed, his leonine countenance, topped by a mass of unruly white hair, looking so sad and drawn that my first impulse was to rush over to him. However, I left it to Stanley to have the first word:

"Samuel, we are here for you, my brother."

When Clemens got up and embraced Stanley, I cannot say if he was weeping (Stanley would never weep), but through his mutterings Mother and I heard him calling Stanley "my dear friend" again and again. Then Samuel, composing himself, came around to greeting us.

"Thank you for coming, my dear ladies, but I wish you hadn't gone to the trouble: I am fairly useless right now, but you are welcome just the same." Then: "Forgive me my appearance. I suppose I should get dressed."

Truthfully he seemed embarrassed both by the unseemliness of his surroundings and, as I have seen with persons in sudden mourning, by the rawness of his pain; he seemed nearly apologetic over his solemn state. "If it's a bit untidy here, its because I've let my housekeeper go, and, as you can see, I've lived a month's worth of bad habits in a day or so." Then, managing a smile, he added, attempting to make a joke of his circumstances, "Oh, don't look so worried about me; I'll get over it in about a hundred years or so."

Mother had commented to me that Mr. Clemens should be "carefully looked after," but as Stanley himself had pointed out on our way to Guildford, Clemens was a very private man. "At best, we can only expect to buck him up a bit: I cannot imagine his sufferings." In the coolness of his sentiments, he had seemed rather matter-of-fact, but as one who had seen much death in the wilds of Africa (sometimes in the cruelest forms) and on the battlefields of the Civil War in his youth, he knew there was not much to be done with that hard fact.

"I have always been good at writing letters of condolence to the family when one of my officers has died. But what to say to a man who has lost his daughter is beyond my abilities," he had told us. And yet, though he did not know just what to say, I had never observed Stanley so willing to offer a man such immediate and (for Stanley) affectionate gestures of support. My husband escorted Samuel into his dressing room and held the writer steadily by his arm, patting him gently on the back, patiently, as Samuel, in a state of shock, moved ever so slowly, slippers shuffling along the floor, as if he had the weight of the world on his shoulders.

"Come on, Samuel, you must be strong now," I heard him say.

After they left us, Mother and I took the liberty of putting some order to the room without disturbing his manuscripts (with their many crossed-out paragraphs, they were obviously the failed attempts of a man trying to find some coherence in his troubled thoughts). But I could not avoid seeing the penciled scrawl written in large letters on a single sheet, in Clemens's hand: "I wish it had been me." Nor could I avoid the discovery of a photograph in an oval frame that had been turned down on its face: It showed a young woman of about twenty, her expression solemn, her large and liquid eyes like that of a startled sparrow—his daughter Susy, I presumed. The sentiment that this tender and troubled face was that of the deceased nearly brought me to tears, but Mother, in her strong way, told me to attend to my duties. Although I was unaccustomed to such tasks, I carried the plates into the kitchen to soak them in a basin; then I gave the floors, which were covered in cigar ashes, a sweep. Mother, in the meantime, had opened the window shutters, and the room was filled with light and fresh air. From her own experience she knew that someone should take the initiative, for when Father died, Mother had sat in her darkened bedroom for a month and had only come around when my brother, Charles, and I finally drew open the curtains for her; now she was doing the same for Clemens. But no sooner had she thrown the window shutters open than we saw why Mr. Clemens had kept them closed: The journalists who had been stationed across the street were abruptly upon us, peering in and shouting all manner of questions at us. We shut them again.

Stanley helped Clemens to dress, which is to say that he picked out his outfit from a closet, a dark frock coat and a pair of Harris Tweed trousers along with a clean white shirt; and although Clemens resisted, so Stanley later told me, he had stood over a washbasin while Stanley shaved him. When he finally emerged from his room, quite improved in his appearance by my husband's ministrations, we heard him saying: "Just look at me, ladies. It seems that Stanley has half revived a dead man." Then: "Though it is a hard fact, I can't believe she's gone."

"Look here, Samuel," Stanley said. "As it's a beautiful day, why don't we get out of here for a while? The ladies have packed a picnic. The fresh air will do you good."

"I will if you think I should," he said. "But mind you, you will be picnicking with a somnambulist; a walking ghost. Yes, let us go: Lead me on, and do make sure that the vultures out there leave me alone."

☀

OF MINOR IMPORTANCE WAS THE conversation that Stanley had with the reporters outside the house just before we set forth. As this small but determined contingent of journalists would have surely followed us wherever we went, Stanley took it upon himself to act as Mr. Clemens's spokesperson. It was a necessity that he attended to with the utmost politeness and patience in the name of Mr. Clemens's privacy. Crossing the road, he gave the journalists a statement, portions of which were published all over England by the next day. In essence, he said:

"Gentleman, as Mr. Mark Twain is in mourning, he has asked me to speak on his behalf. Though he is greatly moved by the outpouring of concern for his well-being and by the natural curiosity that many have about his state of mind, he wishes to inform everyone that he is holding up quite well—as much as any father can be given the loss of a beloved daughter. Above all, to the people of England, he extends his deepest gratitude."

And that was all. Though the reporters asked for more—"Will he be attending the funeral?" "Will he be staying in England?"—Clemens himself, standing in the doorway and seeing Stanley in their midst, walked over and, thanking the gentlemen, led him away. Though they were shouting out other questions, all Mr. Clemens said was, "Good day, gentlemen."

☀

BY HIRED CARRIAGE WE PROCEEDED to a meadow a few miles out of town. There we found a congenial place under a spreading elm near a brook, along which there were some good-size rocks on which we might sit. The brook flowed with some vitality out from the surrounding woods; in the distance, beyond a long fence that spanned the horizon, a herd of Devonshire cows lolled in a pasture. All manner of bird life twittered and sang about us, butterflies occasionally came lilting through the air, and there was an agreeable scent of the deep woods wafting briskly out from a hollow. Nature could not have been more cooperative, for upon coming to this place, Clemens, stretching his legs and looking around, allowed that it was as pretty a spot as he had ever seen. As we sat to have some bread and cheese, Mother serving us all, I asked Samuel if he were willing to speak about his journey to India as a way of distracting him. "Was there any one place you found especially agreeable?"

"'India' and 'agreeable' are not two words I would put together in any sentence," he said. "But I will allow that there are some pretty interesting places—like Benares, their holy city, a city of temples rising in tiers from the sacred and filthy Ganges, with death and the spirit dense in the air and with holy men and pilgrims and burning funeral pyres everywhere. We liked Darjeeling, mainly for its view of Everest, but wherever we went—from Bombay to Delhi and from Muzaffarpur to Jaipur—we were overwhelmed by two things: the poverty and squalor of the people. Abundant in numbers, the people are, judging by their Hindu temples, the most God-conscious—or gods-conscious—people I have ever seen, though I heard I would find an even more religious people up in Tibet. But as to sights, I think we were most impressed with the Taj Mahal at Agra: what gardens, what flowers, what flaming poinciana trees! And all surrounding the vast ivory-white Taj Mahal—a tomb, big as any palace, built by a Mogul emperor grieving for his dead wife, but one did not think of it that way. A majestic place, and so pretty I can remember thinking that Susy would have very much enjoyed seeing it. I don't know if she would have been up to the hard parts of travel, but Livy, frail as she was, bravely got through the whole business. But now my Susy will never see anything beautiful again. And all because of me."

"My friend," Stanley said, "I know what you are feeling is of the greatest difficulty; but remember that she loved you, and that is the best thing of all."

"Oh, yes, she did, certainly she did: And what did she get for it but death?"

"Why would you even think that, Samuel?" I ventured to ask.

"Why? I'll tell you: If I hadn't let my partner, Charles Webster, run my publishing house into the ground, and if I hadn't gone deeper into bankruptcy because of that blasted Paige typesetting machine, I would never have had to go on my world tour. And if I hadn't gone on that tour I would have been with Susy, and she wouldn't have gotten sick with worry and would be alive today."

"Samuel," my husband said, "you're thinking irrationally. Calm yourself."

"Easy to say, Henry; hard to do. The worst of it for me is that I know how my dear Livy will be sorely affected; she is at sea even as we sit here. What she'll do when she finally hears the news worries me most of all. If it doesn't kill her, I'm sure she'll wish it had."

Then: "The hardest thing is that as a family we were on the verge of finding some normalcy again. I finished a new novel, about Joan of Arc—we know how that ended—and my debts were all but paid; it was time for us as a family to go forward. But somehow, even when we settled in town, I had a hunch that things might go wrong—just how wrong I could not have imagined. I'd stay in the house with Livy and Clara until about five, writing—or trying to write. Supper would be at seven, but in the few hours before that I would venture forth into town to have a half and half in the pub: Few knew me, and no one had read my books, but just the same they were awfully friendly."

In seeking to change the subject, Mother brought up the writer Gustave Flaubert, whom she had once known in the days of her youth in Paris, but Clemens didn't seem to hear a single word of what she said, his sad eyes looking off into the distance. So great was his melancholy that Stanley also seemed affected in a way that he was not with others: His hardened soul somehow always softened in the presence of that man. We sat in that place for around an hour or so, and at around four, as I remained with

Mother, Clemens and my husband went for a walk along a trail in the woods. Upon their return we accompanied Clemens back to his rented house, where we said our good-byes, Stanley assuring Clemens that should he be needed he would drop everything else to see him. "No need to," Clemens said. "I've gotten accustomed to my bit of purgatory."

"Well, we will see you again," Stanley said. "I hope under better circumstances."

"Will there ever be better circumstances?" Clemens asked.

LATER, ON THE TRAIN BACK to London, I asked my husband about what he and Clemens had talked about during their walk in the woods; they had been gone for about half an hour.

"It was not so much what we spoke about that was interesting," Stanley told me. "It was what happened. During our walk he spoke mainly of his daughter, as if there had been nothing else in the world: I could not blame him, his tragedy being so recent. I listened, admitting that I would not know what I would feel if something happened to our little Denzil. But as always, our paths diverged on the subject of God and the afterlife, as I tried to offer him the solace that a heavenly reward awaited her. He had no use for such ideas, though he wished that what I said was true for his wife's sake. He then told me that in the midst of all his misery the only time he felt any relief was during a fleeting dream from the night before, about a blue jay alighting upon his arm. In that dream the delicate little creature had somehow managed to lift him up off the ground into the air—the sensation of floating free from the troubles of the world having greatly pleased him. When I told Clemens that I thought it was a dream about Susy's spirit, about this he also disagreed. But no sooner had I mentioned it than a blue jay appeared before us on the path, picking around for seeds; and then, strangely enough, it lifted off the ground and alighted briefly on Samuel's shoulder before taking off again. When I said, 'Ah, you see, dear Samuel, there is someone listening,' he allowed that it was a memorable coincidence but left it at that. I suddenly pitied the man as I never had before—even after the passing of the years, his is still a godless world. We continued our walk in silence."

From Stanley's Notebook

SAW SC TODAY AT HIS home in Guildford, two days after he learned about his daughter's unexpected death. Made the journey with Dolly and her mother, though in retrospect I wish I had gone alone, as Samuel would, I think, have preferred to sit quietly and drink with a friend. Despite this we managed a reasonable afternoon, spent partly in the countryside, and I think Samuel was better for it. During the short time we had to speak intimately, while taking a walk through the woods, Samuel circled again and again around his terrible guilt over the whole business. It was not his fault, but knowing him a bit, I think he tended to blame himself for the great tragedies of his life. I was reminded of the way, many years before, he had blamed himself for the death of his younger brother. I could only try to offer him the solace that Providence has its ways and a purpose: Clemens would have nothing of that—and I could not blame him. The world, beyond the confines of one's own family—if one is fortunate enough to have a family—is a wicked and unforgiving place, and when that illusion of safety and permanence is disturbed, and most unfairly so, as in the case of his daughter, what defense can be made of the notion that God is good and that God cares?

It has, to say the least, been upsetting, and today I wish that I could have known the words to soothe his heart—my own stoicism is of no help in these matters. Between his outbursts of sadness and interludes of peaceful reflection, the woods, like thoughts of youth itself, seemed a sanctuary, a place to stand still and look around and take in the magnificence of nature. A small story: As we walked in the woods, Samuel told me a dream he'd had—"the only one, besides imagining Joan of Arc burning at the stake," wherein he had been visited by a blue bird that had given him the magical ability to fly. Knowing a little of dream symbols, I tried to plant the notion in Clemens's mind that it had been about Susy's soul, newly released into God's universe; but just as he began to take it as a more or less pleasant thing, along the trail in front of us we came across a gravely injured creature—a blue bird, in fact, writhing upon the ground, its pellet eyes twitching with helplessness, the sight of which saddened Clemens even more. He nearly wept then, but being a manly sort, he restrained himself. I broke the spell by offering him a cigar, and we made our way back. Later, for Dolly's sake, I reported the story about the bird differently so as to conform with her optimistic belief that in life there are always happy endings. I disagree, and so does Samuel.

From Lady Stanley's Journal, Autumn 1896

WHEN MR. CLEMENS'S WIFE AND daughters arrived in England, they remained in seclusion with him in Guildford for several months, seeing no visitors, not even my husband. "Dear Stanley: I hope you understand this, but 'life has stopped' for us for the time being," Clemens wrote in those days. Of course we understood their difficulties: Stanley himself had made several attempts to bolster Clemens's spirits by way of sending him parcels of books, and Mother and I, with great concern, saw to it that the family received some baskets of special foods from our better shops—we could do no less. (Mrs. Clemens wrote a note of appreciation.) As to what they must have been feeling in those days I cannot imagine, and as much as we would have liked to help, we naturally respected their need for privacy. But thankfully their stay in Guildford was not a prolonged one, and by early October they had taken up residence here in London, renting a house on Tedworth Square, in Chelsea, though we had yet to see them again.

From Stanley's Notebook, December 18, 1896

I'M NOT GIVEN TO SENTIMENTALITY. Nor am I particularly given to weeping over a grave. Dead men whom I have known have not risen, no matter how much I grieve for them, but some come back again and again in dreams. In my slumbers last evening, I found myself in the vast anterior room of a palace, the dark space around me dimly lit by distant lanterns, and everywhere I looked there were wooden columns arranged in endless rows, much like those in the Alhambra. Stepping from behind one of these columns—or abruptly appearing in front of one—was the butcher said to have been my father, wearing a bloody apron and looking at me sadly. Just as I was turning toward him, he stepped away; then, as I went to look for him, I saw Mr. Stanley of New Orleans, my adoptive father, wearing a tall hat and dark suit, emerging from behind another column. He regarded me with the sternest and most disapproving expression—why I cannot say; and even then, as I moved closer to him, he slipped into the darkness. Then I turned to find the dear and saintly Livingstone, a shadow of himself, gaunt and as sickly as I remembered him, in safari garb, holding out his bony hands toward me; then he stepped away and I could not see him anymore. But as I sought to find my way out of that place—I think it was Hades—I turned in another direction and saw the three of them circling around me and (I think) speaking sorrowfully of the loneliness that comes to the dead, and I was greatly agitated. Everywhere I looked I saw them; if I closed my eyes (in the dream) I still saw them. And then they were gone— back into the farthest recesses of that place, I presumed. How long I searched for them in that gloomy darkness I cannot say, and why this dream should have taken yet another turn is a mystery, but as I made my way along the endless procession of columns, I came across my friend Samuel Clemens. He neither spoke nor looked at me, nor did he answer me when I asked him the name of that place. Then, as with the others, he, too, began to step away from me; not vanishing suddenly, as the others had, but floating off, as would an apparition, his form becoming smaller and smaller as it receded and then disappeared in the distance, a ghastly dream.

I do not know what it means, and was most grateful to awaken in the real world in my bedchamber, to smell the newly delivered evergreen that the servants were putting up in the parlor, to hear Dolly and Mother chatting away, and to look in and play, as fathers should, with my little son.

⁂

THAT CHRISTMAS, DOROTHY, HOWEVER TROUBLED she may have felt over Clemens's sufferings, remained her resolutely cheerful and optimistic self. As she did every holiday season, she presided over a campaign to raise funds for charity and spent several mornings visiting the households of her affluent friends to solicit donations—successfully so, for within a fortnight she had raised more than a thousand pounds, a sum that did not include her and Stanley's own substantial contribution. (These funds she distributed equally among three relief agencies: the Destitute Children's Dinner Society, the London Orphan Asylum, and the Home for Friendless Young Females of Good Character.) But just as dutifully, she threw a party in mid-December for a gathering of her favorite urchins, those children who had been her subjects: About eight of them, in their Sunday best, turned up at the mansion with their mothers or older sisters to partake of a grand feast that included a roast goose, mince pies and cake, and many other niceties, including a plum pudding into which Dorothy had secreted coins of the realm. To each of these children, from "Little Mary" to "Sad Tim," she had given a toy—a pennywhistle or a tin drum, a doll or cup game—and each, regardless of sex, received a picture book, gloves, and woolen caps and scarves. For the families themselves there was a basket of tinned jams and biscuits and other sweet viands along with an envelope containing a five-pound note. She served a sweet punch, and with the fireplace blazing and the children in an ecstatic state over the wreaths and holly set out here and there along the mantel, she presided over one of the most satisfying luncheons of her year.

This fete began just after noon; by two, with many delights having passed their lips, the children had become raucous. It was an affair that Stanley, off in his study, largely ignored, though at one point, while sitting down to work on some correspondence— nearly daily he wrote at least a short note to Clemens, inquiring after his well-being—he, somewhat distracted, decided to look in on the proceedings. When he appeared by the parlor doorway, white-haired, his expression stern, and with the gravity of his commanding bearing pouring forth, the children, in the midst of a happy reverie and playing their toy instruments, at once stopped making their cacophonous music. While he had thought to request that they quiet down, once he saw their little stunned faces, not a one yet ruined by the harshness of the life awaiting them, he simply looked around and mumbled, "Don't mind me, lads and little misses; just carry on."

He pretended to look around in a drawer for a cigar cutter, then sat down in a corner chair for a few minutes, a cigar in hand, taking it all in, with both sadness and joy, such a scene reminding the explorer emeritus (as the RGS referred to him) of what "might once have been" at St. Asaph's.

✺

DESPITE THE HAPPY DOMESTICITY AROUND him, he was greatly disturbed by what he had been reading in the newspapers recently about the Congo. The reports were not a constant feature, appearing intermittently, but now and then, as he would sit down at his home on Richmond Terrace to look over the morning dailies, there would be some item relating to alleged colonial atrocities in the region. One such report came by way of an American missionary named Murphy, who, traveling in the region, had testified about the methods used by the Belgians for the harvesting of rubber in order to meet their weekly quotas.

> It is collected by force. The soldiers drive the people
> into the bush. If they will not accede to this forced labor,
> they are shot down, and their left hands cut off and
> taken as trophies to the commissaire. These hands are
> then smoked in small kilns and, thusly preserved, laid
> out in rows before the commissaire, who counts them to
> see that the soldiers have not wasted cartridges.

Other accounts, including one by a pious Swedish missionary named Sjoblom, claimed that rapes and kidnappings were common events and that entire villages were burned down and their inhabitants either taken into slavery or killed. A certain Englishman named Parminter, who had traveled in the upper Congo, spoke of seeing detachments of Belgian soldiers carrying, slung over their shoulders, lengths of hemp cording to which were attached a succession of severed human ears. He claimed he had witnessed a Belgian lieutenant putting two native women to the lash of a chicotte, a whip made of hippopotamus hide with edges like razors, before ordering his men to cut their breasts off, leaving them to die.

Now and then, while out in public, where people once stopped to shake his hand or ask for his autograph, Stanley would occasionally be approached by persons who wished to take issue with him if not insult him outright. While strolling along Oxford Street one day with Dolly and his mother-in-law, he was approached by a man who was brazen enough to spit at Stanley's shoes, and it took great restraint for Stanley not to administer him a beating with his cane—the man ran away in any case and was soon lost in the crowd. Stanley blamed the erosion of his reputation not only on the contradictory reports that had come out about Africa (how was it that some said he was the cruelest man to have trod African soil while others said that he was the kindest, in the mode of Livingstone?) but also on one particular penny pamphlet that was, unfortunately, being widely read in England at the time. It was called *Stanley's Exploits, or, Civilising Africa*, and it had been written by one D. J. Nicoll, a socialist; its tone was set by its frontispiece. In it, Stanley is shown in a jungle clearing, his hands clasped in prayer, while behind him, dangling from a tree, hangs an African native.

As Stanley sat in his study that Christmas of 1896, the very idea that he, after all his efforts in Africa, might be associated with such allegations or that his explorations had in any way led to such things depressed him greatly.

"No—it cannot possibly be," he said over and over to himself.

From the parlor came the tinkling sound of a Swiss music box playing, with bell-like tones, the melody of a Mozart sonata; the scent of the Christmas tree, fresh as the morning air; the gleeful cries of the urchin children; his wife's voice, with its patient schoolteacher's tone—"Now please sit down!" In the crib was the darling presence of the cherubic Denzil: "Your fingers are so little, your ears so delightful," Stanley said, visiting him.

From Lady Stanley's Journal, circa 1896

ON CHRISTMAS EVE AT FOUR o'clock, Gladstone came by for a few minutes to greet the family in his gentlemanly manner (he had congratulated Stanley on his election into Parliament and for a change there had been no evident tension between them). Later, William James and his timid but brilliant brother Henry arrived: So did Bram Stoker, Lady Ashburton, the Edwin Arnolds, and the Arthur Conan Doyles as well as several artists of local repute, among them the tall and handsome Sidney Paget, illustrator of the Sherlock Holmes tales, and that most whimsical of composers, Mr. Arthur Sullivan. Also in attendance were my sister Eveleen and her husband, Frederic Myers, along with my brother, Charles, and his wife. Then, by way of a special honor, I had the opportunity to greet Reverend Benjamin Waugh, founder of the National Society for the Prevention of Cruelty to Children, who, making the rounds of many a household that evening, graced our proceedings with a blessing and a prayer, after which he tendered a well-responded-to appeal for funds.

Altogether it was a congenial gathering; cocktails were followed by the singing of traditional carols, with Mother at the piano, and all our participants were in a merry state. We had, of course, put the house in very good order for the holiday. Just a few days before, my husband and I had passed an agreeable afternoon instructing the servants as to the decoration of the evergreen, which was wrapped in garlands and glowed majestically with fine German glass ornaments and tin-cupped candles; holly was strung along the ceiling moldings and fireplace mantels. In the afternoon, a bar had been set up in the corner of the parlor, where our fez-wearing Swahili boy, Ali, made drinks to order—and strong ones at that, as by dinnertime most of our guests were loosely and happily conversant and speaking of many things.

Throughout the evening Stanley, for his part, remained in good spirits, which is to say he did not break into an argument with anyone. He seemed rather subdued, in fact, and Mother and I noticed that he was in a somewhat quiet and introspective mood. I cannot say if some matter of health bothered him (the day before he had taken to his bedroom quite early in the evening, complaining of some discomforts), but it was likely that Clemens's absence from our celebration disappointed him, as Clemens and his family, despite some hints that they might possibly come, had, in the end, decided to remain at home. But for a few hours at least, as our guests arrived, Stanley had been cheered by the prospect, though by the time we sat down to dinner and the seats we had set aside for them remained vacant, he had withdrawn into himself, content to simply take in the conversation. This was dominated by a lively debate about the spirit world between Arthur Conan Doyle, a member of the Society for Psychical Research and a devoted spiritualist believer, and William James, the renowned psychologist and theoretical theologian, who viewed such beliefs as inward projections—a debate enriched by my brother-in-law's savvy participation. (I thought it a pity that Samuel had not been present to absorb the many credible arguments about the immortality of the human soul and other matters relating to its "peripheral molecular consistency," as Frederic called it; such notions might have cheered him.)

Later, as we bade farewell to our guests and gave them each a basket of "good cheer"—containing a bottle of fine Champagne and other niceties—Stanley, somewhat restlessly, made it a point to head out with a lantern onto the flagstone road fronting Richmond Terrace to officiate the orderly progress of carriages that were pulling up one by one to receive their passengers. Stanley sent off each of our guests off with a cordial farewell. I watched him from our front window—the little man, my darling, despite the chill of the night, in his commanding fashion seeing to their orderly departure.

As the last carriage left it began to snow, and as the feathery white fell around him I noticed Stanley looking up into the sky. Then he began turning in a circle, his head arched back, spinning slowly around, as would a child, and if I am not mistaken, he was laughing—I thought it a good thing that no other persons were on hand to witness this uncharacteristically eccentric act, but I doubt he would have been twirling around had he known that I was watching him from our window. For a few minutes he continued in this fashion, then he started back toward our door, pausing by the top step to take another look; though he was hatless and wore no overcoat and must have surely been chilled, it was if he did not want to come inside, much enjoying his exposure to the purity of the elements. But thankfully, his common sense prevailed, and he came back into the house; he was shaking from the cold but made nothing of it and quickly settled into the comfort of our parlor's warmth.

Mother had gone to bed, so Stanley and I sat alone in front of the fireplace. Having occurred to me that he might have had too much to drink that evening—for every time I had looked at him during dinner he seemed to have yet another glass of brandy in his hand—I asked him if he might want a cup of tea. This he declined, testily, calling in one of our servants to bring him some brandy instead. Then, in a deeply pensive mood, staring into the fire, he loosened his cravat and warmed his brandy with a lit vesta, sipping the drink slowly, his eyes widening. In such moments I always supposed he was remembering some distant place or some moment of great enchantment or grief.

ON PSYCHICS

CHRISTMAS DAY, 1896: WHILE THE Stanley household bustled with visitors, Stanley himself spent much of that afternoon in an idyll of pride and wonderment as friends came by to look upon their infant, who, like a princeling, lay in his crib under a silken canopy in the parlor. Meanwhile, Clemens and his family sat inside their flat, estranged to any Yuletide cheer—the writer huddled in his study; his wife, Livy, sitting by a window and staring out as a fresh snowfall came drifting down over Tedworth Square. But the loveliness of it all, that whiteness that purified the gutters, turned into slush after a cold rain. They passed the time reading aloud Tennyson's *In Memoriam*. Clara practiced scales upon a rented piano, but there was not a single mention of Christmas, their solemnity being so resolute and great. They gave out no presents and had no tree, not even a simple wreath; their only shopping trip in those days yielded, for the females, black ladies' mourning hats affixed with widow's veils. Even several of the parcels they'd received from Richmond Terrace they left untouched, waiting until well after the New Year to open them.

Sunday was their main day for excursions, when Clemens and his daughters took their constitutionals in the city's parks. Upon occasion during the week, they visited one museum or another. In the great hall of the Natural History Museum in South Kensington, Clemens, in seeing the skeletons of animals as they lay in their glass cases, thought about coffins. The truth that everything living in the world was meant to die configured sadly in his fecund mind into a vision of his daughter as she lay in her final rest. That he had not been able bring himself to travel back to Elmira, New York, for the funeral of his most favored daughter, Susy, he put down to its being unbearable to his soul: Yet wherever he ventured in those days, he could not, for the life of him, stop thinking about what she must have looked like as she lay at rest. In dreams he often saw her ghost wandering through the rooms of their house in Hartford, helplessly. To contemplate her sufferings so pained him that, as he once wrote in a note to Stanley, he thought about taking his own life—and he might have had he not Livy and his daughters to look after.

What pleasures he had were of an intellectual sort. When he was not holed up working from seven in the morning until seven at night, without so much as breaking for a meal—the heavy fumes of his cigars, smoked one after the other, clouding his study—he tended to read voraciously, as if words would smother his sad emotions. Carlyle's history of the French Revolution he read for the sixth time; then he took up William James's *The Principles of Psychology*, then Stanley's *In Darkest Africa*, a book whose prose, although engaging, he found as dense and tangled as any jungle. Other books—about science, history, biography—he consumed as well, his desire for them so strong that, fearful of being left to his own devices in the evening, when his thoughts would surely drift to "her," he would sometimes drop whatever he was working on and pay a fleeting visit to the London Library, where he took comfort in seeing and being surrounded by the purest evidence of the better side of man. Sometimes he would stroll over to the Chelsea Library, from which he always returned home with a bundle of treasures (these were often related to his research for the manuscript he called "Another Innocent Abroad," which became *Following the Equator*). Then he would stay up to a late hour, reading until his eyes grew red-rimmed and he fell asleep—that "little nightly death" another of his refuges—a book slipping from his hands.

Often he raged about God, or the foolishness of believing in God, mainly around his daughters, who had to contend with this sentiment every time they went out with him, for their father, at this point, was bent upon obliterating from their minds the idea of any presiding deity.

"There is nothing there, no kindly being attending to us. What is called God is but a projection of a dismal mankind hoping for more." And what were churches to him? "Artifices of superstition, monuments of ignorance, the refuge of the dim-minded and gullible." On their walks, he spent much of his time lamenting the "damned human race," eternally corrupt, privately likening life on earth to living in hell. ("Even my well intentioned H.S. doesn't, in his blindness, see or want to believe what he has set in motion in Africa: In his well-protected shell, he hardly grasps that the natives, whose lot he might have sought to improve, are being enslaved, mutilated, murdered at whim. Now, I ask you, if as moralistic a chap as Stanley, who seems to really believe in all that stately fluff one hears from the pulpits, and if *even he*, who cares, in his way, for those Africans, can allow the wool to be pulled over his eyes—then what hope is there for this world?" he wrote.)

꙳

"I AM FAR FROM A perfect man," he wrote to Stanley. "I blow my top over a lot of things. I suppose it's the effect of Susy's death on me, but there's more: I've still got some debts to settle—perhaps I might have to take on yet another wearisome tour, but then Livy has so withdrawn from life these days that I doubt if she could bear the idea; and she, in any case, is not so well. I think her heart has somehow been damaged by all this, and she seems bent on becoming an invalid, sitting all day and doing nothing except staring out at empty space. Neither books nor the prospect of even taking a walk holds much interest for her. I am thankful for my own work, and she has been helpful as my editor—it's the only labor she undertakes—but even then I don't think she ever stops thinking about Susy for a single moment of the day. I, at least, can lose myself in the recollection of distant climes and the research attached to my writing: Still, I am almost afraid of finishing the book for that reason alone. And my daughter Jean's epilepsy has been acting up—she hardly leaves the house because of it, and, aside from my own work, I really don't want to leave her or Livy alone, so I rarely go out myself; which is to say, dear Stanley, that there are innumerable reasons why we have not seen you and your own. I keep hoping, at any rate, that future months will bring better things with them, mentally speaking."

꙳

Dear Samuel,

During my recent voyage down to South Africa, I often thought about what you said to me—that no worse a thing can happen to a father than losing a child. I know that this is true. In adopting our own little boy, Denzil, a Welsh

orphan, the fact that he is hardly of my own flesh hasn't mat-
tered very much to me or my wife. He has become the light
and center of my world, as your daughter had always been to
you. Though he was far from me during my journey, I spent
most of my time trying to find a semblance of Denzil among
the young passengers on deck. On the way back to England,
I saw his sparkling eyes in every child's face. Thus reminded
of the beauty of innocence and the fineness of the beginning of
life, I became forgetful of my own self-importance and made
it a habit to speak to the little ones during my constitution-
als along the deck, each smile, each laugh, lifting my great
loneliness away. Sadly, during that voyage, one of those fair
children died suddenly of a fever, and as the customary funeral
at sea was held, with the ship's chaplain saying the appropri-
ate words, I watched solemnly as the little casket, wrapped
in the Union Jack, was committed to the sea and nearly wept
thinking of my Denzil and how thin is the fabric that separates
all such children—and all of us—from an uncertain, perhaps
glorious, destiny.

Surely I know that your grief must be a thousand times
greater than what I felt that day, but I must tell you that not
all is over with her, that for those of us who truly believe in the
compassion of heaven, she is surely in His hands and in that
realm where there is neither pain nor suffering but only love:
And though her physical absence from this world presses upon
your waking days, I suspect that she is the very air around you
at every moment, watching and loving you as surely as any
fine daughter would her loving father.

※

BY THE TIME CLEMENS VISITED the Stanleys again, in mid-1897,
he had already reluctantly made the decision to rejoin the world.
In April, allowing that it would not be so bad for his daughters to
get about without him, he purchased two bicycles by mail order

from Manchester so that the girls might ramble through London, as young girls should. (Clara took to her new freedom, attending London piano concerts, but Jean, with her delicate health, confined herself to ambles around the square.) He tried to encourage Livy to get out as well, but she, save for a few excursions to a local market to pick out cuts of beef and some vegetables, preferred to stay home. Despite the secrecy surrounding him, his whereabouts were eventually discovered: While only a handful of people knew where he was residing in London, he had been in correspondence with Stanley's old employer James Gordon Bennett, publisher of the *New York Herald*, for whom both men had written, about a few lucrative assignments (one was to cover the queen's upcoming Diamond Jubilee), but there was also, to Clemens's embarrassment, the matter of a subscription fund that Mr. Bennett, perhaps for the sake of publicity (Stanley said of Bennett that he "did not have one kind or selfless bone in his body"), had started up on Clemens's behalf in America. Reacting to the secrecy that shrouded his life, the newspapers published rumors that Clemens was living in great poverty and illness, or that he had been abandoned by his family; at one point Clemens was rumored to be dead. To all this, Clemens put an end in an interview he gave at his home on Tedworth Square to a reporter who had tracked him down by making inquiries at the Chelsea Library that late spring: "For someone said to be dead I am doing reasonably well. I am writing; my family is indeed with me; and if I am dying I do not know it yet, and in any case I am not doing so any faster than anybody else." And, most famously, he was quoted as saying: "The reports of my death have been greatly exaggerated."

From Lady Stanley's Journal, circa June 3–4, 1897

WE DID NOT SEE MR. Clemens or his family until the late spring, when, at long last, with the weather much improved and with his newest work nearly completed, the harshest period of his mourning had seemingly passed, for after months of notes passing back and forth between us (I often corresponded with his wife, Livy, who was in a laconic state in those days, but she seemed interested in hearing about our doings), there came to us a missive in Mr. Clemens's own hand saying that they would indeed come to visit us for supper—news that my husband regarded with joy. It relieved him greatly to hear that Mr. Clemens would be getting around again, for his own state of mind during the previous few months was somewhat melancholic, mainly because of matters of health. In that period he had come down with two bouts of malaria, one mild, the other, in early May, agonizing. Lost to the world for weeks a time, his body burning with fever and his speech slurred and rambling, his greatest solace remained the company of Denzil, whom, during periods of distress, I would carry into the room and place on the bed beside my husband.

"Ah, it is worth getting well now!" he'd say.

In contrast to my own disposition, he professed little interest in social engagements. As much as I liked to go out, my husband did not, and I made it a habit to attend many a function without him—whether in the company of Mother or one of my platonic male friends (Henry James, John Singer Sargent, and the recently departed John Everett Millais among them).

⁂

ON THE OTHER HAND, I came to dislike the quarrels that we, like all couples, had. We particularly argued about what he considered my snobbish and prissy crowd; there were days when he, somewhat put off by the joy I had for life and its gaieties, as he called them, would lash out at me with such venom that Mother and I feared he might actually strike me. When such disruptions took place in hotel rooms, and were overheard by bellboys, the outbursts were communicated to the snooping press, which explained the rumors that haunted Stanley during our early tours—that he was a wife beater. He shouted at me but never lifted a finger against my person; and in the multiplication of such fables, it was said that he was an adulterer as well—all rumors against which he had to defend his reputation.

☆

WHEN THE CLEMENSES CAME TO our home for supper we were, of course, determined that Samuel and his wife should pass the evening without hearing any mention of their late daughter and were resolved to avoid the subject. Filling the parlor and dining room with freshly cut flowers, we removed from plain sight any reminders of death, such as an early Renaissance painting from Siena that I had always fancied, which depicted Lazarus rising from his tomb. Among other guests, we invited the author Bram Stoker, who had been most charming at our Christmas fete. And as Livy had once expressed to me an interest in spiritualist matters, I took the liberty of inviting my brother-in-law Frederic Myers and my sister Eveleen, should there arise the possibility of Livy's broaching the subject. As an entertainment, we retained the services of one Matilda Pym, renowned soprano of Strand theatrical fame, who was to regale us with several tunes from *The Mikado*, and we hoped that Clemens's daughter Clara, in that artistic ambience, might also perform, for Clemens had often mentioned her talents as a singer and pianist, though we had no way of predicting whether she would be willing to entertain us. I also thought to take the opportunity of showing the Clemenses some of my recent drawings and paintings, which I had displayed in my studio, among them the portrait of Clemens that I had long been working on. This I had set out an easel and covered with a velvet cloth, as it was my idea to formally unveil it for him should the moment arise.

Stanley awaited their arrival in his study, mulling over his autobiography, but mainly he rested, having awakened the night before anxiously. That morning, when I had inquired as to what had distressed him so, he told me about a curious dream in which he was a clock boy whose job it was to crawl about inside the great works of Big Ben, smearing its gears with grease. In the midst of crawling about, while the gears of the machinery were turning, his sleeve got caught in one of the machine's teeth, and he found himself on the verge of being mangled before his own cries of anxiety awakened him.

"Surely as I sit here before you, I am being swept up by time: Dolly, please, let us make the best of what I have left of my life."

He took it as a presentiment that this dream should coincide with the impending arrival, after an extended absence, of a longtime friend whose sufferings had been many. In his heightened awareness of the passage of time, he wondered if he had indeed always acted toward Samuel as a good friend should.

"Dolly, have I ever let him down in any way?" he asked me that afternoon.

"No, I think not."

"We did go to see him at Guildford; this I would not have done for anyone else. Surely he must know that."

"He values your friendship.."

"But why do I sometimes doubt my standing with him?"

"You have that strain in you—a doubtful nature."

"As of late I have been troubled over the way I turned down his offer to publish my last book; perhaps it might have saved his business."

"As you know, Stanley, his list was overloaded with esoteric titles; it was bound for bankruptcy."

"I should have helped him. The truth is that I could have given him something, even a children's tale; or I could have written something with him in tandem—he had often spoken to me of that, but I always turned a deaf ear to that idea. And now I wish I hadn't."

"You are being harsh with yourself, Stanley; even if you had given him *In Darkest Africa* it would not have made any difference in the long run. How many copies of the Africa book did you sell with the Scribner's company in America?"

"Sixty thousand in the first two weeks alone."

"And how many do you think you would have sold through Clemens's door-to-door salesmen, with their clientele of farmers and backwoods people?"

"Not half as many, but we will never know. In the meantime my friend came to financial ruin, and he is suffering for it still."

"Stanley, you are tormenting yourself over something that cannot be changed. Besides, he has remained your friend, despite your fears."

"Oh, Dolly, if you only knew the number of times he wrote to me about the matter. He even sent me telegrams about my book as I was writing it in Zanzibar. Look here," he said, and he pulled from his correspondence cabinet a slew of telegrams and showed me a handful of them.

"It would have been an easy enough thing to do at that time; he even sent his partner, Charles Webster, over to see me, but after he had gone to the trouble and expense, I still turned him down. Why, Dolly, I cannot say, but I have sometimes sensed his disappointment over the matter. Even if it is something that he has not since mentioned, I know that he must have felt let down by me: Had I a way to make it up to him I would, but he has no company now with which to publish anything, and, in any case, I have lost my desire to write."

"Then you must forget the whole matter."

"I wish I could."

※

CLEMENS AND HIS FAMILY ARRIVED at half past seven. The first to come in was Livy, in black and wearing a veil of mourning. She was followed by her elegant daughters, each also dressed solemnly. Then Mr. Clemens himself entered, with his top hat in hand and dressed finely in a dark frock coat and silk necktie.

Mother and I greeted him. "Better late than never, goes the adage," he said. "It's been too long, hasn't it?"

Most evident at first sight, after a scant six months or so, was how much Clemens seemed to have aged, for he seemed to have many more lines of grief about his eyes, and his brow was more furrowed than before: Like Stanley's, his hair had turned white. As for Livy, that sweet, dear woman was thinner than ever and tentative in her movements, though for the sake of her children, she put on a good face, encouraging her daughters to enjoy themselves.

Shortly I escorted Mr. and Mrs. Clemens into the parlor, where our other guests had gathered for drinks, among them Gladstone, who had also just arrived. There Clemens found Stanley engaged in conversation with Bram Stoker, whom Clemens apparently admired and knew somewhat. Mr. Stoker, a short stick of a man with an unforgettable, darkly featured face, had in those days just finished writing a gothic fantasy—some tale about vampires, ghosts, and other spirit creatures entitled *Dracula*. (Stanley had read the thing and dismissed it as a captivating bit of arcane fluff that played upon people's superstitions and fascination with death and their belief in ghosts; he had seen enough truly horrid things in this world to think that reality was cruel enough without help from the spirits.) However, I noticed that Mr. Clemens, who had also apparently read the book, was quite complimentary of it, telling Stoker that "the simple vampire's sleep, out of sight from people and the sunlight," held rather an appeal for him.

"A wonderful fantasy, my dear Stoker, of people coming back from the dead—a physical impossibility, but one that has its appeal in a Christian, Lazarus-back-from-the-grave kind of way. Still, even if the idea is nothing new, I like your book, Mr. Stoker; it fits my mood these days."

"That resurrection business," Stanley said, "goes back long before the days of Christ—to Egypt, of course, but even the ancient Greeks had a number of folktales relating to the risen dead." Then: "Come, Samuel, meet our other companions."

As with all things, certain evenings that start in one direction end up going in another. While we had hoped to avoid any discussion about Susy or the supernatural, and although we had conceived the evening as a belated Christmas for the Clemenses (in one of the anterooms we had several gifts waiting for them—Stanley had bought Clemens a Dutch meerschaum pipe, and for Livy we had a Scottish shawl, while the girls were each to receive various things congenial to the young—hand mirrors, several diaries, perfume, and some soaps), the specter of Susy's passing came suddenly into our house. As merriment was the first order of business, we played some charades, which Clemens's daughters and some of the other young guests enjoyed; but even as we were in the midst of these parlor games, there arrived Lady Winslow and her daughter Lily, whose resemblance to Susy was so great that Mrs. Clemens fell back into her chair in a swoon.

"It is her way these days," Mr. Clemens told me. "She is in an emotional state lately, I'm afraid to say."

But if our original promise to avoid the subject of Susy's passing was forgotten, I owe this to Mother: When Livy, fainting, had been attended to by her daughters, Mother, beside her on a couch, poured out her sympathies—and this, I am afraid to say, opened a floodgate of tears on Livy's part, for she wept unabashedly in Mother's arms. Then, to settle Livy, Mother took her off for a "private talk" in her own study about the spiritual realms.

I was a little peeved—and Stanley was furious. He seemed to feel that Mother had opened a "can of worms," while my reasons were different. Mother only had a wishful belief in such things, whereas my own conviction was based on a careful study of hard scientific facts as pursued by the Society for Psychical Research. Mother had little more than a passing interest in those facts, but she based her general belief in such things on some rather reassuring visits with spirit mediums and on what she claimed were several visitations from Father's ghost when she was first widowed. But I take issue with the idea that Father is a "ghost," in that it implies that he is "dead"—no, I say he is very much alive!

At dinner, Livy smiled occasionally at my brother-in-law, even though she spent much of the time staring down into her plate, rarely eating a morsel or saying a word. Finally she piped up, asking Frederic, "What is it, Mr. Myers, that you do?"

※

UP TO THAT MOMENT, MY husband and Clemens, at the other end of the table, had been holding forth about diverse subjects: As it was the queen's Diamond Jubilee year—the sixtieth of Victoria Regina's reign—Clemens announced that he, on behalf of the *New York Journal* and other American newspapers, would be reporting on the processions and ceremonies as a special correspondent. (This was met with applause.)

Stanley, however, did most of the talking: He had for a time, to Gladstone's bemusement, referred to his peeves with Parliament—I had the sense he did so to remind me that I had, in my overzealousness to keep him away from Africa, pushed him into that unhappy situation. (Indeed I had come to regret it, for it brought him much misery and boredom, but there was nothing to be done: His term was to last until 1899.)

※

IT WAS AT THIS JUNCTURE that my brother-in-law, given the lull at the table, and in response to Mrs. Clemens's question, addressed her.

"Mrs. Clemens, I am a classicist by profession, trained at Trinity College, Cambridge, and among my other credentials, I am one of the founders of the Society for Psychical Research, whose inception dates back to 1882. Our fundamental doctrine, in regard to the division between this life and the next, has always been one of telepathy—that is, communication between the so-called dead and the living through a process called supersensory communion, wherein the thoughts of the departed are conveyed through the 'ethers,' which I define as the silence that exists between our waking thoughts. It is our belief, Mrs. Clemens, that in death the consciousness we call the self and refer to as the 'I' never disappears but is transferred into a realm contiguous with the present; from that realm come communications, and these mainly enter our minds not through ghostly apparitions but through the phenomena of hallucination and dreams. Signals are sent out, which, without a system to decode them, are hard to make sense of. However, I have in my studies developed a system for interpreting such things. To hear an unexpected word or sentiment that suddenly intrudes upon one's waking thoughts is to receive the verses of another world. I have advocated that the recipients write these down. This has fostered an activity called automatic writing, which, contrary to its mechanistic sound, is very humane and recognizes the value of such words. I also believe that when a person has passed on, his spirit will transmit fragmented parcels about the afterlife to the living—fragments that are received and interpreted, piecemeal, by psychics all over the world.

"That is the most complicated aspect—studies of which are pursued by a scientifically based coordination of such information. But on a more practical level, we at the society address the means by which most ordinary people, without knowledge, might benefit from our beliefs. And so we hold in esteem the much-disparaged practice of medium augury, which has many adherents, including, if I may say so, such notable persons as H. G. Wells, Arthur Conan Doyle, and our own forward-looking and very wise prime minister, William Gladstone."

Clemens, I noticed, was somewhat put off by this business, fumbling about his pockets for a match with which to light his cigar, even when there was a lit candle before him. I heard him muttering to himself: "Now, where is that thing?" and "Where are you?" as if to distract himself from the importance of what he refused, in his godless way, to believe. Livy, on the other hand, seemed raptly engaged: I cannot say if it was Frederic's eloquence that held her so, but she, rising above her timidity, said, "Please do go on."

"I am often asked," he said, "if there is anything to divination. Consider crystal balls, for example—they cost but a few shillings and can be ordered through a catalog. Most people use them as handsome paperweights, yet there are professional mediums who have explored their practical effects: I have heard of—indeed witnessed—a medium staring into such a crystal until a faint pink and gaseous light seemed to form inside of it; from this will be divined some event, some foretelling of a distant simultaneous or future happening. But what is this act? It is the idea of it that matters most. The scientific explanation is that the peculiar effect upon the optic nerve provokes to activity some latent clairvoyant function of the brain, but the crystal itself is not a necessity. We've seen such practices in pagan rites and find instances of them in the Old Testament: A cup, a mirror, or a blot of ink can be used, as they do in India and Egypt. The Africans use a bowl of water. Any shining surface—a pond, or even the very surface of a river when it is caught in a certain light—will do. In such instances the mind enters into a receptive state, receiving, if the practitioner is skilled, signals—mind you, many of them are false; that is, erroneously or incompletely constituted or falsely and purposely misconstrued by the medium—but when they are accurate, and many successful transmissions have been noted, there is only one explanation: they are real. The scientific exploration of such matters is one of the things we do at the Society for Psychical Research; it is our mission to get at the heart of that reality, difficult as it can be in an age of skepticism."

"And you truly believe in such things?" asked Mrs. Clemens.

"I do; and should you need assistance in any way," Mr. Myers said, "we will be glad to offer it."

Mr. Clemens, having listened with impatience, then asked: "Well, then, Mr. Myers, if I may ask, aside from so-called communications with the other world, just what do you seek to gain from such information?"

"Contact with the other realm, which goes against all logic and scientific reasoning, is real: In our mechanistic age, few have the gift. But as to your question, well, the answer, in a word, is hope. And not just for an individual but also for the world at large. Not long ago, one of our best mediums in London, Mrs. Peabody, predicted that the coming century will be one of unimaginable change and scientific advances; she foresaw great improvement in daily life but at the same time great advances in the destructive powers of weapons. In a séance, one of the messages she received, allegedly from the poet William Blake, spoke of 'exploding suns, to the woe of living man,' a message we have construed to be about the necessity of peace. Surely that is something all of us want, isn't it? And from her communications she has ascertained that unless mankind changes in some fundamental fashion, our futures—and she mentions the span of several centuries—will consist of much carnage and suffering."

"But sir," Mr. Clemens said, "such generalities seem to be always true. What century hasn't had its share of carnage and useless suffering?"

"None. But we believe that science, with all its practical benefits, especially in the realm of medicine, comes with a price—which is the deadening of the human spirit."

Having brought in our little toddler, Denzil, then nearly two and anxious to run about, Stanley had been standing by the dining room door for some minutes, taking in these words. Denzil, in breaking away from his father's hand, ran over to Clemens, hurtling himself onto his lap. Clemens said, "Well, now, dear boy, perhaps you need a more comforting lap." And with that he stood up and carried our son over to Livy, who held him tenderly.

Then Stanley, with whom I had had my differences over the subject of the spirit world, said: "Frederic, thank you for your enlightening talk about an unsolvable mystery. You would surely like Africa, where such things are taken for granted, but if I may, I would like to take the opportunity to raise a toast to my friend Mr. Samuel Clemens and his gracious family."

WE HAD DESSERT, THEN AS we reassembled in the parlor for after-dinner brandies, I offered to show Clemens the portrait I was making of him. Because many of our guests were leaving, we waited awhile, then I took Clemens and his family into my studio. With Stanley by my side, and with Clemens waiting somewhat patiently, I withdrew the velvet covering my canvas on its easel. It was an oil study, some twelve inches by sixteen inches, that I had begun the year before, though more work was needed. Looking it over, Clemens said, "I look younger in it. Seems I've turned into a gargoyle in the meantime."

"You are as refined-looking a man as I have ever seen. Are you pleased?"

"As much as my worn-out self can be."

But his daughters were delighted.

"What do you think?" I asked Livy. She hardly seemed to look at it or any of my other paintings. As she moved about my studio, it was as if she were moving through a room packed with heavy drapes.

"It looks like him. I like it," she finally said.

⁂

WHILE WE WERE SAYING OUR farewells in the foyer, Samuel took me aside.

"Do you remember, Dolly, when I told you once about the 'little commuter' in my head?"

"Of course."

"I told you how he waits and waits for that train. Well, since Susy died, when that man gets on the train and enters the car, I always see the back of a female head sitting in one of the seats—before Susy died, the car was empty. So I move up the aisle, and when I go to take a look, the head turns, and it's Susy. She always recognizes me and says, 'Papa.' What do you make of that?"

"I don't know, but she must surely love you."

☇

June 7, 1897

Dear Stanley,

Thank you for the delicious and welcoming time at your house. And thank you and Mrs. Stanley so much for the wonderful presents. A curious thing: In a private moment, I fell into further conversation about the psychic world with your brother-in-law, Frederic; and since he (like everyone else in the world, apparently) knew about our tragedy, he kindly made the suggestion that we, as a comfort, look into the medium business, and he recommended several to us, as well as a Hindu palmist of some great reputation. I should say that his professorial manner and the great weight of his learning make all the otherworldly stuff sound credible. I liked him—his kind and intelligent eyes give him something of an air of a vicar, and I can see why your wife is so attached to him. He made a good enough impression on Livy at dinner. Just hearing him hold forth about "spirit molecules" and "transmissions" and "ethers," as if he were describing well-known facts, is very soothing. My conjecture is that if you are around enough people who believe in the same thing, it seems to be so.

In any event, Livy came away from your party feeling enchanted—not just by your family's warmth and cheer but also by the hope of "contacting" Susy. She is so bent on finding proof of an afterlife—what with her mother and now Susy gone—that even my most cynical side is rooting for that nebulous cause: Though it doesn't make all that much sense to me, she wants to pursue this foolishness, and I am willing to oblige her for the sake of easing her mind. But I take no great stock in the afterlife and, in any case I cannot really buy into all the business of "telepathy" and the transfer of thoughts, etc. Granted, Livy and I upon occasion have seemed to have had the same thoughts at the same time—this Myers ascribes to telepathy and "transmissions," electrical charges that can be plucked from the air—yet I am pretty sure that in our case, any semblance of similar thinking no doubt owes more to the fact that we have been like a pair of bookends wrapped around the same activities, people, and travels for most of the past twenty-five years. (You know she is my first reader and my strongest editor and that she combs over my every word, much to my texts' betterment.) Anyway, I am not sure if it will be worth doing, but we are going to visit one of these spiritualists for the sake of diversion: Will you and Mrs. Stanley come? We will attempt to breach the unseen bridge at some point, and who the heck knows what there might be awaiting us?

As always, I tip my hat to you.
Samuel Clemens

September 3, 1897

Dear Father,

Frederic and I have arranged for the Clemenses to visit a psychic, a certain Mrs. Turner on Grosvenor Square, in order to obtain information about their daughter Susy's situation in the afterlife. Stanley and I are planning to accompany them tomorrow afternoon, though I do wish that Stanley would remain behind, as he is somewhat skeptical about such things.

Good night, my dearest.

From Lady Stanley's Journal, the Evening After the
Séance at Mrs. Turner's

WE ARRIVED AT MRS. TURNER'S around four. Her parlor was
largely bare save for a circular table and some six or seven chairs, a
cabinet containing crystal balls and some "star" stones from Tibet,
and a nearly transparent screen made of rice paper, which stood
on a Chinese lacquered frame against one of the walls, through
which, it has been said (by my sister Eveleen, who has assisted
Mrs. Turner on occasion), the faces of the departed have sometimes suddenly appeared, glowing. On the table itself was a slate
board, some chalk, and some paper and pencils.

Mrs. Turner was a rather matter-of-fact sort of lady—from
Kent, I believe. Around sixty, she wore an ordinary dress, her only
spiritualist affectation a crystal that hung off a leather cord around
her neck. When our party walked in, she could not have been
more welcoming, and she seemed, in fact, quite flattered to meet
the famous couple. Since Frederic and I were well known in such
circles as believers but were not direct participants, she allowed us
to sit off in a corner to observe. But a problem arose with Stanley,
whose "energies" put Mrs. Turner off.

At least she was forthright about it: "Sir, with all due respect,
I must ask you to wait outside; yours is such a powerful presence
that you may confuse the communications." Which is to say that
she sensed immediately Stanley's skepticism. And so, to his discontent, he left, advising us that he would wait to hear news of the
outcome at home. (I was quite relieved.) However, another skeptical
subject was on hand—Mr. Clemens himself, who, having dabbled
with Livy (so she once told me) in spiritualist communications at
the Lily Dale colony in upstate New York, remained unconvinced
that there was anything to this practice. (The irony, I should say,
was that they had often taken Susy to spiritualist healers to cure
problems with her throat and had perhaps relied upon them a bit
too much; despite my beliefs, I always went to doctors when I felt
unwell.) Clemens and his wife, while courteous about the whole

business, were sheepish at first and, as Mrs. Turner instructed them, took their place around the table somewhat reluctantly—I think with a little embarrassment, which is a normal thing.

"Have you something that belonged to the person you wish to contact?" she asked.

Livy did—one of her daughter's brooches. This she passed to the medium. Mrs. Turner then instructed Mr. and Mrs. Clemens, who were sitting across from her, to join hands and close their eyes and concentrate on the object as a means to open the channels of communication. She then pressed the brooch against her heart, then held it against her forehead for several minutes, then set it down on the table before her. For some several minutes more she said nothing, her face in a grimace of fierce concentration. Though she had asked them to remain still, Samuel shifted in his seat several times during the twenty-minute or so lull. Once, he turned quickly toward me and winked; however quietly he had done so, and though her eyes were closed, Mrs. Turner noticed it and whispered, "Be still, sir, or I will end this now." Another twenty minutes passed. A great silence prevailed—not a sound from the outside world penetrated the heavy drapes over the windows. Since it was September—and a warm one, I should add—the room became stifling, nearly unbearable. However, after another twenty-minute interval, the temperature in the room became noticeably cooler and a slight scent of strawberries wafted into the air. The atmosphere changed, without a doubt, and once this had taken place, Mrs. Turner, who had been still as a statue, with her eyes still closed, began to scramble about the table for her writing implements. Taking both chalk and pencil in hand, she began to scribble various words down on both the slate board and the papers. Coming out of her trance, she sat back in her chair and exhaled deeply, as if exhausted. At first, when she looked about, it seemed that she did not know where she was.

But she gathered herself and, instructing Samuel and Livy to open their eyes, began her interpretation of what she had received. On the slate board she had written, in wildly scripted letters, one word: "Train," which in her confusion she had spelled "Twwain," as if an infant had written it. Beneath that were two letters, *P* and *W*. And on the paper she had scribbled other words—"Mama," "My book," and the letters *P-P.* The rest, as often happens, consisted of indecipherable bits of script.

"Well, then," she cheerfully said, "Open your eyes to the revelation that your loved one is thriving." Then, without so much as a pause: "Without being able to ascertain everything, I can tell you with confidence, Mr. and Mrs. Clemens, that your daughter Susy was in this very room, having been conducted through me."

"You know her name?" gasped Livy.

"Of course," said Mrs. Turner. "I read the newspapers. But what matters most are the other communications."

Then she said: "Does this first word, 'Train,' have any relevance to you?"

They conferred. "Well, yes," said Livy, somewhat hopefully. "We last saw our daughter waving good-bye to us from the Elmira train station, some sixteen months ago."

Livy bowed her head and did not look up for some time.

"And the letters *P* and *W*—have these any meaning?"

"No," Clemens said. "Nothing."

"And 'My book'—what do you make of that?"

"Well," said Samuel, "she was the most gifted writer of the family, really."

"Was she writing a book at her end?"

"She'd already written one, as an adolescent, about our family."

"Ah," said Mrs. Turner. Then: "But 'Mama,' what does that bring to mind, Mrs. Clemens?"

"Her last word," said Livy. "She spoke of me, then she died."

And Livy began to weep in Clemens's arms, gasping so deeply and with so many convulsions of her slight body that I, looking at Frederic and thinking that it had been a mistake to bring them there, despaired: The purpose of contacting the spirit world was not to conjure past grief but to give hope. But then, to my relief, Livy calmed down and awaited the rest of Mrs. Turner's questions.

Mrs. Turner, holding up the slate board, then asked about the letters *P-P.*

"And these initials, have they a meaning for you?"

Neither Livy nor Samuel could arrive at any answer, though Samuel, slightly peeved, said: "They can mean anything."

"You may say so," said Mrs. Turner, "but such received things do have meaning. Does anything come to your minds?"

"No," Livy said.

"Well, then," said Mrs. Turner, "if I may take the liberty, I will give you my interpretation of what I received. First of all, Susy, your late daughter, is in the hands of loved ones. Since she is in a timeless place, both of you were by her side. What years you will die in I cannot say, but they will be as fully relevant to your souls as were once your birthdays, and those dates you will also celebrate in the afterlife, by her side. As to the first word I wrote down, 'Train,' erroneously spelled—but then, you must understand, I was in a trance and blindfolded—I will say this: It seems to me to be about more than just that last parting. I would imagine that in the other world, she is often journeying with you, but without the grief and discomforts that accompany our earthly travels. What else I have perceived is this: If she wanted to be a writer, then she will be writing; and she is doing so right now. But I also sense that she was a creature of great talents—did she sing?"

"Yes," said Livy.

"Then she is singing there as well."

She stood up.

"Please do believe me: My line goes back to the sibyls. I promise that what I have told you is truthful." Then: "It has been a pleasure to meet you and your daughter: Please do come back. And the fee is two guineas. Thank you."

Frederic lingered with his notebook to scribble down the more or less indecipherable scribbles that had eluded interpretation, many of the letters not even looking like letters at all. For my part I tried to forward the idea that it had been a successful outing, but Samuel was incensed. Walking along with him on the street, I was startled to hear him carry on in a manner that made me feel bad.

"Not a thing she said could not have been derived from the newspaper accounts of her passing. The only thing she came up with of interest was the 'my book' business, but then it would not be a wild impossibility for someone, even a half-baked medium, to suppose that Susy—the daughter of a writer—might have wanted to venture into such territories. All in all, Mrs. Stanley, while I appreciate your efforts on our behalf, please be careful—and not in regard to me, as I have taken every harsh thing in life—but with my wife, who is too delicate for this world. Please do be careful."

"Are you angry with me?"

"No: just stating my point of view."

From Samuel Clemens's Notes

MRS. STANLEY, DESPITE MY DEEPEST allegiance to Livy, strikes me as some kind of lady, eccentric as she seems to be. Even if she gets on my nerves sometimes and goes through life like a kid, with the attitude that there is a Santa Claus (God and afterlife; happy endings), and even though she often annoys me with such optimism, I enjoy her company. Mainly I like looking at her— never directly, but in a passing way. She is beautiful in the sense that her most attractive qualities come not from her surface but from within. When she is eighty, I am fairly certain that she will be just as engaging and enticing in an eternally female way as when she was young. Livy has the same qualities but not so much control over her physical aspect, which is to say that she has been set back a bit, having suffered so much from various chronic maladies. (When I see Livy coiled up on a couch feeling so sad, I want to throw myself on her and protect her from the cruel realities of life forever; I wish I could fend off all sadness, all illness, and death from this angel. I would cut off my right hand to protect her.)

But Dolly . . . when I'm around her, despite her frivolous ways, she always reminds me that there is a difference between prettiness and timeless beauty. While the young have the advantage of possessing smooth and untroubled features, which passes as a kind of loveliness, the real truth of beauty has to do with a timeless expression of physical and psychic soundness. I have to say that Mrs. Stanley seems to possess it. She not only looks young—somewhere around forty—she also never seems to age (the advantages of an untroubled life, though I can imagine that Stanley can be a handful). She seems younger and more ebullient each time I see her: For all her aristocratic affectations—her "How *dooo* you dooo?" and other mannerisms of speech—she seems self-assured. Stanley, on the other hand, at a relatively young age, seems old. How that union happened, aside from the allure of fame, I do not know. Seems an instance of pure luck—what a soul she is, ever so cheerful. When I'm around her, I feel a tinge of envy toward Stanley, for no matter what she says sometimes, she somehow brings me a feeling of comfort.

☙

DURING THE WANING MONTHS OF 1897, Clemens went to pose for Dolly again. While hoping to exhibit her portrait of him at the National Gallery, she had come to view her painting as a means to express her warm feelings for the man. His sitting for her that autumn was a highlight of her days.

"MR. CLEMENS—"

"Samuel to you—"

"While I know that you have had your share of hard times, is there—and forgive my curiosity—any one memory you have of yourself from a time of happiness that enters into your mind when you are feeling troubled?"

"I don't get what you're asking me."

"Whenever I am feeling melancholy I like to recall the walks

I would take as a little girl with my father in Scotland. I would prance after him, for he had a quick pace, over the meadows, and run into his arms as he, smiling sweetly, awaited me. Sometimes I dwell upon my youth, when I posed for various London and Parisian artists. I would feel overwhelmed by the way they looked at me, as though I were beautiful."

"You are."

"Well, if you think so, then I am flattered, but if you could have seen me thirty years ago—I am but a shadow of that now."

"You never age, Mrs. Stanley. You are as fresh as when I first saw you; if anything, you look younger to me."

"Thank you, Samuel. But as to my question . . . can you answer it?"

He gave it some thought, then said the following:

"There is something I think about fairly often. It goes back to my piloting days: I used to bound down the stairway from the pilothouse to the boiler deck and from there to the lower deck. Sometimes when we came to the landing of some river town and we only had an hour in that place to take on cargo, I would want to make my way to whatever bookstalls might be around. So I'd sometimes just leap off the riverboat railings onto the dock with nary a concern for tearing the tendons in my heels and spring off in my mad searches. I'd make my way into the town, nearly gal-loping like a pony. And I would do this again and again, without the slightest infirmity—no pains in my hands, hips, or knees then. I was light as an angel. You see, Dolly, in my youth I was made out of rubber, it seemed, and able to bounce around without the slightest benefit of conscious exercise."

And before Mrs. Stanley could say another word, he added, "I mean jumping down and landing hard on the planking in boots! I have sometimes seen myself doing this in a kind of silhouette— again and again—it would kill me now, of course. Takes me back to more fanciful times, when passage through this world was a dream: Even when I knew I was not made of rubber, I was barely conscious of it; it was just what it was, the vitality of youth, pure and simple. I don't know if my memory of that easy leaping and landing down hard somehow soothes my aching limbs now, but I hold that memory in esteem just the same. Keeps me going sometimes. Wish I had the same elasticity now, but the years have taken that away from me, along with the hawk-pretty looks I once had."

"I disagree; you are still a handsome man."

"Excuse me while I guffaw, Dolly. One thing I do know is that you are a nice lady—and Stanley is a lucky bloke."

He then made some mention of having first met Stanley on a steamboat around 1859, which much intrigued her.

⁂

IN THE GRIEF OF THOSE years, his was a restlessness that led him and his family to extended stays in various locales—in Switzerland, in an idyllic spot called Weggis; in Budapest, in Prague, and then in Vienna, where they took up residence at the Hotels Metropole and then Krantz. Clemens chose that city of great music so that his daughter Clara might study piano (and it was there that she met a brilliant fellow student, one Ossip Gabrilowitsch, with whom she later fell in love). As for Livy, she had, in those few scant years, aged in even greater increments than Stanley had in Africa—she was thin, frail, and grandmotherly, already ancient-seeming beyond her time, a gaunt and haunted relic of her own youth, a hundred years of anguish having transformed the once delicate and youthful countenance that Clemens, while traveling to the Middle East as a young man, first spied in a cameo carried by her brother.

Part Three

LETTERS 1897–99

Dear Stanley,

   I greet you from a small village in Switzerland, Weggis
(about a half an hour from Lucerne). Here I am writing a new
novel about my old and reassuring friends Tom and Huck—a
detective story—and am getting along very well with it. My
Joan of Arc book is behind me (more or less). We've rented a
small house on a hillside overlooking a picturesque lake, the
whole scenario, I think, the loveliest in the world. We have a
rowboat and some bicycles, and good roads, and no visitors.
Nobody knows we are here. Sunday in heaven is noisy compared to this quietness.

                                        Sincerely yours,
                                             S.L.C.

                        ☀

                              Hotel Metropole, Vienna
                              December 20, 1897

My dearest Mrs. Stanley,

   What new nails have been hammered into my palms. First
Susy, then my older brother Orion, who'd always wanted to
make something of himself—he is gone at the age of seventy-
two. A more tiresome and mournful yoke cannot be put on
anyone. If I take any solace it is in the way he went out—
without pain, without any particular awareness; like a clock

whose springs and gears have suddenly wound down and then stopped at a certain hour and minute and second. He was working on a book, a novel about Judas Iscariot, when the very same soul who was robust and hardy in my youth simply ceased existing. Strangely, when I heard of his passing, I could not help but wonder about the last word he wrote, for his wife found him slumped over his desk in the midst of his work. Was it the word "the" or "an" or "morning" or "night," among the countless possibilities? We will never know. (And, of course, I wonder which last word will be my own.)

Forgive my melancholy—it's been with me for some years now. Think more about our painting sessions at Richmond Terrace, which were pleasant interludes—when I was younger! For what it is worth, Mrs. Stanley, I wouldn't mind the idea of coming through the darting and cold rain to sit again for you once we are again in London.

As always, give my best to your mother and Stanley, my most famous friend.

Regards,
Samuel Clemens

☙

Hotel Krantz, Neuer Markt 6, Vienna
February 15, 1898

Dear Dolly,
We've moved to the Hotel Krantz—and lo and behold, while we're settling in, Livy looks around the lobby and sees over the concierge's desk a picture, in oils, that looks suspiciously like me. The exact double, but dressed up, of the one you showed me not long ago in your studio—the initials D.S. in the corner giving it all away. How on earth did you do it? At any rate, I thank you heartily for making me more

handsome than I am and for elevating the standards of good
taste in that hotel.

Samuel

꧁

Richmond Terrace
February 19, 1898

My dear Samuel,

I don't want to disappoint you in any way, but it was
your dear friend Stanley who first thought you might get a
charge out of it. Hearing that you were moving from the Hotel
Metropole to the Krantz, I wrote the hotel manager, who was
delighted to put your picture up.

With best wishes from Stanley and me,

Dolly

꧁

Hotel Krantz
February 20, 1898

Dear Stanley,

Surely you are aware of the incident in Havana harbor
a few days ago (February 15), when the US battleship Maine
was blown up, allegedly sunk by a Spanish torpedo. Since I
have known of many a riverboat exploding over some careless
act—like a fellow smoking in a munitions hold or a boiler
overheating—I'm inclined to think that it was an accident
of some kind, but whatever the cause, the American papers I
have been reading over here (the Hearst papers in particular)
are calling it an act of war and are banging the war drums, as
if this action was akin to the bombing of Fort Sumter. At any

rate, the coals are being stoked in reprisal, even if there's no definitive proof. If it turns out that the Spaniards are the cause and our boys go in, I would support them, though given all the blarney going around, I would not be surprised at all if it turns out to be a pretext for invading and annexing the island, which, as you know, has been on Uncle Sam's list of things to do for many years now.

And speaking of Cuba, by my internal calendar it is thirty-seven years since you and I were in that now-infamous city, sailing the harbor where that battleship went down, and thirty years since I paused briefly there on my way to Panama in 1866. My, how the clock ticks, even as the world goes on its one-minded way.

Yours,
Samuel Clemens

❧

Hotel Krantz
March 17, 1898

Dear Stanley,

Vienna is beautiful, but I have never seen as much anti-Semitism in any other place as I have here. These days there's much talk about the "Jewish question." Here, in one of the most civilized and expensive cities in the world, the mayor, Karl Lueger, and any number of earnest and devoted family men—members of the Christian Social Party—hate the Jews! Riots are breaking out over the ethnic rights of the Germans and Czechs, and the Jews, however they stand on the issues, are caught in the middle. If I had time to run around and talk about such things—even understand what the commotion is about—I would do it; for there is much politicking going on, and it would be interesting if a body could get the hang of it. But it's a strange atmosphere to be in. Even my first name,

Samuel, has attracted the attention of the right-leaning press as sounding suspiciously Jewish—can you imagine the fuss they would make about Moses, your Welsh grandfather? I suppose I should take it as a compliment—it's a marvelous race—by a long shot the most marvelous that the world has produced, I suppose.

In the meantime, the merde *piles up higher and higher; it seems as if all this hatred, at the Jews' expense, will cost heavily sometime in the future.*

I wish I could understand these quarrels, but of course I can't.

I will now end these few lines of my grumbling: Livy calls me a grouch, and my daughters try to stay out of my way, probably with good reason.

With best wishes,
"Mark"
(a.k.a. Samuel the Jew)

᠅

Hotel Krantz
May 20, 1898

Dear Mrs. Stanley,
You will notice that I begin this note with an actual date as absolute proof that I am capable of such subtleties. In your house in London a hundred years ago you said that my occasional omission of dates (or years, anyway) is a bad habit—and I have since tried to reform, as I would not want to disappoint you. Your remark has cost me worlds of time and torture and buckets of ink; but I thank you for the fine advice.

I hope it will interest you (for I have no one else who would much care to know it) that here lately the dread of leaving the children in difficult circumstances has died down and disappeared. I am now having peace from that long, long

*financial nightmare and can sleep as well as anyone. It seems
that with one thing and another and with much good management and advice from my benefactor, Mr. H. H. Rogers (head
of Standard Oil), I have finally come out of debt. Every little
while, for these three years now, Mrs. Clemens has sat down
in the evenings with pencil and paper to tally up our accounts.
Two nights ago I was still a worrier, but last night, she
reminded me that we own a house and furniture in Hartford;
that my English and American copyrights pay an income that
represents a value of $200,000; and that we have $107,000 cash
in the bank. What a boost to my spirits! I suddenly feel like a
free man again.*

Lovingly,
Samuel

*P.S. I have been out and bought a box of six-cent cigars; I was
smoking four-and-a-half-centers before.*

☀

Hotel Krantz
August 24, 1898

To the Stanleys,
    *We've enjoyed Vienna to a point, but since the war in
Cuba has ended, and on the heel of our "liberating" invasion
of the Philippines, most folks around here (including myself)
have gotten the notion that the United States is playing the
empire game. The Austrians, who once flocked to our parlor—
and have not been shy about heaping admiration upon me,
despite my known disapproval of their local politics—have
been receiving us far less warmly than before, even coolly.
As we are being lumped in with the brutish notion of American aggression, and as Clara has finished her piano studies
(her teachers have concluded that her hands are too small to*

overcome the technical demands of certain pieces, so she has
decided to become a singer instead) we are planning on leav-
ing soon enough—to sightsee, take some cures (Livy and I and
Jean) where we can, and eventually to settle in England again,
for a short time, at least.

Of course, we will see you then, dear friends.

Lovingly yours,
Samuel

THE COUNTRY LIFE

From Lady Stanley's Journal, Regarding the Years
1898–99

DURING OUR YEARS OF MARRIAGE, for our occasional escapes,
we had prevailed upon the respite of inns at seaside resorts such
as Brighton and Llandudno or upon the generosity of friends
who would invite us out to their estates, where Stanley indulged
in hunting small game and I made studies from nature, Denzil
always by my side. Stanley, however, had grown dissatisfied with
our life in London and, seeking a permanent retreat we could
call our own, decided to look for a property in the countryside.
Mother was none too happy about the proposed change; Stanley
felt otherwise. While there were certain advantages and comforts
to be had in the capital, with its societies, theaters, and gentlemen's clubs, he had lost his taste for the public life and perhaps
wished to put some distance between himself and his detractors,

of which there were many. After a long period of professional torpor, in which he seemed to move through his days with little interest in the tedious duties awaiting him in Parliament, Stanley awakened one morning to announce his intentions. Mainly he desired, at long last, "a home to call my own," a home that he could configure in his own image and where he might spend his last years, whenever they might come, in peace amid his family and the things he loved the most—his books, his artifacts, and his maps, all of which brought him comfort.

Much as Mother disliked the idea, Stanley stood firm.

"By God, woman, do you not know that it is now my time to find some peace at last? Do you not know that I am tired and in need of a rest?"

Over the summer and into the first weeks of autumn in 1898, when Parliament was in recess, he spent many days looking at various properties, some fifty-seven of them in total, outside London, in the Home Counties, mainly in Surrey. But there was one estate of some seventy acres, near the town of Pirbright, thirty-five miles southwest of London, in the midst of farm country, that he returned to again and again: Furze Hill.

A "real beauty," he said, "but one in need of a little care, I will admit."

The photographs of that place were, frankly, a bit off-putting, for the house, a rather grotesquely overwrought Tudor ruin some two hundred years old, seemed to be falling apart. With its overgrowth of ivy, and with trees and bushes that practically enveloped the whole premises and crept up its turreted towers—for the grounds had apparently not been attended to for years—it seemed the kind of dwelling where a coven of witches might live; yet Stanley had his heart set on it.

"The price is quite reasonable," he told me. "Besides, it seems like me."

Whatever my original reservations about the property were, they were only enhanced by the journey we made there one day by train in the early autumn of 1898, just before Stanley was about to purchase it. ("Of course I will buy it only if you approve," he said.) When we arrived at the Brookwood station from Waterloo, and made our way by hired carriage to Furze Hill, as we entered the grounds, not only did the stony mansion seem more dilapidated and gray than it was in the photographs (it did not help that the weather was grim), the surrounding property seemed covered with an oily greenish scum. At least it seemed to be a quiet sort of place. But then, too, on that day, we heard from the distance the firing of cannons. "What is that?" I asked Stanley.

"Oh, the cannons? Just a bit of a military exercise in progress. You see," he said rather happily, "the properties surrounding us belong to the British Army: they come out here every several months to drill. The main thing is that we will be absolutely left alone, with few neighbors to disturb us."

Mother was speechless. Proceeding toward the ruins, she looked at me several times, as she sometimes did, as if to say, "Stanley is mad," but as much as this suspicion also occasionally entered my mind, I realized that for the first time in years, Stanley seemed happy. Taking us through the house itself (some forty rooms), up half-collapsed stairways and into musty chambers whose ceilings had fallen down—many a room filled with piles of debris as well as the remains of private belongings, including beds, cabinets, and chamber pots—he seemed not at all perturbed. What most enchanted him was the evidence of craftsmanship, which he, with his sharp eye for detail, found everywhere.

Whatever it lacked in aesthetic grace, the mansion must have been a solid enough structure to have lasted so long—like Stanley—and the amount of stonework in the entranceways, the fireplaces, and the friezes seemed fantastic to him. Every room had an elaborate wrought-iron gate in the doorways, and, rusted though they might have been, Stanley delighted in swinging them open. "Can you imagine the man-hours involved?" he asked. Of course Mother was aghast at the thought of anyone except ghosts living there, but I remained tolerant of his interest.

"Can't you see," he said to me one day, "that with a little work it could be as fine as any house I have ever seen—as fine and individual a house as what Sam Clemens built in Hartford?"

I did not particularly like that place, but then, to that point, Stanley had never denied me anything I had wanted. And so when he asked me, "What do you think?" even when I found it one of the gloomiest houses I had ever visited, I told him, "It's wonderful."

⚡

HIRING A CREW OF SOME twenty masons and carpenters, Stanley, like the commander he had once been, presided over the yearlong renovations at Furze Hill, his architect and foreman often by his side. Around its outer walls went up scaffolding, and for five and sometimes six days a week, in the manageable seasons, the sounds of sawing and hammering and winches pulling up old bolts and nails and pieces of flooring could be heard everywhere.

He'd come home on Saturdays (usually by six) and spend an hour soaking in a bath to get the grit out of his skin, thereafter sitting down with Mother and me to dinner and reporting the details of his progress with the house. (I always listened patiently, often eager to head out to some affair in which Stanley had no interest.) Sundays he spent with Denzil, taking him to church in the morning and, in the right kind of weather, strolling with him though the Zoological Society's gardens at Regent's Park in the afternoon. (I still have that enviable but disintegrating photograph of Denzil and Stanley in a howdah, riding the massive African elephant Jimbo along a circular dirt track in that park, Denzil cuddling in Stanley's arms and my husband looking somewhat bemused in the course of participating in London's famous zoo ride: "I have shot elephants, but never ridden them before," he said to me that day.) Otherwise, when at home with the child, Stanley attended to his education, reading aloud some Latin texts and teaching him mathematics, as if that boy, at five, were already an adult.

Still, despite his pedantic manner with the boy, Stanley had a soft spot for Denzil and was not immune to the fatherly impulses of spoiling him. Coming in from Furze Hill, sometimes after two weeks' absence, he'd turn up with some wooden horses or a castle that he had made himself and painted during his evenings alone. But no matter what, he always came home with something for Denzil—a top, a cup-and-balls game, some miniature soldiers— even if he had to prowl the neighborhood around Waterloo station for toy shops. As he'd come into our entranceway, calling out, "Anyone here?" Stanley always looked forward to the moment when our blond cherub, Denzil, would come charging down the hall into his arms, crying out, 'Father!'"

The cool weather found Stanley at night in the mansion's front entry hall, where he slept on a cot with some blankets amid the piles of timber and slating and dust, or reading some book by the light of a kerosene lamp, the fireplace blazing. But in good weather, he'd pitch a tent in the field and sleep under the stars (Stanley wrote me many notes about the "glistening, and knowing, character of the constellations"). All this he found invigorating and almost regretted when, after so many months of labor, the tasks at hand were nearing completion.

But transform the place and its grounds he did. Most capriciously, huddling with his architect, Stanley—in fulfilling some boyhood fantasy that had been born of his liking for gothic novels and the strange devices that were found in those fictional houses—had his carpenters install trick sliding walls and cabinets, which, with the press of a button, would open onto a hiding place. Though these installations were costly, Stanley thought them worthwhile, for, as he told me, "If I am bothered by company, I can simply disappear."

As a final touch, he had a stonemason carve a crest bearing his monogram, HMS, into the entranceway portico; under it was a date, 1899.

※

OVER THE COURSE OF THE restoration, Stanley had overseen the transformation of every walkway, every crumbling wall and cracking cornice, into a monument of artisanship. The fences were of the strongest and best description; even the ends of the main gate and fence posts he had dipped in pitch so they would better resist decay. He built footbridges for the many streams that flowed through the grounds; he also constructed a boathouse, which he stocked with canoes for the large pond that Dolly had named Stanleypool. Envisioning Furze Hill as a kind of utopian refuge, Stanley created a sheep farm and brought in bulls and cows to laze about and procreate in a bucolic meadow. While his wife planted rose gardens and put down the seeds of an apple orchard, he made footpaths and set benches and tea tables out so that their future guests might rest after their leisurely strolls. A pine woodland they named the Aruwami Forest after the dense jungle that the tireless Stanley had once penetrated in Africa as a younger man. A brook that meandered across the property his wife christened the Congo—the naming of such places a happy diversion. (They even gave the surrounding fields African names; there was Wanyamwezi, Mazamboni, and Katunzi, among others, each with its own place in Stanley's illustrious history of exploration.)

The property itself he called the Bride, in honor of his marriage to Dolly.

※

AND IN OTHER WAYS 1899 was a good year; for despite Stanley's decline in relevance to the popular imagination of the British nation, for whom the age of African exploration had become passé, he, having renounced his American citizenship to stand for the House of Commons, could at long last accept a knighthood from the queen. In a ceremony at Windsor Castle, Victoria, stocky and jowl-chinned (she bore a remarkable resemblance to Gertrude Tennant in that regard), wearing a black velvet dress, stood up and, assisted by a royal page, placed around the neck of the kneeling Stanley a golden chain to which was affixed the weighty ornament known as the Grand Cross of the Order of the Bath. In that moment he became Sir Henry Stanley.

"Receiving me at me at Windsor Castle, the queen actually looked at me with kindness," he wrote.

⁂

SETTLED IN AT FURZE HILL, Stanley seemed most happy to pursue the life of a country gentleman. Often he rode a horse over the property, or else he just hiked off by himself over the hills, returning home many hours later with some wildflowers gathered from a field for his wife.

He'd come back in a reflective state and, in his reserved manner, retire to his study, where he would sit, at times motionless, before his desk and the quires from his autobiography, the work he had long since lost his desire to write.

And on many a day, in the appropriate seasons, in the hours before he would make his various excursions, Stanley would look from his study window and watch Dolly, in a shepherdess bonnet and florid silk shirtwaist dress, sitting out on their lawn before an easel with a palette of watercolors, executing the most delicate works of nature, renderings that engendered the deepest pride and wonderment. He'd find himself marveling not only at her God-given talents but also at the many pleasures her gentle and vivacious character had brought into his life, even if they had come late. For her presence, and for all the things he had been given— his fame, his wealth, and the adopted son on whom he doted—he often thanked God.

How lonely did Stanley feel when wife and son made their inevitable return to London.

From Lady Stanley's Journal, circa 1899

IT WAS BY AN AGREEABLE coincidence that the autumn of 1899 found the Clemens family back in London, having returned from Vienna and other places, and in residence at 30 Wellington Court, Albert Gate, a household that my sister Eveleen and I occasioned to visit, namely in service of Mrs. Clemens's continuing interest in the psychic realms. However disappointed she had been with the failure of various mediums to summon forth her daughter—"The spirits sometimes sleep for a hundred years before venturing into the world," I once told her—she seemed to enjoy our lunches and romps to local galleries, where my knowledge of the Pre-Raphaelite painters seemed to interest her greatly, as did any subject that took her mind off her daughter.

In the shadow of her famous spouse, she seemed perpetually humble, but, as I got to know her somewhat, I sensed that under the many layers of her demure personality there resided a tenacious and forthright being, a strong spirit. She was, after all, her husband's first reader—in effect his editor—and I could sense, knowing Samuel's mind a bit from his always charming but rambling reflections on his past, that she was invaluable to him, perhaps by way of helping him to organize his thoughts. (Stanley, on the other hand, was loath to show me anything, considering himself a "man's man" who had no need of assistance.) While she would never say so, I sensed that his books would never have been the same without her.

In the various letters and notes I had received from them in years past, their handwriting seemed identical, though her letters were much more compact: The same note, word for word, that Samuel would need three leaves to write—his handwriting being large—would, in her hand, fill a single page; and so it seemed to me that where he was LARGE she was small. Years of this ratio—which played out, I imagine, in every area of their lives—seemed to account for the way she carried herself.

And yet we got along well enough, despite her lack of interest in social amusements. I wanted to rejuvenate Mrs. Clemens's female vivacity by taking her to some of the better shops in London to buy new dresses. But however much I tried, she was intent upon her mourning, remaining doggedly in black and wearing her hair, when not under a veil, pulled tight in a bun. A pair of wire-rim spectacles continually reaffirmed the impression she gave of a woman who had not only entered into but also lovingly embraced her premature old age.

<hr>

NOW, WHILE LIVY WAS MAINLY content with her life at home, often quietly entertaining visiting family members from America, Samuel had completely embraced London society. Coming out of his gloom over Susy insofar as he could, he not only went out in public willingly but also gave many well-attended talks in every major club, from the Blackfriars to the Savage.

He was sometimes a bit brusque with me, however: I do not know if he was peeved over our spiritualist outings with Livy—though we were only trying to be help her out of her grief—or perhaps he was truly overwhelmed with appointments (to the detriment of his writing, as Livy told me), but in those days, during our fleeting encounters, I began to get the distinct impression that he was trying to avoid me. Why I cannot say.

Still, I would often take the liberty of sending him invitations to lunch with Mother and me at Richmond Terrace, with or without Mrs. Clemens, but time and time again came the polite refusal.

Giving this matter further thought, I wondered if he had begun to feel some discomfort in my presence. While this was not the case when Stanley was around (which he often was not, for he mainly liked to stay out in Surrey in those days) or when we headed out with Livy and the girls to a museum or to visit a psychic, or when we were on some other group excursion, but when we were alone, even if we were just speaking in passing, he would seem to become very sad. And sometimes he would look at me with a tenderness that was heartbreaking, as if through his fiercely intelligent mind there raced a variety of dreams that would take his mind off his sorrows. (So I conjectured.)

The last time he posed in my studio, a few years before, I noticed a terrible solitude and longing in him, and though I did not believe that it could have anything to do with me, Samuel, despite his vivacious facade, seemed especially melancholic at our parting. It may have been my fantasy, but I believed that under other circumstances, this kind and moody genius, ageless in his own way, may well have wanted to have a good cry in my arms. It was an impossibility, of course, as we were each inextricably entwined in our own lives, but it occurred to me that he had perhaps come to regard our friendship as something to be carefully managed; along the way I believe that his admiration for my artistic and feminine qualities, which he'd always commented upon favorably, had perhaps blossomed into some kind of autumnal infatuation, which neither of us had any use for.

One evening, however, when I shared these thoughts with Mother, she tried to set my mind straight on the subject.

"My dear daughter, yours is a remarkable vanity to think that a man like Mr. Clemens would have any interest whatsoever in your person beyond a mild and socially amicable friendship, which exists because of Stanley. If Samuel is sad it is because he is getting old, which is never easy on anyone, and because he has an ailing wife and has lost his most beloved daughter. What man wouldn't ache in such circumstances? Mr. Clemens, however famous he might be, is no exception." Then: "But my God, what a dreamer you are."

※

ODDLY ENOUGH, A FEW DAYS later, Mother informed me that she had invited Mr. and Mrs. Clemens to lunch and that they had accepted. On a Saturday in late November, they arrived with their daughter Jean. At the outset, Clemens had been most apologetic for his long absence from our household and seemed disappointed that "Sir Henry," as he liked to call him since his knighthood, had not been able to make it in from Furze Hill. Indeed, Stanley had planned to come home for the occasion, but, as often happened in those days, he had been in no condition to travel, even over such a short distance. (The journey took about two hours, including carriage rides to and from the stations.) Aside from regretting Stanley's absence, Clemens seemed to be in good spirits. And as it seemed that the Clemenses' sojourn in England would likely end soon, perhaps by summer, for they were longing to return home, I insisted that they promise to visit us at Furze Hill in the spring, for by then the winter's frost would have passed and, God willing, Stanley would be better.

"Well," said Mr. Clemens. "Stanley has written to me about the place; it sounds as if he is building a little kingdom there; so perhaps we will."

FURZE HILL, EASTER WEEKEND, 1900

From Lady Stanley's Journal, the Evening of
April 14, 1900

OVER DINNER THAT EVENING, SAMUEL told a humorous story about his family's stay at Dr. Kellgren's spa, in Sweden, where they had gone the year before in search of an osteopathic cure for various ailments. It was an awful place that he likened to a "Nordic hell" because of its primitive facilities and terrible food. "But it does make you forget your infirmities," he said drily. He also held forth about his latest investment in some kind of new carpet-weaving machine and his continued interest in a food supplement called Plasmon, a nutrient derived from curdled skim milk, which he saw as a means to eliminate the scourges of famine in places like Africa.

Stanley listened attentively. Having tried Plasmon himself, thanks to Samuel, Stanley had noted some mild improvement with his own Africa-born gastric difficulties (I believe he was just being kind, as this "wonder powder" had not really made much difference), and then, intrigued by the notion, he questioned Samuel as to the practical matter of the organization and distribution of such a product. "How would such a wonder food be distributed in the countries where it is most needed, such as Africa?" he asked. "And what would prevent the unscrupulous from profiting? It seems that for every good soul there are three to undo his best intentions."

"Well, I am taking this one step at a time," Samuel gloomily answered.

(Privately Stanley thought that Clemens's altruistic views about saving mankind from itself were half-baked; by his lights, any solution to the world's problems would only spring forth from a universal moral order—sadly, based on his experience in the Congo, I don't think he really believed such an order was possible.)

During that meal, Samuel brought up a quite touchy subject: It began with a discussion of the Boer War. Samuel had mentioned a recent visit to London's docks, where teeming crowds gathered daily to bid farewell to the British regiments as they boarded ships bound for South Africa, all in defense of the empire's citizens residing in Kruger's realm, the Transvaal. Their relief was a matter of liberation: Already many brave British young men had died, but Stanley, a die-hard British nationalist, saw it as a just cause, even if he thought it was already lasting too long, for, as he told Clemens, "we have overwhelming armaments." He added, "If it is dragging on, it is because of the incompetence of our unseasoned generals, who are perhaps not used to fighting against forces who will fight and die for their beliefs in the way that a Yorkshire infantryman in a strange land might not."

But Clemens saw it differently: "As much as I love England and the way it has treated me as a writer—far more kindly than America—and as much as I believe in the queen and in my Stewart forebears, my heart goes out to the underdog Boers. They are farmers mainly and will surely be crushed sooner or later. And that makes me weep."

Then, to Stanley: "Do you not see the injustice of a militarily superior nation like Great Britain invading some backwoods territory like South Africa? Whatever momentary defeats are suffered, we all know that Britain, with its Maxim machine guns and cannons, will prevail, and in the meantime, many lives—both Afrikaners and British—will be lost. It disgusts me."

"My dear Samuel," Stanley said. "Profess as loudly as you will the very best of sentiments toward people with whom you desire to be on amicable terms, but do not forget, for even a single minute, that human beings are not angels or children to be restrained by sentiment alone. Ours is a predatory world: To invade, to consume, to conquer—and then to rewrite history—is in every people's blood. Even this war, viewed years from now, will be considered but a step toward the progress of civilization. I, for one, have seen such disputes played out again and again. Believe me, Samuel, however noble you may feel about a cause, there is a contrary and just as adamant opinion. These conflicts just go on and on."

Then, as he was quite fond of Clemens, he added: "I can see your point, but just remember that however benevolent the intentions of any nation, the actual course of action is inevitably influenced by human failings. Or, to put it differently, Samuel, no matter how noble the cause, once the d—d twits take over, greed presides and morality goes out the window."

⚜

RUMINATING OVER THIS SUBJECT, AS Mother and I were trying to cheer the proceedings by pouring a very good port into their glasses, Samuel said:

"But consider Cuba. We invaded the country with good and noble reasons in 1898—to save the long-suffering Cubans from Spain. We overran the island with troops and heavy armaments, and, of course, we eventually won. But in the meantime we— I mean the American forces—by way of a ridiculously abstruse diversion to the Philippines, provoked a war of endless carnage in the name of American imperialism: I can think of no other reason. That we crushed Spain is a fact; but that we had 'noble reasons' I doubt."

"But Samuel, the Philippines will provide the United States with a major port into Southeast Asia—that's all you have to know. In the end, regardless of the casualties, both liberty and trade will benefit that godforsaken region."

"Stanley, as much as I respect you, I think you're a bit narrow in your thinking sometimes! Don't you care about the innocent people who are hurt and killed during such so-called liberations?"

"I do, but no amount of good sentiments will protect them from the difficulties of war. Whatever you may think, that is the way of the world, Samuel."

"Nevertheless it's our flag that is now stained; the eagle of freedom has become a predator."

Later Clemens referred to himself as an anti-imperialist, a statement that perhaps should have greatly offended Stanley, but he seemed not to mind it at all and gently told Clemens: "Just remember that what is called imperialism today will be meaning-less in a hundred years, when the world will be changed in ways that neither you nor I can begin to imagine. What happens now,

in our lifetimes, will, in the context of history, only occupy a footnote for future generations, who will by then have long forgotten
the events that made their world. History just goes its own way,
and all one can wish for is that it proceeds onward with a mini-
mum of human suffering—and in that, I am in total agreement
with you, Samuel."

Thankfully, the Congo was a subject that Clemens never
brought up, though it must have been very much on his mind. If
he and Stanley did not speak about the controversy it was, I think,
because neither man cared to risk endangering their friendship
with a discussion that could easily turn adversarial. In general,
however they may have felt about each other's views on politics—
that decidedly complicated and dreary subject—a kind of gentlemanly neutrality based on their friendship and mutual admiration
seemed to be the rule, at least publicly. (I am not sure if they
were really far apart on that many issues.) And, in any case, my
husband, at that point in his life, after spending so many years
in the midst of various debates about Africa, and frankly preferring to savor his newfound domesticity, had little fight left in him
and not much of a taste for the venom of such arguments, certainly not with such a close friend. Besides, except for the letters
he sometimes angrily sent off to one newspaper or another, most
of which were toned down by the editors, he had largely given up
on the struggle to extricate himself from what I had heard him
call "Leopold's mess."

"One day," Stanley once told me, "People will look back and
think what I did was a good thing."

※

SUNDAY EVENING FOUND THEM GATHERED in the parlor,
Clemens, to everyone's joy, performing spirituals on both the
piano and guitar. The songs he played ("Go down Moses," "I got
shoes, you got shoes," "I know the Lord has laid his hands on
me") seemed to take him and the family back to better times,

when such performances were part of any gathering of friends, for this was something that Samuel had not done in years. Then the evening took a turn toward literature, for Lady Stanley asked Clemens if he might read something aloud to them; he did so— first, a curious bit of fiction in which a man is transformed into a microbe and travels through the innards of a distressed intestine, a clever tale that, however imaginative, left Livy mortified. But then he followed it by reading from one of the chapters of his *Huckleberry Finn* book, prevailing upon Stanley to retrieve his copy for him. (Knowing it to be the very one that Stanley had taken with him to Africa, he was impressed by its pristine condition, as if it had been cared for tenderly—although it did not smell neutral, having a foreign fragrance to it. He was also quite intrigued by Stanley's penciled notations in the margins of certain pages, and though he did not mention it, his expression conveyed an interest in reading all of them.) He chose one of Stanley's favorite sections, the chapter (23) wherein Nigger Jim recounts the story of how he learned that his daughter 'Lizabeth was a deaf mute. Throughout this recitation, for reasons he did not know, Stanley could not take his eyes off Clemens. When Samuel, in his mimicry of the Negro dialect, recounted how Jim slapped the girl's face for not responding to an order, and then, standing behind her, yelled "Pow!" in her ear and discovered that she was deaf—enunciating carefully the passage, "Oh, de po' little thing! De Lord God Amighty fogive po' ole Jim, kaze he never gwyne to forgive hisself as long's he live!"—Stanley was overcome with emotion, and Dolly noticed the first glimmerings of tears in his eyes. Whether it was Jim's grief or 'Lizabeth's suffering that Stanley related to we will never know.

When Clemens finished, he looked around and asked: "Who's next?" Then to Stanley: "My dear man, please: Why not grace us plebeians with something from your own pen? Otherwise I'll read more, and who would want that?"

Stanley, deeply touched and perhaps emboldened by the

reminder that there was something noble and beautiful and deeply human about literature, then stood up, and, with his eyes most sad, excused himself from the parlor and headed into his library, where he kept some sections of his autobiography in a drawer. Written in longhand and converted into typescript, those pages were much expanded from the days when he had first begun them, in the early 1890s (that version proceeding after his "cabinet" manuscript), and though he had since rarely added anything more than a few sentences a day, despite the hours he had devoted to the book, he chose, in an effort to please Clemens, to plunge forward and read from its beginning. But it was no easy thing. When, after some fifteen minutes, and after gulping down two shots of a fine Napoleon brandy, Stanley returned to the parlor, the discoverer of Livingstone and the conqueror of the Congo—"the new Alexander," as Leopold had once called him—sat down humbly and, with his hands shaking, began to read a section involving his own youth titled "Through the World."

Tracing the beginnings of his lowly childhood in north Wales, it was a rather fanciful collage of vaguely remembered people and scenes from his earliest days—the interior of a peasant's cottage, with its ordinary objects: some Chinese pictures, a window set in lead, a teapot hissing, an old clock with chains and weights beneath it, a fly alighting near his cradle—all such things described with care and read in a halting but clear voice. The progress of those pages was marked with various hesitations, his words hardly audible as he stated that he had no father, the man having died a few weeks after his birth, and, with his gut tightening and breathing laborious, his pace slowing whenever he came to any references to the mother who had abandoned him. His face would redden whenever he mentioned that shadowy presence in his narrative.

Then, with the apparent exhaustion of a man who had marched out of a swamp, he simply stopped. "However well, mechanically speaking, I may write, and however many books I have sold—for

I have earned my living mainly from literary output—nothing I ever create will be as heart-wrenching as Mark Twain's tales." In a solemn mood, he added, "Still, this is what your humble servant has been doing."

He may have felt bad about his writing, but there was much excitement among his listeners. Clemens's daughters, although spoiled by their exposure to famous people, knew that it had been a special moment, and they applauded his efforts: Gertrude had often nodded approvingly, and Dolly, greatly pleased and wanting to see and hear more of his autobiography, hoped the recitation would be the beginning of a new phase, one in which he might feel emboldened to finish the "chimerical story of his life." And Clemens? Touched by Stanley's timidity in reading from that work aloud, drew him aside and said: "Look here, Henry, if you should need me in any way to assist you, then I am at your disposal. If you care to, I would be glad to be your editor."

Stanley, shaking Clemens's hand, answered, "Thank you, Samuel, but this book feels like it will be my coffin. What I have written of it will remain where I left it. It is just my way."

With that, he and Stanley went out onto the veranda with some brandies and cigars in hand, and there, while luxuriating in the beauty of the night sky, Stanley bared his soul to Clemens.

⚹

PERHAPS HE HAD INTUITED THAT he might never see Clemens again, but on that Easter Sunday evening, Stanley, not feeling long for the world, said:

"Now, Samuel, may I ask you something?"

"Surely."

"What do you really make of the doings in the Congo?"

"I've heard both good and bad things about it, like most folks."

"But the bad things—do you believe them?"

He thought for a moment and said: "I do, sometimes."

"You know it's the ivory and rubber trade behind it. I've been made sick over the whole business. And yet some people are saying I've profited greatly from it. But what money I have, Samuel, I've earned from my lectures and books, mainly."

"I believe you."

"Then why do I think you don't?"

"Sir Henry, I have my own highly developed peeves. The likes of Leopold, your friendly king; the Russian czar; the missionaries in China. America as well these days. I would sooner drink piss than fall in line with the acquisition-mad parties who have made the world a misery for so many. But even if I distrust the motives behind the Africa game and deplore imperialism—well, I've said it: Not once have I ever thought you implicated as the planner of such things."

"Some have accused me of cruelty."

"You've told me that, but do I believe it? My God, Henry, I would imagine that, in the circumstances you've been in, you did what you had to do."

"I've never awakened any one morning and thought I would have to kill someone to survive the day, but I have killed again and again."

"So your conscience is bothering you?"

"No, my conscience is clear. Yet...in the midst of my days, even when I am taking a stroll with little Denzil, some part of my mind is always racing and taking account of the number of lives I have personally brought to an end. Some days I come up with a modest figure—thirty-seven; then the next day I will remember another incident. The number shoots up to one hundred; then on yet other days, I tally up five hundred and more graves and fall into a vague sense of remorse. That's not counting the hands I've lost to malaria and other diseases and those who have starved to death or been shot with poison darts or rifles or drowned, like my poor Kalulu. Nor does it account for the many animals who've died on my expeditions—hounds, donkeys, horses, and birds. I don't lose sleep over it, mind you, I just have odd dreams, in which I am a harbinger of death. Yes, I know that my efforts have contributed to making central Africa what it is today, but never did I dream possible the sufferings that have been reported. Even if only ten percent of the stories are true, as I know them to be, that is hard for me to live with. And though I do not feel at fault—for I was never given a chance to run things there—I have some moments of misery just the same."

Then: "And here I will tell you how I get beyond it. The first way is through prayer."

"You sincerely pray?"

"Yes, but sometimes I feel I pray to nothing. Then I think of my family and how I am blessed, and I ask, if I had brought evil into this world, as some accuse me of doing, than how can it be that I am now more or less a happy man?"

"Are you?"

"For a good portion of my days; but then the other moments creep in, and that's when, Samuel, I must tell you, I will chew on my dream gum and otherwise prevail upon the resources of my wine and spirits cellar. The fact is that it is the rare day when I am not, let me say, in a more or less salubrious state by supper without such spirits."

"It is your business."

"Yes, I know, but then even as I count my blessings, I still feel preyed upon by my worst doubts. Along the way I am reminded that I am no longer much of a writer. Tonight you heard a bit of my so-called autobiography, but as I've told you, it is something I never expect to finish. You see, I've been unable to progress beyond a certain point; if you must know, I have been barely able to proceed beyond the years when you and I knew each other and journeyed to Cuba."

"So you've told me. Why don't you just get on with it?"

"I have lost the celestial spark for such ruminations."

"Is it the story of your American father that halts you?"

"I sometimes think so, but it was such a distant thing. How can that be?"

"The truth cannot proceed if it's distorted. Have you told the truth of that tale?"

"I could, but I have chosen not to."

"Then how," asked Clemens, "can you pass through a door if you do not even describe it? My God, Stanley, do you not see that?"

"I do, but my own history, outside of Africa, which I have written about endlessly, should be of my own making. Do you think me a fool for declining to state every hard fact about myself?"

"No; I have done the same myself."

"Then let me ask you another question. As I don't think I will ever live to see that book completed—the truth is that whatever I write one day I undo the next—can I still feel confident in my trust that you will never betray me by writing your own account of our journey to Cuba?"

"As I promised you many years ago, despite the times you have annoyed me immensely, I will always keep to it."

"That relieves me, Samuel. I never want my son, or any future generation, to read what I do not consider the truth about myself." And then, to lighten the discourse, Stanley added, "For that I will be eternally grateful. Should there be something to Dolly's speculations about the spirit world, I promise that should you outlive me, Samuel, and I come back as a ghost, I will be as a tail to your back, protecting you in every way."

"Good, my dear fellow," he said. "Come now and accompany me while I shoot some billiards."

Later, as Samuel was happily shooting billiards, he heard a high-pitched voice coming from behind one of the wood-paneled walls: "Find me!" With it came what seemed to be the giggles of a small child; then the voice again. "Come and find me if you can!" it said. And so Clemens, putting aside his cue and bridge (for he had been in the midst of lining up a shot when he heard the voice), moved about the hall, which was lined with elaborately carved seats and cabinets, tapping here and there on the walls. But even when he came to the place where the voice seemed to have originated, it would sound again from somewhere else; and while he had been momentarily intrigued, Samuel, wishing to return to his game, finally said: "All right, Stanley, where are you?" And with that a high glass-fronted cabinet, which was filled with mementos of Stanley's illustrious past, swung out from the wall; behind it, in what seemed to be a passageway, stood Stanley and Denzil, who, with great pride, exclaimed, "We fooled you!"

STANLEY'S LATER DAYS
1901–4

A lifetime of journeys has left me chronically indisposed, and while I do not relish the lapse in my physical powers I rather enjoy the concentrations of thinking that come to one with such limitations.

—STANLEY

STANLEY NEVER SAW CLEMENS AGAIN. His world, in those years, was largely reduced to the grounds and surrounding woods of Furze Hill, and his moods, along with his health, were becoming more and more unpredictable. On certain days Stanley seemed beyond fatigue and spoke happily of future journeys and the years he had yet to savor with his wife and son, but just as often, he would become forgetful and irascible. The household staff would avoid him whenever possible, and even Dolly suffered from his sudden outbursts of anger—such as when Stanley, for no good reason, accused her of being a dilettante, an overindulged lady of leisure. Alternately he became extremely pious, spending entire nights rereading his favorite sections of the Bible; just as abruptly, he would grow gloomy at the "nonsense of thinking there is a God."

Even his stays in London during the winters had not made much of a difference to him, for he kept getting sick, and though he managed to visit some of his old club haunts, his had become the life of a recluse.

That his vision continued to grow weaker troubled him, as did the deterioration of his once fine handwriting. As for his own work, the great autobiography: That had long been abandoned. Even his daily habit of keeping a journal fell by the wayside—for after December 19, 1901, he never made another entry. What he otherwise produced—short letters to dear old friends—he had to painstakingly write out, his right hand afflicted with a trembling that required him to steady his forearm with his left hand just to sign his name. The elegant flourishes of his youth were gone forever. Convinced that he had perhaps suffered a mild stroke, he consulted with various doctors and after subjecting himself to a complete physical examination was presented with the news that he might at best have another ten years to live, the prospect of which left him even more covetously disposed toward time and the reassuring surroundings of Furze Hill.

He had maintained a correspondence with Clemens, his letters conveying the general drift of his quiet days at Furze Hill, the progress of his son's growth, and the ordinary pleasures of the domestic life he had always wanted (as well as his continuing bouts of illness). By then, Stanley had intuited that Clemens was in his past for good.

FOR HIS PART, CLEMENS WAS undergoing his own mounting tribulations—for in tandem with Stanley, his beloved Livy had also begun to enter her final decline in those years. But despite his great distractions, Clemens, in thinking about his friend, had made several attempts to entice Stanley into crossing the Atlantic.

The first had come by way a letter that arrived at Furze Hill one morning in the spring of 1901.

Stanley sat down on a high-backed chair, looking about the room, tapping the floor with a silver-headed cane, a gift from Lord Marlborough, as Dolly stood reading the note by the window.

19 May, 1901
West 10 Street, New York

Sir Henry—or would you prefer Sir Hank?

I bid you a respectful hello from the shores of your old digs.

In case you haven't heard, I am a newly elected vice president of the American Anti-Imperialist League, and, given the powers of my august position, I have decided, for reasons of mutual interest and friendship, to invite you to this fair city to address the league at the Century club on whatever range of subjects you so desire. I would be lying if I tried to conceal from you my truest motive, which is to publicize our good cause—yours is a name to be reckoned with, and any discourse, I am sure, would draw attention to our concerns. Lest you should feel that our adversarial opinions on many a matter would drown our friendship in venom, I assure you that you will be treated in the manner to which you have become accustomed—and paid well for your troubles to boot.

Of course, I hope you will forgive the impertinence of this invitation. We'll put you up at the Waldorf-Astoria, take you around town to mingle with my literary crowd, and, should you decide to honor me with your and your family's presence, I would be happy for you to stay as long as you like in my town house if that would suit you.

Whatever you should decide, we send you and Dolly all our love.

Yours in friendship,
Samuel L. Clemens

*   *   *

IT WAS DOLLY WHO MADE the reply, citing innumerable projects awaiting them at the estate and expressing the wish that she and her mother might make a trip to New York without Stanley, if that would interest him, but for the time being, it was Stanley's failing health that made all the difference. He added his own note to the same effect:

> *Dear Samuel,*
>> *The plain fact is this: In another time I would do it, but, old friend, my health prevents me.*
>> *I send you my devotion.*

※

STILL, A YEAR LATER, THERE came yet another invitation from Clemens, and this one, greatly intriguing Stanley, was very hard for him to turn down.

> *Dear Stanley,*
>> *I send you this brief note to mention a leisure cruise of the Caribbean I will be making with my good friend (and financial savior) Henry Rogers in April, to which you are herewith summarily invited. We are planning to head out next month. I mention this because it is our plan to make Cuba a part of our route, and I thought you and I, sailing there, might find it of quite special interest. I am making this journey sans Livy, who is not at all well. (In fact, as I have written to Dolly, I am only allowed to see her for brief periods of time, so I guess I will not be missed if I am gone for some few weeks.) I know you are nailed down to your estate these days, but do let me know if I can tempt you. It would be a nice way to pass the time.*
>>
>> *Regards,*
>> *Sam*

Stanley truly lamented that he could not go; a fall while roaming the estate had badly twisted his ankle, and, in any case, he never knew when he would be visited by an attack of gastritis. He had become afraid to leave the estate, as if it were keeping him alive. And yet it took him several days to make up his mind.

※

April 1, 1902
Havana, Cuba

Dear Stanley,
A note from Havana—en route to Nassau and New
York—to say once more that I wish you had been able to
join us. But here I will report my journey. We sailed down
to Santiago de Cuba (port city on southeastern tip of island,
nestled in a bowl between two mountain ranges), a fine and
most ornate place; we spent a day there, and with my very
distinguished party were given a first-class tour and taken
around to the most interesting sights—the old cathedral, etc.,
with a side trip to San Juan Hill, where Teddy Roosevelt
made his famous charge and where stands the Peace Tree,
where US general William Rufus Shafter accepted the Span-
ish general Toral's surrender in July of 1898. Aside from a little
sun-baked Spanish fortress at the top of the hill, along with
some pieces of eighteenth-century ordnance, there wasn't much
to see. Nevertheless, this was the place where the Spaniards
defended against the charge made by the Rough Riders. There
were many florid trees about—the air perfumed—and yet
what most lingered was the sense that the hill was a roadway
of death, of lives wasted. Of ghosts. For as the Rough Riders
advanced up the hill they were met with a fusillade of bullets
from the Spanish trenches around the fort, a slaughter on both
sides ensuing. You can feel the dead around you, as you do at
places like Gettysburg.

Later, we were hosted at a dinner at our hotel by some of the more distinguished persons of the city: On hand was an admiral who gave a vivid description of the naval battle that had taken place between the US fleet and the Spaniards. To make a long story short, the Spaniards, while trying to escape the Santiago harbor, were trapped between two flanks and bombarded; they lost four hundred men, with many more wounded, while the United States only suffered one casualty— what a score! And so there it is: In the ocean, along the coast east and west of Santiago, lay the husks of numerous Spanish ships, the bones of their men at the bottom of those blue and beautiful waters.

I would have liked to have visited more places—at my age, I don't think I will ever have the chance again—but, as with everything in my life, I was locked into a schedule of receptions, press interviews, etc. As I was traveling in the company of Mr. Rogers and T. B. Reed, former Speaker of the House of Representatives, the fluff of much of that business fell equally on them, to my relief, though I ended up drinking too much rum, attributable mainly to intermittent periods of boredom and resentment. (You know what I mean.)

Most interesting was our cruise over to Havana. From our yacht, the Kanawha, as we came along the south coast toward Matanzas—remember it?—I could not wait to see that Moorish city's pearly buildings glowing in the distance, but as we passed its harbor, I saw that much of it had been destroyed. There were ruins everywhere, a result of one of our superior fleet's bombardments during the war. That depressed me: I nearly came to tears with the unique melancholy that old folks like me get when they see things so dreadfully changed. But then we passed on, along the stretch of coastline toward Havana, with its many coves and beaches and harbors—which you once likened to the snout of a crocodile—and lo and behold, as we approached the city of Havana itself, whatever feelings of melancholy I had were amplified tenfold! For looking

*out, I saw the mangled, twisted, rusting carcass of the battle-
ship* Maine *rising out of the water—it was dark and ugly and
protruding in so many directions that I was reminded of a
dying crab: a strange sight.*

*Everywhere I looked there was row after row of American
battleships along the harborside, and many soldiers and sailors, too: Stanley, the country is occupied 100 percent!*

*But we had come into port for no more vital mission than
to meet with some local officials and then have lunch, so we
dined in a mansion in El Cerro—a neighborhood on a hill.
Journalists were on hand to interview Mr. Reed, who declared
the island "safe and sound."*

*Afterward I visited the plaza: I found an English-speaking
bookseller there, and when I asked him to recommend a volume of Cuban literature, he came up with a book of poetry
called* Versos sencillos *by one José Martí. It's a funny thing,
Stanley—apparently the poet is considered a very great Cuban
patriot, for he died in an early battle against the Spaniards,
but as I looked over his poetry, in Spanish, which I will take
pains to translate, it occurred to me that I had once met him
before, perhaps in New York or Boston, where he was said to
have lived for a time.*

*In any event, old friend, I wish that you had been able to
come along. We might have fooled ourselves into thinking we
were young again and could have traipsed about Havana like
Huck and Tom along those streets, beautiful as ever.*

Faithfully,
S. L. Clemens

Furze Hill, April 17, 1903: Another Special Spring Day

STANLEY HAD NOT BEEN FEELING particularly well when he
took Denzil for a walk; they had gone out into a meadow to fly a

box kite, as there had come some good winds that late morning—
the British and American flags Stanley kept on the lawn were flap-
ping gloriously in the breeze—but he should have known better,
for just the day before, while coming down the mansion staircase
with a drink in hand, on his way to take the hounds out and shoot
some birds, he had experienced a bout of giddiness. His face had
heated up, and all at once the walls around him suddenly turned
a bright red, as if he had been staring into a sunny lake for too
long; for a few moments he had to steady himself on the banister.
Sitting on the landing, as he looked around the mansion and saw
his many possessions, and as he looked through a window at the
fields and woods, ever so radiant at dusk, he began laughing, his
joy so pure and timeless that, in those moments, he considered
himself nearly immortal. One of the servants found him there,
and no sooner did he inquire after his master's well-being than
this brief ecstasy passed. Helped up to his feet and insisting that he
was perfectly fine, Stanley took a stroll though his gardens. Their
loveliness inspired him to believe that he was an especially blessed
man and that Providence had, for whatever reason, rewarded his
difficult life with that little moment of earthly happiness.

Walking the grounds that evening he had felt deeply contented; the months he'd passed apart from London society he had
spent peacefully—reading when his eyes were up to it; forgetting
all the bad news about Africa; choosing only to remember his
good experiences. And he spent as much time with Denzil as the
boy could tolerate, teaching him about plants and the nature of
gardens—in short, behaving with him in a manner that Stanley
had missed as a child.

He considered his friendships. In the previous few years he
had become quite amicably disposed to the company of Henry
Wellcome, and his amity with Edwin Arnold and Frederic Myers,
for all their eccentricities, provided him with more pleasure than
annoyance. And when he reflected upon his other friends, like
Samuel Clemens, whom he considered a unique and kind man of
astounding talents, he smiled at the thought. In such moments,

when he felt that all was good with the world, he wished that his old American friend were by his side and that he could somehow magically convey his wondrous feelings to him, for he knew that the poor fellow had suffered so much. It was as if, in an unexpected way, he could feel a "benevolence" all around him. And this benevolence made him feel nearly saintly. For all his grumblings to Dolly about feeling unappreciated by the world—for by then he had become a relic of the past—he found himself, in fact, feeling no malice toward anyone—not even King Leopold, who had deceived him with his sanctimonious prattle about bringing peace and prosperity to the Congo. Suddenly he was so charitably disposed that were his mother-in-law present, he would have shocked her with a bounty of kisses upon her face. It was as if he had been suddenly freed from all self-restraint: He felt young and loving, dashing and wildly handsome; and though he knew he could not, he wanted to celebrate. And there was Dolly. When he last saw her, in the late morning, she was sitting in her studio at Furze Hill, at work on one of her paintings—it happened to be one of the portraits of Clemens she had been working on—and although he sometimes felt a slight twinge of jealously about her fascination with him, for she had always behaved coquettishly around Clemens, it did not bother Stanley. Instead he wanted to seek her out and sing the praises of her talents and beauty—and then, in imagining that alternate self, he wanted to overwhelm her with the long-recessed powers of *amore* that he'd always known he had within himself.

But all that, too, turned out to be an illusion, for shortly the elation he had been experiencing was followed by a severe headache, which laid him so low that he dropped down onto a walkway bench, remaining there until one of his farmhands found him slumped over in agony and helped him back to the mansion, where he spent the evening in bed, a strong dose of brandy, along with some grains of quinine, which he had taken as a precaution against malaria, seeing him through the night. Yet by the morning, as that severe pain had seemed to have receded to a mild ache, and as his son had a rejuvenating effect upon his waning vitality, Stanley, never wishing to disappoint Denzil, went to find him in his nursery, where he had been playing with a set of wooden grenadiers, a gift from the king.

"Come, my boy," he had said to Denzil. "Let's go outside. This time, we will get it flying."

In his hands was the box kite that he had constructed for his son from a kit. And so, even if he could only move ever so slowly, and even if the effort of keeping his head up taxed him, he did not let on. Denzil, in the joy and sprightliness of youth, could barely keep himself from leaping up and down even as he ran forward.

They had come to one of the meadows somewhat east of the house. As Stanley stood, watching the boy scamper forward with the string and kite floating over his head, his father wished that a strong breeze would come along and lift it upward—and it did. As the kite ascended, low clouds drifting along the horizon, Stanley again felt himself fading—a sudden paroxysm so numbing his left hand that he let the string he was holding fall away. The kite pulled up on the current and slowly rose over the fields; Denzil watched it lift beyond the clouds and out of sight.

☀

SOMEHOW HE MANAGED TO MAKE his way back to the mansion, where, begging his son's forgiveness—"I am sad that I cannot play more with you, but I will get you another kite soon enough"—he retired to his bedroom. Along the way Dolly, seeing his pallid face and drunken manner of walking as he entered the front hall of the mansion—for even with the assistance of a cane he swayed slightly from side to side—was so alarmed that she wanted to send for the local doctor. But Stanley, who had grown tired of doctors and treatments and medicines, told her: "With a little rest I will be better." Then, to further ease her mind, he added, a slight slur in his voice: "Haven't I always gotten over things? I may be worse for wear, but I will recover; perhaps it was something I ate."

He managed to sleep for several hours, and as the dinner hour came and went, with Stanley only taking a few sips of broth in bed, Dolly, as was her habit when he was indisposed, came to sit by his bedside and read aloud from whatever he might desire. Lately he had wanted to hear passages from his book about Livingstone, but that evening, Stanley could barely sit up and open his eyes, and though she had begun to read to him, Dolly decided there was no point in continuing, as he had hardly noticed that Denzil had come into the room to sit beside him. When he asked, "Is there something wrong with Daddy?" she thought it best to tell him that he was simply napping; then, as Stanley indeed had seemed to have fallen asleep, she left him in the company of their nurse and went off to attend to Denzil's bath.

Later she sat down in her small study to write several letters, and then, at around ten, when most of the servants had gone to bed and with silence prevailing, save for the ticking of the mansion's many clocks, she also retired for the night, in the large boudoir next to Stanley's, hopeful that he would be better in the morning.

※

May 22, 1903

Dear Samuel,

    I know that you have your own ongoing difficulties with Livy's health, but I feel it my duty to inform you that last month my beloved husband suffered a stroke. It came to him at Furze Hill in the middle of the night, his cry for help awakening our household: Of course, we sent for a doctor, who arrived at four in the morning, but as with such things there was little that could be done save for the usual recommendation of a sustained period of rest. If I have not informed you sooner, or if

Mother has not, it is because we had hoped for a sudden turn for the better, but for the last month Stanley has been unable to speak with coherence and unable to move—my great and brave explorer as helpless as an infant. The doctors say that time will perhaps restore his energies, but it is hard to look at him; one side of his face seems normal, the other dreadfully still or else pinched. I have spent many an hour administering massages to the afflicted areas, as per Dr. Kellgren's methods, but there has been no result so far. Still, we have tried to make him as comfortable as possible; more frustrating is that he knows not who is attending to him and seems lost to the world. That is what is hardest to endure.

For my part, however, I remain hopeful. Not long ago I consulted a London doctor who also happens to be a spiritualist, and he has assured me that Stanley will greatly improve in the coming months; surely once this recovery begins we will have much to celebrate. In the meantime, on behalf of Stanley, I send you and your family much affection.

Yours always,
Dolly

※

June 1, 1903

Dearest Lady Dolly,

I am truly sorry to hear about Stanley's illness; believe, me I can commiserate, for we are both tethered to the same burden of seeing a loved one suffer. As you know, Livy has been laid low these past few years—with gout, a weak heart, and a general malaise of the spirit that has its origins in Susy's passing and our daughter Jean's worsening epilepsy and fainting spells. Worries about Jean's condition have been a great drain on Livy, and so as a rule we have tried to keep Jean's continuing seizures a secret. Our decision to finally sell our old house in Hartford has not helped matters, because it is filled with Susy's spirit. It is impossible for us to return there—we closed on the sale, at a considerable loss, just a few weeks ago—but I am also much vexed by the fact that some doctors seem to think my moods have somehow aggravated Livy's condition of "nervous prostration." And so for a good part of the past seven months I have only been allowed to see her for a few minutes a day—and sometimes not at all. Even when I do visit her, the nurse stands by with a stopwatch, restricting me to two minutes a day. On our wedding anniversary we were allowed five minutes, and just this past February, when Livy seemed to improve somewhat, this was increased to fifteen minutes—though by then our Riverdale house had been turned into something of a sick ward. Back in December, Jean had come down with pneumonia (which we kept a secret from Livy) and then, once she finally recovered, both Clara and Jean came down with measles and our house was quarantined; it was one of those ironies that on top of it all, even as Livy seemed to improve, yours truly fell into an agony of toothaches, bronchitis, and rheumatism, all of which left me in bed for five weeks. It was only a few weeks ago that I was up and about again.

In the meantime, Livy has been well enough for our servants to occasionally bring her downstairs to our front lawn to take in the sun; and although she cannot get around without a wheelchair, it is our hope that a change of scenery to a warmer clime may help extend her life. We have been considering a move to sunny Italy, perhaps by the fall, if she is well enough to endure the crossing. But am I optimistic or hopeful? The truth is that my wife is slowly dying—that is clear to us all—and as a result, when I contemplate it I am drawn to the conclusion that sooner or later, in a sunny clime or not, I will become one of the loneliest men in the world.

Forgive my maudlin ramblings—I turned sixty-seven last autumn, and if I cannot be frank at this time of my life, when will I ever be? I am feeling more than a little upset to hear about Stanley; I hope you do not mind that I did not share your letter with Livy, for I know she would be greatly saddened to hear about him, and that is why she has not written to you herself. I am simply trying to protect her from anything that would bring further aches to her heart. Stanley remains one of the lights we both look to, and whatever controversies have swirled about him in recent times, I think him a very great man and count myself lucky that he is a good friend. So when he comes around, as I am sure he will, please tell him that Samuel Clemens looks forward to the day when the two of us will sit out in some sunny place, sipping drinks and swapping stories.

And please do keep us apprised of Stanley's health, as I will keep you informed about Livy.

With all best wishes and love,

S. L. Clemens

⚶

THE MONTHS PASSED, AND SLOWLY Stanley began to come around, an improvement that Dolly attributed to the stream of spiritualist healers whom she had brought to his bedside—their hands passing over the ailing magnetic fields of his body, their voices summoning the spirits of the great healers of the past to breathe new life into him—or perhaps he had been heartened by the continuous attentions of Dolly herself, who rarely left his bedside and often spoke to him sweetly or read aloud from his favorite books. Denzil, too, entirely bewildered by his father's condition but obedient to his mother's wishes, sat with him for at least an hour a day. Then, after many weeks of the deepest unconsciousness, some movement came back to him: He could open his left eye, had some feeling in that hand, and slowly began to emerge from the dark and claustrophobic room. With the movement of his eyes, there slowly returned the faculty of his speech, although his words were slurred and labored.

His first full phrase consisted of a question: "Where am I?"

"Oh, Stanley, my love, you are at home, safe and sound!"

"Safe and sound?"

"Yes, my love!"

"But is this Cairo?"

"No, you are home, at Furze Hill."

And he looked at Dolly with confusion, having trouble recognizing her.

"And you are?"

"I am your wife, Dorothy."

"So I am married? How did that come to be?"

"Oh, Stanley, do you not remember? We have been wedded now for thirteen years!" And she pulled the boy close to his side. "This lovely cherub is your son, Denzil. And look there, through the windows: You will see the spreading meadows and woods— they are yours, as is everything you see around you."

"Ah, yes, I suppose that is so." Then: "What's happened to me?"

"You've fallen ill."

"From malaria?"

"No, my love; you have suffered from a different a kind of affliction."

"And you say that my name is Stanley?"

"Yes! Henry Morton Stanley."

"Why does it seem odd to me?"

"Because you have been ill."

And when he turned away sadly, Dolly, in her most hopeful and cheerful manner, said: "The main thing is that you are getting well! And if you do not remember everything clearly now, it will all come back to you, day by day; that I promise you."

A former schoolteacher from Pirbright, a slight fellow with a soft voice and the patience of a saint, was brought in to sit by

Stanley's bedside every afternoon to reacquaint him with his own life and read aloud from Stanley's own book of travels and his most recent articles about Africa. Dolly made it her habit to bring her husband various photographs and objects: "Stanley, this is the jewel box the queen gave you in 1872; here is her picture. And this, Stanley, is the Bible you brought from England when you first journeyed to America; and here is the inscription: 'To John Rowlands.' And this is a picture of you in Zanzibar; the black boy by your side was called Kalulu." Then: "And this one is of you and Denzil taken a few years back—you rode the howdah on Jimbo the elephant and attracted great crowds."

"Ah, yes," he would say, seeming to dimly remember.

Dolly read to him from her own diaries, reminding him of the names of their many friends and social acquaintances (for she kept always kept track of everyone they encountered). But when he heard Dolly mention "Samuel Clemens, an old friend," a number of images simultaneously converged upon his thoughts, as if from every direction: a steamboat; the Mississippi River at dusk; riding horses on a narrow jungle road; a billiard table; a kind and loquacious man with a shock of red hair puffing incessantly upon cigars; and books, wonderful books, among them the tale of a runaway slave named Jim and a raffish boy, Huckleberry Finn; the memory of taking that book on expedition to Africa, with its rivers, ravines, and jungles; the pleasure of recalling how those words once soothed him during moments of deepest sorrow entwining with the general memories of having him as a friend; yes, he was one of the first persons whom Stanley seemed to recall more clearly than the others.

"And this Samuel Clemens, he is also called Mark Twain?"

"Yes!"

Such small advances elated Dolly and boded well for the fuller recovery of his mind, its faculties having been dimmed by several months of listless inactivity and sleep. And with that improvement came progress with the physical aspects of his recovery, with which, however, she was only marginally involved, for she had left the indelicacies of the bedpan and sponge baths and the exercising of his limbs to their hearty Irish nurse, leaving for herself the easier acts of shaving his white bristles daily, which he had insisted upon, for even during his worst bouts of malarial fever in Africa, a shave always made him feel better. And she washed and cut his hair—even brushed his teeth—with such tenderness and affection that even if he had forgotten he was once in love with her, his love was renewed, for daily he looked more and more forward to her visits and the time they spent together.

Slowly the movement of his jaw returned, and with mastication possible, he could begin to take in nutriments beyond just the soups and broths he had been spoon-fed; and with his strength building, he could finally sit up in bed. The improvement of his circulation brightened his mind: His thoughts suddenly connected, and a lifetime of memories that seemed mysterious and obscure flooded in with the ferocity of the cataracts he had once traveled. The facts of his existence—with its glorious adventuring and the many wants and sadnesses of his youth—coming back to him all at once both cheered and made him despair, for in recalling who he was, he realized the finitude of his days. He had a certain suspicion about himself, and this he verified, some three months into his recovery, by asking Dolly to bring him a mirror.

"But why, my love? You are looking splendid."

"Bring it to me."

This she did: It was a hand mirror she had purchased in Florence, its delicate neck a swirl of fine-wired filigree. As he held it up to his face, all his illusions were gone, for, looking at it, he told her: "My God, Dolly—but I am old!"

☀

BY LATE JUNE HE WAS well enough to be carried downstairs from his sickbed in an invalid's chair to take in the sun on his lawn at Furze Hill. Once out through the entry hall's door into the open air, he nearly wept from joy. It was a glorious day, teeming with life: a flight of sparrows flocking across the woods; the tapping of woodpeckers and the churning of a brook sounding from a forest hollow in the distance; a monarch butterfly dallying over a rose. In the fields, some of his men, a hearty crew, were digging out a well. Cows, sheep, and horses lolled in a meadow; dogs were barking; his farmhands were going about their business in attending to the estate. And around him—everywhere, he supposed, in the very radiance of life itself—was God's unseen presence, of which the miracle of the world's existence in those moments was proof enough.

Although he was no mystic, his stroke had left him predisposed to wild imaginings, for whereas before he had once looked at the horizon and saw it, geographically speaking, coming to an end, in whatever direction he now looked Stanley fantasized that he could follow the terrain beyond its apparent boundaries, as if, radiant with divinity and the promise of youth, he could roam the world from his chair. Though he could not move without assistance, for he did not yet have the strength to wheel himself about, he spent many a day reveling in mental adventures, the likes of which he had not experienced since he was a boy and dreamed of following the road out from St. Asaph's to the rest of England. Just looking out at the horizon brought back the wanderlust that had driven him throughout his life—how else could he have journeyed so far and wide? He felt blessed to have seen so much of the world, and whether it had been good or bad, he reckoned that he had experienced more than most men ever would. If he felt sad at all, it was out of a longing for the days when the future was a mystery to be pursued and explored.

How he wished he could get out of that chair.

He read quite a bit then—Dickens, Blake, Gibbon—his son often by his side, playing with some puppies on the lawn. With the sun suddenly emerging from behind a cloud and filling the world with light, his son would come with some drawings in hand to show him: "This is Mother"—as a hen. "This is you, Daddy"—as a lion. Day after day went by in this fashion, and he always lamented the coming of night: Even if the mansion was a most comfortable and homey place by then, the world's darkness distressed him, as the night could only bring him sorrow.

His farmhands often came to pay their respects to him and to see how the old man was doing. One of his builders came by to tell Stanley that he was naming his new house Bula Matari, and one of his housekeepers, having given birth to a little boy, tried to cheer her employer by christening her son Henry. The local vicar, Lamb, and his wife came to visit weekly. And certain friends from London ventured out—Henry Wellcome, H. G. Wells, Edward Marston, and dear old Edwin Arnold.

Often he would simply sit looking out into the woods in a daydream of his past. Once, while drifting into sleep, he conjured a riverboat on the lawn, and, looking up beyond its various decks, he saw Samuel Clemens as a young man in the pilothouse. Samuel was considerate enough to wave and gesture for him to come up and take the wheel, the Mississippi waiting. Then he had a dream of being on the Congo River, along one of its tranquil stretches, its serpentine course drifting past verdant tracts of jungle, friendly Africans clustering on its banks, clacking sticks to get his attention, and holding up baskets of food they wished to barter for lengths of merikani cloth and coils of wire and beads—ah, yes, it was not all bloody hell. Somehow he grew sad to think that some of the Africans might end up slaves: He saw them being herded off by the Arabs, transported in chains through the jungle, their robes dropping off of them; then, just as suddenly, the Congo would turn into the Mississippi, and he would see these same natives on riverboats as the vessels, their great horns blowing, would come into the port of New Orleans or Natchez or Memphis—the two rivers, the Congo and the Mississippi, merging as one in his mind. Along the way the native Africans were turned into the slaves of the South, the sorrowful and beautiful souls he had once known—"At least, in my small way, I have perhaps spared some of their predecessors from a similar fate." And then, just then, he might hear a voice and open his eyes to see that it was all an illusion, a great sadness coming over him as he realized that he was confined to a chair.

The view from Mount Craig, the African highlands, a stampede of zebras and antelopes in the distance, and much more came to him during such enforced idylls.

DAILY, WITH THE HELP OF his nurse and a servant, he attempted to stand up, his legs and coordination having gone out from under him. Giving such exercises his all, by September he could, with considerable effort, walk short distances—down a hallway, across a room, from one end of the veranda to the other—but only with a cane and the assistance of Dolly, the only one to ever hold him closely, to help him along. Sometimes, in order to keep up the strength of his one good hand—his right—he would spend hours kneading a small rubber ball (his left hand was never strong again). And while he consoled himself with the fact that he was making some progress, many a dark thought entered his mind, and so it was that against his doctor's orders he'd bribe one of his servants to bring him a glass of whiskey or some other strong spirits.

The Carriage Ride

That winter, back at Richmond Terrace, Stanley, in wishing to settle matters for the future, made up a final will (his fifteenth), leaving most of his estate to Lady Stanley and Denzil, but in it, he also provided small bequests to his valet Hoffman (three hundred pounds) and his former officer Arthur J. M. Jephson (five hundred pounds) to repay their loyalty as well as token amounts to several distant cousins in Wales and some of his servants; and it satisfied him to give the St. Asaph Union Workhouse (last visited in 1899) an annuity of one hundred pounds for its library, a portion of which would go into a holiday fund to buy the juvenile inmates some special cakes at Christmas. Many of his geographical books, maps, and travel notebooks he left to the RGS; informally, he prevailed upon Dolly, who did not care for such talk, to send, upon his demise, certain items to friends—especially Samuel Clemens, for whom Stanley had set aside a very old edition of the *Twelve Caesars,* which Clemens had once admired while visiting him, and a vest-pocket watch and gold chain, the inner case inscribed with BULA MATARI so that his old friend would perhaps remember the man known as Stanley. Much else of what he possessed he left to Lady Stanley to keep or dispose of as she pleased, though he expressed the hope that she would "take care of and cherish" his collection of Mark Twain books, in particular his copy of *The Adventures of Huckleberry Finn.*

Although he was not at all prone to speaking about the future, on some days, when he could slowly amble about the mansion and settle into his study, he spent many an hour searching through old papers, as if to see whether there were overlooked portions of narrative that might be easily be put together for a new book. On one such afternoon he came across the forgotten fragments of his autobiography that described his journey to Cuba from years before; with his memories of that distressing and disappointing time reawakened—and with his own uncertainty about just how much of the tale was true—he was tempted to throw the sheaves into the fire, and yet, because they contained some happy bits of portraiture about the young Samuel Clemens, he could not bring himself to destroy them. Thinking that his illness was affecting his judgment, he decided to put them aside for the time being, stashing them in his cabinet for future contemplation; these, however, he never returned to, and the pages were to remain undiscovered until years later, when Lady Stanley found them.

* * *

FOR DOLLY'S PART, IN ATTEMPTING to maintain some semblance of normalcy among her friends—Stanley's illness being something she would not rather mention—she remained the ever-buoyant grande dame of social occasions, often attending fetes around the city and having acquaintances over to the mansion for lunch. Both she and Stanley were acting a role: Even when Stanley knew his demise was just a matter of time, he would speak of future trips—to Switzerland, to Paris, and to Florence, as Samuel Clemens had in recent times moved to a villa outside that city. Stanley spoke of traveling there "as soon as I am better, if Livy is well enough." And Dolly never failed, when seeing him, to remark, "You look well; better than yesterday." Or to convey some glad tidings: "My astrologer says that once we have gotten through this rough patch with your health, better days await you." Bent upon cheerfulness, and trusting that she was allied to a great number of benevolent spirits, she never lost her hopefulness. "You will get better, my love: Think of yourself six months before, barely able to move, and think of yourself now. Yes, you will get better."

He wanted to believe this was so: As a stroke had so suddenly befallen him, he still held out the hope that one night, as he slept, the malady would be suddenly lifted by God "in the twinkling of an eye." Yet he would hear no talk about religion or an afterlife, dismissing them as subjects of pure conjecture.

"I'll find out, soon enough, won't I?" he told her one evening.

THAT DECEMBER, AS STANLEY HAD grown fond of Christmas, and for the sake of their child, Dolly decided to hold a dinner as of old. The invited guests included H. G. Wells, George Bernard Shaw, Lady Ashburton, and various colleagues of Stanley's from the RGS. She also extended an invitation to the new king, Edward VII, but whether he would be able to show up or not was of minor consequence, for, as in better days, the mansion was gaily decorated, and that was what counted to her. A good bar was set up, and gift baskets were laid along a table for their guests, each including a handwritten note from Dolly requesting donations for her favorite charities. The first visitors arrived around seven; by eight the parlor was crowded, with Lady Stanley and her mother greeting everyone, and as dinner approached and their company retired, one by one, into the dining room, Stanley rested in his bed. Rising up the winding staircase and down the hall into Stanley's room were the murmur of voices, clinking glasses, and toasts—"To England!"—and laughter and piano music as well the clamor of servants coming and going from the kitchen and pantry into the dining hall. Stanley was moaning and feeling sad when Dolly, tapping at his door, told him, "Come and meet our guests, my darling."

"I must dress."

"I will come back, then."

In her crimson velvet dress and pearl earrings, Lady Stanley helped him along; an observer who did not know them would have thought that Dolly was escorting her elderly father into the dining room. White-haired and eyes bloodshot, Stanley had lost a great deal of weight: His skin had thinned so that it had a nearly transparent quality, and his evening suit hung loosely on him. He seemed more like a bird-boned child than an intrepid explorer—in fact, making his way slowly down the hallway, he was bemused by the thought that such a small passage was as exhausting as any he had ever made in Africa. To rely upon anyone, including his dear wife, embarrassed him, but whenever he tried to make his way alone, he tottered as if he would fall. Eventually they made their way into the dining room, their guests standing up and applauding him: From guest to guest he went, whispering a few words of thanks to each, then taking a seat between Gertrude and Dolly. He sat in silence, barely picking at the various plates put before him and preferring to sip at the brandy while taking in the conversations around him. As it was Christmas, Stanley, however great his indisposition, rose to say a few words—his last before any gathering in that mansion.

"To count the blessings of my life: First there is my family, who has bestowed upon me the healing love of angels. From them, despite my waning powers, I have regained the celestial spark of trust and affection; it is especially so with my boy, Denzil, who in reminding this old man of the purity and joys of youth, with all its innocence, has made me feel like quite a wealthy man. And all of you, in your friendship with me and my wife, have made me happy as well: It is to you—to us, to the season—that I raise this toast. May God bless you in all your days. And yes, Merry Christmas."

That's when someone stood up and said, "Long live Stanley!"

※

AFTER THAT LAST "PUBLIC" DECLARATION, Stanley and his family withdrew into nearly complete isolation: Stanley did not once leave the confines of the mansion until April, when he departed London for Furze Hill, in the last spring of his life. There, in the company of his wife and son, he calmly approached his waning days; Dorothy, reading aloud to him, rarely left his side. The change in setting had, at first, a salutary effect, and for two of the most peaceful and happy weeks of their lives, he seemed to be regaining his strength. His spirits were raised, books and the good memories they brought him all but obliterating the sad aftertaste of the Africa controversies. Given that he appeared to be slowly improving, death was seemingly kept at bay.

But that same April, he, Dolly, Denzil, and Gertrude went out for a carriage ride; a piercing chill came abruptly over Stanley, who, despite the blankets in which he'd been wrapped, began to shiver, and by the time they returned to the estate, he was feverish, his lungs congested so badly that he could only breathe sitting up in bed. The good doctor from Pirbright diagnosed a case of pleurisy. Were he younger and his system not compromised by years of illnesses, he might have had some chance of recovery, but for ten days he struggled just to open his eyes. Up until then Dolly had maintained some hope, but one evening as she sat beside him, she had a premonition of his death—a black shadow passed quickly across the room behind her; she had just caught a fleeting glimpse of it—and with that she turned to her husband and embraced him dearly, as if to do so would ward off death itself: "Now, what is this?" he asked her.

"I will never leave you alone again, I promise you."

And she didn't, believing that somehow her love would protect him.

By then, however, he was preparing himself for what he called the final liberation, and as he wished to pass his last days in his first true home he asked to be taken back to London. He was too ill to contend with the train, and was thus transported back to Richmond Terrace by a private ambulance, his world, at last, reduced to the confines of his bedroom, where he was to take comfort again in his love of literature and family. Often he slept, but awake one evening, he sat up and said to Dolly:

"Where will you put me?" Then: "When I am gone?"

"Stanley," she told him, "I want to be near you, but they will put your body in Westminster Abbey, next to Livingstone's."

He told her, "Yes, it would be right to do so," but then, even as he said so, there was doubt in his eyes. "Will they?"

From Lady Stanley's Journal

MY DARLING IS SINKING, SLOWLY and painlessly. His dear mind wanders gently at times, and his eyes look far away.

FOR ANOTHER TWO WEEKS HE lingered, lost to the world. He'd gotten over his pleurisy by then, could breathe more or less normally, but everything else he had suffered from had taken its cumulative toll: His body was simply giving out. Often he thought, "I am looking forward to the very great rest." Sometimes he would look across the room, as if seeing some invisible being standing there; in one instance, Livingstone himself came up from the underworld to tell him, "Come, now, Stanley; it won't be so bad." He even fancied seeing his own Welsh father in tattered rags, with a bottle of ale in hand, sitting beside his nurse in the corner of the room, trying to gather himself to say a proper few words to his son. "When will he speak?" he'd ask himself. His father, a dark-haired man with thick hands and a bristled face, ever so timid, in the way of drunks, finally spoke up one afternoon: "You may not think much of me, but I have ever been proud to see you done so good in the world." Others came to tell him that he had done right: Even his mother, dressed in the very fineries he'd once bought her in Paris, told Stanley: "I may not have been much of a mother to you, Johnny, but I was your mother, and in the end result, making you who you were, I didn't do so badly, did I?"

Through this process, Stanley was surprised by how peaceful he had begun to feel. Lethargic, unable to leave his bed, he slowly slipped away, his days and nights spent dreaming. Mainly he liked to think about the way life would go in the household even without him; he liked to imagine Dolly sitting before her dressing-room mirror each morning, brushing out her hair, or bathing with a scrub brush in hand, the door always left slightly ajar, as if she wanted him to look in and see her naked body. He would miss the sheer joy of looking in at her in her studio, as she pensively and serenely contemplated a drawing. Would that wonderful sensation be transferred to some other life? he wondered.

If he had any great regrets, they came down to the sad prospect of never seeing his son again, for when he contemplated an afterlife, it was a shadowy zone where souls wandered in darkness, longing for the world, much as the Greeks of his boyhood readings had imagined. Yet in Denzil he saw pure light. In giving him what he, an abandoned child, had never received—the best of his affections—Stanley felt renewed. In fact, no greater pleasure came to him than when, while resting in his bed, he would feel the atmosphere of his sickroom changing, the ever so slight weight falling on the mattress, and his one good hand, his right, feeling upon its knuckles many soft and moist kisses—Stanley opening his eyes and seeing the gentle manner in which his son was trying to awaken him.

"It's me," he'd say. "Are you happy, Father?"

"Always, when I see you."

And then a whole new ritual would begin, Stanley slowly shifting his body to the side in his bed to make room: "Come lie beside me." Denzil's lithe and nearly weightless body with all its warmth snuggling close to him, his hand laid tenderly across the right side of Stanley's face, the boy asking all kinds of questions: "When will you get up, Father?" and "Can you read something to me?"

All of that he would miss.

FOR DAYS HE DREAMED ABOUT Africa. He often spoke in Swahili; at times he seemed to be at the head of a column, shouting out orders that could be heard throughout the house. Once he awakened in a sweat, convinced that he had a pith helmet upon his head. His flannel undergarments were drenched with moisture, and his body throbbed from the impossible heat that rose in shafts from the jungle floor around him. He believed, in such moments, that he was a younger man again, and as such, reliving those discomforts did not bother him, for sooner or later, the small ecstasies of such journeys came back to Stanley as well. He would find himself perched on a ravine overlooking a waterfall, its spray shooting up great clouds of rainbowed mists that settled coolly and lovingly upon his face; or he would be on the fortieth day of a trek in the continuous twilight of a forest, bringing his column to a halt, astounded to discover a single radiant shaft of sunlight coming down through a clearing in the treetops, a cluster of tropical orchids gleaming like church lamps before him, God's handiwork illuminating the darkness.

One afternoon when Stanley opened his eyes, in the corner of his bedroom was sitting his plump Irish nurse, praying over a rosary; then he saw Kalulu—no longer a pile of bones residing somewhere at the bottom of the Congo rapids but rather standing straight and tall at the foot of his bed, smiling. And this cheered him greatly:

> "Kalulu, I am happy to see you again."
> "And I you, master."
> "But why have you come?"
> "To bring you some water. Are you not thirsty?"
> "I am."

And with that Kalulu, wearing nothing more than a pair of linen pantaloons, drew from a water bag a cup's worth, which he brought to Stanley's parched lips; and then, as if to baptize him, he dampened his fingers with water and anointed Stanley's brow and eyelids, as if in a gesture of final peace.

"Thank you, Kalulu. But why are you being so kind to me when it was because of me that you drowned in the rapids?"

"Even as I am dead and drowned, as you say, it was you who, in bringing me to London and to England, showed me a new world. I would never have seen it without you; and though I miss life itself I will never forget the things I have experienced."

"Then you are not angry with me?"

"No, Bula Matari. I have only come to welcome you."

In that parting, a simple embrace: Then a blink of the eyes, and Kalulu was gone.

STANLEY HAD NO AWARENESS THAT he might have set into motion a colonial machine that, as rumor had it, was responsible for the mutilation and death of hundreds of thousands of

Congolese natives. The *London Herald* and *Le Monde* were writing continually of atrocities, and world opinion was shocked by the release of the Casement Report—but Stanley never saw it.

As his end approached, he was not bitter, only wistful at not being able to say good-bye to old friends. Among those he most dearly wished to see again was Samuel Clemens; he asked that Clemens's books be placed beside him, and, in a final effort, he asked Dolly to write Clemens a letter to see if he might be persuaded to visit them in London.

> *Dear Samuel—*
>
> *As I send you these words, I am on my way out of this nonsense. What you once described to me as the "lowly dirges of life" I have come to. God bless me, brother, if you can.*

Then he began to fade.

From Lady Stanley's Journal

IT WAS THIS MORNING, MAY 10, that my beloved died. But I had not expected it to come so soon, for we still held out hopes for his recovery. In those early hours, he suddenly cried out, "Oh, I want to be free! I have done all my work...I want to go home!" He told me then: "Good-bye, my sweet love; good-bye."

❈

STANLEY'S FUNERAL WAS HELD AT Westminster Abbey on May 17; as with his and Dolly's wedding, tickets were given out only by written request and at the discretion of the family. The nave was filled to capacity, and Stanley was carried toward the altar by a distinguished group of pallbearers—from the RGS, mainly: Arthur J. M. Jephson; David Livingstone Bruce; James Hamilton,

Duke of Abercorn; Alfred Lyall; George Goldie; Henry Hamilton Johnston; John Scott Keltie; and Henry Wellcome. The service had been appropriately respectful, and yet for all the ceremonial pomp and reverence accorded the old explorer, the abbey's dean, Joseph Armitage Robinson, a man not entirely convinced of Stanley's innocence in the "rape of the Congo," had denied him the one honor that he had most wanted, which was to be buried alongside Livingstone. Later, his cortege wound through the crowd-lined streets in its silent and solemn march toward Waterloo station, whence his ashes were taken by train to Surrey and laid to rest in the cemetery of St. Michael and All Angels Church in Pirbright.

Thereafter, as the kind of woman hard put to openly grieve or even admit to any finality about death, Lady Stanley had at first devoted her energies to finding a monument appropriate to her late husband's status as a "great man." For three months she conducted a search for a monolith with which to mark the grave where Stanley's ashes had been buried and, to that end, contracted a certain Mr. Edwards of the Art Memorial Company to scour the quarries, fields, and riverbanks of Dartmoor for a sufficiently grand stone, the kind that in the days of ancient practices would have been put up to mark the passing of a king—a druidic monolith that in its blunt majesty and permanence would fly in the face of the slight that had been rendered toward her husband by the sanctimonious powers that be. Various localities were visited—Moreton, Chagford Gidleigh, Walla Brook, Teigncombe, Castor, Hemstone, and Thornworthy—and thousands of stones were examined for their suitability; the search was a matter of such popular concern that many local farmers and their tenants joined in, with the happy result that by the summer a proper mass of granite, some twelve feet high and four feet wide and weighing six tons, had been located on a farm called Frenchbeer. Hauled to the churchyard and put up, its face bore the following inscription:

Henry Morton
Stanley
Bula Matari
1841–1904
Africa

Above the inscription was carved the symbol of life everlasting, a Christian cross.

CLEMENS IN THAT TIME

Yours has just this moment arrived—just as I was finishing a note to poor
Lady Stanley. I believe the last country house visit we paid in England was
to Stanley. Lord! how my friends and acquaintances fall about me now in
my gray-headed days!

SAMUEL CLEMENS TO THE REVEREND
TWICHELL, 1904

CLEMENS HAD BEEN SITTING ON the veranda of his rented palazzo in Florence, the Villa Reale di Quarto, when he read in the late afternoon papers of Stanley's death. By then, no bad news surprised him, for since he had taken up residence in that poorly heated and damp building, with its cavernous halls and chilly floors, few good things had happened. If there had been a high point, it had come with the singing recital that Clara had given in early April, but even then, his joy quickly vanished, for that same evening, Livy suffered a sudden heart seizure and would have died had not a subcutaneous injection of brandy revived her. Altogether, this sojourn in Italy, during which he had hoped to recapture the pleasantness of an earlier stay—one that took place some ten years before, at the Villa Viviani—had been a fiasco of discomforts. It rained continually, and daily fogs, like a "blue gloom," enveloped the grounds so completely that their rose and holly garden—the most charming feature of the property—seemed, with its crumbling walls and arches, like a haunted cemetery. And their landlady, the Countess Massiglia, who lived in an apartment on the grounds, was a foul, proprietary, and bitter woman, seemingly bent on making their lives miserable. Despite the fact that she knew Clemens had arranged for a doctor to attend to the ailing Livy daily, she ordered her servants to keep the front gates locked so the physicians would have to wait endlessly. When Clemens, complaining of bad odors that filled the lower floors, asked her to have the cesspools under the villa drained, she ignored him, and Clemens had to have his own dredgers come in. Incensed by this poor treatment, he was, in any case, already gravely distracted, for instead of helping Livy recover, that bleak and inhospitable Tuscan setting only seemed to have made her worse.

As his old friend Stanley had begun to fade in the early months of 1904, so did Livy. Various attacks of breathlessness and torpor and depression came over her, and oxygen and morphine had to be often administered. Worse was that he could rarely see her: Livy's doctor limited his visits to two minutes a day—once again!—as if he, the love of her life, were somehow harmful to her. For those months she had remained in bed, attended by a nurse, Margaret Sherry, and by Katy Leary, their housekeeper, who had joined them from America.

Occasionally Clara went into her mother's room to pass an hour by her side, as her presence seemed to calm her; but neither Samuel nor Jean, with her own continuing frail health and tendency toward fainting, was allowed to freely visit her. Clemens was so grieved by their separation that he would sometimes go into her room to quickly embrace her and cover her neck with kisses: Then suddenly, fearing that he would harm her, he would just as quickly leave.

To assuage his misery—and the long wait—he worked on his autobiography, dictating aloud to his secretary.

⁂

AT LAST, BY MAY, THE weather became glorious; the gardens went into bloom, wisteria fell over the walls, and butterflies came lilting over the blossoms. And the palazzo itself, while never entirely warm, had, with its fireplaces burning, at least lost its constant chilliness. With the appearance of the sun and Florence gloriously vivid to the west—the *duomo,* the campanile, the Medici Chapels, and the beautiful tower of the Palazzo Vecchio glowing in the distant plain, and with many villas and houses vanishing in and out of the light, as if time had dissolved them—the dreariness of that setting was transformed by a peculiar Tuscan magic. (Clara had the best of the views, because from her room, she could look out at the scenery through ten-foot-high windows.) Clemens, newly invigorated and inspired by the change of weather, began to search anew for a villa near Fiesole.

Livy seemed to become better by early May, but during one of Samuel's brief visits with her, she looked at him with haunted eyes and said: "I don't want to die, but I will, won't I?"

Sometimes Clemens would take long strolls along the pathways of the villa, enjoying the gardens and the beautiful decay of its moldering, ivy-covered walls. His passage meandered under arbors heavy with grapevine; or he would head out to the stable to watch his daughters ride around the estate on the gray mares that their mother had given them. But at around four, he always waited for his servant to bring the papers in from Florence, among them the London *Times* (always a few days old), *La Stampa,* and *Corriere della Sera,* which he would go over with an Italian dictionary in hand. But on that day—May 11, 1904—he had no need to, for even with his quite limited Italian there was no mistaking the

headline: IL ESPLORATORE HENRY MORTON STANLEY È MORTO A LON-
DRA, IERI MATTINA.

Greatly saddened by the news, Clemens called forth his memory of first seeing Stanley, so many years before, standing by the
railing of the boiler deck of the steamship—the scene coming
back to him with an immediacy that confounded him. It was as
if, as they had sometimes discussed, the past, as cumbersome as
it was in memory, seemed only separated from the present by the
thinnest of lines, and more so as one got older—a tautological
folly. Like free-winging angels, exempt from the linear constric-
tions of time, memory did as it pleased. As he thought about his
friend a few tears came to his eyes; these he brushed away. For
by that time in his life so many old friends had passed on—just a
week earlier he had read of the death of Antonin Dvořák, whom
he had gotten to know in Vienna; there were others, but Stanley
went back so far in his life that he immediately set out to write
Lady Stanley a letter of condolence, despite the fact that he would
have preferred to not dwell on the subject at all.

Villa di Quarto, Firenze
May 11, '04

Dear Lady Stanley,
I have lost a dear and honored friend—how fast they fall
about me now, in my age! The world has lost a tried and true
hero. And you—what have you lost? It is beyond estimate—
we who know you, and what he was to you, know that much.
How far he stretches across my life! I knew him when his work
was all before him, fifteen years before the great day when he
wrote his name faraway up on the blue of the sky for the world
to see and applaud and remember. I have known him as friend
and intimate ever since. I grieve with you and with your fam-
ily, dear Lady Stanley. It would be "we," instead of "I," if Mrs.
Clemens knew, but in all these twenty months that she has
lain a prisoner in her bed, we have hidden from her anything

that could sadden her. Many a friend is gone whom she asks
about and thinks is still living.

In deepest sympathy I beg the privilege of signing myself,

Your friend,

S

༄

Wherever she was there was Eden.

—SAMUEL CLEMENS, "EXTRACTS
FROM ADAM'S DIARY," 1904

Not a month later, a shout was heard coming from Livy's sickroom: "Come quickly, Mr. Clemens!"

And with that Clemens rushed to her side. Not a few moments before, she had said to Katy Leary, "I've been awful sick." And while Miss Leary, holding Livy in her arms, told her, "You'll be all right," she gasped, then slumped forward, her chin resting on her housekeeper's shoulder. Samuel knelt before her; as her eyes were still open, he hoped she would recognize him. But she said not a word, neither did she move; in that instant, as it occurred to him that she had been released into her final peace, his heart began to beat rapidly; then his right eye and cheek began to twitch and his stomach went into knots, and while he could hear what was going on around him—his daughters, now beside him, wailing out in grief—he felt himself at a far remove from that room and only came around when Clara and Jean huddled around him, weeping. Then indeed, when he realized she was gone, he staggered from the room, opened a liquor cabinet, his hands shaking, and bolted down two full glasses of whiskey. Her visage, with her lips so tightly pursed, neither smiling nor contorted into a frown, haunted him in its lifelessness. Everything seemed lifeless then; though he knew that a mantel clock was surely ticking, its hands seemed frozen in place, and through the windows he could see that the gardens were absolutely still—in those moments, he wondered if he had been the one to die; but this was not the case, and he began to weep and weep. What else could he do but go back into that room and sit helplessly before her throughout the night and into the next day? The doctor had come in at five with all manner of arcane devices and closed the doors as he made preparations to embalm her. At least, in those hours, he consoled himself by thinking that in the repose of sleep and release from her sufferings, the gauntness of her features had faded and she became, in his eyes, beautiful again—an angel.

"Just remember, if you can, wherever you have gone, that I adored you, and not only for the way you helped me raise our children but also because you never abandoned me; not once did you falter, and I will never forget that. And when you are in the other world, with Susy, I hope that you will always remember the day we met, in New York City in 1867, when an organ grinder was playing 'In the Sweet By and By' on the sidewalk across from the St. Nicholas Hotel, and the way you, in your beauty and quiet ways, looked at me, as if I would certainly be your man."

SUFFERING A SEVERE DEPRESSION, CLARA did not leave her mother's bedroom for days; Jean was visited by a sudden epileptic seizure. Clemens occupied his time writing letters, among them this one to Lady Stanley in London.

Villa Reale di Quarto
June 10, '04

Dear Lady Stanley,
   As you no doubt already know, Livy is gone, and I am numb, as you must have been over Stanley. Even now we are preparing for her transport to America—to Elmira, where she will rest beside Susy and others of our family. What can I say

but that hers was the best heart that ever beat beside my own?
I blame myself for her premature passing. She should have had
a much easier life than the one I gave her. But she put up with
me, my irascible personality and all, and her reward for so
many kindly efforts was nothing less than heartbreak. At least
her death was instantaneous: I do not think that even after
twenty-two months of suffering (by my count) she expected it
to come so suddenly, but it did.

As to your deeply held beliefs in spiritualism, though I am
numbed, I still see Mrs. Clemens in my every waking thought.
I dream about her—perhaps she is a ghost, but I doubt it:
I don't sleep much in any case. But she comes to me all the
same, not so much as a spirit who might be contacted—what
I know you believe in, with your spiritualistic societies—but
as a calming note during my nights. And so I thank you for the
abundance of your thoughts in that regard.

Yours,
Samuel

◈

TOWARD THE END OF JUNE, when the Clemenses finally
departed for America on the steamship *Prinz Oskar,* they arranged
to transport the two gray mares that Livy had bought for her
daughters. Their Italian butler and maid had also come along with
their party. On that journey his daughters' faces remained hidden behind mourning veils so thickly meshed that one could not
see their eyes. Clemens spent much of the transatlantic journey
stretched out on a lounge chair on the deck, bundled up against
the high winds, ever aware that his wife, in a lavender dress and
velvet slippers, lay in her coffin in the ship's hold. Looking out
over the horizon and the endlessness of the churning waters, he
was so stunned by the depth of his sadness that he hardly ever
spoke.

THE CABINET
MANUSCRIPT AND
OXFORD
1907

When you and I are dead and forgotten, the name of Stanley will live!
—DOROTHY STANLEY TO A RIOTOUS MOB DURING STANLEY'S

FIRST CAMPAIGN FOR PARLIAMENT, 1895

IN THE YEARS THAT FOLLOWED Stanley's passing, his widow lost her taste for visiting Furze Hill but continued to do so in good weather for Denzil, who had grown fond of the outdoor life. Not far removed in temperament from Stanley, he was a lonely-seeming child, despite the tutors and the smothering attentions of his mother and grandmother. Delicate in his manners, and already better educated than most children of his age, he seemed to come to life only when he was out in the countryside and free to consort with the farmhands and their children and roam the property's gardens and woods. Even if his father had once survived the most rugged terrains in the world, Denzil, their precious treasure, was guarded closely, as if he were a young prince. He was never allowed to climb trees or swim in the pond Dolly had named Stanleypool, and he could not venture out without a servant trailing behind him at a discreet distance. But he was already an enthusiastic, if not entirely accomplished, horseman, having been taught to ride at the age of seven; his equestrian pursuits were always conducted under the vigilant eye of a foot-man who led him along by the reins.

Still, he was turning into the kind of fine and well-bred adoles-cent that Stanley would have wanted him to be—not too foppish or spoiled or overly aware of his high social standing. Never told by Stanley that without his and Dolly's intercession he would likely have ended up as a ward of some parish orphanage in Wales, he moved through his childhood as humbly and happily as possible for a boy who'd witnessed his own father's gradual death. Among his interests were the language of French and collecting *cartes de visite*: he wrote to many a family friend requesting such items and amassed a great variety of stamps and butterflies as well. While lacking any genetic link to the drawing talents of his adoptive mother and father—she'd always admired Stanley's hand-drawn maps and illustrations of the various arcane objects he wished to record in his travels—Denzil seemed to possess some natural abil-ity of his own. It helped that his mother had taken considerable joy in teaching him the rudiments of drawing with pencil and water-colors and that he had had much exposure to the artistic habits she resumed after the upheavals of her husband's final illnesses.

Even in her widow's life, she rarely refrained from spending at least an hour or two every day in the room known as the bird-cage, working on some unfinished portraits or scenes; and while she did not take long strolls around the city, as she once used to, Dolly, commissioned by friends to make new illustrations for books and articles about the life of poor children in London, still visited her favorite squares by coach, looking for more urchins to sketch. Dressing in black for a year, she had not allowed her sadness to keep her from renewing that practice, nor did she abstain from wearing jewelry, for, while wanting to seem in mourning, she never wanted to appear drab or commonplace. And while her mother, Gertrude, continued to disapprove, as she always had, of bringing such children into the mansion—"It is below your station," she would say—when those often unruly children came into her studio, Dolly remained open-minded enough to allow Denzil into the room while she drew her subjects. She even allowed him to make his own sketches and talk with the children, though they did not have much in common. They were the children of beggars or washerwomen or garbage pickers, while he, as she was wont to remind him, was the son of one of the greatest men who'd ever lived in England.

Only ten years of age, this slight and long-nosed boy seemed to understand this. The hours he had spent with his father, listening to him describe the "dark" regions he'd traveled, listening to his lectures about the making of maps or where a particular spear or arrowhead had come from—all these he had not forgotten. And there were his father's books in the library—rows and rows of them, in many languages, and while he had not yet developed the taste or patience for actually reading them, he sometimes picked one of them off a shelf and would sit, its pages opened before him, astounded by the sheer magnitude of words and thinking that his father was still alive because of them.

Dolly remembered how well composed Denzil had been through all the eulogies at Westminster; he sat without moving for most of the service, only turning once when the shadow of some bird traveled across the stained-glass windows and seemed to cross the floor toward the altar. Afterward, during the recessional, he slowly marched out of the church with his family, clouds of incense preceding him, his hand in his mother's. Then their progress toward Waterloo station: On public buildings the Union Jack fluttered at half-mast, and the streets were lined with people, many of them working-class folk who counted Stanley as one of their own. Most were standing on the curbs solemnly; some applauded, and some dabbed their eyes with handkerchiefs. Through all this Denzil had been well behaved, even stoic; but even so, he asked his mother, "Where will Father go?"

☀

BY THE SPRING OF 1907, Dolly had not only overcome the loss of Stanley, whom she believed still lingered around her, but had decided, being a social creature and thinking of Denzil's welfare, to marry again. The object of her attentions was the Harley Street surgeon Dr. Henry Curtis, whom she had met while accompanying Stanley to the doctor's office for treatment of gastritis. She found it a pleasant coincidence to discover, in the course of several conversations with Curtis, that he had a great interest in the general field of psychic research; the doctor had attended, in his time, various séances through which he had hoped to contact his late mother. But there was something else: While not a handsome man, and somewhat stout, and rather upright and self-effacing in his demeanor, he seemed the sort of well-heeled gentleman, eleven years younger than she, who, with a practice to keep him busy, would not impinge upon her independence.

IN THOSE DAYS, DOLLY WAS sad to realize that Samuel and his surviving daughters had become distant figures in her life. It sometimes stunned her to think that she had not seen him in seven years, and while they had exchanged Christmas greetings, much of their correspondence seemed to consist of letters of condolence. Though the familiarity with which they had once written each other had given way to a more formal tone, her affection for Clemens had never faded. Following his political writings, as she received from friends copies of "Mark Twain's" articles and open letters to the public, she was quite aware of his outspokenness about certain matters, for since Livy's passing his patience for the insane cruelties of the world had ended; what had been private opinion had become public. She knew that he supported an anticzarist revolution in Russia, that he deplored the partition of China by Western powers, and that he blamed the Boxer Rebellion on the missionary influence there. She also knew that he strongly disapproved of the British war against the Boers in South Africa and had felt ashamed by America's slaughter of innocent people in the Philippines in the name of bringing them democracy.

Without a doubt he had grieved over the loss of Stanley, but with his friend's death had come a certain liberation; while he would have never written such a thing on the chance of offending his old friend while he was alive, once Stanley had gone to the peace of his grave (or the constant wanderings of a spirit) Clemens took up his pen and addressed, most caustically, the situation in the Congo by means of a pamphlet entitled *King Leopold's Soliloquy*, which was published by the Congo Reform Association in Boston.

One day, Dolly received a copy of the pamphlet from Samuel Clemens himself. With it came a letter.

21 Fifth Avenue
May 2, '06

Dear Lady Stanley,

Inasmuch as my anti-Leopold pamphlet seems to have gone into the world, I thought you should receive a copy from me if you have not received one already. I wrote it as an American citizen with the intention of simply asking its American readers to realize how misguided and greedy and callous the Belgian king has been in regard to the Congo. Knowing that he was Stanley's friend, I hope you do not find its contents too upsetting, but by my lights, the greater truth about what has been going on in that region, as reported by various eyewitnesses—and by the greatest witness of all, the camera—is well worth telling.

My previous interest in Africa mainly consisted of curiosity about an unknown region; Stanley's spoken and written tales about his exploits and the peoples and trials he had encountered have always fascinated me—and I am still tickled by the notion that he took my Huckleberry novel with him during one of his journeys. And of course I have always believed in your late husband's stance in opposition to the slave trade there; as to his "preaching" about Christianity, I have been neutral, trusting in his faith in the missionaries, whom he knew well. However, I have been not at all convinced that Leopold wanted to accomplish anything except the enrichment of himself and his own small nation through the exploitation of the Congo and its hapless people.

However you may view Leopold, he should be called into strict account for his actions. As you know, such actions were forbidden by the proclamations of the Berlin Conference of 1884, in which Stanley was a participant—the natives were to be protected and their well-being was to be advanced in various ways. But in all this the International African Association has failed miserably—I believe that even Stanley knew this, deep down.

Freedom of trade in that region, without the molestation of the natives, was supposed to be the main goal of the conference, but Leopold has managed to turn it all into his own cruelly and mercilessly run enterprise. As an absolute sovereign in the Congo and a plunderer of its resources, he has overridden all the restrictions put upon him at Berlin and at the conference in Brussels in 1890. He has thus, in taking over the Congo, which is twice as large as the German Empire, become very rich—but, like a Machiavelli, he has done so through devastation, robbery, and massacre of the natives. Unfortunately, the Christian powers have been negligent in holding him responsible, and my own imperialistic nation, like Pontius Pilate, has washed its hands of the affair. Our government cares to do nothing about it, even as the evidence of wrongdoing comes forward—as if it has forgotten its duty, as one of the first nations to officially recognize Leopold's realm, to see to a morally responsible handling of such affairs. (My goodness, but now I am sounding like Stanley!)

As I know that England is already somewhat outraged by the news that has been consistently coming out, I hope you will understand my intention in publishing this pamphlet, which is to motivate the American people to press our government into doing something about the situation. Whether this will happen I cannot say, but Dolly, I want you to understand that my pamphlet is by no means intended to implicate Stanley in any way. He was a great man—and my friend—and because of that something has been stirred in me that refuses to

see the seeds of what your brave husband planted turned into a
sham.

I intend that the pamphlet shall go into the hands of every
clergyman in America and therefore to their pious congrega-
tions, with the hope that our ordinary citizens will move to
make our government use a firmer hand in relieving Leopold of
his profitable satrapy.

There is not a single word in the pamphlet that would
implicate Stanley. His deeds, I believe, will always stand apart
and above the tawdry machinations of this world.

With fervent admiration and affection,

Yours always,
S.C.

If Dolly had any regret, it was that she had witnessed Stanley's misery at hearing his name associated with such reports, for he had lived and breathed and loved Africa. As for the pamphlet itself, she had nearly written to Samuel to verify that his portrait of the indignant king, with whom she had spent some time, was truer than he might realize. Yet there was something that ultimately disturbed her about the photographs. Their inclusion somehow felt offensive to her husband's legacy.

Still, she was grateful that Clemens had waited until after Stanley's passing before going public with his long-brewing feelings.

※

ONCE CLEMENS FINALLY CAME OUT of his deepest mourning, he shed his dark serge suits, with their sagging frock coats, and his stiff black bow ties for snow-white swallow-tailed outfits. An instantly recognizable figure on the streets of Manhattan, he'd walk up and down Fifth Avenue in an "efflorescence of white," as a local paper described the impression he made on passersby. In his beatific quest to purge the world of imbecilities, he may have wished to present himself as the purest of spirits or as an angel with a flaring shock of whitening hair and lightning-bolt eyebrows; but he may have picked up that manner of dress in Bermuda, where white linen was supremely practical, during one of his journeys to the Caribbean with H. H. Rogers aboard the *Kanawha*, the same yacht on which he had visited Cuba in 1902. And he may have thought white more hygienic, or he may have simply tired of his mourning, but whatever his reasons, he thereafter rarely appeared in public, save for formal occasions, in anything else.

AFTER LIVY DIED, CLEMENS SUMMERED at a retreat near Mount Monadnock, in Dublin, New Hampshire, where he had hoped the setting would help his daughters recover from their own grief. Poor Clara, who had been closest to her mother, had suffered several nervous breakdowns and spent a year in sanatoriums in New York and Connecticut, and Jean, tossed from a horse in a trolley accident, which could have easily killed her, continued on in ailing health, and bouts of violent hysteria and epilepsy had prompted her own stays at various institutions. And Clemens, despite the fact that he spent many a day fighting depression and wishing himself dead, found that he had risen to new heights in the public's affections. Steamboats and cigar brands had been named after him, and, as with Stanley in his heyday, he was often approached by strangers on the street who simply wanted to shake his hand or to pose beside him for a photograph. His friends were the most important people in America: Andrew Carnegie, Teddy Roosevelt, and Thomas Edison. Numerous invitations to luncheons and dinners proliferated—the banqueting life, as he called it, taking up many of his days.

BY THE TIME HE HAD been informed that he would be given an honorary doctorate in letters by Oxford University, in the spring of 1907, his ardor for the political arena had somewhat abated, for with his dedication had also come endless invitations to speak before various groups on behalf of the Congo Reform Association—travel commitments that he, at his age, found exhausting.

Withdrawing from such duties, save for producing the occasional foreword to a book or pamphlet about Africa at the behest of the American Anti-Imperialist League or the Congo Reform Movement, Clemens continued work on his autobiography. Having no preconceived plan or scheme for the narrative, he began each session in his Fifth Avenue home by simply talking about whatever memories or images happened to come into his head, much as he had done while sitting for Dolly during their portrait sessions. Often he did so while shooting billiards. Meandering to wherever his mind took him, he began, bit by bit, to improvise the long and digressive narrative of his life. No particular event was more important than another, and his method was founded on the premise that anything he spoke about would be later configured into a meaningful sequence. Intending that the book would be published posthumously, he would take liberties with the truth sometimes, especially in the segments regarding his days during the early Civil War and the period of time—only three or so weeks—when he accompanied his friend Stanley to Cuba, a subject he was never to mention to anyone except Dolly. It happened on an afternoon in late June of 1907, when, wearing his newly acquired Oxford robes, he once again sat before her in her studio at Richmond Terrace.

�☀️

A FEW WEEKS PRIOR TO their meeting again, Lady Stanley—having married that past March 21, nearly three years after Stanley's death—read with delight the news of Clemens's arrival in England, for his landing at Tilbury aboard the SS *Minneapolis* on June 8 was met by a considerable crowd of admirers and journalists; harbor bells had rung, and even the stevedores were whistling

and cheering as he made his way onto English soil. But that accla-
mation was just the beginning. As he stood on the dock, waving his derby and umbrella at the crowds, he thought that such
attentions had come about from his London publisher's efforts
to make known his return, for he had many events to attend to
and publicize; but he had no inkling that his writings against the
wrongs of the world—the very same that had been met tepidly by
the American public in regard to Africa and other places—were so
in tune with the general mood of the English public, who, in any
case, already revered him for his books.

Indeed, from the moment he took up residence at Brown's
Hotel in London, Clemens found himself constantly besieged by
people. Within a few days of his arrival its lobby had become a
second American embassy. While on most ordinary afternoons
one would enter the public room and find most of the club chairs
and sofas unoccupied—except at four o'clock tea—they were now
all filled, and dozens of people were always standing about with
books or gifts in hand, anxious to speak to or get a glimpse of
the famous man. He received a steady flow of illustrious visitors,
and once his address was known, letters poured in from all over
England, along with numerous gifts. So great was England's welcome that the papers were comparing his popularity to that of
Charles Dickens at the height of his fame, when he could only get
around London anonymously, wearing a theatrical disguise—a
false beard, an eye patch, and an oversize top hat pulled low over
his brow. Holding court and consenting to many an interview,
Clemens only found peace when he lay in bed at the end of his
long and busy days.

WITHIN A WEEK HE HAD to engage two additional secretaries
to handle his correspondence. For about sixteen hours a day, his
assistants went through the mail, reducing the massive influx of
letters and requests to the few that Clemens might directly answer.
Among them—because he had left instructions that anything

from Richmond Terrace should be put aside—was a missive from Lady Stanley.

2 Richmond Terrace
June 12, 1907

Dearest Samuel,

G. Bernard Shaw has told me that he recently made your acquaintance on a platform of the station at Tilbury upon your arrival and that you later spent a few hours with him, James Barrie, and Max Beerbohm at Claridge's. I imagine that he must have told you about my marriage ceremony, since he was one of the few guests invited. It was an austere affair, and since then Dr. Curtis and I have been living quietly at home. And while I am joyfully embracing my new circumstances, I have been very aware of your presence in London, the papers being full of accounts about your every doing. (Even our little Denzil has been excited!) I know that you are impossibly busy, but here I must remind you of your promise to visit me at Richmond Terrace. I still want to continue painting you and have been savoring the thought of a new session all these years: As always, I would like to present the "Mark Twain" whom I have known and been greatly fond of in all his glory. Can you come here, and soon?

And there is the matter of the manuscript I sent you. As much as I wish to address its curious contents—for Stanley is still always foremost in my mind—you must know that I want to see you and join right hand to right hand. I must see your dear face again. Otherwise you will have no peace, rest, or leisure during your stay in London, and you will end by hating human beings. Please do come and see me before you feel that way, my dear sweet man.

Yours,
Dolly

☽

WHEN HE THOUGHT ABOUT LADY Stanley, with all his admiration for her as an artist and friend, he never once forgot that she was quite a woman. Tall, buxom, and with a great handsomeness about her Pre-Raphaelite features, she had always seemed the opposite of Livy, who even in her prime, before gauntness and severity arrested her features, had never been a voluptuous beauty. Delicate, yes, and angelic, but not the sort to stir a man's appetite. (After all their years of marriage, he had never seen her naked in the light; their sessions of love had been conducted in the dark, under sheets and blankets.)

At night in his hotel, when he was finally alone in his bed, after shooting billiards—the hotel had installed a table exclusively for his use—and exhausting himself to the point where he might finally sleep, he sometimes wondered what drew him originally to a creature who was so frail, for from the day he first met her Livy had never been in robust health and was often ailing. But he remembered looking at her and thinking, "This woman is as elegant and austere as a poem." And he, loving literature, though he did not know what it was, became enamored enough to marry her.

And yet at his ripe old age, Clemens sometimes thought about Dolly. He had always imagined that her breasts would be full and pendulous, her physical persona forward in a "Western" kind of way. Her femininity had always reminded him of the blunt physicality of the brothel women of the West and New Orleans, the salons of which he, in his youth, with his curiosity about life and youthful vitality, had enthusiastically explored. He found himself, in his old age, sexually curious again.

Though he had never uttered as much as a word about such doings to Livy, long before their honeymoon he had been an experienced lover. If he never told her of these experiences, it was because he had his pious husbandly image to preserve. Before he met her, his favorite consorts had not only come from New

Orleans, Denver, or Fort Collins but also, to his chagrin, from many a mining camp and from San Francisco, where he would play cards and drink until the early hours of the morning in the back room of a brothel. As those ladies were friendly and inviting and gentle and accommodating, and prone to kissing a card player's neck, how could one resist? He'd further amused himself with some Polynesian consorts in the Sandwich Islands, their seedy boudoirs situated in long palm-thatched houses along the beaches. Once, those many years ago—1867—he had nearly gone into a brothel in Jerusalem after a day's excursion to the holy sites, but by then he had fallen in love with the image of Livy, which her brother, Charles, a fellow passenger on that journey, had shown him in a cameo; She seemed to be purity incarnate. And because he knew that Charles was somewhat aware of his doings, as they and his fellow "pilgrims" kept nearly constant company, he had not only abstained from his curiosity but also swore thereafter to reestablish a vow of chastity, which he mainly kept to during the years of their courtship and never once violated in their many years of marriage.

⁂

WHEN CONTEMPLATING THE PRIVATE SEXUAL life of a man, especially famous men such as Stanley and himself, Clemens recalled a conversation he once had with Stanley, God bless his soul, regarding the untarnished image of David Livingstone. They were at Richmond Terrace on a Sunday in 1899 when Dolly, Gertrude, and Livy had gone off to church.

That Stanley remained behind to partake of a leisurely breakfast with Clemens had surprised him.

"How is it that you, of a most pious bent of mind, are abstaining from the service?"

"Oh, I never go. My church is in here," he said, touching his heart. "Besides, I did not want to leave you alone."

"I would have been fine."

"That is so. The truth is, Samuel, as often as I have spoken to church groups from the pulpits, I've tired of the stuffy doings of the services." Then: "Here, have some Champagne." And Stanley poured him a glass.

"Isn't it a bit early?"

"Samuel, if you must know, given a period of sound health, I begin every morning with a glass of Champagne, followed by a shot of brandy, in the Spanish fashion. It brightens my spirits and in its way brings me closer to God than any dreary service. In fact, if I have attended church at all in recent times it's because of Denzil, but mainly I leave it to Dolly and Mrs. Tennant to take him: As I think a boy should know about such practices, I allow it. You see, Samuel, even though I was raised in that way and had salubrious teachings rammed down my throat as a boy at St. Asaph's, my once naive views on divinity and the necessity of churches have long since become artifacts of my past."

"But when we first knew each other, you were different."

"Yes, I would say so: But I was then an innocent to the world—we both were."

"Now, tell me, Stanley, do you really believe in God?"

"Ah, that great subject. Before addressing it, let me fill your glass." Then: "Cheers!"

"But do you believe it, Stanley?"

"To be truthful, Samuel, even as we sit here, I do. And do not. Which is to say that even at the highest-pitched moments of belief, it has sometimes slipped away from me. And yet I have still always aligned myself with the faith, I suppose because of a few encounters with truly devout men. My father, Mr. Stanley, was one of them, as you know, but even his influence faded gradually with the passing years. How could it not when I have seen so much carnage? But then, as such things have a way of working themselves out, just when my faith was at its lowest ebb and I was as cynical and selfish as any man can be, it was my destiny to know Dr. Livingstone. If you have read my book about him—"

"I have, Henry."

"Then you will know of the profound change in my person

that transpired. But here is the twist: While in his company, I saw that even the most pious of men, like Livingstone, can have a side that seems contradictory to the usual expressions of belief in a Christian God."

"How so?"

"A little bit of history for you: In all his years of wandering through central Africa, Livingstone's survival often depended upon his honoring of local tribal customs, becoming a 'blood brother' with chieftains, which I did many times myself. But Livingstone, it has been said, also took concubines among the native women. The queens of these tribes thought him possessed of special powers because he was a white man and would, as the Bible might say, 'lie down with him.' This was considered a special honor, and he, to stay in their good graces, could not refuse it. But if these rumors are true, he had no problem with this practice. For Livingstone would have put such sensate activities as . . . well, to put it bluntly, copulation into the same category as eating and digestion—a bodily affair, to say the least, one kept separate from the effort to bring Christ's teachings to the savages.

"In that way, Livingstone was of two minds, but his religious side was so great and inspiring that after I had gone slogging through the swamps and jungles to reach him, and had despaired so often that in my malarial states I thought God a bit of a myth, it was his faith that revived my own.

"Mind you, he was an endlessly restless man—a foot tapper, like me, even when he tried to sit still—how else could he have trekked through uncharted regions for so many years? That energy and his appetites were one side of him; the other, the religious, was absolutely serene. He hung on to his faith even after watching his wife die of malaria in Africa just a few months after she had arrived to join him in his missionary work. One would think he would have resented the idea of a God then, but he did not. And when he died, after years of solitude in some desolate village in the Congo, he was found pitched face forward to the ground, his hands held in an attitude of prayer.

"Now, dear Samuel," Stanley continued. "If he was an undeniably great man—a much greater man than I—who am I to dismiss his final opinion? And so it is that even when I have little faith, his influence changes my mind."

"Do you suppose he was praying to clear himself for Judgment Day?"

"Possibly."

"And the afterlife, Stanley?"

"Ah, now, I know you don't believe in it. As for me, when I am in my cups, I will say there is one. But in my everyday waking life, I don't imagine it exists, although I really don't care—at heart, as much as I have come to love certain human beings, I think the human race so despicable that I almost welcome the idea of having no more dealings with it."

"I am with you on that."

"But who is to say?" said Stanley, filling Clemens's glass with more Champagne. "What I most often believe, dear friend, is that what awaits me will be a merciful darkness."

"That cheers me up," Clemens said. "As you and I are sitting here on this beautiful morning, another sacred day commemorating the hearsay about the risen Christ, I remain as skeptical as I have ever been, much as I have tried lately to put on a good face about all that business for Livy. Simply put, I am a reluctant atheist, and as much as I wish it were otherwise, it is so."

※

ON HIS NIGHTS BY HIMSELF, a terrible loneliness overwhelmed Clemens. Restlessly he would think about Susy and his beloved Livy, then of his remaining daughters—his little family. Clara had not accompanied him to London because he had insisted that she make the journey with Isabel Lyon, his secretary, whom she had come to dislike; Jean was then in a sanatorium, and in any case her doctors seemed to believe that, as with Livy, Clemens, in his moodiness, would only aggravate her symptoms of hysteria and epilepsy. Mainly he brooded about death and reflected unwittingly upon the passing of old friends, Stanley among them.

AS FOR STANLEY AND THE general subject of sex, Clemens remembered asking him once about the wilds of Africa and whether he had ever consorted with any women there. He recalled an evening in 1900, when Stanley, mumbling, had said, "Yes, I suppose I have." At first he was guarded, but after some questions, and with Samuel filling Stanley's glass with brandy again and again, the great explorer elaborated: "As much as I would not like to admit it, in my early middle age, I have lain with African voluptuaries. Mainly in Zanzibar. But what I say to you, Samuel, should not be known. As beautiful as these women were sometimes, I was as a shepherd would be with his flock: I attended to them as briskly as possible." (At that, Clemens laughed.) But then Stanley added, "These were only occasional events undertaken at moments of great boredom and torpor. I do not regret them, nor do I particularly remember them."

And had he ever lain with Lady Stanley? This, of course, he could never ask. Clemens imagined not, for in those years, when Stanley's luck with the female sex seemed to finally have changed, he had often been sick; but to imagine what Dolly might have been like intrigued Clemens. Sometimes, as he shot his billiards in the middle of the night, he saw her stretched out naked in a chair, like *La maja desnuda*—her Rubensesque form a pure enchantment. Of course, he was too old to linger long on such thoughts, but for a few moments, he envied Stanley for having found such a vivacious specimen of good health for a wife.

But all in all, as much as his mind drifted, he wished that Livy were still alive to ease his passage through those lonely nights and to share in his glory.

Often he drank until he began to miss his shots and could barely see across the room.

꙳

June 14, 1907

Dear Lady Stanley,

First of all, forgive the tardiness of this reply. And yes, I absolutely intend to visit you, but as I am like a fish in a barrel and up to my neck in engagements, our reunion must wait until after the Oxford ceremonies, to be held, as you know, on the 26th, at the Sheldonian Theatre: Will you be coming? I hope so. Otherwise, why do we not set aside the afternoon of the 28th? I promise to clean off the slate of my engagements.

I did meet Mr. Shaw—a poised, wonderful, self-effacing sort of fellow, whom I would gladly count as one of my friends. He spoke highly of you and Stanley and said that your wedding to Dr. Curtis was indeed a quiet affair. A question: Is it true that Mr. Shaw wrote a play about you? He claimed to have done so in Candida, which I have not seen. If this is so, I cannot wait to see it.

If I do not see you at Oxford first, then you will find me at your door at one o'clock on the aforementioned date.

With deepest affection,
The soon to be doctor of letters from Oxford!
Samuel

꙳

ON THE AUSPICIOUS DAY OF his honors, among the audience at the Sheldonian Theatre sat Lady Stanley and her new husband, Dr. Curtis, along with young Denzil and Gertrude. Dolly had been on hand to witness the great standing ovation, of some fifteen minutes' duration, that greeted Clemens as he was escorted up the aisle to the stage. Presiding over the ceremonies was Lord Curzon of Kedleston, chancellor of the university, and seated behind him, in robes of scarlet and gray and wearing tasseled mortarboards, were the honorees: General William Booth, founder of the Salvation Army; Auguste Rodin; Camille Saint-Saëns; Rudyard Kipling; and Samuel Clemens himself, his posture erect and expression unchanging as he solemnly looked out into the theater. When the moment came for Clemens to receive his degree—in recognition of his *artem scribendi*—the great man rose from his chair and sauntered forward to hear the citation. He reverently bowed his head but could not help but shrug and break into a smile at hearing the remarks read in Latin. This show of pure amusement and joy during so formal a ceremony, coming as it did from a man whose travails and convictions were so well known and whose literature was so much beloved in that country, had a compelling effect upon the audience, for once he had received his degree and had shaken hands with Lord Curzon, saying, "My goodness and thank you!" the entire audience of some three thousand people, including the stately and rather reserved dons, who, sequestered in their own section of high-backed chairs on stage, where they sat gravely viewing the proceedings, stood up and gave Clemens another extended ovation, all cheering loudly.

Afterward Clemens walked out from the theater in a procession with Kipling, Booth, Saint-Saëns, and the Duke of Connaught, the king's brother, into the light of day: The other honorees shortly followed. A battery of photographers, poised behind their cameras, were awaiting them on the green: In the crowd, George Bernard Shaw, wearing white kid gloves, spotted Lady Stanley and waved to her, and though she wished to greet him personally, there were so many people in the gathering that it was impossible to easily move across the grounds. Yet she managed to place herself in the front line of well-wishers. When Clemens came to the place where Lady Stanley and Denzil were standing, he stopped for a moment and said to Dolly, "It is good to see you again." And he gave Denzil, in his dark suit and tie, a firm handshake and pat on his head. When he said, "Why don't you come to lunch at the lord chancellor's? I am sure I can sneak you in," she answered,

"Well, there's more than me and Denzil, Samuel. But God bless you on this great day."

As brief as this exchange had been, the Duke of Connaught commanded the drummer to halt, and even though the drummer had only marched in place for a few moments, the thumping of the drum, booming across the grounds, commanded Clemens on; and so he, excusing himself—"Guess I will be beheaded if I don't"—took his leave and rushed ahead to take his place in the procession. Then he vanished into the glories of his day.

IN THE BALANCING ACT OF perusing Stanley's autobiography, Lady Stanley carefully went through all that he had written. Mainly she wanted to lay out for the public as valiant and as honorable a portrait of her late husband as she could. For whatever she may have felt about his failing physicality or the untoward reports about the Congo, "which flowed like spurs and thorns" through her being, she genuinely loved the man.

THE DAY THAT SAMUEL CLEMENS came to visit her at Richmond Terrace, Dolly spent the morning in her studio with a group of young girls whom she had found around St. Paul's and wished to depict in a drawing to be called *The Muses of London*. Somehow, despite the importance of her reunion with Clemens, she had allowed herself to forget the time, so that when Clemens arrived promptly at one, she was running late and was upstairs dressing for the occasion. She lingered for a long time before her mirror, trying on various necklaces and fussing over a selection of skirts, vests, and frilly blouses, for she wanted to appear pleasing before him. Why she had this feeling she could not say, but even given the heady circles she traveled in, there was something about the way Clemens regarded her that she always found flattering. He would look at her in a way that was tender, avuncular, yet admiring of her female qualities; and there was something else—as it was likely to be the last time she would see him, she wanted to leave him with a remembrance of refinement and beauty, even if at the same time she chastised herself for such maudlin thoughts.

He had been let in by their butler just as some of the young girls, having been given lunch in the kitchen, were scurrying out ever so happily.

By the time the butler had taken him into the parlor, which Samuel knew well, and had brought him a drink, Clemens, looking around, had become aware that the house had not much changed since Stanley's passing. No matter which direction he turned, there were monuments to Stanley's achievements. As he waited, there strode into the room a plump, well-dressed man of about forty, a red-cheeked fellow whose dark hair glistened with lotion. Clemens had been tempted to say, "Dr. Curtis, I presume?" but was preempted by the doctor's own warm introduction of himself.

"I am the lucky fellow who is Lady Stanley's new husband," he said. "Henry Curtis. And you, sir, I know, are the one and only Samuel Clemens."

"I am."

"Saw you at Oxford a few days ago; all very touching and well deserved." Then: "Accommodate yourself: Dolly should be down shortly."

Then a voice called out from the hallway: Gertrude Tennant, who had become progressively heavier with each passing year, slowly made her way from her study to greet her friend. She warmed instantly at the sight of him: "My dear young man! Let me kiss you!"

Clemens blushed, sat the old woman down, and, though nodding in his most friendly manner at her remarks about how grand had been his reception at Oxford, he was somewhat discomforted by the way she, assuming a motherly posture, held his right hand in her own. Though happy to be there, he was hungover after a late night with some of the "boys" from the clubs. In fact, he had been so tired in the morning that were his appointment with anyone else but Lady Stanley he doubted he would have kept it, having dragged his heels and barely made his way out of the hotel in time.

There was something about the mansion that he found greatly comforting: the birdsong from the garden; the resplendent light through the windows; the quiet of the house, which was situated in one of the less trafficked parts of London. And it pleased him to look back and remember the times he had visited and the pleasant sessions he had passed with Dolly in her studio. As insignificant as they were to the story of his life, and even given the many other artists he had sat for in his day, there was something consoling in being reminded of earlier, perhaps happier times, no matter how numerous his troubles—his family was intact then! And at least he would be away from the glut of journalists who seemed to track him down wherever he went. His only duty was to engage in a little polite conversation with Dr. Curtis, who within a few minutes began to sound to Clemens like an ever-cheerful and not terribly clever sort, a strange choice for so vibrant a lady.

"I imagine your life must be a parade of one great occasion after the other—how exciting," the doctor said, and Clemens, with his gift for pleasing strangers, rattled off an anecdote about his recent visit with the king and queen. Then he told the doctor about the time that the archbishop had shown him the supposedly genuine Holy Grail—these stories he related with apparent interest, even while his mind was focused on the matter on hand, which was to see Dolly again and clarify for her the circumstances of his and Stanley's journey to Cuba. Which version he would convey he was not certain. There was the truth, the half truth, and Stanley's own account, all drifting hazily in the mists of time.

AFTER ABOUT HALF AN HOUR, Lady Stanley appeared at the parlor door, wearing a black skirt, a ruffled blouse, and a snugly fitting corset, with a string of pearls around her neck and smelling sweetly of lavender perfume. Though he had seen her briefly at the Oxford ceremonies, the clamor had been greatly distracting, and he had only been vaguely aware of her charming appearance; now, in the mansion, he saw her clearly. In the seven years since he had last laid eyes on her, not only had she not seemed to age a day but, if anything, bestowed with the dignity of a widow, she was also more beautiful than ever. Instantly he got to his feet, and such was his agitation that he spilled his glass of whiskey.

"Oh, my dear, Lady Stanley," he had said. "May I kiss your hand?"

And with that, in a stately fashion, he stood before her, clicked his heels as if to parody a German count, and planted a light kiss upon the knuckles of her right hand. It was at this point that Dr. Curtis obligingly flicked open his vest-pocket watch and said: "Wish I could stay, but I've got an appointment at two." Then: "It was an honor to have met you, sir. Enjoy your afternoon."

※

LUNCH THAT SUNNY DAY WAS held at a table in the backyard, under a large awning. Around three, Gertrude began to doze off in her chair and, summoning her strength, called a servant to help her to her room for a nap. "It's all too relaxing for me," she said to Samuel. At around four, Denzil came by to say hello: He had been out taking riding lessons. A slight and thin-shouldered boy, he had been glad to give, as Dolly insisted, his "uncle Mark" a hearty embrace around the neck, and after answering a few questions about his schooling and interests, Denzil left them alone. And suddenly the most famous American in England was sitting across the table from Dolly. After several glasses of claret, he was beginning to feel "pickled," and in that state, as her face grew brighter and more sharply defined in the shifting of the sunlight through the trees, she seemed to become much softer and more beautiful—and as she did he began to feel older and older, his expression settling into one of stony unhappiness that he was not a young man.

"Samuel, how much time do you have this afternoon?" she asked him, breaking the spell.

"I have an appointment at the hotel at six. An interview that I have twice canceled."

"As you must leave, then we should attend to certain matters."

"You know, Dolly, I wouldn't mind another drink."

"Good. You will sit for me in my studio and smoke to your heart's content! Then you will tell me your impressions of the manuscript."

The Manuscript Explained

"NOW, TELL ME, SAMUEL," SHE said. "What did you make of it—was Stanley writing the truth of those days?"

He fidgeted a bit, relit his cigar. Then settled himself again.

"Well, mainly he did, but some things he got wrong. I can't speak about his early days in New Orleans, but I would guess that the accounts are true: I do remember occasionally passing by the Speake and McCreary dry goods warehouse on Tchoupitoulas Street way back when, and don't doubt for an instant that the place existed or that he worked there. And I believe that Stanley's stories about the poor slaves and the way he claimed to have met Mr. Stanley, the merchant trader, are also true, and I take him at his word, though I find the bit about his Bible being essential to that meeting on the inventive side—but maybe it happened. As for his early love for literature, I believe that is true. And his version of New Orleans I somewhat enjoyed, but I might have added a different detail or two. And what he wrote about the yellow fever, which was quite a calamitous event in those times, could not be avoided, though to be perfectly honest, Dolly, I felt a little suspicious about the fever stories he told regarding the deaths of Mr. Speake, his employer, and Mr. Stanley's wife, for I do not recall him mentioning them to me at the time, and, frankly, from a writer's point of view, the narrative seemed to creak a bit too much from the deus ex machina conveniences such deaths provide.

"But most everything else, to a certain point, I would say seemed plausible enough, though I have to say that in those days, in my recollection, neither Stanley nor I, for that matter, was particularly enlightened or sympathetic about the plight of the Negro slave. If you will forgive my saying so, in that regard Stanley seems to have wanted to come off more nobly than was the case: For we were products of the time, and those times, in the South, were not kind to those folks."

He took a sip of his drink, then, gripping the armrest and pushing himself up a bit, continued:

"Now, as you told me that he may have written some of the manuscript in a haze of postmalarial confusion, I do believe it may have been so. Especially when it comes to him and me. Indeed, we did meet on the boiler deck of a steamship, upriver somewhere between Memphis and St. Louis, in 1860 or so; I have to say that I was touched by the fraternal flourishes and tenderness he bestowed upon those scenes. But as dim as my memory can be at my age, I cannot recall being so forthcoming about certain personal details, especially in regard to my brother Henry's fatal accident on the Mississippi. I take it, then, that he may have simply allowed my accounts from *Life on the Mississippi* to slip into what he may well have construed as his truthful memory of our first meeting; or maybe it was just a dose of plain old wishful thinking, for I was not at all an easy person to get close to—certainly not with some young, straitlaced bookkeeper I happened to meet while having a smoke.

"But about the general drift of our friendship, he was mainly telling the truth. I did like him for his bookish nature, and I did enjoy talking with him. I just don't recall saying the things he said I did, but by now I've forgotten more than enough to fill two or three books, so I don't fault him for that. As for what went on aboard ship during those river voyages, the stories are mainly true; but from that point on his narrative seems to go astray.

"Mr. Stanley of New Orleans, however preachy and inspiring he may have been while speaking about the Bible, consorted with a very rough trade, and as I remember him, he was drunk a lot and not particularly nice to Stanley, whom he ordered about like a servant. Sometimes I saw Stanley in such a dejected state after leaving his cabin that I wondered what verbal abuses and curses his father had heaped on him; sometimes I wondered if he had laid hands on the boy, for I saw Stanley once with a pretty bruised-up eye. From what I remember, his father was plain mean and cantankerous. That he left out."

She looked at him quizzically.

"Then why would he write so respectfully about him?"

"Why? I suppose he liked the air of respectability that being with a riverboat trader conferred, and maybe he didn't suffer as much as I seem to remember. Or maybe he was just trying to cover the tracks of his youthful misjudgment. In any case, Mr. Stanley was not the saint that his adopted son mostly made him out to be." Then: "May I?"

And he poured himself some whiskey from a decanter.

"Now, once we had parted we sometimes corresponded. Stanley was so appreciative of my writing that I sent him old pieces from my early days—that is true—and in the meantime I learned something about his later doings up in Arkansas and the malaria he'd caught. The truth is I never expected to see him again, as we pilots were used to fleeting friendships. Sometimes you saw the same folks over and over again, and sometimes you didn't; that was the long and short of that kind of life. And maybe I was a little curious about him, maybe even worried—for he had no one but Mr. Stanley to depend upon, which was not much, in my opinion. Then a year went by, and I was sitting in the pilots' association house in New Orleans, killing time, when in walked Stanley, a bit down on his luck. He was all skin and bones, and the peachiness of his complexion had turned pale. Anyway, I took him out for a good meal and some drinking, and perhaps we did speak about Cuba and his plans to go there and look for Mr. Stanley; frankly, I could not understand why he should even bother, but his heart seemed set on it. He asked me if I would care to come along with him. Well, that was not the foremost thing on my mind. Hostilities were about to begin between the Confederacy and the Union. And with the commercial steamboat trade coming to a dead halt,

I was trying to figure out just what I would do with myself—maybe head back up to St. Louis with Mother Clemens, who was visiting me at the time.

"But shortly thereafter, Stanley came down with a bad bout of malaria. Coming out of it a few days later, he was still determined to book passage for Cuba. Now, I have never been a particularly kind fellow—though I thought I was doing right by Stanley by putting him up at my hotel—but as I thought about my friend, in his feebleness, making that journey alone, I began to have second thoughts. Maybe there was something about my brother Henry that I saw in him, and maybe I was thinking that by helping Stanley I might find a little peace of mind. In any case, I was restless and curious about the world, and I did not mind the idea of traveling abroad for a short time. And I was not sure if I wanted to set out straightaway upriver, so I kind of made up my mind to go along with him; all that is true.

"Stanley, I noticed, seemed to think it appropriate to invent other motivations—a girl, as I recall, and some fascination of mine with the island. The truth is that in those days I had met many a southerner who had dealings in Cuba, and all of them had some nice things to say about it and some things that were not so nice: but leaving it to fate, I eventually determined to go.

"And it is true that Stanley met my mother—I found it touching to read about her in Stanley's words after so many years; and it is true that she was none too pleased by my sudden decision. However we each remembered it, I do not regret the wonderful exhilaration of setting out to a new and unknown place—that alone, despite the nuisances and discomforts of any voyage, made it all worthwhile. I do not regret a single night spent out on the deck looking at the moon reflecting on the water or at the dusting of the stars."

He lit another cigar.

"Havana itself was a strange, majestic, and run-down city, much as Stanley described it, and our hotel, which I revisited a few years back during my journey there with Henry Rogers, was a tolerable enough place run by a somewhat eccentric southern lady who saw ghosts. In fact, the city was filled to the brim with southerners, and there was a lot of talk among them about how Cuba really belonged to us and how once the Civil War was over the matter would be settled for good. I kind of liked the intrigue—the feeling that every stranger might be a spy—but poor Stanley remained a bundle of nerves and mainly worried about locating his so-called father. I will not comment about his description of our doings in Havana as we tried to track his father down except to say that they are generally true. We did indeed make a call upon a businessman's family who lived above the city, and there was some truth in the statement that I had once met a girl who happened to live there, but romance was not much on my mind in those days. We did meet with a certain Captain Bailey, who had known Mr. Stanley; we visited his old offices and wandered about the American docks of Havana harbor. We did find a man, a dissipated drunk, who knew Mr. Stanley's whereabouts. All that is true, Dolly, though construed through the peculiarities of Stanley's voice.

"Once we reached Limonar by train, we were helped by a French Haitian planter named Mr. Bertrand, who put us up for the night and rented us some horses, and we rode out through a beautiful and rigorous track of mysterious jungle and encountered an escaped slave there. That is all true. And indeed we met Mr. Davis on the plantation-house porch and were shortly led inside, where the reunion between father and son took place. At first we were treated grandly, and the elder Mr. Stanley could not have been more kind to his namesake. Often he called him 'my dear protégé' and said things that would ingratiate himself to Stanley, praising his abilities to high heaven. But from the beginning he made it clear to Stanley that he was only a visitor and could expect his hospitality for no more than a week or so, though we were given the run of the place.

"In fact, Dolly, during our days there, Mr. Stanley did his best to make himself scarce. I had the feeling that he really wanted no part of Henry and certainly had no intention of adopting him. I further imagine that he believed Stanley had come all that way only to lay claim to his estate.

"It wasn't long before the elder Mr. Stanley began to consider Henry's presence more than just a nuisance: My guess is that when he sent Stanley up into the backwaters of Arkansas he never expected—or particularly wanted—to see him again.

"In any event, Dolly, Stanley's depiction of their wonderfully earnest and close relationship, suddenly dismantled by fate, was a fantasy, as was his depiction of Mr. Stanley's death."

"He didn't die?" Dolly asked.

"No! The picaresque episode in which Stanley described our party being waylaid by bandits and his father being shot through the neck was another of his inventions. The elder Mr. Stanley was never wounded, never lingered for days with fever from infection, never died; there was no funeral, no lead coffin to ship back to New Orleans. We did go out riding one day to visit a plantation, on a 'farewell' tour of that wild region that Mr. Davis had initiated, as we were obviously growing bored by our confinement on the mill. Indeed, we did set out along a narrow trail and were accosted by bandits. Those details were as Stanley recorded them. Our progress was halted by some of the most grisly and menacing fellows I have ever seen. They surrounded us and demanded a watch and whatever monies we had. But once Mr. Stanley and Mr. Davis produced their pistols and some shots were exchanged—not a single bullet hitting its mark, on account of the rearing horses— we began to gallop away, back toward the mill and safety. I can remember hanging on to my horse for dear life, Dolly! The bandits, for which that region was known, scattered into the woods. Only the elder Mr. Stanley suffered an injury, and a minor one at that. For as we retreated along the narrow trail, with gunshots sounding behind us, Mr. Stanley's horse threw him from his saddle roughly to the ground, and his left shoulder was badly dislocated as a result.

"Once back in the main house and laid out on a settee, Mr. Stanley was in considerable pain, although nowhere near the brink of death. But his infirmity inspired our young Henry to attend to him as if he were an angel sent from heaven, for once he had been carried into his bedchamber to recover, Stanley, for the next few days, never left his side, much to the man's discomfort. If the truth be told, Mr. Stanley already had two comely female slaves to look after him—women with whom, I noticed, he retired to his bedchamber each evening. A few times I had seen them gently washing his hair and beard as he bent over a tub of water in his inner courtyard: I had seen one fanning him as he rested in a hammock on his front lawn, the other standing by, smiling, with a whisk broom to swat away the flies. I remember them just standing alongside him while he, as Stanley dutifully recorded, seemed to be working on a memoir of some kind. In other words, Dolly, Mr. Stanley was no sainted man: He had his concubines and all the rum he would ever want to drink. Yet as he lay in his bed, there he was confronted with Stanley, sitting beside him, with a Bible in hand, reading from it aloud."

He sipped more whiskey.

"To extricate his namesake from his side became Mr. Stanley's greatest preoccupation. A few mornings later, we awoke to find Mr. Davis waiting for us in the parlor. He was affable, friendly. And then, calling us 'young lads,' he announced that it was Mr. Stanley's wish that we vacate the house—no good reason was given. We were then shown a hut near the stables, with a palm-thatched roof and no outhouse, which we were to stay in before we would leave. 'It is Mr. Stanley's wish,' he said. And that was when I told Stanley that it was time for us to go, but he insisted that we stay until certain matters were settled. He was so intent upon getting his way that Stanley took the liberty of drafting a letter stating the elder Mr. Stanley's intention to adopt him, a bit of madness given the man's obvious indifference to the subject. That night, he visited Mr. Stanley in his room. I was out in the main hall playing cards with Mr. Davis, who, being a good sort, was caught in the middle of the whole affair. I'd gotten to know him well enough to learn that he had barely any awareness of a special relationship between Stanley and his so-called adoptive father; he only knew that they had once worked together, but that was all. In the meantime, Stanley, pressing his point, had it out with the older man, who had been drinking heavily. Distinctly we could hear Stanley saying, 'But you are my father!' and just as distinctly we could hear the elder Mr. Stanley's answer: 'I'm not, nor ever will be! Now, get out of my sight!'

"Later Stanley came out with the letter—unsigned, of course; and even when his father could not have made it more clear that he wasn't wanted, he *still* held out hope. His thick-headedness was mind-boggling to me. 'Cut your losses,' I told him. 'Let's get out of here.' At his insistence, we remained a few more days, but by that point, we were not even allowed back in to the plantation house. Even when I made good use of my time, getting to know the Cuban slaves and the run of the plantation somewhat, after a while, it was more than I could take. And so I told Stanley that I would be heading back to Havana with or without him. One morning, without so much as a proper good-bye, we gathered up our gear and rode dejectedly through the woods to Limonar, solemn as any souls could be, neither Stanley nor I saying much to one another, the whole business having been a great waste of our time.

"Back in Havana, we learned about the bombing of Fort Sumter, and by and by we sailed to New Orleans, where we parted ways."

"So his father's death was a fabrication?"

"Yes, it was. For whatever his reasons, Stanley wanted to kill him off. And if you recall, Dolly, in this account Stanley had him buried under a banyan tree—do you know whose heart was buried under such a tree in Africa? Livingstone's. I remember that from Stanley's accounts."

"But why would he have even bothered to write it?"

"Who can say? Maybe he had convinced himself that it was true, or he wanted to convince others that it was true; maybe it was the way malaria played with his memory. But Dolly, your husband surely knew better. In fact, not only did Mr. Stanley not die in Cuba, he also returned some years later to New Orleans—I suppose after having had his fill of that life. I know this because I ran into him one afternoon along Royal Street. It was about 1877 or so, when I was in New Orleans on a lecture tour. By then he was still a looming but slightly hobbled old man. I approached him and said, 'Mr. Stanley, do you remember me?—Samuel Clemens; I once visited you with your namesake in Cuba.' In the midst of apparent senility he claimed that while he had indeed spent a few years in Cuba during the war, he had no recollection of me and Stanley going there; but I knew better. 'But surely you must be aware of your namesake's great fame as an African explorer?' I asked. To that he professed ignorance as well; but as I read a glimmer of recognition in his eyes, I am sure that he did."

"And you are certain it was he?"

"Yes, he admitted that he was Mr. Henry Hope Stanley, as I addressed him, but otherwise he claimed to have never seen me before. In fact—and get this, Dolly—he went on to say that he had been living for many years on a small plantation outside New Orleans with his wife, the one who supposedly died of yellow fever in Stanley's account. In other words, Dolly, your late husband killed them both off, when they in fact lived on for some years afterward."

"Dear me," Dolly said. "But why would Stanley do that?"

Clemens tugged upon the bristles of his mustache.

"That's a chin-scratcher, Dolly, but my guess is that he just wanted the story of his life told in a certain way. But who can blame him? Why would an orphan whose future was to be as glorious as Stanley's wish to do otherwise? And whom does it hurt? Certainly not the elder Mr. Stanley, who lived to see his name associated with your husband's great explorations.

"That your husband chose to take that name for himself struck me as a greater mystery, considering the way he was treated in the end. What an honor to a man who disowned him! Why he did so I cannot imagine. Once, when Stanley and I were sitting up late drinking, I asked him, 'Why did you take that name?' And he—frankly, in his cups—looked at me and said: 'Which one of us is not the product of circumstance? When I first heard that name it rang to me of accomplishment and gravitas; it signified progress and a commitment to advancing myself. And of all the names I considered for myself, it sounded like a name I would like.' Then he elaborated: 'My original name, John Rowlands, never rang true, nor did the provincialism of my Welsh roots. I wanted to be a man of the world,' he told me."

Dolly looked over her canvas and asked, "But Samuel, do you think his autobiography is a lie? What should I say about Cuba and your travels there?"

"Henry never wanted it mentioned. Especially after we'd become well-known writers."

Another sip of whiskey; Dolly behind the easel, laying brush to canvas.

"Knowing your husband as I did, Dolly, I would say he just could not stand the failure of it. After writing so admiringly of Mr. Stanley in his autobiography, why wouldn't he reduce that affront to his baffling affection for the man to a few lines— 'He later died in Cuba,' as you told me? I don't blame him—writers blur the facts all the time."

"But shouldn't I mention that he knew you back then?"

"It's up to you, Dolly: Naturally, I would be flattered. If you care to, you could write a note to the effect that he and I once met in New Orleans in those days; but what it would add to the story of his life I cannot say. For my part, I once promised him to never write of that episode, and I haven't. Perhaps it is best to leave it alone. Who knows? Maybe one day some enterprising fellow will come across the details of our lives and try to make something of them; but as for me, I will keep my promise to Stanley."

❧

LADY STANLEY HAD BEEN PAINTING Samuel Clemens, a visage she most wanted to have remembered by posterity. With his many sharp features, he was a perfect subject—flaring eyebrows, a shock of white hair, a stony and regal face; the sharp, slightly crooked nose; the intense eyes, their lids drooping like a hawk's. For all the years she had spent contemplating his face, and for all the renderings that would eventually be judged excellent, she, looking him over, as he sat before her one afternoon in 1907, realized that this would probably be the last time he would ever grace her studio.

"All that you have said to me I will consider, Samuel, but I will leave Stanley's account as he wished it to be. The pity, I think, is that neither you nor he ever wrote about one another."

"We didn't. Maybe I will one day."

Samuel Clemens never did, and what was written about their friendship came by way of some brief mentions in the memoirs of Major Pond and Stanley's manservant Hoffman as well as a few newspaper articles referring to appearances Stanley and Clemens made together. But a few days after he left Dolly's company, Clemens appeared before an audience at the famous Savage Club in London, where he spoke of the fact that Stanley had taken one of his books with him to Africa; though he lamented Stanley's passing greatly, that was the last mention he ever publicly made of him.

ON THE AFTERNOON WHEN HE parted from Dolly, Samuel Clemens moved slowly, his limbs, his body weighed down with age and drink. Occasionally, as he would pause along the hallway to look at some photograph or portrait of Stanley, he would pass his hand over it, as if to bid him farewell. And when Dolly escorted him from the mansion, where, by the curb, Lady Stanley's chauffeur and Daimler motorcar awaited him, Clemens looked at her tenderly and said, "As you must know, at my age this will definitely be my last visit to England. In another world, I might come back again and again, but for now, I think this will be it." Then, taking her white-gloved hand in his, he added: "I hope you did not mind my disclosures about Stanley," at which Dolly smiled and shook her head slightly. And with that he embraced her, the scent of his soap, tobacco, and whiskey rising into her nostrils: It was the only time he had ever been so demonstrative with her, but it only lasted for a moment.

"Lest I get teary-eyed, I better go now, Dolly."

With that Clemens climbed into the Daimler's backseat and, to the driver in his top hat and duster, said: "To Brown's Hotel, if you will."

As the motorcar pulled out into the curving flagstone driveway and Clemens waved to her, Lady Stanley, in those moments, was overcome with a melancholy that stayed with her for some days.

WHEN *THE AUTOBIOGRAPHY OF SIR Henry Morton Stanley* was published in 1909, five years after his death, its only reference to Stanley's friendship with Clemens came by way of a footnote that Dolly had added to a chapter entitled "I Find a Father," about his years on the Mississippi. Occurring on page 246, it read:

"During such riverboat journeys with the merchant trader, Stanley made the acquaintance of a young pilot named Samuel Clemens—later the famous Mark Twain—with whom he remained a good and steadfast friend for the rest of his life.—D.S."

The book was received tepidly by a public whose interest in Africa and the great explorers of the Victorian age had long since · waned. Though its sales were disappointing, Dolly remained most proud of her efforts, for at long last, the noble and selfless Stanley with whom she had first fallen in love would be known to all. In her enthusiasm she had taken the trouble to have several special editions printed on handmade paper with elaborate morocco bindings—ten in all. One went to the Royal Geographical Society, another to the royal family. One was sent to Samuel Clemens at his new home in Redding, Connecticut.

With it, she attached a note:

Dear Samuel,

    Well, here it is—a book for the ages! I do hope you understand its omissions, but when you see how I have inscribed it, I hope you will do so with the understanding that Stanley was by my shoulder as I wrote it.

With sincerest love,
Dolly

A frothy shaving brush in hand, Clemens was in his new house—Stormfield—when his housekeeper handed him a parcel from England. In it was one of the special editions of the aforementioned book. The inscription read:

    To my dear friend Samuel,
    Here is my life, contained in some few pages. And tendered to you with love and admiration.
    Henry Morton Stanley

In those moments, reading it, Clemens was amused that Dolly had taken the liberty of signing Stanley's own name, her script exactly as his own, including the florid underswirls that Stanley had always used in his better days.

Well, in a nutshell, he thought, that is the spiritualist in Dolly; later, he wrote her a long note of appreciation.

From Lady Stanley's Journal, April 22, 1910—A Variation on a Letter to Her Long-Dead Father

Dearest Father,

    This morning's papers—Friday's—have been filled with the sad news of Samuel Clemens's passing last night. When I learned of it, I was sitting in our dining room at breakfast. At first I could not accept the news and threw the paper down. Denzil, in from Eton and sitting beside me, retrieved the paper in his gentlemanly manner and asked, "Mother, why are you so upset?" But all I could do was lower my head and weep as privately and discreetly as possible. But in seeing that his "uncle Mark" was gone, Denzil withdrew into the privacy of his room. Then Mother came in, and, seeing my distraught state, also read the news; she, too, lamented the death of that great light, calling him "a dear young man." (But she did not weep.)

Once I cleared my mind of the immediate shock, I clearly saw his circumstances. According to the accounts, he had retreated to the freeing pastures of his home in Redding, Connecticut, at twenty-two minutes past six last night. With him were his loved ones—his daughter Clara, her husband, Ossip, and several others. He went peacefully, from heart failure, and among the effects by his bedside was the same wedding gift he once sent us—a copy of Carlyle's book on the French Revolution. Though his passing grieves me, I remain confident that he has not only found his peace but is also now standing by your side.

Do tell me if it is so.

But the fact remains, I will miss him. Since I last saw him, a few years ago, I'd heard from him rarely. A Christmas card to our family was all, but then, just this past winter, he wrote me about the loss of his beloved daughter Jean. It was Christmas Eve. She had finished decorating their tree when she went upstairs to take a bath; while soaking in the water, she suffered a seizure and drowned. How he must have felt, Stanley, I cannot say, but this past mid-January I received a letter from him, and among his words were these lines in particular, which moved me to tears:

"It was snowing the next morning, on Christmas Day, as I stood by my window watching the hearse take her off into the great silence. Life can be so painful that in those moments, I found myself envying the dead."

It was clear to me that he would not be long for this world—and yet I had hoped it would not be so.

DROWSILY, IN THE WAY THAT people sometimes scribble down a dream, Lady Stanley envisioned a happier alternative to the notion that the spirits and strong intellects of such formidable men should lie buried, extinguished, forever in the ground, existing only as memories. Drawing with pencil a quick sketch of some celestial place, patterned after the visions of heaven that she knew from the etchings of Gustave Doré, she saw Twain and Stanley meeting again at the foot of some great marble stairway from whose highest step one could see every pleasing element of the universe—every star, every planet and galaxy, a great swath of starry light, the radiance of life itself streaming down upon them. (She considered for this fantastic drawing a concept of the two of them, hand in hand, Stanley depicted as the warrior Mars and Twain the father-head and statesman, Zeus—with herself as Venus, representing wisdom and impulse and love—proceeding together into a place that transcended the conditions of this world.)

But after an hour, there it was: Twain in his white serge suit, and Stanley—dear Henry—in his frock coat, mounting those steps together. For what it is worth, at that moment, just as Lady Stanley had to choose between getting up and making her way to her bedroom or simply allowing herself to doze, at about 11:45 p.m., London time, on the evening of October 22, as a dray passed by on the street, Twain and Stanley entered Paradise.

AFTERWORD

AS I WRITE THIS NOTE, I am surrounded by my husband's beloved books, lead soldier collection, ancient artifacts, paintings, guitars, and mementos from our sojourns around the world. Oscar Hijuelos, the man and writer, was a human being of robust convictions and interests. He loved beauty in all its manifestations: the starlings in late autumn as they danced in the Roman sky; the brilliance of a Bach fugue played by Glenn Gould; a portrait by Velázquez; the Himalayas; sunsets on Long Island Sound; a child's knowing eyes. He lived for the purity of art and its transformative power on the soul. And it was this love of art that allowed him to meander inward to the depths of his being and intuition to create so generously for others. He was also an outward traveler who sought adventure in Egypt, Nepal, and Bhutan, to name just a few destinations far away from his home.

Twain & Stanley Enter Paradise is a creation many years in the making—actually, more than twelve. The reading and gathering of documents that Oscar employed to discover truths and little-known details about the lengthy friendship of Twain and Stanley is, in fact, staggering in scope. And yet this novel is a fiction, through and through. And all of the writing is Oscar's; which is to say that—in addition to the narrative—the letter excerpts, diary entries, speeches, and pronouncements in these pages are imagined and created by Hijuelos.

It is a novel that had an unusual and mysterious journey from inception to completion and, finally, publication. It was written in three locales: New York City; Branford, Connecticut; and Durham, North Carolina. And it was informed by several field trips. These trips I arranged in a way that allowed Oscar to better understand the backdrop to his story. New Orleans became a favorite spot. Oscar absolutely loved the city, with all its social curlicues, manners, secrets, and magic. He was charmed by every inch of the French Quarter and the river views along the promenade. He felt Twain's and Stanley's footprints everywhere.

We visited Mark Twain's home in Hartford, Connecticut, a particularly rich experience for both of us. Oscar delighted in the ephemera of Twain's home life and the fascinating details of the furnishings (the handcrafted matrimonial bed from Italy was notable), objets d'art, and the elegance of the grand estate. We went on European jaunts to better understand the life of Stanley—one to Wales and England and another to Belgium. We walked through Welsh forests, gardens, and beachfronts to get a sense of Stanley's boyhood. We studied the facade of Stanley's Richmond Terrace home in London, to the bemusement of some wary guards (the house is now occupied by the Ministry of Defence). While in Belgium we visited Ostend, a resort city, as well as a museum in Brussels that displays African artifacts, a reminder of Stanley's exploits under the patronage of King Leopold II.

My husband was working on the novel's pages up until the day before he died.

It feels somewhat presumptuous to tell you what I believe Oscar "was saying" as an artist in the making of this fiction. Only the author of a work can explain or even attempt to explain the inner workings of his creation with authority. No critic, no scholar, no friend or family member has the knowledge to do this. But I can offer a few insights as to why Oscar chose Mark Twain, Henry Morton Stanley, and Dorothy Tennant as the subjects of his tale—a tale about the vagaries of destiny that I believe was also an investigation into Oscar's two sides: the quiet contemplative and the gregarious wanderer.

Oscar truly admired the work of Mark Twain, especially his *Adventures of Huckleberry Finn*. And this fact is not surprising, given that Twain was one of the greats. But Oscar's fascination with the life, work, and spirit of Stanley is, perhaps, more of a curiosity. It began in his late teens, when Oscar read an extensive biography about the intrepid British explorer. Over the years, rather than diminish, his interest in Stanley grew, and he read voraciously about him. In fact, Oscar read every book he discovered about the Victorian giant. Along the way, my husband found a reference to Stanley's friendship with Mark Twain. And there was something else that struck a chord of intrigue: a reference to the fact that Stanley had, at one time, gone to Cuba in search of his adoptive father, who had disappeared. Whether this escapade was historically accurate did not matter as much to Oscar as the idea that it could have been true. He began researching and writing the novel shortly thereafter.

Soon enough, Oscar encountered the beguiling figure of Dorothy Tennant, an accomplished portraitist who would eventually marry Stanley. Dolly, as she was known, was a mesmerizing vixen. And she was just the kind of female character who could get under Oscar's skin: strong-willed, artistic, elegant, flirtatious. This was the woman who stole Stanley's heart. Oscar had found an interesting triangle of seductive personalities, passions, and friendships.

As Oscar wrote the thousands of pages that he attempted to winnow down to publishable size, even as he continued to expand upon the story, we experienced several challenging and painful events in our lives. Oscar became more philosophical and spiritual, although he had always been an introspective, keenly sensitive man. His loving nature deepened in ways that were clearly obvious to those closest to him. The more difficulties we endured, the more generous he became to those around him, intimates and strangers alike. He was always giving of his time, advice, and material means. The hurts, injustices, and inexplicable tragedies that befell friends, family, and acquaintances affected him deeply. Often, he would begin our mornings, over coffee, with commentary about the cruelty in the world, which he could never understand.

He started to see his protagonists as he would his inner circle.

He cared about them and experienced their joys and vicissitudes. He delighted in the fact that Stanley was able to become a father when he and Dolly adopted a boy from Wales; he suffered the tragedies Mark Twain endured, particularly the deaths of his infant son, two young daughters, and his wife.

Oscar often wondered aloud: What are the elements that conspire to grant one human being privilege and another so much despair and agony? What is fame? Success? Throughout his life, my husband conscientiously wrestled with the difficulty of being human, and in his writing he sought to offer musings on the following subjects: death and its aftermath; moral fortitude; man's inhumanity toward man; the redemptive essence of love and artistic creation; the consolation of family.

For some fans, this last novel of my husband's might seem like an anomaly within his overall work. Many readers have come to associate an Hijuelos title with lively New York City neighborhoods, *cubanía*, amorous passion, a love of music, and the immigrant experience. While these attributes and many more characterize his oeuvre, Oscar was, first and foremost, an American intellectual. His interests ranged from archaeology to physics, from medicine to boxing, and Disney animation. He was a passionate reader of world history and religious discourse. He was curious about all aspects of the world and human endeavor.

ON OCTOBER 12, 2013, OSCAR died of a massive heart attack while playing tennis in New York City's Riverside Park. That day my world came to a stop, as it did for all who loved him. He was not only a remarkably gifted man and a supremely talented novelist but the most soulful person I have ever known. And the sweetest. We were a double helix; my life is only "a half" now. And the world, as noted by journalists and writers around the globe, is a poorer place without his brilliance.

In the months following Oscar's death, I was in too much pain to think about the rituals of daily life or professional obligations, but gradually I summoned the resolve to seek a publisher for *Twain and Stanley Enter Paradise*. (The one and only extant copy of the manuscript was found on top of several boxes of related material in my husband's study.) It has been edited with loving attention and acumen by Gretchen Young. To the entire team at Grand Central Publishing, I say, "Thank you from my heart for the care, intelligence, and passion you have put into its publication." Oscar would be so very grateful to you.

—*Lori Marie Carlson-Hijuelos*